"You don't want to

They were sitting, their [...] wall. Ginger's arms were around the kids, obviously arranged that way.

Their throats had been cut.

The sign said: *Happy Father's Day!*

The seven-shot clip had been fully loaded. He hefted it in his hand, squeezed the checkered walnut grip.

He started for the door, knowing exactly where he was going, what he would do. He hoped it would make him feel better.

He was tired of the same old questions. Now he wanted some answers.

Even the lies would do.

—THE—
REMINGTON
CONTRACT

THE

RAYMOND OBSTFELD

REMINGTON CONTRACT

W☮RLDWIDE ®

TORONTO • NEW YORK • LONDON • PARIS
AMSTERDAM • STOCKHOLM • HAMBURG
ATHENS • MILAN • TOKYO • SYDNEY

THE REMINGTON CONTRACT

A Worldwide Library Book/December 1988

ISBN 0-373-97095-1

THE
REMINGTON
CONTRACT

BEGINNINGS

SHE WAS PURPOSELY BAREFOOT. Each careful step on the ancient warped-wood floor threatened to expose her, creak out an alarm that would alert him of her approach. She liked that challenge.

His door was wide open. The room was dark as usual, except for one bright light over his desk. She could see his shadow flicker in the doorway as she crept nearer. He was writing again, maybe a poem, maybe an essay about some obscure historic battle, maybe some observations on microorganisms in New Guinea tidal pools.

Hardly breathing, she slid her naked foot around the corner, her callused toes brushing bare wood. She slowly added the weight and pressure of her body with the delicacy of someone pouring sand into a wine bottle. When she felt balanced, she slid her other foot over and stood framed in the doorway, watching him. She smiled proudly at her stealth.

He was standing at the antique scrivener's desk, slightly hunched, pen gyrating furiously over paper like a seismograph needle recording a disastrous earthquake. Suddenly he stopped writing, looked over his shoulder. A huge smile spread across his face.

"Very good," he said, signing the words with his hands as he spoke. She was deaf and mute, but he was teaching her to read lips.

Did you hear me? she signed.

"No."

Then how did you know I was here? I know it's not my perfume—I didn't wear any this time.

"I smelled your shampoo. Apple-honey, isn't it?"

She made a disgusted face, then signed, *You're too good.*

"You're better," he said. "You just don't know it yet." He gestured for her to come in. He shut the desk lamp off and the room bloomed into almost total darkness. "The older I get, the darker I like it. I think it's supposed to be the opposite— that's why old people move to Florida."

You're not old, she signed, meaning it, though he was clearly fifty years older than she.

"You think I'm being maudlin." He smiled. "I'm not."

She looked at his tired face, saw the dread in his eyes. Her hands fluttered to life. *You've already done it, haven't you?*

"I had no choice."

She stood still, comfortable in the cool darkness of the room. The edge of her foot itched and she rubbed it against the wood floor. It made a scraping sound, which she could feel though not hear. *Now what?*

"They will send men to kill me."

Clever men?

"Yes."

As clever as you?

He laughed. "We shall see."

She watched him pour her a cup of tea. The ceramic pot and cups he had made himself, on the potter's wheel in the back-yard. The unusual red glaze was his own mixture, the material specially imported from Holland. The tea was a special blend he grew out back in the garden, one that his mother had favored when he was a boy in Georgia. The tea plants had come over from England with her ancestors and had been grown on her family's plantation generations ago when they'd been slave owners. The plantation house had already fallen to ruin by the time he was born, and his father's failing insurance business hadn't gone far in helping to maintain it. His father seemed to resent his wife's legacy, the burden of her heritage. When he was sixteen his father, drunk and bitter, stabbing the air with a glowing cigar, had lamented the abolition of slavery in front of his son's black friend. They had argued. His father had leaped on him in rage and in the fall had broken the last two fingers of his son's right hand. He had left home that night with a ten-dollar bill he'd earned fixing Victrolas. He had never again spoken to his father. Sixty years later, the fingers were still a little crooked.

He handed her the steaming tea, which she hated to admit she didn't much like. She preferred Pepsi. She drank the tea anyway.

Why are you doing this? she signed. *It's crazy.*

He looked at her, his eyes bright and warm. She knew he would never tell her anything so personal unless she asked. He didn't believe in burdening people with unwanted information. But once she did ask, he would never hold anything back.

"It's a long story," he said. "Sit."

She did. He stood in front of her and began telling the story. The room was already dark, so she had no sense of time passing. Minutes. Hours. She didn't know. She clenched her bare feet in her warm palms and listened as she had never listened to anyone before. His long graceful hands swirled and gnashed the air in front of him as if he were conjuring a god, not just telling a story.

When he was done, she wept.

"Now you know," he said. "That makes three of us."

"BETTER HURRY, STAN," she warned. She tapped a red acrylic fingernail on the crystal of one of her watches. She wore three, the colored plastic bands wildly fluorescent and bunched together on the same wrist. They all showed him fifteen minutes late. "They've already phoned for you. Twice."

Standish Ford, the CIA's youngest section chief, shuffled stiffly down the bright corridor toward his secretary's desk. He was hunched over, his mouth grim with pain. Sweat quilted his face. "This is my top speed for today, kiddo."

"Better not be." She made a sour face at the phone. "I could tell from his tone, Stan, there's an evil force loose in the universe bent on the destruction of life as we know it. And you're running late."

"I'm not running at all." He leaned wearily against Carla's desk, catching his breath. One hand was clamped against his churning abdomen. His stomach seized and exploded like misfiring pistons. He was just returning from the men's room for the fourth time in an hour and was pretty sure he had to go right back again.

"I mean it, Stan. You've got trouble."

Stan managed a slight smile. "Trouble is my business, Carla."

"Yeah, right. Here I thought flushing toilets is your business."

"Just my hobby."

She gave him a smile, but it faded quickly. Tiny frown wrinkles stitched the corners of her mouth like sutures. "No fooling, Stan. Everyone around here is edgy as hell."

Stan didn't blame them. So was he. The only difference was, he knew why.

Carla waited, but when Stan remained silent, she prompted him with a demanding "Well?"

"Well, what?"

"'Well, what?'" she mimicked. For the past five years it had been the nature of Carla and Stan's relationship that she tried to pump him for information and that he refused to give her any. "Christ, Stan, the Spy City big shots are acting like they've got alligators up their assholes and all you can say is 'well, what?'" She eyed the red top-secret emergency report tucked under his arm. The source of everyone's edginess would be in there. "So what's going on, Stan? I mean, should I skip low-impact aerobics tonight and start reading *Das Kapital*?"

Stan picked up the ceramic "Honeymooners" mug from her desk and sipped her coffee. As usual it was too strong, too cold and oversweetened with sugar substitute. He drank it anyway. The mug had a picture of Jackie Gleason and Audrey Meadows nose to nose in argument with the caption, "To the moon, Alice." Carla's entire desktop was a crowded museum of canceled television shows: photos of Mike Nesmith from *The Monkees*, David Janssen as The Fugitive, Nick Adams in *The Rebel*. A twelve-inch rubber Gumby held a stack of unsharpened pencils in his arms like logs. One of her watches showed Howdy Doody on the face, another had Betty Boop. The third displayed Rod Serling's grim visage.

"Where did you get all this junk?" Stan said.

"Junk! These shows helped form my adult values." She waved a dismissing hand. "You wouldn't understand."

"I grew up on these shows too, Carla."

"Yeah, but you don't have any adult values."

Stan laughed. Carla could always make him laugh, even today. Unfortunately, the laughter shook loose a knotted ball of barbed wire in his stomach and launched it roller-coastering through his intestines. His insides burned like a grease fire. He spun around and hotfooted it back toward the men's room. Over his shoulder he called to Carla, "Tell the director I'll be there shortly."

She snorted as she reached for the phone. "Fat chance."

Stan trotted down the hall, shoved open the men's room door with his good right hand, while the mechanical hook that was his left hand tugged open his belt. Even the director of the CIA would have to wait this out, Stan thought, elbowing through the stall door and dropping his pants with a sigh.

Yesterday Stan and his wife, Lanie, had been ordered back to Washington halfway through their vacation in Cancun where they'd been celebrating their fifteenth anniversary. When the coded telegram had arrived, Lanie had been sitting on the toilet with a wicker wastebasket clamped between her knees. She was spewing from both ends. Stan had been stretched flat on the bed with a cool washcloth over his clammy face, sucking Lifesavers to scrub the rancid taste of vomit from his mouth.

After packing hurriedly, they'd waited at the tiny jungle airport in absolute misery, never straying too far from the rest rooms. They'd fanned themselves with their airplane tickets; the humidity was so high that they felt as if they were waiting inside a clenched fist. One indication of the seriousness of the emergency was that the director hadn't sent a private jet. He didn't want anyone to suspect how desperate things really were.

They'd arrived back in Washington late last night. Lanie had bolted right from the taxi to the upstairs bathroom and had still been in there moaning, with *Newsweek* spread across her lap, when Stan finally fell asleep. When he woke up this morning Lanie was sleeping wedged between the toilet and the tub, her cheek pressed against the cool white porcelain. She was naked, her clothes from last night balled into a knotted pillow under her head. Though he was running late, Stan carried her to bed and dabbed her face with a wet washcloth. She didn't open her eyes, but smiled up at him as he left. "Go save the world, honey."

Save the world. Stan grimaced. He felt like etching that phrase into the side of the toilet stall with his hook. Come to think of it, this was the only men's room he'd ever been in where there was no graffiti. None. No exaggerated penis. No sexual pleas. No phone numbers. No racial slurs. Surely these must appear every so often, even at Langley, but someone must immediately sand and paint them into oblivion.

Save the world.

At Langley, that would be the most obscene phrase of all.

And maybe already too late.

Stan balanced the secret report on his knees, though he didn't bother to open it. He'd already read the damned thing three times this morning during his imprisonment in this very stall, and each reading raised more questions than it answered. Something was wrong with this report. Too much vital information was missing. Curiously, the report had been prepared by Director Aaron Leland himself.

Stan leaned over the sink and washed his one hand. The other had been blown off seventeen years ago, back when he'd worked the bomb squad for NYPD. A stockboy had found a crude pipe bomb hidden under a pile of women's bras, size 36s, in Bloomingdale's. A former employee, fired for stealing a carton of panty hose, had planted it. She hadn't been very good at selling bras or stealing panty hose, and she was even worse at building bombs. It blew up in Stan's hand, ripping off the hand, a couple of yards of freckled skin and his left nipple. There had been other superficial damage, long since sanded and painted as smoothly as the stalls of the CIA men's room. In fact, Lanie insisted he was even more handsome since they'd straightened his dog-leg nose and bobbed his ears. The skin grafts had taken immediately and his tousled blond hair had grown back thicker than ever. Now at 39 he looked square shouldered and robust, like a young Spencer Tracy. He'd adjusted to the artificial hand. The missing nipple he'd never bothered to get rebuilt. When he took his shirt off it looked like one nipple was staring while the other was winking. It didn't bother Lanie and it didn't bother Stan.

He splashed some cold water on his face, looked into the mirror and said, "Let's go save the world, honey."

"YOU KNOW what we need, don't you?" Director Aaron Leland was saying as Stan entered the room. Carla was right, he looked edgy. They all looked edgy. "You know what we really need right now?"

"A miracle," Stan said, closing the door behind him.

"Didn't bring one back with you, did you, Stan?" the director said.

"Just the miracle of life."

Collins grunted. "How about the miracle of a cigarette?"

Stan shook his head. "Nicotine stains my hook."

Collins laughed. Big and bearded, he cultivated his resemblance to Ernest Hemingway. He and Dubus were sitting at the conference table, just to Leland's left. Collins was absently twisting the staple out of the top-secret emergency report in front of him. Dubus was polishing his glasses with a monogrammed handkerchief. Stan decided Dubus was the only man in the country under fifty who still carried a hanky.

All three watched Stan as he crossed the room, slightly bent over, obviously in great discomfort. He didn't try to hide his condition from these men. No point. They were three of the smartest men in the country. Not just book-smart IQs, but field smart. Stan knew the Russian and Chinese counterparts to these men and, all things considered, was glad he was on this side.

"Good morning, gentlemen," Stan said and took his seat at the table. He poured himself some hot coffee from the pot in the middle of the table. His mouth felt parched, as if lined with fleece.

"We ate the doughnuts already, Stan," Collins said.

"I was hoping you would."

Dubus stopped polishing his glasses and glanced uncomfortably at Stan's hook as if he expected it to leap out from under the sleeve and go straight for his throat. He'd been giving it that same look every time he and Stan met for all these years.

"Stan," the director said, swiveling around in his chair to face him directly, "I feel terrible about hauling you and Lanie back like this. Some anniversary, my friend."

"It'll keep," Stan told him.

"Unfortunately, it'll have to. But I'll make it up to you both as soon as this mess is over. You name the place, we pay all the expenses. That's a promise."

Collins finally plucked the stubborn staple free from the report and tossed it at Stan's coffee cup. It pinged off the saucer. "Where's your Mexican tan, Stan?"

"In the bathroom."

Collins laughed. "Kaopectate. Don't leave home without it."

Dubus made a humming sound of appreciation. A dapper little man with the blackest skin Stan had ever seen, Dubus never laughed outright. Nor did he ever raise his voice in anger. He expressed emotions by the warbling sounds in his throat, like some exotic species of bird.

Leland's mouth stretched into a weary seam. "You've read the report, Stan?"

"Yes, sir."

"Then you know that calling you back on a national emergency was no exaggeration."

"I agree."

"Good. Then let's get started. Ideas, gentlemen?"

Silence. There was some shifting in chairs, some rustling of papers, Dubus trumpeting at the back of his throat. But no one actually spoke. No one was anxious to target himself in Aaron Leland's cross hairs. Not that he was vicious or cruel. Quite the contrary. Aaron displayed a serenely patient demeanor, qualities retained from his years as a Jesuit novice studying for the priesthood. But his honed logic was ruthless, tearing through suggestions and opinions like a jagged iceberg shredding the hull of a ship. You could almost see the poor man who was his target taking on water and sinking quietly out of sight. Every man in this room had spent some time underwater. The worst part, Stan thought, was that Aaron was almost always right. That was what made him so effective as director. Yet even after he'd sunk someone, even someone ill prepared and deserving the treatment, Aaron Leland always took time to soothe his tattered ego, cajoling him back to confidence. Collins referred to him, behind his back of course, as the Reverend Father Leland, and adopted a ludicrous Irish brogue whenever imitating him.

"Well?" Leland repeated. "Ideas, gentlemen?"

More silence.

Leland smiled. "At this point I'll even take bad ideas."

"In that case," Collins said, "Dubus might as well start."

Dubus gave Collins a sharp look. Collins laughed, a deep rumbling sound like potatoes rolling down a cellar chute.

Stan poured more coffee. His body craved liquids. "Are the lab boys still certain there's nothing they can do?"

"So far. They've been at it since it happened." Leland glanced at his watch. "Thirty-two straight hours. Once the ransom note came in, I added another seventy-five experts from the private sector. Had them flown in from all over the country. No breakthrough yet."

"How much do they know?"

"The bare minimum. Just enough security clearance to do their jobs and find the bathrooms when they have to."

"The Pentagon?"

"Need-to-know basis," Leland said. "Right now, they have no need."

"They'll be pissed," Collins said.

"If they find out. Which they won't." Leland smiled brightly and Dubus and Collins nodded, appeased. Leland had that kind of smile, that kind of charm. His good looks reminded Stan of men in glossy magazine ads for cologne, the guy holding a tennis racquet and grinning over his shoulder at an unseen but undoubtedly vanquished opponent. He was tall, six-three and trim. His wavy black hair was as dark as carbon paper, interrupted only by a tiny island of fine white hairs on his left temple. A birthmark no larger than a half dollar.

Aaron Leland's rise to power was one of the inspirational stories of Washington. Terrorism had spread across Europe, slopped over into Latin America and Canada, and finally even penetrated the United States. Several poisonings of packaged breakfast cereal in Denver, aspirin in San Francisco, coffee in Miami had been traced to Libyan terrorists. To prevent public panic, false suspects had been announced, bogus police sketches broadcast on TV news, even phony arrests made. Eight months ago, Aaron Leland had convinced a desperate president that he could curb this terrorist problem without causing an international incident. The president, facing a tough reelection campaign in fourteen months, accepted the sudden resignation of the director of the CIA and immediately appointed Leland as replacement. Aaron Leland was given everything he asked for. The problem was, since then there had been no evidence that he was attacking the situation. Terrorist acts had continued, even increased, though most were still kept from the public. As far as Stan knew, Leland had never discussed the specifics of his plan with anyone other than the president. Stan didn't know if he was in fact doing anything at all.

But in other areas, Aaron Leland had not been idle. Since becoming director, he had embarked on what Stan referred to as a "glitzkrieg." A complete overhaul of the Agency's image. Everything from personnel shake-ups to higher media profile to somehow finessing a substantially increased operating budget from Congress. New buildings were already designed and set to begin construction within the year. Morale had never been higher. Most of the CIA's 16,000 employees admired and adored the director, considered him a protective father figure. Stan had the impression that Aaron himself looked upon the Agency as if it were his very own parish. Indeed, performance efficiency had increased dramatically. He personally listened to individual employee grievances and often straightened them out the same day. No detail was too small. Upon Stan and Lanie's arrival at their Cancun hotel, champagne and caviar had been iced and waiting for them, compliments of Aaron Leland. Stan suspected that even Collins, the resident cynic, admired the man.

Stan tapped the report in front of him with his hook. "Our boy sent a hell of a ransom note."

"He's a fucking comedian," Collins said angrily.

"He's crazy," Dubus said.

Stan looked at Leland. "Who else knows about it?"

"The ransom demand?" Aaron Leland leaned back in his chair and absently touched the white patch of hair at his temple. The white ones weren't the same texture as the rest of his hair. They seemed silky, shiny. Like down feathers. "Just us. I prepared the report myself at home. I printed only three copies, one for each of you, then destroyed the disk. Before you leave this room, I want each of you to shred your reports too. We're the only ones who know, and I want it to stay that way." He gave each man a stern stare. "Understood?"

"Christ, Aaron," Collins grinned. "If we can't keep a secret, who can?"

Leland didn't answer. He looked distracted, as if he were thinking of something else entirely.

"What about the president?" Stan asked.

Leland shrugged. "He'll keep. He's got other problems right now. Terrorists in every corner."

Collins and Dubus exchanged uneasy expressions. "That's risky," Dubus said.

Leland smiled. "Only if we get caught."

Dubus put his glasses back on. The thick black rims squared his otherwise shapeless doughy face. He had begun to go bald a few years ago, then suddenly within the past six months the process had escalated until the entire top of his head was bare and as shiny as vinyl. To counteract the balding, Dubus had recently grown a mustache, but wore it so narrow and close-cropped it arced razor-thin over his lips like one of Garbo's eyebrows. The glasses were also a new addition. Stan had secretly tried them on once and hadn't noticed any magnification from the lenses. He suspected the glasses were merely a prop, a dress-for-success device Dubus affected.

Aaron Leland, on the other hand, ignored the shiny business suits and ties worn by his predecessors and subordinates, preferring instead to dress drably but comfortably, like a tenured history professor. He wore plaid cotton shirts under huge cardigan sweaters with thick shawl collars. His shoes were honest-to-God penny loafers, complete with shiny dimes in the slots. The shoes alone had won Carla over to his side, Stan noted with amusement.

"He should've asked for money," Dubus said. "A couple million maybe. Something reasonable. Saved us all a lot of aggravation."

"Money we can deal with," Collins said.

"He doesn't need money," Stan reminded them. "He's already rich."

"Net worth of $6.7 million," Leland said, consulting a file in front of him. "That we know of."

"You can never be too rich," Collins said.

"Certainly he knows we won't meet this demand. It's too—" Dubus grappled for the right word, curling his pudgy lips with distaste "—grotesque."

"Then he must have something else in mind," Collins said. "Something he's not telling us. Something he'll spring on us later. He was always clever." There was admiration under the anger, still some of the old hero worship they all felt.

Stan shook his head. "I don't agree. I think he wants just what he asked for. The question is, why? You all know him. Hell, just about everyone in the world knows him. He's the last person we should be having any trouble from. Don't you think so, Aaron?" There was a slight challenge in Stan's voice, a flex in the vocal cords to let Leland know Stan was aware information had been left out of the report. He hadn't meant it to come out that way, but it had and Stan wasn't about to back down.

Aaron Leland sighed, adjusted the collar of his cable-knit sweater. The white wool accentuated the patch of white hair. "The man was a national hero, Stan. But men don't stay the same. Wish to God we could. 'All is flux, nothing stays still.' The Greek philosopher Heraclitus said that in the sixth century B.C., a hundred years before Socrates, and the words apply even to great men, national heroes. At this point, all we can do is judge him by his most recent deed. And as you all know, that deed has been devastating. If we don't correct the situation immediately, this whole country is in serious trouble. The kind we may never recover from. Am I wrong, gentlemen?"

There was another long silence. Stan looked at Collins and Dubus, but both avoided his gaze. They had to be just as aware as Stan that Leland was holding back. Only Leland knew why this was happening. And he wasn't telling.

Stan didn't know why Aaron was playing it this way, but he assumed it was for a good reason. And if Aaron bent the rules sometimes, who better than Stan to defend him? After all, it was Stan himself who had benefited most from Aaron Leland's methods. Stan had been rotting for years in semiobscurity as one of three assistants under the ponderous and burned-out carcass of Philip Crenshaw, who'd been a mediocre section chief for twenty-three years and, because of excellent genetic heritage, threatened to continue as one for another twenty-three years. Stan's career had dead-ended—until Aaron Leland, in a move as bold as firing J. Edgar Hoover, had forced Crenshaw into early retirement and promoted Stan to Crenshaw's job. Leland had undoubtedly taken a lot of high-octane heat as a result, but he'd never mentioned that once to Stan. Out of loyalty and gratitude, Stan had worked harder than any other section chief ever had, and had proved himself a worthy addition to the inner sanctum. According to Carla, gossip had begun circulating that Stan was being groomed as Aaron Leland's eventual successor. That was okay with Stan.

"We could just blow the bastard away," Collins suggested. "We have the trained personnel. Hunt him down, make it look like an accident. Like he had a nuclear meltdown in his microwave oven." He pointed to Stan. "Hell, Handy here's had some demolition experience."

Stan had, in fact, done demolition work for the Agency, even with his one hand. That was how he'd gotten started there. Collins had nicknamed him Handy a dozen years ago, not just from his usual frat-house humor, but because Stan had solved some tricky political problems with a few ounces of expertly placed plastique. His assignments had always been well planned and perfectly timed. Most important, they'd always been successful.

"Whatta you say, Stan?" Collins teased. "Like to climb back into the saddle again? A little field work?" Collins laughed harshly. "Bet you'd rather have your asshole sewn shut. Am I right, Stan?"

Stan smiled but didn't say anything.

Dubus studied a pink thumbnail. "Actually, that's not a bad idea. A hit squad to go in, finish him off, make it look like an accident, heart attack, whatever. The world mourns the loss, still thinking of him as a hero. They don't have to know what a traitor he became." Even Dubus couldn't keep the mixture of admiration and disappointment out of his voice. As if he'd discovered Mother Theresa dealt drugs out of a brothel.

Leland nodded wearily. "Which leaves us with another problem. How do we find him? Since he disappeared from the public eye twelve years ago, nobody knows where he is or even what he looks like now. There are no recent photos. His friends and relatives get letters postmarked Hong Kong, Berlin, Rapid City."

"He thinks he's Howard fucking Hughes," Collins said.

"But smarter," Stan added. "Much smarter."

There was a silence that spoke agreement.

"You know what we need?" Leland said. He was leaning forward now, his long narrow hands spread out palms up like an evangelist about to deliver a fiery sermon. "You know what we really need?"

Collins nodded glumly. "Like Stan said, a miracle."

"Stan is too pessimistic," Leland said. "Probably due to the tender condition of his bowels." He looked at Stan and smiled. "Seriously, you know what we need?"

They didn't.

"A whipping boy."

Dubus frowned. "A what?"

"A whipping boy. Like they used to have back in England. Rich boys would have a male playmate, a commoner who was raised and educated with the titled child as his best friend. Whenever the rich boy did something wrong, his commoner friend was punished. Whipped. It was supposed to teach the gentry responsibility."

"Better not let my kids hear about it," Collins said. "They'll want one and then I'll have nothing to look forward to at the end of the day."

"Barnaby Fitzpatrick," Stan said, pouring himself more coffee.

"What?" Collins said.

"He was the whipping boy for Edward VI. And Mungo Murray took the lashes for Charles I."

They all looked with surprise at Stan. Because he was a lowly ex-cop, a mere New York City College graduate, they never could get used to the extraordinary breadth of his knowledge. Despite the group's apparent chumminess, they were an elitist bunch. All except Stan were from wealthy or upper-middle-class families. Collins was a former California fraternity party animal with a movie studio head for a father, who went directly to the Agency from Stanford University. Big and brawny, he still liked to vacation at the beach, surfing with the kids and pretending his IQ wasn't fifteen points past genius. Dubus, son of a white father and black Jamaican mother, both journalists, had been recruited out of Cornell by a political science professor long on the Agency payroll. As for Leland, after leaving the Jesuit seminary without any explanation six weeks before his final vows, he'd gone on to graduate Harvard Law. Leland's reasons for abandoning the Jesuits and for his odd seguing to the CIA were still mysterious, a topic for speculation around Langley water coolers.

"So what's the connection?" Dubus asked. "Where does this whipping boy fit in?"

"We find someone," Leland explained. "Someone removed from the intelligence mainstream who they don't really know much about. We set him up as a whipping boy to take the heat off us."

"I don't see how that will work," Dubus said.

"Christ, Dubus, the top of your head is brighter than what's inside." Collins smirked.

"Please confine your remarks to the matter at hand," Dubus returned.

"Oooh, tough guy, huh? I bet you and your wife have a cute name for your dick, don't you? Marvin, maybe? Dorchester? Rambo?"

Dubus's face darkened even more. "You're ridiculous, Collins."

"Yo mama," Collins laughed.

Stan and Leland watched the interchange without comment. These two often chewed on each other like this, sometimes seeming to be on the brink of throwing punches. But it was just the way they worked. The results of their antagonism were often quite brilliant. They were also top-ranked bridge partners who played together four nights a week, cleaning out generals and senators and journalists with regularity.

"Who do we get?" Stan asked. "How do we select?"

"I've been up all night going through the files. I found somebody who fits our needs." Leland flipped through the stack of papers in front of him. Stan watched with amazement and envy. He had no doubt that Leland had indeed been up all night, though he looked as sharp and neat as if he'd just returned from a restful two weeks in Hawaii. After only two hours at Langley, Stan knew his clothes were already rumpled. Under the clothes his skin felt rumpled.

"All we have to do," Leland said, "is bait the hook and lead our whipping boy to water."

"And if he doesn't want to drink?" Stan asked.

"We nudge him a little. Or a lot. Whatever it takes."

Collins nodded at Leland's stack of papers. "Who's the lucky winner?"

Leland opened a red file folder and slid it down the dark mahogany table.

Collins leaned forward, his big hand clamped on the photograph. He read the name. "Clifford Halsey Remington."

Stan immediately shook his head. "That will never work, Aaron. He's been out too long. They'll know it's a setup."

"Remington," Collins mused. "I know that name."

Dubus began vigorously polishing his glasses again. "That Moonshadow mess a couple of years ago. All those citizens who died."

"Jesus, yes. The biochemical stockpile."

"Remington terminated the renegade agent responsible."

"Well, then," Collins said to Stan. "He's not totally incompetent."

Stan felt his stomach churning again. Small sharp-toothed animals were burrowing through his raw intestines. He needed to get back to the bathroom, quickly. But not before this was settled. "Remington isn't an agent anymore, Aaron. He's been retired for years. Two years out of this business is like twenty in any other. He owns a landscaping company now, for Chrissake. There's no way we could send him against someone as formidable as Cronus." Out of habit, Stan used the old code name.

"We're not," Leland said. "We set it up so Cronus will come after him."

"Remington couldn't survive."

"That's the point," Leland said gravely. "He's not supposed to."

No one said anything. Stan studied Leland's unreadable expression and wondered for the thousandth time why the man had dropped out of the Jesuits. What had happened six weeks before he took the final vows?

Leland leaned forward, his voice soft, a somber whisper. They all had to lean forward to hear him. "In the *Soliquiorum, Animae ad Deum*, St. Augustine said, 'Necessity has no law.' Look around you, gentlemen. We are up to our armpits in necessity. I wish there was another way, Stan, I truly do. Something sensitive and humane. I wish we had the time to think of one. But we don't. This country doesn't have the time. We have to act now or risk losing everything. I'm not talking about careers here, I'm talking *lives*. Millions of them." He spoke to all of them, but he made a point of focusing on Stan. His eyes were heavy-lidded, as if with sadness. "If we need a bad guy in all this, okay, I'll take that responsibility. As long as we succeed."

Suddenly Leland stood up, gathered his papers and walked briskly to the door. Under the fluorescent lights the patch of white hair looked for a moment like the bleached white bone of his skull showing through. He appeared unbearably tired. Deboned. Then he straightened, as if he'd just had an injection. He turned and gave each man a steady no-argument stare. "Get started on it right away, gentlemen. Top priority."

He left, his back stiff with burden.

Three of the smartest men in the country stared at each other without speaking.

Collins scratched at his pockets for a cigarette.

Dubus brought a flat gold case out of his jacket, popped the lid and rolled a cigarette across the table. Collins was torching it before it was all the way to his mouth. He took a deep drag as if to calm himself.

"Well, me lads," he said, affecting a thick Irish brogue. "You heard Father Leland. Our objective is to find this poor son of a bitch Remington and hang him out for the squirrels to gather his nuts." He puffed out a cloud of gray smoke. "Ideas, gentlemen?"

PART ONE:

THE COMEBACK

• 1 •

"MY GOD, I thought for sure I'd killed you." The pretty young woman handed Cliff a plastic bag of chipped ice she'd fetched from the snack bar. "You okay?"

"Fine."

"You don't look fine."

"I have that kind of face."

She looked down at him without a smile. "You'd better not get up yet."

Cliff Remington pressed the bag of ice against the tender bump rising Vesuvius-like over his right eyebrow. He held it there a couple of seconds, letting the sharp cold penetrate and sting as punishment for his stupidity. The bag stuck to his sweaty skin and he had to peel the plastic carefully from his forehead. He looked at the bag. A pinkish smear dripped down the side. Blood.

The Samoan was going to be pissed.

Cliff sat cross-legged on the floor of the racquetball court. The back wall was thick tempered glass, and some of the other club members eating lunch were staring in, wincing at his injury as they nibbled salads and sipped green Gatorade. Cliff clamped the ice back against his forehead, pressing until it hurt.

"God, I'm sorry. I'm really sorry." The young woman kept going on like that, waving her racquet so excitedly that Cliff was afraid she might accidentally clobber him again. She was about twenty-five with long tan legs that stood just inches from his face. She shifted and the taut muscles in her legs flexed impressively. They smelled pleasantly of baby powder. "I don't know what to tell you," she said.

Cliff started to get up but her hand pressing on his shoulder stopped him. "Maybe you shouldn't." She leaned over for a better look at the wound and made a face. "That's nasty. You might need stitches."

She wore her blond hair short and brushed back, in a manner attractive women do sometimes to be taken seriously in business. A thin white scar easily mistaken for a crease in the skin arced over the apex of her upper lip. Like a white check mark. Hardly noticeable, but somehow suggestive. "I want you to know, I've never done this before. I mean, hit someone with my racquet. I guess I got turned around when the ball came off the back wall."

"Don't worry about it," Cliff said. He started to get up and felt her fingers on his shoulder again. Her thigh brushed his cheek.

"You think you should?"

"I'm okay." Cliff stood up and backed away from her a little. The adrenaline pumping through his stomach made him slightly queasy, but otherwise he was fit enough to walk. He took a couple of steps and the young woman grabbed his wrist. Her grip was surprisingly strong. He could feel his pulse beating rapidly against her warm fingertips. She wore no makeup, no polish on her nails. She didn't need any. The sweet scent of baby powder hit his nostrils again.

"I mean it. I've never done this before."

"It happens."

"Not to me. You believe me?"

"Sure," Cliff said, gently freeing his arms. He just wanted to get out of there. He was running ten minutes late because of this accident. He'd already skipped lunch to exercise, and now he'd have to skip his shower, too. The gashed forehead was going to be hard enough to explain to the Samoan. Being late would make things even worse.

"You know, you really should wear safety goggles," she said, holding her own up for inspection. "A few inches lower and I could've put out your eye." Her tone was no longer apologetic but rather parental, as if now she'd decided the injury was Cliff's fault.

In a way, Cliff agreed. He should never have played someone so dangerously clumsy, flailing around the court like a runaway propeller. But the club had been dead today and he'd been warming up alone for forty minutes, his allotted exercise time almost gone. So when she'd wandered in asking if he wanted a game, Cliff had actually been grateful.

"Really, when you think about it, you shouldn't have played me that tight," she lectured. "You probably stepped into my backhand."

Cliff felt the tiny patch of skin at the back of his neck start to burn and tingle—what Ginger called his Rabid Patch. "Better than litmus paper," she would tease. Then she'd wet her fingertip, touch it to that little spot and make a sizzling noise. "Maybe we can market a whole line of dolls. The Rabid Patch Kids. Their necks light up when you beat them at tennis."

Cliff smiled as he thought about Ginger, his anger ebbing away. Certainly this incident wasn't worth getting mad about. Not like tennis with Ginger, all those damned dink shots of hers.

The young woman was following Cliff out of the court now. "I mean, God, you were practically in my shorts. If you think about it, you're lucky you weren't hurt worse."

Cliff stopped and eyed the woman a long cold moment. She didn't flinch, matching his stare. It was the first time Cliff noticed her eyes, the pale blue stained with dark red, as if blood had somehow seeped into the iris when she was still an embryo. She cocked her head defiantly, planted one hand on her hip. Cliff felt an urge to twist her safety goggles around her throat.

As if reading his mind, she backed up a couple of steps. When she spoke there was a threatening timbre to her voice.

"I'm a lawyer, you know. So I'm not liable for this type of accident. If you're thinking about financing another car by suing me, buster, forget it."

Cliff turned and walked away.

She caught up, her hand on his arm, not grabbing this time, just resting gently. The smell of baby powder swirled around him again.

"Look, I'm sorry," she said, her tone apologetic again. "Occupational hazard. Someone's always suing over Mickey Mouse shit like this. The whole thing was my fault and I really am sorry." She offered a warm smile and her hand. "No hard feelings?"

Cliff studied her face. He could see now she was older than he'd first thought, closer to thirty. He shook her hand. "No hard feelings."

"You really should have that cut looked at by a doctor. Least I can do is drive you to the clinic down the street. My Porsche's right outside. We'll go in style."

Cliff shook his head. "I'm fine, thanks."

"I'll drive slow. I'm a better driver than a racquetball player."

"Really, I'm okay."

"You sure?"

He nodded.

"Okay then." She shrugged. "See ya."

Cliff picked up his battered racquetball bag and headed for the checkout desk. On the way he dumped the blood-smeared bag of ice in the trash. At the desk he exchanged his locker key for his membership card and started for the front door.

That was when he spotted the first assassin.

The man was standing near the front door, hands deep in the pockets of his white sweat pants, trying to act casual. He wore Air Jordan hightops and had a basketball tucked under one arm. He was tall, somewhere in the six-four range, with red hair buzz-cut high over his ears. The hair on top stood straight

up and was mowed into a flat plateau. He had so many freckles on his face that they were arranged in clusters rather than
individually, giving him a spotted look.

He was reading the poster tacked to the bulletin board near
the front door. A club-sponsored trip to Las Vegas. Three
nights, two days at Circus Circus. Transportation by double-
decker bus, the Joan Rivers show at Caesar's Palace. Squinting thoughtfully, the redhead was pretending to concentrate
on the poster, as if trying to decide whether he and the family
could afford this bargain package, whether he'd get the time
off from his computer sales job. Who'd water the plants, feed
the dog? Only he wasn't very good at pretending and ended
up looking as if he was calculating how fast he could pull out
that ankle gun he was wearing under the baggy sweat pants.

Cliff turned, started down the corridor toward the emergency exit.

The second assassin was leaning over the drinking fountain, sipping water, splashing some on his glasses as he tried
to look everywhere but at Cliff. He was a little better at acting
dumb than his partner. He was about Cliff's height, but
packed about twenty more pounds of bulging muscle, most
of it in his neck. He wore a maroon Adidas running suit with
the jacket zipped all the way to the throat. His watch was
strapped to his right wrist, so he was probably left-handed. If
his left hand started moving toward the zipper, he'd be reaching for the gun Cliff could tell was holstered under his arm.

Cliff looked at the clock over the snack bar and sighed. The
Samoan was going to be *really* pissed now.

2

CLIFF STEPPED UP to the snack bar. "Diet Coke."

"Machine's busted," the attendant said. "How about a cold beer?"

"Milk."

"The milk's not so good, neither. A little electrical problem knocked both of them out. Guy won't be here to fix them for an hour. Beer's cold, though."

"How's the juice?"

"What have you got against beer, man? You a surgeon or something?"

"A vet," Cliff said.

The attendant brightened. "Yeah? Me too. Marines." He tugged up the short sleeve of his white polo shirt. A faded blue marine tattoo covered his thin upper arm. He flexed his arm but not much changed. The eagle looked hung over, the anchor rusted. The globe appeared to be in the midst of a nuclear winter. He shrugged, pulled down the sleeve. "Looked a whole lot more impressive when there was some muscle under it. Been sick, though. Agent Orange."

Cliff looked at the man's face. Late thirties, about the same age as Cliff, but his skin was loose and mottled, and he had the rheumy eyes of an alcoholic.

"Orange juice," Cliff said.

"Coming up." The attendant's name was Jerry. Cliff had passed a few words with him over the past month while waiting for a Diet Coke after his daily workouts. Mostly they chatted about sports, who would the Lakers get to replace Kareem, should Sugar Ray Leonard stay retired or risk his eye for a few lousy million. Jerry had strong opinions about both, though they changed from day to day.

The two assassins hadn't moved yet. They were still standing at their posts, practicing acting casual. The one wearing glasses was in charge, and he hadn't decided yet what Cliff was up to.

Cliff hadn't decided yet either.

Jerry set the orange juice down on the counter. The Styrofoam cup was overfilled and some slopped over to the edge onto his fingers and the counter. He licked his fingers. "Eighty-five cents." He took Cliff's wrinkled dollar, ironed it flat against the counter with the palm of his hand and laid it gently in the cash register like someone building a nest. He slid back a dime and a nickel. He looked sad. "That Agent Orange stuff I told you? Bunch of crap. I never was in Nam. Never made it out of El Toro."

"That's okay. I'm not a veterinarian."

"I knew that, man. I was pulling your leg. I'm dumb, but not that dumb."

Cliff dropped the fifteen cents in the torn tip cup and walked off sipping his orange juice. It was warm and sour. He stood in front of one of the glass-enclosed courts and pretended to watch the game going on inside. A gray-haired man about sixty-five was running a kid in his twenties around the court. The kid was puffing and hustling, diving for dinks, scrambling for passing shots. The old guy stood in the middle of the court flicking the ball wherever the kid wasn't, hardly budging.

Cliff tried to think. Not about who these gunmen were or who they worked for. That didn't matter. What was important now was staying alive.

In a way, Cliff was grateful to the two assassins. They had proved his point. The Samoan had convinced Cliff that his years away from the Agency had dulled him mentally and physically. His marriage to Ginger, being father to her two children, running the landscaping business had made him no longer fit for the kind of work the Samoan had in mind when they formed their partnership a month ago.

"What about the Moonshadow business?" Cliff had pointed out a little angrily.

"Luck," the Samoan had said.

Down deep, Cliff wasn't sure he disagreed. He was only ten pounds heavier than in his prime years with the Agency, but he was slower and softer. More like a family man. Volleyball with the kids wasn't quite the same as a fifteen-mile jog with full gear. A bucket of balls on the golf range wasn't the same as a box of bullets on the rifle range. That was why he was working out daily at the health club. Swimming laps, jumping rope, running the rooftop track, lifting weights, racquetball. His partnership with the Samoan was going to change everything, and he was determined to make it work, despite Ginger's skepticism. Still, he'd thought it would be easier than this.

At least he'd spotted the assassins. That proved something. Proved that his instincts were still sharp. True, these guys weren't world class, but they were still professionals. Farmers. That's what Cliff and Drew used to call themselves. "Like farmers we toil in the fields, we get our hands dirty," Drew would say. "And we plant the bodies."

Cliff stood halfway between the two killers, still sipping his warm orange juice and watching the racquetball game in front of him. Okay, he'd spotted them. Now what?

Both were big men, late twenties, solid athletic builds. They looked as if they could run for miles without tiring, a full marathon if they had to. There was no chance he could outrun them on foot. And direct confrontation didn't look promising. It wasn't like the old days, that game he and Drew used to play when they were on assignment together. A variation of "Name That Tune." They'd be following some hulking foreign agent on his payoff rounds through West Berlin or someplace, and Drew would size up the guy from a distance and say, "I can kill him in ten seconds." Cliff would say, "I can kill him in seven seconds." Then Drew, with a game-show host flourish, would point and say, "Kill that spy!"

Mostly, they just killed time. Mostly.

Cliff shook his head at the memory. He hardly believed that arrogant naive youth had been he. They'd swaggered around like smug jocks on a winning football team. Gimme a C. Gimme an I. Gimme an A. What's that spell? *What's that spell?* The two men stalking him now could just as easily have been Cliff and Drew ten years ago. Before the incident in London with Drew, when everything changed. When things went bad.

The redheaded assassin by the front door was now kneeling, retying his hightops. Easier access to his ankle holster. His partner was still slurping water from the drinking fountain. So much had splashed onto his glasses that the cluster of drops made his eyes look many faceted, like a fly's. He must have realized Cliff had spotted them, because he suddenly stopped drinking, stood straight, wiped his mouth with the back of his hand and stared directly at Cliff.

"Damn," Cliff said aloud. He had no idea why they were here. He'd given up all that childish crap long ago. All the old excuses—patriotism, adventure, loyalty—had wilted one by one with each new assignment until there had been nothing left but instinct and habit. After London even that had changed. Now his sinister past was something even Washington wanted to forget. They had buried his files deeper than hot plutonium. Since the Moonshadow episode, they'd each accepted a kind of unofficial truce. Peaceful coexistence. Cliff was free to play with his family and his landscaping business; they were free to play with the rest of the world. But why come after him now? He'd stuck to his part of the bargain.

The redhead stood up, nodded to his partner. They both started a slow march toward Cliff.

Cliff crumpled the Styrofoam cup and tossed it in the trash. Now came the tricky part.

Quickly he unslung his racquetball bag from his shoulder and walked back to the second court. The young woman who'd hit him was bent over, stepping into a pair of black sweat pants. Her red shorts were cut high on the hips and the elastic from her blue panties peeked out.

"How about one more game?" Cliff asked.

She looked around startled, the sweats halfway up her thighs. "What?"

"Another game. We never did get to finish."

"But your head . . ."

"I'll try to stay out of your way this time."

"I don't know. I really should go. I have clients—"

"One more," Cliff said. "Quick one to eleven. My appointment just canceled, and I have some free time on my hands."

"I don't know," she repeated. Then she made a mistake. She glanced, just for a fraction of a second, down the hall toward the man by the drinking fountain.

Christ, Cliff suddenly realized, *she's with them!* The whole thing had been a setup. A minor injury to get him out of the building. Ideally, he would have agreed to let her drive him to the clinic. Of course he would never arrive. The Samoan was right about him, after all. He was dulled.

"Come on." Cliff smiled at her. "Take ten minutes. You can serve. You came here to play, didn't you?"

She shrugged, trapped. "One game," she said. "Then I've got to get back to the office." To her credit, she was still trying to maintain her cover.

She peeled off the sweat pants, grabbed her racquet and goggles and followed Cliff onto the court. He handed her the blue ball and she looked into his eyes, as if searching for something. He noticed for the first time that she was nearly as tall as he was. Other than a passing appreciation of her face and body, he hadn't really paid much attention to her before. Passing appreciation was all he allowed himself; he loved Ginger too much to linger. A bad sign. He'd acted more like a husband than a professional. But now he examined the woman much more closely. As an enemy. The strength in her grip and the muscles flexing in her long legs indicated more athletic ability than she'd displayed during their last game.

"Well?" she said with a forced smile. "Are we going to play or are you trying to psych me out?"

"Let's play."

They lagged for serve. Cliff won. As he strolled to the server's box, he glanced over his shoulder, watching the two gunmen closing in outside the glass wall. The redhead spoke to his partner, and Cliff noticed for the first time that he wore thick silver braces.

"Zeroes," Cliff announced cheerfully. He served a high arcing lob that barely cleared the back wall. She smacked the ball with a perfect backhand that fired it to the front wall for a perfect roll-out kill shot. Nervousness had made her forget to play badly.

"Nice shot," he said, tossing her the ball.

"Lucky," she said. She served.

Her shots were so accurate, only Cliff's speed and reflexes kept him barely in the game. She was leading 8 to 7, having just pinched a ball into the corner that sent him crashing into the wall trying to retrieve it. Obviously she was anxious to finish the game and get away from him now that she suspected things had gone wrong.

It took a few more points before Cliff found the opening he'd been waiting for. A ceiling ball rally had kept them crowding each other in the back corner. Finally, she hit a ceiling ball that allowed Cliff to fade back, trapping her in the corner behind him as he brought his racquet back for an overhead smash. Sensing exactly where she was, he snapped the racquet back over his shoulder and cracked her sharply on top of the head.

She dropped to her knees with a moan. Blood immediately seeped into the blond hairs.

"Oh, my," Cliff said, rushing to her. "Are you okay?"

"You did that on purpose, you son of a bitch," she said.

"Better let me have a look." Cliff bent over her as if to check the injury. Her back was to the glass wall. Over her shoulder he saw some of the horrified patrons watching. Including her two partners.

"Get away from me," she snapped, pushing at him with one hand. The other dabbed the top of her head. She examined her fingertips and saw the bright blood. "Shit!" She looked into Cliff's eyes. The red flaw in her own eyes seemed to expand. "You think you're cute, don't you? But you've just made a big fucking mistake. A big goddamn—"

With her body shielding his movement, Cliff reached down and clamped his fingers around her jugular. To those outside it looked as if he was comforting her. He squeezed. His fingers sank into the soft flesh as if they were pinching a garden hose, closing off her air. She grabbed frantically at his arm, but even with her considerable strength, she was unable to loosen his grip. This particular move had once been Cliff's specialty. Ten years ago he'd managed to crush another agent's windpipe even though the man had stuck a Swiss army knife through Cliff's hand. During the infamous London incident.

This time he squeezed only hard enough for her to droop into semiconsciousness. Cliff immediately slipped an arm around her waist and lifted her to her feet. She sagged against him, dazed, her eyes half closed. The scent of baby powder was mixed with a heavier musky smell of fear. Her lips moved, but no sound came out. He guided her off the court. Instantly a short but thickly muscled teenager pushed through the crowd. On his short body the mass of muscles looked silly, as if his body were overinflated. A plastic name tag identifying him as a club employee was pinned to the pocket of his too-tight shirt. His name was Larry.

"She okay?" Larry asked. His voice had a squeak of teenage panic in it.

"Just dazed," Cliff said.

"I'd better call the paramedics."

"No need," Cliff assured him. "She asked me to drive her to the clinic down the street."

"That so, Mrs. Fawley?" Larry asked her.

Her eyelids fluttered, her lips twitched. Otherwise nothing.

Larry looked uncertain. "I don't know. Mrs. Fawley's a lawyer, you know. The club doesn't want no trouble."

Cliff used one hand to hold her up and the other to rummage through her bag. "She owns a Porsche, Larry. You know which one?"

"You kidding. That white 930 Turbo with the whale-tail spoiler."

Cliff tossed him the keys. "Bring it around front. I'll take her to the doctor." He pointed to his own gashed forehead and smiled. "Maybe he'll give us a two-for-one deal."

"Yes, sir," Larry said happily. He dashed off with the keys clutched tightly in his hand. The thrill of driving the Porsche had replaced concern for Mrs. Fawley.

"Why don't I give you a hand, sir?" the tall redheaded assassin asked politely. He stepped toward Cliff, hands the size of lobsters reaching for her.

"I've got her," Cliff said, stepping around him. "But I would appreciate it if you'd see to someone getting her clothes from her locker." He handed him the locker key from her bag. "We'll meet you outside."

The redhead grimaced, his saliva-slicked braces catching the light like silver-scaled fish flickering under the surface of a lake. He looked questioningly at his partner, who nodded for him to go. The redhead grabbed the locker key and hurried off downstairs to the locker rooms.

Two down, Cliff thought, half carrying Mrs. Fawley down the hallway toward the front door. Some of the crowd stayed with him, including the assassin in glasses. As they passed the snack bar, Jerry winked a rheumy eye. "Finally bagged one, huh, Doc?"

Cliff kept walking. The thing about a bluff was, once started, it fed on momentum. Any slowing down and the whole illusion collapsed under you. He pushed through the front door and walked Mrs. Fawley to the curb.

Larry had taken the long way around the parking lot, circling once before doubling back and pulling up to the curb. Cliff noticed that her license plates were personalized: SINNER. Larry pumped the gas a few extra times, revving the engine to a muffled roar, before hopping out. He rubbed his hands gleefully and gave the car a lustful look. "Man, I'm in love."

Cliff opened the passenger door and was about to lower her into the seat when he seemed to suddenly remember something. "Damn. I forgot our bags." He turned to the crowd, looking them over a moment, his eyes landing apparently at random on the man with glasses. Cliff smiled at him. "Would you mind running back and getting them for us? Just take you a minute."

The assassin hesitated, his blue eyes locking murderously onto Cliff's. The muscles in his neck were jumping.

"My hands are kinda full," Cliff explained, nodding at Mrs. Fawley.

All eyes were focused on the assassin now, and he managed a curt nod before racing back into the clubhouse. Cliff figured he'd be back in about ten seconds.

Cliff instantly handed Mrs. Fawley over to Larry. "Hold her a minute, would you, son?"

"Yeah, sure," Larry grinned. This was his lucky day, first driving the Porsche, now holding Mrs. Fawley. He wrapped one muscular arm around her slender waist to hold her up, but she slipped a little until her breasts rested on top of his fore-arm. Her soft hair brushed his face and he took a deep breath of baby powder. Her head rolled back against his shoulder, her eyes opening now, her lips forming words. Faint muttering sounds were coming from her mouth. "Hey, mister, I think she's trying to say something."

"Yeah?" Cliff said, climbing behind the wheel of the Porsche.

"Want me to slide her in?" Larry asked through the open passenger door.

"No need," Cliff said. He gunned the motor, popped the clutch and roared away from the curb, the passenger door slamming shut from the force. In the rearview mirror he saw the crowd watching dumbfounded, Larry still holding Mrs. Fawley, shouting something nasty after him.

Cliff urged the car into the traffic on the busy boulevard just as the two assassins sprinted through the crowd and ran for their car. Whatever car they were driving, it would never catch this one.

He stomped on the pedal and rocketed onto the freeway.

So much for being mentally and physically dulled.

"HI, IT'S ME."

"What's wrong?" she said immediately.

Cliff frowned into the telephone. He'd tried to keep his voice as casual as possible. But she'd read him easily. Another bad sign that the Samoan was right. "Got hit with a racquet."

Ginger let out a relieved sigh. "God, is that all?"

"Thanks for the concern. Wait till I tell you where I was hit."

She laughed. "You know what I mean."

He did. She usually managed to hide it, but she lived in constant fear that somehow his past would reach back to pluck them out of their comfortable lives, just as it had two years ago with Moonshadow. When they had first fallen in love she hadn't known anything about his former life. After she found out, after the terrible adventure he'd put her and the kids through, she'd still stuck by him. He admired her courage.

"How bad's the damage?" she asked.

"Forehead. Probably leave a little scar."

"We'll add it to your vast collection. Did you at least win the game?"

"Yes, I won." He paused as a semi carrying produce to Ralph's supermarket roared past the phone booth. The glass rattled as it blasted by.

"Jesus!" she said. "Where are you?"

"Anaheim."

"I thought you had a meeting in Irvine."

He looked down the busy street. From this angle he could see the tip of the Matterhorn ride in Disneyland. The train of bobsleds darted out of a cave. Half the people in it waved their hands over their heads to prove they weren't afraid. "I do have a meeting. I'm late."

This time Ginger paused. "Come on Cliff. The last time you were late was when you were born."

"Something unexpected came up."

"You're scaring me, Cliff."

Cliff gnawed the inside of his cheek. He wasn't handling this well. Out of practice.

"Just come out with it, okay?" she said. "What's going on?"

"Any strangers been by?"

"This is a landscaping business, Cliff. We're open to the goddamn public. Yes, strangers have been by. I neglected to fingerprint them, however."

"I'm trying to make this easy."

"It's not working."

Cliff used his finger to draw a big G on the glass of the booth. The G shimmered for an instant then faded like a ghost. He breathed on it and the G reappeared. "I ran into a couple of guys at the club. Professionals."

He heard her quick intake of breath. When she spoke her voice was shaky. "You okay?"

"Yeah. I lost them. But if they know I work out there, they must know everything else. The house, the business, the kids' schools."

"Have you called the Samoan?"

"Not yet. Right now I want you to leave the store. Denise can run it. Go collect the kids from school and check in to that motel in Laguna. You remember the one."

"What about you?"

"I have a plan," he lied. "Probably have everything straightened out by the time you and the kids have argued over what TV show to watch."

There was a tense silence. Finally, Ginger spoke. "I love you, Cliff. I wish there was something more useful I could say."

"That's pretty good for starters."

"Are you scared? Truth."

"Some."

"Good. That makes me feel better. Now I know you won't do anything stupid."

Cliff was startled by the loud knocking behind him. Heavy metal clunking on glass. He spun, already knowing what he'd find.

The tall redhead was standing there, his snub-nosed .38 pressed against the glass at waist level. Around his metal-jacketed teeth he mouthed, "Hang up."

"Gotta go," Cliff said into the phone. "Do what I told you."

"Cliff?" she said.

He hung up.

3

CLIFF WAS SANDWICHED tightly between the two big men. Each had a meaty hand choking one of his arms as they marched him silently up the brick walkway. The squat one-story beach house was barely visible behind the sprawling foliage that surrounded it. Three-leaf clovers grew between the weathered bricks. Moss or mold, something blackish green and slippery, coated most of the bricks. A eucalyptus root as thick as an elephant trunk had stretched out under the walkway and buckled some of the bricks up out of the ground.

The redhead stumbled over one of the broken bricks. To keep from falling, he tightened his grip on Cliff's arm until the whole arm went prickly numb. The tall redhead cursed, kicked the offending chunk of brick with his hightops. The piece of brick tumbled into the grass and Cliff cringed a little to think what would happen when an unsuspecting lawn mower rolled over it. When he caught himself in the middle of that thought, he realized with a little shame just how far he really had come from the hot-shot agent he'd once been.

They were in the tiny beach town of Corona Del Mar. The cool briny breeze from the Pacific half a mile away offered some small relief from the hot September sun. All three men were sweating as they hurried toward the house. Next to the front door lay a pair of worn rubber flip-flops with dozens of animal teeth marks puncturing them. A dusty layer of beach sand where someone had brushed himself off was sprinkled around the porch. The three men had just climbed the porch when the front door jerked open and an angry face jutted out at them.

"What the hell did you bring him here for?" she snapped. She stood blocking the doorway, her short blond hair dripping wet and plastered straight back over her head like an Olympic diver's. She was wearing a short red-and-black Japanese robe and had obviously just stepped out of the shower. Some shampoo suds still foamed in her left ear. A drop of water clung to the white checkmark scar above her lip, magnifying it.

The assassin with glasses muscled open the front door, jostling her out of the way. "Relax, Tory," he said. "This won't take long."

The redhead nudged Cliff in the spine with his fist. The impact pitched Cliff forward into the door. He caught himself on the doorjamb. The back of his neck was fiery as if he'd been bitten by red ants. He wanted to slug the redhead, maybe break a major bone, but he let it pass. When it came to revenge, timing was everything. The redhead immediately went to the kitchen phone, dialed, mumbled their present address and hung up.

The woman just stood there, dripping and glowering.

"How's the head?" Cliff asked her.

She ignored him, concentrating her anger on the man with glasses, who was looking around the room with a shocked and angry expression. "Listen, Ed, I let you bully me into helping corral this guy, but that's it. Now you can just—"

"What the fuck have you been doing here?" he asked, a threatening edge to his voice. "The place is a fucking mess."

Indeed the walls were bare with patches of white Spackle where nail holes had been filled in. Half of one wall was freshly painted a deep lavender; the rest of the room was a faded green. Cliff thought the lavender looked better.

"Where the fuck's the furniture?" Ed growled. "All that fancy white rattan crap you insisted we spend a fortune on. That bastard salesman who jewed us on the price."

"I got rid of it after the divorce," she said. "Sold it at a garage sale."

"Yeah? Where's Mike? You sell him too?"

"He's napping in the bedroom."

"Mike!" Ed hollered. "Mike, come here!"

Cliff turned to the redhead. "Not exactly Ozzie and Harriet."

The redhead bared his braces. "Shut your hole, man."

Cliff went over to the bar stool next to the counter separating the kitchen and living room. He had to step carefully because the carpeting was in the process of being torn up. He perched on the tall stool and waited.

"Where's my Porsche?" Tory asked.

"Mike, goddamn it!" Ed yelled. "Get your ass out here."

"It's at a gas station in Anaheim," the redhead said. He tossed her the keys and gave her a nasty look. "Fucker must have cost you some hard bucks."

"I make monthly car payments like everyone else."

"Everyone else doesn't drive a Porsche."

"Out here they do," Cliff said, glancing up from the *New Yorker* magazine he'd found on the counter.

"I told you to shut your hole."

Cliff sighed. "Listen, sonny, if you were going to kill me, you'd have already done the job. If you were going to work me over, you'd have tied me spread-eagled to the kitchen table by now and would be heating up the potato peeler over the gas range. So you've been sent to intimidate me, remind me of the long reach of your employers and then ask me for something. Okay, I'm impressed. I didn't think you guys would be smart enough to put a homing device in her car. Now if we can cut through this episode of 'Divorce Court,' I have a real life to get back to."

The muscular man with glasses grinned at Cliff. It wasn't a friendly grin. He had wavy black hair and the pampered good looks of a high school football hero who'd found life after high school rough. He'd probably been terribly handsome once, his initials embellished with medieval flourishes in girls' biology notebooks. But now he was starting to look a little puffy under the eyes, like a leading actor slowly going to seed, reduced to taking character parts. Cliff had the feeling the man spent a lot of time in the mornings at the bathroom mirror, reassuring himself. He wore a thick USC class ring with a red stone and was absently twisting it on his finger while grinning at Cliff.

"They told me you were a smartass," he said to Cliff. He made it sound like a disease. He turned to Tory. "Go get Mike."

Tory started to argue, then sighed resignation and disappeared down a carpetless corridor, her bare feet hushed on the foundation padding.

"Come on, Fawley," the redhead said. "Let's just stick to the job."

Ed Fawley turned and shot the redhead a look that shut him up.

Tory appeared again, her arms filled with a long fat basset hound weighing at least sixty-five pounds. She held the stocky tubular hound effortlessly, balancing his hindquarters and front in both arms. Slowly she lowered him to the floor, where he lay still a few seconds, then struggled to his short stubby legs.

"Come 'ere, Mike," Ed called. "Come on, buddy."

Mike stared impassively, ear flaps drooping to the floor.

"Apparently he still remembers you," Tory said.

Fawley went over to the dog, petted him, grabbed him roughly by the ears. "Yeah, you remember me, dontcha boy. Sure ya do." Ed straightened up, grinning as if Mike had shown him a lot of affection. Now that he'd made his point, though, he seemed to forget the dog was there, almost stepping on him as he crossed the room to the stereo, which was the only piece of furniture in the room besides the huge speakers in opposite corners. He began flipping through the records. "Hey, here's my Meat Loaf album. I been looking for it."

"You had your pick of records when we separated. You took half. More than half, I remember."

"Yeah, but this one's *mine*. I bought it for the party, remember, the housewarming party when we moved in here."

"We both bought it, Ed. And, you already took your share."

He continued flipping through the albums.

Mike yawned, made an awkward turn and ambled back down the hallway. Fawley looked angrily at the dog as if he would run after him to give him a kick.

"Where are your contacts, Ed?" Tory asked, distracting him. "You haven't worn glasses in years."

He touched his glasses self-consciously. "Wore the contacts too long. Scratched my eyes."

"You were always too vain."

"You were always a cunt."

She stared at him a long moment, as if he were a species of animal she didn't recognize. When she spoke, her voice was unnaturally calm, but firm. "Get out now, all of you. If not, I'll call the cops. Maybe they won't arrest you, but your bosses will sure be pissed at you."

The redhead smirked. "You aren't going to call the fucking cops."

"No? Ask Ed. He knows better."

Ed Fawley was standing next to her now, the muscles in his neck jumping again, the hand with the big ring flexed as if he were about to strike her. She tensed reflexively, a flash of conditioned fear. The red flaws in her eyes ballooned. Then with a visible effort of willpower, she shrugged off that fear and stared back at him, the look in her eyes saying, Try it, asshole.

Fawley was smart enough to read her expression and let his hand drop to his side. He started twisting his class ring again. Cliff noticed that the ring had just the right heft and shape to cause a scar like the one that rode Tory's upper lip.

"Listen, Tory," Ed said. He was smiling now, trying some of the old locker room charm. "This isn't going to take long. Maybe you're a balls-out lawyer now with a Porsche and IRAs, but you were on the inside once. You wore the Company colors."

"Yeah, black and blue. And red."

"You know what I'm saying. Just give us a few minutes. Take Mike down to the beach."

"He hates the beach this late. He always has."

"Okay, then you go. You used to love it when we body-surfed together, remember? Rubbing in all that tanning oil?" He tried a lustful smile; it came out as a smirk.

She shook her head as if at a child. "I can't just run down to the beach any time, Ed. I have an adult job now." She leaned over the counter next to Cliff so she could glimpse the kitchen clock. Cliff smelled fresh baby powder. "I've got clients to see this afternoon. Give me five minutes to dress and I'll get out of here. Don't start anything before then. I don't want to know anything or overhear anything I shouldn't."

"What about your car?" Cliff asked, without looking up from the *New Yorker*. "How will you get to work?"

"The Mustang. Thanks so much for asking." The look she gave Cliff suggested she held him in slightly more contempt than she did Fawley.

Five minutes later she was walking toward the door, dressed in a light blue suit and white hose that made her look extremely competent and gorgeous as well. "Remember our deal, Ed."

"Sure, Tory. See you Saturday."

She looked at him as if trying to decide whether or not he was lying. She shrugged. "Lock up when you leave," she said, closing the door behind her.

While she'd been dressing, no one had spoken. Cliff had continued leafing through his magazine while the bored red-head leaned against the unpainted wall, occasionally looking out the window as cars approached and went by. Ed Fawley kept fingering through the record collection.

Once Tory Fawley had gone, though, the redhead straightened up as if ready for business. Fawley pulled out the Meat Loaf album and put it on the stereo. "All Revved Up with No Place to Go" blared from the speakers. He sang along with it a couple of lines, eyes pressed closed, strutting and pretending to strum a guitar. Then he opened his eyes and turned to face Cliff, that malicious smirk still on his face. "Some lady I married, huh?"

"Good racquetball player," Cliff said.

"I taught her," he said.

"You get her into the Company too?"

"Damn right. I'd been in a year. They had me doing some recruiting work at colleges, you know, talking about how we hardly do any cloak-and-dagger stuff anymore and what an upstanding group of Americans we were. Like some kind of Christian social club or something. Anyway, Tory was graduating with a degree in criminal justice and wanted to go right into law school, be a public defender, for God's sake. I talked her out of it." His smirk widened to suggest a wide range of sexual activity he'd used to persuade her.

Cliff nodded. It was clear Fawley was the kind of guy who would claim credit for any of her success and accomplishments. That would be a heavy hand to live under.

"She's pissed at you, man," Fawley said.

"I have that power over women." Cliff was watching the other assassin staring nervously out the window. A car was coming and the redhead was craning his neck for a good look.

"Yeah," Fawley continued. "Tory was supposed to charm you into her car and you end up splitting her goddamn skull. Insult to injury, man. She's not used to men shining her on." He chuckled.

"He's here," the redhead said, squaring his shoulders.

Ed Fawley turned off the stereo.

A minute later the redhead opened the front door and a pleasant-looking blond man entered the house. Cliff recognized the face and especially the black metal hook on the end of his left wrist.

"Everything went just fine, Mr. Ford," the redhead blurted immediately. "No problems."

Standish Ford ignored him, kept walking toward Cliff. His right hand gestured to Cliff's forehead. "What happened to your head?"

"Watching these two clowns work. I split the skin I was laughing so hard."

Stan half smiled. "You know who I am?"

Cliff studied Standish Ford. They had never met, but he knew of him, of course, had seen him a few times years ago, when Cliff still occasionally went to Langley for briefing and debriefing. Standish Ford had the reputation of being a good man, both professionally and personally, a rare distinction there. "Yeah, I know you. Assistant section chief under that lardass Crenshaw."

"Not anymore. He's out, I'm in."

Cliff nodded approval. "Quite a promotion. They had to jump over a lot of good people who'd been waiting longer than you."

"I got a break."

"Good for you. Now give me one."

Stan picked off a loose thread stuck to his hook, balled it up and laid it neatly on the counter. "I'm sorry if the boys were rough, Cliff. Their orders were only to ask you to come to a meeting with me, not to force you."

Cliff smiled. "Come off it, Stan. Their orders were to escort me to this meeting by any means necessary, including gunpoint or knocking me on the head, if it came to that."

Stan's face stiffened as if he was insulted, and his eyes locked onto Cliff's. But slowly the muscles around his mouth shifted into a grin. "Okay, I see you haven't forgotten everything since your retirement. That's good."

"I assume things haven't changed that much up at Graceland."

"God, I haven't heard it called that in a while."

"Old habit," Cliff said. Every generation of agent seemed to have another pet name for the CIA. When Cliff was active, the older guys called it the Agency, as if it was some kind of Madison Avenue ad firm. They even talked and dressed like ad men. The next generation had called it the Company, imagining they were part of General Motors or something, the country as one big corporation. Drew, though, had been the first to refer to the CIA as Graceland. An Elvis fanatic, who actually looked a little like Presley, Drew used to do a remarkable singing tribute to the King. When they were stationed in Berlin, he'd dressed like Elvis one evening, greased back his hair and walked into a small club. He began singing "All Shook Up" in German. The crowd loved him.

"March 1957," Drew had said that night, mopping sweat and drinking free drinks the patrons kept sending to Drew and Cliff's table. "Twenty-five years ago today. That's when the King bought Graceland, a church that had been converted into a twenty-three-room mansion. Kinda like the Company, huh? Started as something reverent and decent, and now it's a fucking mansion on the hill." He'd winked at Cliff, a devilish grin on his lips. From that night on they'd referred to the CIA as Graceland. Soon all the younger employees did too. After Drew's death, though, the irony seemed too bitter. The next generation were corporate thugs, and the Company seemed more appropriate again.

Stan tapped his hook on the counter. "We'd like to hire you for a little consultancy work. Interested?"

"No."

"That was a quick answer."

"Wasn't much of a question."

Stan glanced around the living room, looking for someplace to sit. "Isn't there any furniture in this house?"

"She's remodeling," Ed Fawley said. "My wife. Ex-wife."

Stan climbed onto one of the bar stools next to Cliff. "I've always hated these things. Make me feel like a schoolkid being punished. A dunce chair."

"I get the same feeling hanging around Gracelanders."

Stan gave him a sharp look. "Knock off the sarcasm, Remington. You and I both know that you're going to hear me out. On that you have no choice. When I'm finished, you can make your own decision about our offer and we'll both live by that. You're not going to be forced into anything."

"No pressure, huh?"

"None. You either take the job or you don't."

Cliff stared back at Stan. He believed him. "Whose idea was it to come to me?"

"Aaron Leland thought you could handle it. He's the director now, in case you don't keep up with Company news."

"I don't," Cliff lied.

"You ever work with Leland?"

Cliff tried to keep his face expressionless. "Once. Years ago. In London."

"Well, then you know he gets what he wants. He wanted me. Now he wants you."

"Why me? Christ, you've got plenty of regular agents. They're not only willing, they're in better condition."

"This is a special situation."

Cliff suppressed a smile. Stan Ford was pressing all the usual buttons, hoping to tease Cliff into accepting. Most ex-agents would jump at the chance for active status. Drew used to say he'd never retire. "People outside think we all burn out after a while and become cynical husks trying to quit. Truth is, the real problem is that we *don't* want to quit. We like being who we are, living on the Inside. Kinda like emergency room doctors or cops or journalists. Reporters get off on knowing news first, even if it's only a few minutes before the rest of the world. Maybe it makes us feel important. Important equals Immortal? I don't know, man, I only know one thing. . . ." Then Drew would curl his upper lip into a Presley sneer and drawl, "'You can do anything, just get offa my blue suede shoes.'"

Stan continued, "We need someone who's been out of the business for a while. An unknown factor."

Cliff leaned his elbows back on the Formica counter. "Make me an offer."

Stan looked over at the redhead and Fawley. "Wait in the car, gentlemen."

The redhead opened the front door and waited for Fawley. Fawley removed the album from the turntable, slid it into the jacket, tucked it under his arm and walked out, grinning at Cliff.

When they'd left, Stan said, "Excuse me," and disappeared down the hallway. A door closed. A few minutes later a toilet flushed and Stan reappeared looking a little pale. "Mexico," he said disgustedly. "Never again."

"You need liquids." Cliff went into the kitchen and opened the refrigerator. "We've got Poland water, V-8 juice, Pepsi." He pawed through some of the Tupperware containers, each neatly stacked on another. It was the cleanest, neatest refrigerator he'd ever seen. "That's all the liquids."

"Some Poland water. The carbonation seems to help."

Cliff found a glass and poured the Poland water.

"Thanks," Stan said, taking a big swallow. He settled himself back on the stool, his face suddenly grim. "Since you spent most of your time in the field, I don't know how much you know about the base operations at Langley."

"Not much."

"Well, every piece of data we gather, whether from field agents or satellite cameras, gets fed into Fat Boy."

"The computer."

"Right. Except calling Fat Boy just a computer is like calling New York just a village. The thing is immense, handling everything from research and analysis to payroll. Every secret ever gathered since the golden days of the OSS all the way up to and including what was served for dinner at the Kremlin two nights ago is in there. Every agent in our employ is in there, every file, every goddamn detail about anyone we ever opened a file on."

Cliff shook his head. "Let me guess—the Soviets broke the code and have found a way to access the computer. I saw that last week on a TV movie."

"No, it's impossible for an outsider to access the computer. Our security system is completely invulnerable. We even brought in a bunch of child hackers from Dayton who'd broken into the Pentagon computer once. Gave them free rein to enter if they could. Nothing."

"Then what are we here for?"

"The computer is being frozen."

Cliff shifted around in his seat. "Frozen?"

"Information in the computer is coded in sections. Payroll is one section, South America is another, and so forth. Information isn't being stolen, it's being frozen so that even we can't get into the damn thing. It started two days ago—the payroll section was frozen so that we couldn't issue checks. You can imagine how that went over. Sixteen thousand people waiting to get paid, but instead they're told the computer jammed."

Cliff laughed.

"Yeah, I laughed at first too. I figured the glitch would be fixed within a day or two. Then other sections began closing down. Files on our own agents in the Middle East. Files on foreign agents in Washington. Without those files, we can't operate."

"I'm no computer expert," Cliff said.

"We have experts working on the hardware and software. But this isn't an accident, Cliff. It's a deliberate act of sabotage. Every day another section closes down. If it continues, soon we won't have any CIA. The whole country will be completely vulnerable. We'll be like chickens with a big hole in our coop. The coyotes will be nosing through that hole in no time.''

''Just go back to the old-fashioned way. Hard copy. Coffee-stained files in ragged manila folders. Microfilm libraries.''

''Of course we are doing that to some extent. But so much information has been coming in during the past few years we haven't been able to keep up with hard copies or even with microfilming. The computer held the bulk of the crucial information.''

Cliff stood up, went back into the kitchen and stuck his head into Tory Fawley's immaculate refrigerator. It was so clean and bright it reminded him of a hospital. He grabbed the last can of V-8 and shook it, then peeled the foil tab and sipped. ''I guess the next logical question is who's doing it and why.''

''Cronus,'' Stan said.

Cliff stopped drinking, licked his lips. ''Jesus.''

''We'd be better off if it was Jesus. He'd be easier to find.''

Cliff was impressed. Cronus was the code name for Vatican Towne, the man who had helped create the CIA. An old OSS crony of Wild Bill Donovan, though most thought Vatican Towne was the wilder of the two. Also the smarter.

''If anyone could do something like this, it would be Cronus,'' Cliff said. ''But that doesn't make any sense. How is he doing it? More baffling, why?''

''Vatican was one of the major forces in establishing the billion-dollar Fat Boy computer. He helped lobby for the money and was involved in the selection of the computer company that built it. He even named it Fat Boy, after the first atomic bomb. He joked that this computer would have a greater impact than a dozen atomic bombs. Our experts now figure that when the computer was first installed, he mined the program with code words that only he knows. Each time he activates one, another section of information closes down. Hell, he could be activating it from a home computer anywhere in the world. He wouldn't have to break into the computer to do that."

"That's a little like accusing Davy Crockett of dynamiting the Alamo to let the Mexican troops in. What does Vatican have to gain? What does he want?"

"Maybe he's just gone crazy?" Stan said.

"Maybe. But I'd sooner believe that you're crazy."

"Yeah, me too." Stan shifted on the stool trying to get comfortable. When he couldn't, he slid off and began pacing. "Okay, here's the deal: we want you to find him for us."

Cliff laughed. "Find Vatican Towne? Yeah, sure."

"You'll have the complete resources of the CIA to back you up."

"Which apparently don't amount to much right now."

Stan's eyes narrowed. "Look, Remington, you had your troubles with the Company—maybe I even think you got a raw deal. Maybe. But your hurt feelings aren't what count here. We have a serious security problem. We can't protect our agents abroad, and we're going to have trouble following foreign agents here. We can't access satellite photos so we can't monitor enemy troop movements. Our whole Latin America campaign is now shattered. By the time we recover, half the countries could be overthrown. When the Middle East section closes down, Israel could fold within a month. We won't be able to follow terrorist activities. God, the list goes on and gets worse."

"And you think I can do something about it?"

"Yes. We negotiate with him, play along, distract him. Meantime, you try to locate him."

"And if I find him?"

"We take it from there."

"No wet work."

"Not from you."

Cliff rolled the V-8 can between his palms. "What does Towne want? He wouldn't do this without saying something, making some demand. World peace, an end to nuclear weapons, cancel Star Wars? Feed the starving children of Ethiopia? What?"

Stan stopped pacing. He sighed. "He wants Aaron Leland's head."

"He wants Aaron fired. Easy enough."

"No. He literally wants the head. He wants us to send him Aaron Leland's severed head."

Cliff stood up and walked to the door.

Stan followed, hooking Cliff's arm to stop him. "Where are you going?"

"My answer is no."

"Have you thought it over? Thought about what this means to the whole country? To your family?"

Cliff clamped his hand around Stan's prosthesis. "Is that a threat?"

"It's a reality. You can't hide from this. It affects all of us."

Cliff released Stan's hook. Both men faced each other with flat stares. "Okay," Cliff said. "You wanted to hire me as a consultant. Here's my advice. Give him Leland's head." He opened the front door and walked through. Without turning he said, "I'll bill you for my time."

Cliff walked past the redhead and Ed Fawley, who were sitting petulantly in the car. Behind him he heard Stan Ford's footsteps clopping across the moldy brick walkway.

"Remington!" he called. "Goddamn it, Remington!"

Cliff kept walking.

4

"THIS IS WEIRD," Ernest said.

"What is?" Gibb didn't look at Ernest. He was busy polishing the glass display case that lined the wall of the Animation Building on the Walt Disney Studio lot in Burbank. The Animation Building was located on Dopey Lane and Gibb always got a kick out of putting Dopey Lane down as his work address on loan applications and such. It always got a startled look from the loan officers, who would immediately lean away from him as if he was rabid. Even after he explained, they smiled kind of stiff and waxy. But Gibb's philosophy was you shouldn't take such things seriously. If they couldn't laugh at the joke, then he didn't want to borrow their lousy money. Money didn't matter that much to him.

"Jesus H. Christopher," Ernest said and whistled. He was supposed to be helping clean the display glass that ran almost the entire length of the hallway, up and down both walls. Inside the cases were nifty displays of old drawings from the great Disney cartoons. Gibb had the left side of the hall, Ernest the right side. Gibb always finished first and did the better job.

"How about a little less mouth manure and a little more elbow grease, Ernest?" Gibb triggered the Windex bottle, misting the glass. He polished with a wad of newspapers, rubbing out each streak and fingerprint. "We're supposed to clean with the newspaper, Ernest. Not read it."

"This is weird, Gibb."

"What is?"

"This. Look."

"If it came outta your nose, I don't want to look."

"I mean it, Gibb. Another guy escaped from the funny farm over in Camarillo. Add that to the one six months ago who disappeared from the babbling ward at the V.A. hospital in L.A. and you got three looney tunas roaming around Southern California in the past year."

Gibb's scalp tightened and his heart expanded until it seemed to be crowding the other organs. He felt his pulse fluttering in his throat. Turning, he grabbed the torn hunk of newspaper from Ernest and scanned the page randomly, unable to even follow a pattern. The print went crazy, squiggly patterns of microscopic bacteria. Flotsam on paper. Then his eyes focused on the tiny article, just the kind Ernest liked to read; he usually skipped the front pages' stories of national or international interest, preferring what he called the "human interest" stories. The article blurred away—only the escapee's name remained clear and bold: Jonathan Peppler.

Gibb's hands dropped uselessly to his sides, fingers opening, the paper rocking back and forth through the air as it floated to the floor.

"What's the matter, Gibb?" Ernest laughed. You afraid they'll give those guys our jobs just 'cause you got to be crazy to work here?"

Gibb fell back heavily against the display case, his right shoulder cracking the glass with an eight-inch zigzag like a bolt of lightning. The first time he'd read about one of the escapes he'd thought nothing of it. The second time he'd thought it an odd coincidence. But now, a third time. A third familiar name.

Something was going wrong. Someone knew.

"Jesus, Gibb, you okay?" Ernest rushed over and put an arm around his friend. Ernest was about sixty years old and maybe a hundred and twenty pounds. Gibb was twenty-eight and two hundred pounds. Ernest struggled valiantly, but the older man couldn't quite keep Gibb from sinking to the floor.

The best he could do was hold Gibb's head as he dropped, keeping it from bouncing off the display case.'

"You better go home, Gibb. You don't look so good."

"Yeah," Gibb muttered. "Yeah."

A LITTLE LATER Gibb drove straight down Buena Vista Boulevard to the first bar he saw, a little dump called Captain Midnight's. It was dark inside and the walls and ceiling had some glittery stuff embedded in them so they were always sparkling and winking. He ordered a whiskey sour.

Gibb was not a drinker, but he gulped the drink down in two swallows and ordered another. One more, he promised himself. He hadn't had a drink since being released, first from the Army prison, then the Army hospital. At first he'd abstained because of the medication. The insides of his arms were permanently scarred from all the injections; later they'd taken to sticking him in the legs, hips, buttocks. By then everyone had already been split up. All the old gang. The Junkyard Dogs. That was what everyone had secretly taken to calling them. Even the brass.

Gibb finished his second drink, paid and left. He'd permitted himself two drinks and he'd stuck to the limit. Discipline was one of his most prized character traits. It was his discipline, they had told him in the hospital, that got him through his earlier ordeal. It had made it possible for him to be released four years ago while others remained locked up, each being treated in a different location across the country. Never two together.

Three. Three had escaped. That wasn't possible. Not without help.

Gibb walked through the parking lot toward his car, jangling his keys against his leg with each step. Even if it wasn't a coincidence, what did it matter to him? He was out of it now. He had a job, a clean record, an apartment a couple of miles from Disney with a swimming pool and spa, a sometime affair with the pretty Thrifty checkout woman who lived in the apartment over his and wanted to mother him. Sometimes he liked that, sometimes not. They had a date tomorrow night to play miniature golf.

There were only four cars in the lot. His was the 1980 Datsun of indeterminate hue. Gibb had bought the car for its vague color, just as he bought his clothes for blandness. Grays, blacks, browns. Clothes, car, apartment, girlfriend—everything had to blend in with the surroundings, not call attention to itself. Camouflage.

Maybe he should tell someone. But who? If they'd started gathering the Junkyard Dogs again, no one could be trusted. They'd promised it was all over fifteen years ago. Over forever. Vatican Towne himself had given his word, shaken each man's hand through the bars.

Gibb unlocked the Datsun's door, climbed into the driver's seat. If only Cavanaugh were around. He'd know what to do. Cavanaugh would do something, that was sure.

"Hey, Gibb?" He suddenly heard a deep voice next to him. The man owning it had wedged himself between the open door and the car, leaning one hand on each.

"Who are you?" Gibb asked, though he could guess.

"I heard you guys were bad, man." The guy talking wore glasses and was powerfully built. "Isn't that what you heard, Onan?" He said this over his shoulder and Gibb noticed a tall lanky redhead standing a few feet away.

"Fuck you, Fawley," the redhead said. Braces reflected red neon from Captain Midnight's flashing sign. Gibb thought of blood-soaked teeth and winced.

"What's the matter, Gibbsy?" the muscular man in glasses asked with a smirk. "Tough hombre like yourself so easily spooked. It's not right."

"Jesus, Ed!" the redhead said impatiently.

"Fuck, man. You read the report. Gibbsy here is some kinda man. Nuts the size of bowling balls. They got him down as a MAXCAP."

Gibb looked into the husky man's cold eyes. A word floated lazily from Gibb's lips. He didn't even know he'd opened his mouth until he heard his voice. "MAXCAP?"

"Yeah, bro. Maximum Cautionary Approach. That's the highest rating you can get. Like getting a double thumbs-up from Siskel and Ebert."

"For Christ's sake, Ed!" The redhead was nervous.

Now Gibb knew why. Looking at the two men, Gibb felt his body cry out for action. Inside, he shook and twisted and seethed and burned. His blood was reaching a molten state that screamed to erupt into movement. Gibb fought that urge, fought it the way he'd been taught those years with drugs and counseling and isolation, and finally on his own. Fought it to prove he could fight it. No matter the cost.

"You don't know, do you?" Gibb said. He could feel the words now, barely tickling his tongue and lips as they popped out. "They didn't tell you?"

"Tell us what?" the man, Fawley, asked. He looked curious.

"The Junkyard Dogs. You don't know."

"The fuck's he talking about?" he asked the redhead. "Junkyard dogs?" He laughed. "Fuck, man."

"Let's go, Ed," the redhead insisted.

Ed nodded.

Gibb smiled. It would have been so easy to kill both of these men. So easy it was funny. But he'd beaten them. Finally, he'd beaten all of them. Beaten them by doing nothing, proving he could do nothing no matter how provoked, no matter what the cost. He wished he could tell Cavanaugh. Cavanaugh would be pleased.

Fawley and the redhead pulled out their guns with the thick sound suppressors and each fired a shot into Gibb's head.

Gibb's head snapped backward but there was surprisingly little blood or outward damage. Still, Ed and the redhead stared in disbelief as they watched Gibb pull himself upright, stare at them with wide-open eyes, smile and whisper, "Is that all?"

Then he slumped sideways, dead.

Ed and the redhead ran down the alley behind Captain Midnight's to their parked car, jumped in and sped away onto the Ventura Freeway as fast as possible. Neither spoke a word until they'd driven sixteen miles. Finally, Ed Fawley broke the silence, though his voice was a little shaky. "That takes care of our sector. Everyone on the list."

"Why do you always have to mind-fuck them, man? Just do them and get the hell out of there. That was our job."

Ed turned his head from the road to his partner and grinned. "This isn't just a job, man. It's an adventure."

5

CLIFF'S RUBBER SOLES shrieked against the waxed tile floor as he jogged across the lobby of the office building toward the elevator. The elevator door was being held open by a short old man wearing a plaid sport cap cocked jauntily on his bald head.

"Howdy, Cliff," the old man called as Cliff neared.

"Hi, Fender."

"You're late. They've been waiting over an hour. The Samoan don't like to wait."

"So I've heard."

"You heard right, son. Get your butt on in here and I'll express you up." Fender kept his bony veined hand cupped around the elevator door until Cliff was safely inside. Then he adjusted his plaid cap just so and thumbed the black button for the fourth floor. The elevator shook and rattled and lurched like some sluggish giant waking from a deep and troubling sleep. Slowly it started to drag itself up the shaft.

Cliff leaned against the back of the car to catch his breath. He closed his eyes and listened to the arthritic creaking of gears and cables. The cut on his forehead burned and throbbed. Right now he didn't want to think about Standish Ford or Aaron Leland or Vatican Towne. He didn't want to think about Tory, or the redhead with braces, or Ed Fawley stealing his ex-wife's Meat Loaf album. He didn't want to think about the national secrets he'd been told. None of it was his problem. He had enough to worry about right here at home. Problems of a husband and father. For the past six months he and Ginger had been seriously discussing having a baby together. He loved Liza and Beau, Ginger's kids, as if they were his own, but Ginger and he wanted to create and raise a child

together. Corny maybe, but the prospect always made him
surprisingly happy. And then there were the kids to worry
about. Liza, fifteen, who'd started dating boys from the local
university who talked about venture capital, real estate and the
merits of the BMW. And Beau, thirteen, who'd been getting
in bloody fistfights at school lately but refused to tell anyone
what they were about. Those were the kinds of problems Cliff
wanted to handle now. They were infinitely more important
than spies or computers or governments.

The elevator seemed even more sluggish than usual,
wheezing as if it were bearing a couple of grand pianos instead
of two men. Cliff didn't think of this building as the type that
would ordinarily employ an elevator operator. The building
was nothing special, an old square box designed by someone
with no imagination and built by someone with no pride.
Compared to the sleek gleaming black monoliths that made
up most of Irvine's commercial sites, the Carpathia Building
was the architectural equivalent of a nerd. Even its location was
in legal dispute. The ultramodern planned community of Irvine claimed the building was on land that really belonged to
their older and less flashy neighboring city of Tustin. Tustin
claimed the building was on Irvine property. The courts had
been trying to decide for eight years. Seems no one wanted it
but the Carpathia Realty Corporation which collected the rent.

The building had only four floors, and the tenants were a
mixture of struggling young professionals, seedy entrepre-
neurs and outright hustlers: a family dentist with a drill that
echoed down the halls like a chain saw; a travel agent who
specialized in South American trips to drug-exporting countries; a mail order house selling only one album, *The Best of
Connie Francis*; a few threadbare lawyers; a plastic surgeon
who was being investigated by the medical board and was on
the verge of losing his license. The Samoan's office was on the

fourth floor all the way to the back. The smallest and cheapest office in the building.

"What happened to your head?" Fender asked.

"Racquetball."

"Never played the game myself. Prefer golf. Statistics show that fewer people have heart attacks playing golf than any other ambulatory sport."

"I didn't know that."

"It's a fact."

Fender stared up at the ceiling of the elevator car as if he could see through it straight up past the greasy lumbering cables all the way to the fourth floor. He stood oddly erect, almost at attention. He always stood that way. Cliff had never seen him lean or sit. There was no stool in the elevator, no magazines, no books. It was as if the elevator was powered by Fender's will and that took his complete concentration. In the month that Cliff had been coming to see the Samoan, Fender had been there every day, working from 8:00 a.m. to 5:00 p.m. He never seemed to take even a lunch break or go to the bathroom. Currently the wiry old man was the center of a major controversy. Many of the tenants wanted to fire him because they thought he was a waste of money, even though the building owners apparently paid his salary. The elevator didn't really require an operator; it was fully automatic like those in all the other buildings. Many complained that he gave the place a kind of nonprofessional, shabby appearance. Some feared he was some kind of pervert or reformed drunk, though he showed no signs of being either. Who else would take such a boring and unnecessary job so seriously? The controversy had heated up until there had been actual meetings to discuss the matter.

Cliff was new here, having paid only half of one month's rent on the Samoan's office. But he liked Fender and would be sorry to see him go if it came to that.

"Almost there," Fender said, tilting his plaid cap. As always he was smiling as they neared the floor, as if they were arriving at some exotic destination after a long and arduous journey. "Important meeting, huh?"

Cliff shrugged.

"Come on, Cliff. You got your first client up there. Mr. Cromwell."

"You know a lot."

"I keep my eyes open." He looked Cliff's clothes over and shook his head. "These eyes tell me one other thing, son. That's no way to dress to impress a client. This isn't Hollywood."

Cliff looked down at his T-shirt and shorts, both stiffening from dried sweat. "You're right. Thanks."

"That's what I'm here for."

The elevator slowed even more as it prepared to stop. Fender waited in front of the doors. Cliff figured him to be in his seventies, but wouldn't have been surprised if he was off by ten years in either direction. Fender didn't look so much old as lived in. Cliff wasn't even sure if Fender was a first or last name.

The door opened. Fender held it for Cliff. "There you go, son."

"Thanks," Cliff said, exiting.

"Don't let the Samoan get to you," Fender advised. "Samoans are a touchy bunch, but once they claim you as a friend, you're a friend for life. That's a fact."

"I'll remember that."

Fender smiled, stepped back inside the elevator. The doors closed, a great shaking and rattling echoed up the shaft, and the elevator began its slow descent. Down the hallway, Connie Francis warbled, "Where the Boys Are."

Cliff approached the wooden door with the discreet white lettering that said simply:

L. VAIALA & C. REMINGTON
CONSULTANTS

He checked his watch. He was well over an hour late. After leaving the beach house in Corona Del Mar, Cliff had phoned Ginger at the motel with an all clear. She had tried to sound light and cheerful, talking about the hotly contested Monopoly game she and the kids were playing, about the ham-and-pineapple pizza they were eating, about the jerk on *Donahue* who was advocating vasectomies for all males on food stamps. Underneath, Cliff could hear the aftermath of terror, the tremble in the voice, the shortness of breath, words tripping clumsily on her tongue. Cliff had felt those same feelings himself a few times when he'd first started. But that was all behind him now and he was determined that his family would never suffer from his past again.

He opened the office door and walked in.

The Samoan was sitting behind the small wooden desk, huge hands lying on the desktop like paperweights. The client was sitting on the small overstuffed sofa. All the furniture in the office looked small, especially next to the Samoan.

"Sorry I'm late," Cliff said to the client. "Got whacked on the head and taken to the hospital."

"My goodness," said the client, a thin nervous-looking man. "You didn't get that on a case, did you?"

Cliff shook his head and smiled. "Nothing so dramatic, Mr. Cromwell. Racquetball."

"That's why I play tennis. Been playing thirty years, never been hit." He tried on a thin smile, but it evaporated quickly. The man looked troubled.

"Mr. Cromwell has been telling me about his problem," the Samoan said. "Haven't you, Mr. Cromwell?"

"Yes. I certainly hope you'll be able to help me." Cromwell wore a stylish blue suit that Cliff admired. The gold Rolex wristwatch peeking out under his cuff was worth at least a thousand dollars.

The Samoan stood up; her six-one height seemed to swallow a large gulp of the room. She walked around the desk and sat on the front edge, hovering slightly over the much smaller Mr. Cromwell. None of her size was fat. She was just big, oversize in every respect, but perfectly proportioned. She'd once told Cliff that a boyfriend of hers had said being with her was like watching a woman in a movie theater, the size magnified on the screen. She'd laughed telling him that.

"What exactly is the problem, Mr. Cromwell?" Cliff asked.

Cromwell's face seemed to get even thinner, the skin collapsing around his sharp cheekbones. "I own a small company. Well, not that small, really, but not as large as some."

"What kind of company?"

"Video," the Samoan said. Her long black hair hung down her back all the way to her hips, forming flat coils on the desktop.

"Well, more than just video," Cromwell said, a little insulted. "We actually produce our own instructional videotapes as well as those for others. Quite a lucrative business, I should add. Our 'Baby-sitter' series has sold over half a million units each."

"You do those?" Cliff asked, impressed.

"Yes indeed. Three in the series and another five in preproduction."

Cliff nodded. The "Baby-sitter" videos were four-hour videos designed to act as surrogate baby-sitters while the parents were busy elsewhere in the house. An actress played games that the child could play along with, even speaking directly to the child. Children were known to talk back to her, answering her questions and playing her games for hours at a time. There was even a nap time during which she would coax the viewing child to lie down and sleep. If the child awoke and looked at the TV, he'd see her sitting there in a chair, reading, and usually go right back to sleep. Naturally there was a lot of controversy about the wisdom of such videoparenting, but glowing testimonials from satisfied customers had helped make these videos best-sellers.

"With that series, you won't be a small company much longer," Cliff said.

"I've had offers," he said mysteriously. "Larger companies wanting to buy me out. And of course there are the imitators, other videotapes trying to duplicate our success. But to no avail so far. It was my idea and I intend to keep producing these tapes my way. No shortcuts. No fancy graphics. No violence. Just wholesome fun."

"Then what's the problem?"

"Pirates," Lily said. Lily Vaiala was the Samoan's name, though most people referred to her as the Samoan because that's how she referred to herself. When she called Cliff that first time more than a month ago, she'd left a cryptic message with Ginger, "Tell him the Samoan called." She'd given a phone number. Cliff hadn't had the faintest idea who the Samoan was. He thought it might be some charity selling plastic trash bags.

Lily looked at Cliff, her large brown eyes revealing nothing. "Many of Mr. Cromwell's tapes are being pirated and sold without his company getting any of the revenues."

"The FBI handles that kind of thing, Mr. Cromwell," Cliff said.

"Yes, they do. That's how I know about it. They raided some warehouse in Chicago, confiscated a few thousand copies of *Aliens*, 'Jane Fonda's Workout,' the *Rocky* tapes and some of my titles."

Cliff walked over to the desk and sat behind it. "I understand there are ways to prevent a tape from being copied. Electronic coding or something."

Cromwell nodded emphatically. "Yes, yes. I'm doing that. Every videotape that leaves my company is protected from being copied."

Lily said, "Mr. Cromwell believes that the tapes are copied before they've gone through this process. By someone in his company."

"Do you have any suspects in mind, Mr. Cromwell?"

"That's the point," he said. He puffed with frustration. "No one in the company who has access would do such a thing."

"Who has access?"

"Myself, of course. My wife. My nephew."

"That's all?"

"Yes."

Cliff looked at Lily. Her eyes glinted like oiled ball bearings. She was excited about the case. To be honest, so was Cliff. This was their first job as partners in Vaiala and Remington.

"What is it exactly you want us to do, Mr. Cromwell?" Cliff asked him. "We're security consultants, not private detectives."

"I realize that. I'm not expecting you to track down who did the copying before, just make sure it doesn't happen again. Especially now."

"Why now?"

"Well, as I told your partner, we've just finished another in the 'Baby-sitter' series, and I expect it to be our biggest seller yet. We've managed to secure endorsements from three major child psychologists as to the benefits of our tape. I'm expecting it to go platinum in less than a month."

"That means one million sales," Lily explained.

"I'll have finished the last of the editing tomorrow. I'm worried about the master tape being copied before I've been able to protect it."

"Take it home," Cliff suggested, "or stick it in a safe-deposit box."

"There are insurance restrictions, Mr. Remington," Cromwell said a little haughtily. "Not to mention the temperature and environmental conditions."

Lily spoke to Cliff but stared at Cromwell. "Mr. Cromwell believes the thief will make his move tomorrow night, while the tape is locked in the company vault. He wants us to prevent that from happening."

"I'm sure we'll be able to do something," Cliff said. He studied Cromwell briefly and asked, "How'd you hear about us, Mr. Cromwell?" Cliff wasn't sure that if he were in Cromwell's position he'd have come to a place like this for help.

Cromwell shifted uncomfortably, tugging his trousers at the knee. "Well, I hope you don't take this the wrong way, but I have a friend on the police force, a tennis partner. He told me you used to be with the government. An agent of some kind."

People didn't like to say CIA aloud. It sounded a little corny, and yet a little threatening. Cliff was annoyed that word had spread through the police department, but it was bound to happen after Moonshadow and the bodies the cops had had to clean up.

"Anyway, I figured you'd be experienced in this kind of, well, industrial espionage I guess you'd call it."

Cliff stood up to indicate the meeting was over. "My partner and I will discuss the best way to handle this matter and call you later." He offered his hand.

Cromwell stood up. His thin sliver of a hand disappeared within Cliff's. They shook. "I hope you can help me," he said a little desperately.

"We will," Lily said, ushering him out of the door.

They listened in silence to Cromwell's shoes clicking down the hall. When the elevator swallowed him and carried him away, Lily turned to Cliff and punched him sharply in the stomach. The blow was enough to take his breath away.

"You aren't doing enough sit-ups," she said casually.

Cliff clutched his stomach, straightened, breathing shallowly.

"You want to hit me in the stomach?" she challenged, smacking her flat middle. It thumped like a watermelon. "Go ahead. Give me your best shot."

Cliff shook his head. "I don't play childish games."

She laughed. The sound was surprisingly girlish, considering her size. "Who are you kidding?" She pointed to the scab on his forehead. "You were too slow. Bad reflexes. You need to work out more."

Suddenly Cliff grabbed the front of her blouse in his fist, stuck his leg behind her and flipped her backward off her feet onto the desktop. She landed with a solid crash that shook the desk violently, knocking papers, pens and a stapler to the floor. His fingers pinched her throat. "Talk about slow. I thought you Samoans were supposed to be catlike, not cattlelike."

He released her and she hopped off the desk with a big white smile on her face. She was startlingly beautiful with her long dark hair, brown skin and high cheekbones. But most men were too intimidated by her size.

"Our first job," she said. "Don't you want to tell Ginger?"

"I'm not so sure she'll celebrate."

"You don't give her enough credit sometimes," Lily said. "She's tougher than you think. Tougher than me, sometimes."

Cliff smiled. "Tougher than both of us, I think."

"Let's find out."

"What do you mean?"

"I've got an idea. I'm taking you all out to dinner tonight. My treat. Liza and Bogie too. We'll surprise Ginger, she likes surprises."

"All right," Cliff said. When Lily had first barged into their lives with her proposal for a partnership in this security firm, Ginger had been politely hostile to her. For her part, Lily had been aggressive with Ginger. But eventually their first impressions wore off and the two women started to become friendly, even chummy. They occasionally shopped together, went to a movie without Cliff. Lily even acted a little protective of Ginger, like a big sister.

"You have any ideas on how to handle Mr. Cromwell's problem?" Cliff asked as they locked up the office.

"Not yet. I do my best thinking while cracking a lobster's back. You have any ideas?"

"A few."

"Good. That's why I came to you in the first place. I told you your spook background would help our reputation."

Cliff looked at her with sudden realization. "It was you, wasn't it? You've been spreading word about me at the cop house."

"That's called promotion, Cliff." She grabbed his arm and led him out of the office. They headed for the elevator, walking to the sobs of Connie Francis's "Who's Sorry Now?"

The door lettered Dr. Grundel, Chiropractor, flew open and the white-coated chunky figure of Dr. Grundel ran after them waving a piece of paper. "Hold up. You two haven't signed yet."

Cliff and Lily waited for Dr. Grundel to catch up to them.

"Here," he said, thrusting the paper and a pen at them.

"What is it?" Cliff said.

"The petition to get rid of Fender. Half the people in the building have signed."

Cliff looked at the paper. "That doesn't look like half to me."

"Well, the others have pledged to sign. I just haven't dropped by yet."

The Samoan took the petition and began reading it carefully.

"Why don't you leave the guy alone?" Cliff said.

"Look, Remington, you've only been in this building a month. You don't know. The guy shows no respect. I'm a doctor, for Chrissake, and he calls me Bobby."

"That's your name."

Dr. Grundel's chubby cheeks reddened. "Don't hand me that proletarian bullshit, pal." He whipped out his wallet and flipped through the plastic windows, finally shoving one in Cliff's face. "See that. I belong to the ACLU. I care about everybody's rights. I was in Chicago at the '68 convention getting my head cracked by Daley's pigs. Where were you, man?"

Cliff said nothing.

"I was in the fucking trenches," Dr. Grundel continued. "But now I'm talking about my business here. I earned professional status, and I expect this place to be run in a professional manner. You want that old fart to be the first thing your prospective clients see?"

Lily suddenly crumpled the petition in her fist and popped the ball of paper in her mouth and chewed it vigorously.

"Hey!" Dr. Grundel protested, grabbing for her. Lily clapped her huge hands over his ears. He let out a scream and stumbled backward, clutching his ears and grimacing in pain. Lily spit out the soggy wad of paper onto the floor, turned and walked toward the elevator.

Cliff shrugged at Dr. Grundel and walked after Lily.

6

STAN SAT NAKED on the bed. He wasn't even wearing his
hook. On the bed next to him was a white Styrofoam ice
bucket. He opened the lid and pulled out the washcloth that
he'd earlier buried under the ice cubes. Even in the chilly air-
conditioned room, the icy washcloth smoked with cold. Stan
pressed the nubbled fabric against his forehead, then mopped
the back of his neck. It felt so good he wanted to phone Lanie
and tell her to do it too.

He looked at the clock radio next to the bed and added three
hours for Washington, D.C., time. Lanie would just be getting out of work now and hitting the heavy downtown grid-
lock. Unless her boss, Hampton Andrews, had taken a good
look at her pallor and had the common sense to let her go home
early.

Common sense wasn't something you could count on with
Hampton. He was one of the country's most famous political
cartoonists and Lanie was his only staff. Usually he was en-
dearingly thoughtful, but when deadlines approached or he
was feeling a little insecure, time stopped and Lanie got out
late. Stan didn't blame Hampton. Though Stan lacked any
artistic ability himself, he greatly admired Hampton's talent
and intelligence. Even at seventy-three, the old bastard had
made a halfhearted pass at Lanie during her first week working for him, almost four years ago. She'd teased him out of it
and that had been the last attempt, except for his harmless
verbal flirting. Stan thought Hampton had grabbed Lanie's
ass that first day more out of a sense of obligation than real
sexual interest, as if he was afraid she might be insulted otherwise.

Stan stood up and looked out the huge plate-glass window of the Irvine Marriott. Fourteen floors down, the cities of Irvine, Santa Ana, Newport Beach and Costa Mesa overlapped as if without borders and spread out to the flat horizon where a thick band of brown smog seemed to wall in the cities. Stan tossed the washcloth back in the ice bucket and reached for the phone. He dialed a coded number that would automatically activate the scrambler. Three seconds later Aaron Leland was on the line.

"So?" the director said. "How'd it go?"

"Not well."

"He didn't bite?"

"Oh, he bit, all right. But not the story."

"He didn't believe you?"

Stan wedged the phone between ear and shoulder. He reached for his prosthesis, the Hosmer/Dorrance MA-200, and began strapping it onto his stump. "I don't know what he believed. I told him mostly the truth, just as we'd planned. Everything about Vatican Towne, the ransom, Fat Boy on the fritz. All true. Though I did manage to leave out the part about his being a whipping boy."

There was a long silence.

Stan spent the time tightening the leather straps around his upper arm. A little more than his hand had been blown off when that pipe bomb exploded in Bloomingdale's. Six inches of wrist and forearm had also disintegrated in a mist of hot blood and sticky tissue. A special mold had to be taken of what stump remained and the prosthesis fitted and modified. The stainless steel hook on the end looked like two rounded pincers, the metal tubing a little thicker than a pencil. The hook was controlled by cables connected to the harness sheathing the stump. By rolling his shoulder forward, he opened the hook. It hadn't taken him long to master the technique, especially with Lanie's help. She'd made him practice unhooking her bra with the hook. When he could do that, she'd said, he could have what was inside. He smiled at the memory, felt a tingling of desire for her. Aaron Leland's voice vaporized desire.

"Don't worry about it, Stan. You did your best."

"I don't think he's the right man for us, Aaron. He just doesn't care about this stuff anymore. He's more interested in crabgrass than national security."

"What about patriotic duty?" Leland said angrily. "Or did he think that just an old-fashioned notion?"

Stan tightened one of the straps on the prosthesis. "The funny thing is I think it was tearing him up inside. I think he felt a genuine desire to help. It's just that he's too experienced to fall into that trap." Stan paused. "He seemed to know you, though. Had strong feelings about not wanting to help you. Mentioned London."

Leland's voice was distant, a distance not caused by the telephone wires. "Maybe you're right. Maybe Cliff doesn't have what it takes anymore. Too domesticated."

Stan didn't respond. Aaron Leland would decide either to pursue or to abandon Remington, regardless of what Stan said.

"Come home, Stan," Leland said wearily. "I need your sane head to balance Collins and Dubus's bickering."

"What about Remington?"

"You're right about him. He's not the same man I knew."

Stan was relieved. For some unknown reason he'd felt protective of Remington. Maybe because the files indicated he'd been through enough already, that he'd give more than most while in service to the Agency. His life seemed so right now. His wife, stepchildren. Stan had seen photographs, read the reports. They seemed truly happy together. Stan and Lanie had tried to have children, tried every conventional and unconventional way. Now they were looking to adopt, but the process was slow and complicated. And frustrating.

"I'm booked to fly out in four hours," he told Leland.

"I'll have a limo waiting for you at Dulles. The bar fully stocked and a hot meal simmering. Least I can do, my friend."

"Thanks, but Lanie's picking me up. She likes to."

Leland chuckled. "Best thing that ever happened to you, marrying Lanie."

"I know."

Another long silence hovered between them.

"Stan, I know I haven't told you everything on this one. I'm aware that you realize it. I'm asking you now to trust me."

"You don't have to ask," Stan said, meaning it. Though he was pleased that Aaron was finally admitting he was hiding something.

"See you in the morning, Stan," Leland said and hung up.

Stan immediately punched in the number to his home. For some reason he couldn't explain, he just wanted to hear Lanie's voice.

AARON LELAND pushed the phone away and leaned forward. "Comments, gentlemen?"

"Are you sure Stan doesn't suspect?" Collins asked.

"I see no indications that he does."

"He's a smart man," Collins said.

"He's a good man," Dubus added, removing his glasses and rubbing his eyes. "I hate doing this to him."

"We're all smart men," the director said. "And we're all good men. This country is filled with good men and women, many of whom may soon be dead or worse, rotting from nuclear poison, if we don't do something." His jaw tightened and his eyes narrowed angrily. "This is not a job of just good intentions, gentlemen, it is a job of results! The American people don't want to hear your excuses later, once we've been plunged into a nuclear winter and their hair and teeth are falling out and their skin is flaking off and blowing away with each breeze. They'll want to know why we didn't do whatever was necessary to prevent it."

Dubus polished his glasses. Collins raked his Hemingway beard. Both men looked as if they wished they were someplace else.

Leland's face looked melancholy. "I know what you're thinking. But Stan will get over it. I also know you agree that what we're doing is the only option we have right now. I'm so certain, that I will leave the final decision up to you. If you think what we've planned is so morally wrong when balanced against the lives we're risking, I'll call the whole thing off right now." He reached for the phone, lifted the receiver to his ear, poised his finger over the array of buttons. "Well? Your choice."

Leland waited, crossing his legs. Light glinted off the dimes in his loafers. His eyes stayed on Dubus and Collins.

Collins cleared his throat. "Maybe we should have told Stan about the Junkyard Dogs."

"No point. What was to be gained?"

"I'd feel better, for one thing."

"We're close. Very close. Ed Fawley phoned in his report. The last of the group is accounted for. Everyone except Cavanaugh, and we're working on that. We'll find him too, before long." Leland's finger was still poised over the phone. "The operation is right on schedule. Even Vatican Towne hasn't stopped it."

"That's another thing, Aaron," Dubus said. "What does Vatican Towne have to do with this?"

Leland sighed. He blinked slowly, sadly, like a man going through immense psychic pain who was going through even greater pain trying not to show it. He spoke precisely, as if each word had been hand selected, carved and polished. "Vatican and I have had differences in the past."

"Differences don't explain *this*," Collins said.

"Philosophical differences. Let's just say, Vatican Towne is not the hero everyone thinks he is. There were signs of instability years ago. That's why he dropped out of sight when he did.''

"Then all this shit with Fat Boy has nothing to do with the Junkyard Dogs?''

"Not a thing.''

Dubus and Collins exchanged looks. They communicated silently, as they did during bridge games. Each knew what the other was thinking. They returned their gazes to Aaron Leland but said nothing.

Leland replaced the phone receiver. "Then it's settled. We proceed as planned. Stan stays in the field and continues to lead Remington where we want him to go.'' He unbuttoned his sweater. "After all, two whipping boys are better than one.''

7

ELI SCHWARTZ couldn't take his eyes off her breasts. They weren't particularly large breasts, but they were squeezed together and pushed up until they swelled out of her tight dress like overraised bread dough. Schwartz did not ordinarily consider himself a tit man—he went in more for the shapely ankle and contoured calf—but there was something about her that was unusual in a way he couldn't yet identify. The mystery of it all aroused him.

Embarrassed by his own boldness, he pulled his ivory pipe and calfskin tobacco pouch from his jacket just for an excuse to drag his eyes from her breasts. She was busy driving the car, her eyes firmly affixed to the dark road, cruising at two miles per hour under the speed limit, her hands charmingly at two and ten on the steering wheel.

"I offered to drive," he reminded her.

"What?" She seemed startled by his voice. Then she laughed. "No, no, I don't mind. Everyone always makes fun of me, I'm so intense when I drive. Ignore me."

His eyes drifted over to her breasts again. He smiled, realizing that soon he would probably have his lips on them, his teeth and tongue teasing the nipples. His pants were tightening uncomfortably at the crotch, so he returned to his pipe, tamping in fresh tobacco. "You mind?" he asked, holding up the pipe.

"My father smoked a pipe," she said without inflection.

He wasn't sure whether that was a yes or a no. He returned the pipe to his jacket pocket and saw the slip of pink paper on the floor. He was a big man, tall and thick chested, and the car was a Nissan Sentra, smaller than he was used to, so it took him a little twisting and shifting to reach over and finally snag the piece of paper. It was the rental receipt for the car. He read the name, and twelve years of instinct as one of Israel's top agents sent a cold shiver across his curly scalp. "I thought your name was Karen."

She looked over at him with confusion, saw the receipt and laughed. Her eyes returned dutifully to the road. "It's pronounced like Karen."

"C-H-A-R-O-N. Pronounced Karen. What kind of name is that?"

"Greek. Back in the time of Plato it was pronounced like Leslie Caron's name. Now if I only looked like her. Hell, I'd settle for dancing like her."

Eli Schwartz smiled. He allowed himself to relax, his scalp still itching from the chill that was fading away. His eyes latched onto her breasts again, then lifted to her face. Her hair was very short and black, moussed up so it stood straight and spiky. She wore maybe just a little too much makeup, but she was definitely an attractive woman. It wasn't any single feature that made her that way, nothing exceptional in her nose, or eyes, or cheeks. It was a certain tilt of her head, a confidence in her gaze, an aggressiveness in her stride. She seemed to know what she wanted.

Eli Schwartz had met her only four hours ago at a party celebrating the opening of Rico Enrico's Fine Foods in Georgetown. The restaurant was run by a Cuban refugee and financed by the Israeli government through one of the dummy corporations Eli had set up. The Cuban was a dapper little man from a once-wealthy family. His manners and charm made him the perfect front man for this elaborate drop. Plus, the restaurant was bound to turn a nice profit. Everyone benefited.

The party had been attended by the wealthy and powerful in business and politics. Several movie and TV stars had been there to ensure the right amount of exposure. When it came to publicity, one sitcom star was worth ten U.S. senators.

Eli had stayed pretty much to himself, chatting briefly with a few acquaintances, telling jokes here and there. Although he personally hated parties, he was avidly sought after as a guest because he had one party talent. He told good jokes. For some reason he didn't understand, he remembered every joke ever told to him and managed to improve it with each retelling. Whatever group he joined, he eventually was cajoled into telling a few jokes and everyone would laugh with great enthusiasm. It was a gift he neither understood nor appreciated. He merely used it as a tool to enhance his cover.

Charon, pronounced Karen, he reminded himself, had been a part of one of the groups he'd drifted into, where he'd unloaded a few risqué jokes. She too had laughed, though with less gusto than the others. Instead, she had kept the amusement in her eyes as she watched him. Later in the evening they had somehow come together again, just the two of them. She told him her name, he told her his.

"I know who you are," she'd said. "I know who everybody is."

"FBI?" he teased.

"*People* magazine."

"Even better."

She'd laughed, a somewhat husky, throaty laugh. "Go ahead," she said. "I've heard all the jokes about *People* before. Let me have 'em."

He had in fact heard some himself. "I don't know any," he said.

"Thank you," she'd said, her look appreciative of his lie. "The thing that gets me is, I really like my job. I like meeting all these new people, writing about them. I admit it, I'm a bit of a gossip-monger." Then, as if she thought she'd let something slip, she frowned and added, "Not that I think *People* is a gossip magazine."

"Of course not."

She'd smiled. "Okay, okay. I won't bullshit about journalistic integrity, you don't bullshit about whether or not you're married."

"Would it matter?"

Her eyes got very serious. "Yes, it would."

"Good," he said. "It should." He'd touched her hand, felt an unusual thrill that surprised him. "I'm not married. My wife died eight years ago. A terrorist bomb in Tel Aviv. That's why I moved my two children and my business here. Now you know everything."

"I know you're a rich clothing manufacturer."

"Does it matter? My being rich?"

"It doesn't hurt."

"Excellent," he smiled. "Because I like being rich." He wasn't, of course, really rich. The money belonged to Israel, and they allowed him and his daughters to live like millionaires because it suited his cover. But someday he would have to give all that up. That was something Charon need never know.

"Well, that's enough small talk for me," she'd said suddenly. "How about you?"

He'd laughed, taken her arm.

Now they were in her rented car driving to her hotel room. He'd offered to take her back to his home, but had been relieved when she suggested her room was closer. He didn't like to bring women home where his daughters would know. At sixteen and seventeen they certainly knew what went on in the bedroom, and that embarrassed him. Since his wife died, there had been only one woman he hadn't felt embarrassed to bring home. She had stayed for three months. There had been wedding plans. But then orders had come down that such a wedding would be impossible. Matrimony would compromise his status as a wealthy bachelor, make him less attractive as a guest in certain circles. He'd come closest to quitting then. In the end, he had obeyed orders and broken off his relationship. It was the first time he'd cried since his wife was killed.

Charon parked the car with precision, and Eli smiled when she let out a deep sigh of relief. "Safe," she said. She passed him a naughty look when she caught him staring at her breasts. "I think."

Eli smiled, though he was embarrassed. It wasn't like him to be so adolescent, so boldly desirous. There was something about her that made it all so wickedly delicious. He just didn't know why. Neither of them was married. She was in her late thirties, certainly no innocent virgin being seduced by a fiftyish millionaire. Still, even as they exited the elevator and walked silently down the plush carpeting toward her hotel room, he couldn't help looking over his shoulder. He just couldn't shake the feeling of forbidden fruit. He grinned at his romantic foolishness.

Her room was a bit too chic for his taste—black lacquered platform bed, white sofa splashed with pastel colors, crystal chandelier, twenty-five inch Sony TV with VCR. "Your magazine is very generous," he said. "When my salespeople travel they stay at the Ramada Inn."

"Yes, well, my magazine saves so much on salaries they can afford an occasional splurge. Besides, they heard that I've had an offer from *Us* magazine, so they're being especially nice."

Eli sat on the sofa, uncertain how to proceed. He had never been very good at initiating sex. He decided to let Charon set the pace. He leaned back, looked as if he were settling in for a long conversation. "Will you change jobs then?"

She shrugged and kicked off her black pumps. "Maybe. *Us* is owned by *Rolling Stone*, and I used to free-lance for them. Interviewed Joni Mitchell, Buffy-Saint Marie, Kris Kristofferson. God, now there was a sexy man." She flopped playfully onto the sofa next to him, curled her black-stockinged legs under her. "I've always been a bit of a groupie, I guess.

I was one of the 400,000 naked muddy screamers at Wood-stock. Now I wear push-up bras and garter belts. Go figure.''

Eli felt the stiffness in his pants again. He pushed his left hand across the sofa to brush against her stocking feet. She smiled at his touch, and he felt bold enough to slowly massage her toes through the black stockings. He cleared his throat. ''You said Charon is Greek, but your last name is O'Grady.''

''Greek mom, Irish dad. Quite a combination, I'm telling you. Oil and water.''

His hand slid up to her ankle. He felt as if his whole lap were on fire.

Charon suddenly turned off the lamp next to her, and the room was dark except for the white haze from the streetlights below. Her smile broadened. ''Enough chatter,'' she said. ''Time for that later.'' She reached back to unzip her black sequined dress, stood up and let it slide off her shoulders and down her hips to a shadowy puddle around her feet. She stood in the semidarkness, her slender body clothed only in bra, half-slip, garter belt and black stockings. She walked over to the bed, lay down and laughed. ''You going to make me start without you? Not that I'm against it, if that's what you like.''

Eli stripped off his jacket, tie and shirt with only a few movements. His T-shirt gave him a little trouble. He was not, after all, a thin man. His belly had blossomed in the past few years as befitted a middle-aged man of wealth. Certainly he was not in the iron-muscled shape he'd been in as a young Nazi hunter stalking through the jungles of Peru. If only she could have seen him then. But there was something to be said of age too. He would make love to her slowly and completely, not resting until she could bear no more pleasure.

He removed the rest of his clothes and climbed onto the bed next to her. His thick arms encircled her immediately and they kissed with open mouths and eager tongues. Eli felt an almost painful tightening of the skin all over his body, unlike any-thing he'd ever experienced before. It was thrilling. Their mouths stayed fastened together, and Eli's hands finally cupped one of her breasts. The soft mound barely filled his large hand, but it aroused him more than any other breast ever had. He felt giddy and light-headed, as if under the influence of some potent aphrodisiac.

Deftly using one hand, Eli unhooked her strapless bra and released her breasts. He could wait no longer and lowered his mouth over one, then the other. His tongue and lips pulled at the nipples, hardening them. He felt her breath on his hair, her fingertips easing down his back.

Eli's left hand brushed over her taut nipple, continued down over the ribs and hard stomach and up again across the ridge of the hip. He was pleased by the tight skin and conditioned muscles. "Aerobics?" He smiled, trying to pinch the skin at the waist but finding little to hold.

She just smiled, reached her arms back over her head, her hands grasping the headboard provocatively. She stretched her legs out, toes pointed, the half-slip rising above one thigh to reveal the stocking top and garter strap.

Eli looked for a long hungry moment, then slipped his hand under her slip. Slowly his fingers crept up the thigh to the silk panties. He eased his hand under one leg, fingertips brushing the stiff pubic hairs.

He jerked back as if bitten.

"My God!" he gasped. He scrambled frantically backward, trying to escape on hands and knees. He clumsily turned away, tried to jump from the bed. Suddenly something was looped around his neck, something thin and unyielding, biting deep into his throat. He felt the metal wire slice through the skin and burst the capillaries. He could feel the warm blood drench his neck.

He fought, struggled against the tightening wire, tried to twist his bulk around so he could grab his assailant. But everything was happening so quickly, so expertly, he knew his struggle was just a matter of form. It would all be over in a few seconds. In a way, he was glad. Before tonight, he'd never thought he'd ever feel that way about death.

His elbow swung around, caught Charon in the rib, but there was no longer enough strength to do any damage. Charon maintained a firm grip on the wire, stockinged knees buried in Eli's back for leverage while the hands pulled back on the garrote like a rider reining in a stubborn stallion.

Finally Eli Schwartz slumped into death, his bowels emptying onto the bed.

Charon quickly stood up, ran into the bathroom, stripped off the stockings, garter belt and slip. A hot shower and shampoo scrubbed off the makeup and mousse. Five minutes later, Charon was dressed in a dark blue three-piece business suit, knotting a maroon silk tie, looking every inch the senator's aide or banking executive, a darkly handsome man on the rise.

He adjusted the elastic band he wore around his chest to keep the breasts flattened out of sight. Sometimes it pinched and he could sympathize with what Judy Garland went through during the filming of *The Wizard of Oz* when they'd bound her breasts so she would look younger, less developed.

On his way out of the apartment he glanced over at the crumpled heap of clammy flesh on the bed that once was Eli Schwartz. He shook his head and smiled ruefully. Being a hermaphrodite was like Halloween every day. No matter what you dressed as, it wasn't really you. The soft round breasts that had lured Eli away from the party had been real; but so had the small flaccid penis Eli had touched with horror as his hand had groped inside Charon's panties. The terror on Eli Schwartz's face had been real, but less directed at Charon than at himself.

At a phone booth down the street Charon made a quick call. He confirmed the assignment had been completed, and the man with the Saudi accent on the other end confirmed that $200,000 had been transferred to Charon's Swiss bank account.

There was a pause from the Saudi, and Charon knew what would come next. The usual question.

"How did you do it?" the Saudi asked.

"Garrote."

"That's not what I meant."

"I know what you meant." Charon hung up. He knew that the Saudi himself enjoyed women but preferred boys. Perhaps someone would put a price on his head someday, and he could find out firsthand how Charon did it.

Charon thumbed in another quarter and dialed a number that was so electronically wired that it would be impossible to trace. The number was for a phone that sat on an answering machine in an otherwise bare studio apartment in Virginia.

The number rang once, then the answering machine clicked on. His own voice came at him sounding, as always, a little too masculine and a little too feminine: "Leave your message after the tone." The tone hummed and Charon tapped in a numbered code. He heard the tape rewind. There was just one message.

"Charon, you have a go. Terms agreeable."

Charon smiled. Aaron Leland's voice sounded firm, resolute. Good. He phoned the airport, made a reservation for the next flight to Los Angeles and asked for a rental car to be ready for him. From what he'd heard, Clifford Remington would be a much more challenging quarry than poor old Eli Schwartz.

PART TWO:

SHADOWLAND

8

CLIFF DROVE UP the driveway and punched the button on the garage door opener that was clipped to the visor. The wide wooden door slowly yawned open, recessing upward like a heavy eyelid. Cliff pulled into the garage, carefully guiding the Honda hatchback between Liza's overturned bike with the flat tire and Ginger's giant bag of potting soil, most of which had spilled onto the cement floor and been used by the cat as kitty litter.

The garage was built to house two big American cars, but the clutter of junk barely left enough room for one Japanese compact. Cliff kept promising Ginger that one day he would clean and organize the garage, hanging garden tools and tennis racquets on spray-painted pegboards like the neighbors. But secretly Cliff enjoyed the mess, the stacked jumble of the unnecessary. Cardboard boxes of the past. Lives in the making. It was such a lively contrast to the cold streamlined existence he had endured for so long.

Cliff arrived at his house ahead of the Samoan. Lily had driven him back to the health club to pick up his car and had then announced she would stop off at the Stonecreek Farmers' Market for a bottle of wine so the whole family could toast their success. Just as well. Cliff needed the few minutes alone with Ginger.

He walked through the front door, expecting to find Ginger waiting nervously in the living room. She wasn't. "If anybody's interested, I'm home!" he hollered.

"Out here!" Ginger yelled from the backyard.

Cliff walked through the house. Liza and Beau were in the kitchen, both wearing dirty aprons, both armed with sharp little German knives. Liza was slicing chicken breasts into little strips. Beau was dicing onions and green peppers.

"Hi, Dad," Liza said. She'd only started calling him Dad six weeks ago, when he'd told the kids he had begun adoption procedures. Beau still called him Cliff. Cliff understood this wasn't meant as disrespect; Beau just hadn't yet figured out how he felt. His real father was a successful psychiatrist, a decent and pleasant fellow, but not very close to his children. One of the highlights of young Beau's life was when Cliff dubbed him with the nickname, Bogie.

"What's going on here?" Cliff asked, stealing a sliver of green pepper and eating it. "You sacrificing animals to the voodoo gods again?"

Bogie turned around, grinning. The bruise under his eye from last week's fight was still slightly visible. "Prepare yourself for a tempting taste treat, a delectable dining delight. Right here in Chez Bogie."

"Chez Liza," she corrected, rinsing her fingers under the tap water.

"Chez Bogie."

"Chez Liza." She flicked her wet fingers at him and water splashed his face. She giggled.

Bogie took a sip from the can of Sprite next to him and spat a little stream in her face. "Chez Bogie," he said with finality.

"How does Chez Grounded for a Week sound?" Cliff said.

"He *spat* on me," Liza complained dramatically. Lately, every emotion from Liza was exaggerated, as if she were on stage projecting to the cheap seats in the balcony.

Bogie pulled a paper towel from the roll and handed it to her. "Here."

She began wiping her face. "What happened to your forehead, Dad?"

"Have anything to do with us hiding out at that motel?" Bogie asked.

"Racquetball," Cliff said. "Didn't your mother tell you?"

"She said you'd explain it when you got home."

Bogie gave him a wary look, concentrating on the cut forehead. "You back in the spy business?"

"No," Cliff said. "Never."

"That's what Sean Connery said about playing James Bond," Bogie pointed out.

"He didn't have Chez Nuthouse to come home to, like me." He grinned, grabbed another green pepper and walked out the back door. Ginger was balanced precariously on an old swivel desk chair from the garage. It turned slightly under her feet as she reached up and hammered a nail into the rafter above the patio.

"Shouldn't stand on swivel chairs," he warned. "We've got a ladder."

"This was handier." She knotted a length of string to the nail, climbed down and tied the dangling loose end of the string around a fluffy ball of cotton. When she was finished, she stood back and studied her handiwork. The cotton ball swayed in the light breeze. "What do you think?"

"What's it supposed to be? Art?"

She laughed. "It's a cotton ball. You hang them on the patio and flies think they're spiderwebs and fly away. Keeps the patio free of flies."

"Does it work?"

"I don't know. I read about it in a short story in *Redbook*."

Cliff came up from behind and wrapped his arms around her, his hands clasped together at her narrow waist. She leaned back into him, her mussed brown hair brushing his cheek. For the first time that day, he felt complete. Her weight against him was like joining with the piece that he'd sensed was missing, the part that made him whole. Batteries in a flashlight. She turned her head slightly, looked up at him, and said, "I'm horny."

"Lily's on her way. Wants to take us all out to dinner."

Ginger's face was expressionless. "You got the job."

He nodded.

"You're not going to believe me, but I'm happy for you."

"Lily said you would be."

She smiled, touched the scab on his forehead. "Does it hurt?"

"Terribly. I'll need lots of attention and constant nursing."

She kissed his cheek. "All better." She went into the kitchen.

Cliff followed. "I had a little more than a quick kiss in mind. At least a little tongue action."

"Okay, guys," Ginger said to the kids. "Lily's coming over for dinner. We're going to have to make this stretch. No second helpings until she's done. Got it?"

"She wants to take us out to dinner," Cliff said. "Seafood."

She smiled at Cliff, stroked his cheek. "Men don't understand anything." Then she walked off toward the bedroom. "I'm going to take a quick shower."

"What did Mom mean by that?" Bogie asked, his eyes red and watering from the onions. "I don't get it."

Cliff shrugged.

They looked at Liza. Adopting a patient expression, Liza said, "Lily doesn't want to go out to a restaurant. She likes it much better when we're all sitting around home together. She only said she'd take us out because she feels guilty coming over all the time. Jeez, don't you guys know anything?"

Cliff and Bogie looked at each other.

"Now that I think about it," Bogie said. "Maybe she's right."

"You bet I'm right," Liza said.

Cliff gave Liza a kiss on the forehead. "What would we do without you?"

"Live in caves and eat with your fingers."

"I'm willing to take that chance," Bogie said.

"You're already halfway there, you little piece of dried snot."

Cliff heard Ginger's shower starting. "I think I'll take a quick shower too," he said, tugging at his grungy T-shirt.

"Dinner will be ready soon," Liza said. "Better make it a quickie." She gave him a sly look and she and Bogie giggled.

"Kids," Cliff said. "Can't live with 'em, can't fit them into the blender." He walked out of the kitchen.

In the bedroom he stripped quickly and pattered into the bathroom. Steam had already taken over in there and was leaking into the bedroom like thick ocean fog. Ginger liked the water painfully hot. He heard her before he saw her. She was singing a medley of show tunes from *South Pacific* and *Camelot*. Her voice bounced erratically from note to note, without much heed to an actual melody. But what she lacked in technical skill she more than made up for in enthusiasm. "Some Enchanted Evening" sounded like a call to arms to muster the rebel cause.

He slid the glass door open and stepped in behind her. "Oww," he said when some of the hot water splashed his skin. "Stick a fork in me, I'm done."

Her back was still to him. "What happened today?"

"A woman tried to seduce me."

"Was she young?"

"Yes."

"Pretty?"

"Very."

"What did you do?"

"I hit her on the head with my racquet."

She laughed. "That may be playing too hard to get." She turned to face him and he couldn't tell whether there were tears in her eyes or just condensation. "Hold me, Cliff," she said and clutched him tightly.

He did. They stayed that way for a while. He could feel the pent-up fear and anxiety that had lodged in her body all day slowly drain from her. At some point their comforting embrace turned hungrier and suddenly they were kissing and touching and groping. She turned away from him, braced her hands against the wall, dipped her head so the hot water ran down her back. His hands glided around her hips, slippery where she'd soaped, then traveled slowly up, bumping over the rib cage until cupping the soft flesh of her breasts. Cliff slid in behind her, the hot water not so hot anymore, not nearly as hot as their skin, their moving bodies.

"THESE ARE the best *fajitas* I've ever had," Lily said. She picked another flour tortilla from the warmer, spread guacamole and sour cream on it and dumped on a spoonful of the fried chicken-pepper-onions mixture. Carefully she rolled the whole concoction into a tube and took a bite. "Best ever." She nodded, chewing as vigorously as she had on Dr. Grundel's petition. She looked at the kids. "Who's the better cook?"

"I am," Bogie said.

"He is," Liza admitted. "But I'm the better baker. He can never roll the dough out even."

"I'd rather twirl it in the air, like pizza."

Lily laid a finger on the rim of her empty wineglass and tipped it toward Cliff. Though she showed no effects, she had already downed five glasses. She noticed the concerned look in his eyes and smiled. "Don't worry, Cliff, I'm not drunk."

"You have a bit of a drive to Mission Viejo."

Lily's face darkened and she started to say something fiery, but stopped, looked at Liza and Beau, and smiled. "You're right. It wouldn't look good for a *taupou* to be arrested for drunk driving."

"What's a *taupou*?" Bogie asked.

"Kind of a princess."

"You're a princess?" Liza stopped eating.

"Don't sound so surprised," Lily said. "Princesses don't all have dainty feet. They come in all sizes."

Ginger scooped up a dollop of refried beans with a tortilla chip. "Lily is the daughter of the chief of her *nu'u*. That means *village*. Did I say it right, Lily?"

"Like a native."

Cliff looked with surprise at Ginger. When had she found out so much about Lily? These were things even Cliff didn't know.

"God, a princess," Liza sighed. "What was that like, Lily? I mean, did everyone bow and stuff like with Princess Di?"

Lily tucked a loose curtain of hair behind her ear, her brown face smiling pleasantly, but her eyes darkening with memories. "The princess game isn't all it's cracked up to be, sweetheart. Whether you're Princess Di or Princess Falevao. That's my Samoan name."

"Falevao," Liza said dreamily. "That's nice."

"What happened?" Bogie asked. "I mean, if you were a princess and all, how come you left Samoa? I know if I were the prince of someplace, I'd never leave, no matter what. They'd have to toss me into a volcano."

Lily turned to Bogie and Liza with her beautiful smile. The kids found her fascinating, but more than that, they seemed to truly care for her, like a favorite aunt. Cliff smiled himself, pleased with the sudden familial warmth wrapping around him. Right now the world outside this house, outside this room, seemed terribly unimportant, petty. He sat back, snacked on a handful of tortilla chips and listened to Lily speak of the past he knew nothing about.

"The *taupou*," Lily explained, "is the ceremonial virgin princess. That was my job, professional virgin."

Bogie lowered his eyes, embarrassed. Liza leaned forward, even more interested.

"I was constantly surrounded by *aualuma*, a group of handpicked unmarried women who served as my handmaidens and chaperons. They did everything for me."

"Neat," Liza said. "All you had to do then was just look good."

"Well, a little more than that. I had to prepare the *kava*, the food used in our ceremonies, and I was the dance leader. Kinda the Ginger Rogers of our village. Other than that, all I had to do was wait around until my father arranged a marriage with someone important."

"Oh, I get it," Bogie said, caught up now. "You fell in love with a common boy and your father booted you out. Right?"

Lily laughed. "No. My father selected a very nice boy, handsome and brave and fairly progressive. Much more interested in bringing more education to the village than in gathering *kava*." She paused, picked at the half-eaten *fajitas* on her plate. "At the time of the marriage there is a public defloration ceremony."

"Defloration?" Bogie asked.

"Like in deflowering," Liza said.

Bogie looked confused a moment, then realized what was meant. His face flushed and he gulped, "Oh."

Lily continued, "During this ceremony, the High Talking Chief wraps his finger in white bark cloth and inserts it in the *taupou*'s vagina."

"Gross!" Liza protested.

"When he removes his finger, the blood is proof of her purity."

"So you told these guys to drop dead," Liza said. "That's why you left?"

Lily shook her head. "I went through with the ceremony. I was proved virtuous."

"I don't get it," Liza said. "You were a princess, you were lined up to marry this handsome guy, you already went through with that weird ceremony. Why'd you leave?"

Cliff leaned closer, also curious.

"I don't know," Lily said. "I guess I didn't want to be a princess. Too heavy a burden."

"That doesn't make any sense," Liza said, disapproving.

"It will," Ginger said. "Someday."

The rest Cliff knew; he'd secretly checked it out himself. Lily had gone from Samoa to Honolulu, become a police-woman, worked undercover vice for a few years and eventually earned her detective's gold shield. Along the way she'd fought sexism and racism in her straightforward bullish way and annoyed quite a few important people. When those people made it too difficult for her to do her work, she quit and moved to Orange County to start her own security business. The business had been struggling along for almost a year, and she'd been forced into taking jobs installing alarm systems for paint stores, investigating employee thefts from drugstores.

Cliff had studied her account books himself. She had the expertise for her small business, but the real money and referrals came from the larger corporations. Orange County was filled with companies on the rise, not yet established enough to insist on the old warhorse security companies, willing to hire someone up and coming like themselves. But they wanted broader experience than she had. So when some local cop friends had mentioned what little they knew of the Moonshadow mess and how a local landscaper with obvious Washington connections had been involved, she had looked Cliff up. She'd liked what she saw and made him a partnership offer.

Cliff had refused.

She came back with another offer. He refused again. She found him planting ficus trees on a client's lawn, showed him charts indicating potential profits. She was convincing, but still he refused.

Ginger offered no advice. She said he should do what he wanted. Yes, she was frightened of that kind of business; it smacked too much of his former life, the one that had almost killed them all, but she supported his decision, whatever it would be. He'd held her close and looked into her eyes and realized she was sincere.

The next time Lily approached him, he'd been sitting under a jacaranda tree in full purple bloom, eating his bag lunch, chicken walnut salad on sourdough bread. He'd been installing a sprinkler system for his client, a Mercedes dealer in Newport Beach. Sweat and dirt were caked on his face, but he didn't mind that. He liked hard work. In fact, sitting under that tree at that moment, eating his sandwich among the trenches and pipes, he was totally happy. Had someone asked what would make him happier, he wouldn't have been able to think of anything. But the moment he saw the big Samoan trekking up the slope of hill, more flow charts and ledgers under her dark arms, he knew that he would say yes.

GINGER MADE UP the sofa bed for Lily, handed her a fresh set of towels and gave her a hug good-night. Cliff watched this from the kitchen, amazed at the closeness of the two women. He had never made friends easily, had never gone looking. The last close friend he could remember from before he joined Graceland was Tommy Springman. From age six through twelve they'd hunted frogs in the creek, explored the remote Pennsylvania woods where both families lived, built tree forts, made bombs from skunk cabbage and even started a neighborhood newspaper together. When the Springmans moved away, there was no one else Cliff's age in the area. School was too far from home for him to do anything with his classmates who lived in town. In college, his roommate, a bearded kid from Alaska majoring in Eastern philosophy, had been even quieter than Cliff. Cliff had always dated a lot, had friendly sexual relationships, but always went home with some relief. Later, Cliff made only two friends: Drew, who died in London, and the man responsible for Drew's death.

Now Ginger was his friend. And the children. And Lily. Had other people been living like this all along?

"When did she tell you all that stuff about her past?" Cliff asked Ginger when she joined him in the kitchen. "That princess stuff."

She shut the door behind her before answering. "A while ago."

"You didn't tell me."

"No."

"Did she ask you not to?"

"No." Ginger opened the refrigerator and studied the contents like an archaeologist unearthing a treasure chest. "God, I'm starving. I hadn't counted on making dinner stretch."

Cliff reached into the refrigerator, quickly grabbed a few jars, a package in white butcher paper, the leftover tortillas. He spread them on the counter and began opening them. "Why didn't you tell me about Lily?"

"It wasn't important."

"That's not the point."

She nodded. "I don't know. I figured it was something she wanted to tell you in her own way. She's kind of adopted us, you know."

"I do know."

"You mind?"

"No."

Ginger patted his arm tenderly. "That's one of the things I love about you."

"Yeah? What are the other things?"

She leaned against the refrigerator and watched him sprinkle olives and bacon bits and onion and cheese on the tortilla. He picked up the concoction and lowered it on the heating iron skillet. "Let the cheese get crisp," she said. "I like it crisp."

A few minutes later, he left Ginger in the kitchen, eating her *quesadilla*. She didn't like people watching her eat when she was hungry, because she tended to chew fast and spill crumbs.

She also hummed when she ate, no special tune, just a happy little ditty she wasn't even aware of. The hungrier she was, the more she hummed.

Cliff started his nightly rounds. Liza was easy—a quick kiss on the cheek and she was done. She was pouting only slightly because she'd asked to stay up late to watch a late movie directed by Truffaut, *Mississippi Mermaid*. She'd insisted she was no longer interested in crass American movies, but preferred the sensitive foreign "films" of the European masters.

"It's after eleven," Cliff told her.

"But I haven't seen this one. It has Jean-Paul Belmondo and Catherine Deneuve."

"Rent the video and watch it this weekend."

"You don't understand. None of the local video stores carry it. All they have are the latest John Revolta movies."

"I remember when you had a John Travolta poster on your closet door and I had to listen to 'Stayin' Alive' ten hours a day."

"Jesus, I was a child then. You're not going to throw that in my face forever, are you?"

Cliff smiled. He knew when he was being put on. "Is your father this easy to kid?"

She smiled, and he saw the quiet strength of Ginger in her face. "He's much easier. You come in second. Mom's the tough one."

"Good night, sweetheart."

"'Night, Dad."

Bogie was harder. He was already in bed, propped up, a library book in his hand.

"Whatchya reading?" Cliff asked.

"*Red Badge of Courage* by Stephen Crane. It's about the Civil War. A kid's afraid he's a coward."

"It's a good book."

"You've read it?"

Cliff nodded.

Bogie thought about that, lowering the book. "You've read a lot."

"Not compared to some people."

"Do you feel smarter?"

Cliff patted his own face. "Maybe a little, around the nose."

"I mean it," Bogie said.

Cliff sat on the edge of the bed. "I used to think it would make me feel smarter. I used to keep a list of every book I read. I'd write the title on a note card and what the book was about. I'd keep the note cards bound with a rubber band. And the thicker that stack of note cards got the smarter I felt."

"You still have the note cards?"

"No. I stopped keeping them as soon as I realized that each book only made me realize how much I *didn't* know. That my paltry stack of note cards was only a monument to my ignorance. The bigger it got, the dumber I felt."

"I'm confused. Does that mean you shouldn't read too much?"

Cliff smiled. "Nope. Just that you shouldn't do it for the wrong reasons. It's not a contest."

Bogie shifted in his bed. His book tipped off his lap and closed. He leafed through it, looking for his place. He spoke without looking at Cliff. "You want to know about the fights, right?"

"Your mom and I are worried."

Bogie sighed. "It's Todd."

Todd Kramer was Bogie's best friend. They biked to school every day. They'd been friends since before Ginger's divorce. Tall and athletic and good-natured, Todd was Bogie's Tommy Springman.

"What about Todd?"

"He's queer."

"Did he tell you this?"

"Yes."

"Did he . . ." Cliff hesitated.

"No, he didn't try anything," Bogie said. "Didn't grab my wad, if that's what you mean. He just came out and told me a couple of weeks ago while we were riding home from school. He tells me he's always felt that way. He said he doesn't have any, you know sexual feelings for me, just friendship, but that he thought I should know. Just like that, 'Thought you oughta know.'"

"Who've you been fighting with? Todd?"

"No. We used to fight sometimes, but never face punches. Just the gut and arms."

Cliff nodded. He remembered when there were rules about such things.

"Anyway, some of the kids at school found out about him. I don't know, maybe he even told them. I can't figure him anymore. Now they've been calling me one too. A fag."

"I don't like that word," Cliff said.

"All right then, gay. They say I'm gay like Todd, because I hang out with him."

"Are you?"

Bogie recoiled into his pillows, his face clenched with horror. "No! Why'd you say something like that?"

"Just want to get the facts straight. Here's the problem then: your best friend is gay, and now because he's your friend, people think you are too. So you've punched a few but that hasn't stopped them. Right?"

Bogie nodded.

"Now you aren't sure whether or not to drop Todd as your friend. Also right?"

"Yeah." Bogie looked up with appeal. "What do I do?"

Cliff shrugged. "Dump him."

Bogie looked shocked. "Yeah? I never thought I'd hear you say that. You think I should?"

"Why not? What's to gain by remaining friends? It's not like you'll ever double-date, right?"

"I guess. It's just that I feel, you know, funny about it."

Cliff remained silent.

Bogie picked at the B. Dalton price sticker on the cover of his book, curling up the edges with his fingernail, then rolling up the sticker like a rug. "He taught me how to ride a bike."

"Then don't dump him. Treat him the way you've always treated him. The way he's treated you."

Bogie made a sour face. "I knew it. I knew you'd lay some double-talk on me. No advice, right?"

Cliff smiled. "Right."

"Okay, what would you do if you were me?"

Cliff felt the sudden weight of the question as if the ceiling had dropped on his shoulders and only his great effort was keeping the entire house from collapsing. The boy wanted advice, had come to him for a straight answer. No bullshit. No adult double-talk. What would you do? Period.

"First, I'd figure out what I want most. That's the hard part. Once you know that, you'll know what to do."

Bogie looked disappointed. "Sounds like the same psycho-bullshit I get from my dad."

If there was one thing Cliff didn't want to hear, it was a comparison of him to Ginger's ex-husband.

Bogie elbowed his pillow. "Dad said to do what was right."

"I said to do what you want. There's a big difference."

"Yeah, sure. You mean if I told you I dumped Todd because he was gay, you and Mom wouldn't give me the leper treatment? Christ, Mom would have my copying the Bill of Rights a zillion times."

Cliff stood up. "She'd get over it."

Bogie cocked his head at a funny angle and grinned grimly. "Sometimes I can't figure you out, Cliff. I really expected you to give me the stick-to-your-friend speech."

"If you did it because I told you to, you wouldn't be much of a friend to Todd anyway. You wouldn't be doing him any favors. I guess the question I'd be asking myself right now is whether, after the way you've avoided Todd, he still wants to be your friend. Maybe he's asking his dad that right now.''

Bogie glanced out the window that, if you leaned at an angle, looked directly into Todd's bedroom. The boys had once rigged two empty soup cans attached with string between their rooms and communicated on their primitive ''telephone.'' Later, they'd sent Morse code signals with flashlights. They'd even tried sending homing pigeons back and forth, but Ginger and Todd's mother had gotten together and put an end to that. Tonight Todd's curtains were shut, but there was light behind them.

''Good night, Cliff,'' Bogie said.

''You decided what you're going to do?''

''Nope. I guess I'll think about it some more.''

''Lights out, pal. School tomorrow.''

CLIFF WAS IN THE BATHTUB when Ginger returned from the kitchen. He'd needed to soak, to stick his head underwater and hear nothing but his own breathing. He tried, but Standish Ford's grim face still hovered in his brain somewhere.

His eyes were closed. Suddenly he felt the cold sting of something dripping on his chest. He sat straight up, slopping some of the water over the edge of the tub and onto the floor. Ginger laughed, standing over him, eating a Creamsicle. He splashed water over his chest, washing away the sticky orange drops.

''Very funny.''

She was still laughing. Some of the ice cream was dripping down the stick onto her fingers. ''Lily is right, your instincts are rusty. What if this Creamsicle had been loaded?''

Cliff stood up, smoothed his hair back so he looked like a fifties greaser.

Ginger made a face. ''I hate it when you do that. You look like a hood.''

Cliff stepped out of the tub, adopted a loose stance and pointed his finger at her. "Rock 'n' roll is here to stay, baby."

She laughed again and he pulled her into his arms, using her to dry himself off. She had the giggles now, and was laughing so hard her Creamsicle dropped off the stick into the toilet. "Now look what you've done, Cliff."

He kissed her, backing her into the bedroom, removing her clothing with each step. When she was naked, she flopped back onto the bed. They made love slowly this time, face-to-face, eyes boring into each other's in the dark room. A faint cool breeze from the window chilled the sweat on their bodies, made them shiver with extra delight.

Afterward they lay side by side, his leg hooked over her hip. Her hand rested on his ribs, and she kept trying to line up her fingers, one to a rib like a piano exercise.

"What happened today, with those men? The whole story, Cliff."

He told her, leaving out only the information that would be dangerous for her to know—the stuff Ford had told him about Vatican Towne and Fat Boy. He watched her face as he recalled the events, looking for reaction, but she lay in a patch of darkness so black he couldn't see her eyes. When he was finished, they lay in silence for quite a while.

Suddenly Ginger hitched herself up onto her elbow. He could see her eyes now, intense but cool. His own eyes were half closed but not sleepy. Sex energized him.

"I'm glad you told those men no," she said. "But isn't this whole security business thing with Lily just a variation on the same theme?"

"In some ways, but not in the bad ones."

Her hand slid up his arm. His arm seemed thick and bumpy under her slender fingers. "The weightlifting has made a difference," she said. "I can feel it."

He liked hearing that, though he felt he shouldn't. The old Cliff would have liked hearing that too.

"I guess I don't understand," she said. "You speak five or six languages fluently. You've been everywhere in the world, you know a little bit about a lot of things. Why can't you be happy? Happy with the way things are?"

Cliff thought that over, considered denying any unhappiness, but Ginger would have known better. "Maybe I don't know enough yet."

"I think it's the action, the fucking danger."

"No," he said quickly. "It's not that. I know enough to assure you it isn't that." His hand cupped her hip, his thumb tapping on the tip of her hipbone. "I just like doing something well. It's just an unlucky circumstance that this is the kind of thing I do well."

"You're a good landscaper, Cliff."

"I'm an enthusiastic landscaper. And I'm an honest businessman, I charge what I'm worth, so I'm successful. But I'm not good. I never have the feeling I'm doing something that a thousand others couldn't do better. Let's be honest, Ginger—you do it better than I do."

She didn't say anything, the same as agreeing. She rolled onto her back, disengaging his leg and hand from her hip. "Why couldn't you have been good at law or something? I bet you could if you tried. You could go to law school."

"It doesn't interest me. I don't have the patience."

"You're making excuses."

"Maybe. Let's give this security consultancy thing a chance. I promise you, if you still feel it's too dangerous after six months, I'll drop out and we'll discuss our options again."

She sat up quickly, her voice happy. "Really, Cliff?"

"Yes."

Ginger dropped the subject, switching to Lily. "She's depressed."

"Why? We just got our first joint client."

"Harold dumped her. Went back to his second wife. She inherited money."

"Too bad. Lily liked him a lot."

Ginger rolled toward him, her arms coiling around his chest. "I like you a lot."

"What's not to like?"

They snuggled close and Ginger drifted off within ten minutes. As soon as she was asleep, Cliff eased himself out of bed, went into the walk-in closet, closed the door and flicked on the overhead light. The bare sixty-watt bulb glared in his eyes. He reached to the top shelf for the old Nike shoebox under his sweaters. He hadn't looked in there in over a year. He sat cross-legged and naked on the floor, surrounded by a mute audience of shoes, and opened the box.

He had already been through the photographs with Ginger, so she knew who most of these people were. He flipped through the recent ones of Cliff and Ginger, Ginger and the kids. They were all in rough chronological order, each layer another year deeper into his past.

About halfway down he found the photo he'd been looking for. It was from his first marriage, back when he was still with Graceland. His wedding day. The ceremony had taken place in London, at a small church near his apartment. Cliff's left arm was around his bride, his right arm was around Drew, the best man. And Drew's arm was around their other friend, the man who performed the ceremony.

Aaron Leland.

They were all smiling.

9

THE SAMOAN handed Cliff a gun. They were standing in the dark empty parking lot outside the square glass building that housed Francis Cromwell's video company. Cromwell had given them all the necessary keys and assured them he would leave their names with the security guard on duty.

Cliff took Lily's gun and turned it over in his hand, examining it as if it were an unfamiliar artifact from an ancient civilization.

"Is it okay? I heard you CIA boys liked the 9 mm."

He examined the Browning Hi-Power pistol with speedy efficiency, checking the magazine first to find it fully loaded. Thirteen rounds. He handed it back to her.

"It's legal," she said. "I have a permit."

"I don't. Besides, we're just checking the place out."

"When I was a cop, we always carried. You never know."

"We're here to evaluate his security system and make recommendations, Lily. Nothing else. Consultants, remember?"

She studied him carefully, squinting. "You're not gun-shy, are you, Cliff?"

"Yes. Also bullet-shy."

She laughed, her little-girl giggle tinkling in the dark parking lot like wind chimes.

Cliff looked into her large brown eyes. She was smiling, but he thought he recognized some hesitation, a flicker of doubt about him. Cops, even female cops, tended to judge others by how they handled a gun. In Graceland, if you needed to resort to a clumsy attention-grabbing gun, you hadn't done your job properly.

Cliff sighed, grabbed the Browning from her hand, held it up in front of her face like a Marine arms instructor. "First of all, you've picked a pretty good gun. However, this is brand-new, which on this model means the trigger pull is stiff. But after a couple hundred rounds it should be smooth and manageable. The problem is this new claw hammer they've developed—you almost always cut your thumb on it. And the magazine disconnector is too easily removed. And, for God's sake, it's a shiny steel composition that reflects light. Maybe that's okay for dumb cops busting down a door and charging in, but not if you're sneaking up on someone. Next time, pick up an H&K P9S." He pulled her hand up and slapped the gun into her palm. "Can we go to work now?"

She dropped the Browning into her purse and said, "Okay." Then they headed across the parking lot toward the building.

The security guard inside the main entrance looked as though he'd been half napping; the unfiltered cigarette in his hands had burned down almost an inch of ash. When Lily and Cliff unlocked the front door with Cromwell's special coded card, he perked right up, jumping to his feet. His right hand dropped to the heavy .38 in the holster at his side. The cigarette in his left hand spilled the inch of ash onto his desk.

"May I help you?" he said flatly.

"Cliff Remington and Lily Vaiala," Lily said. "Mr. Cromwell said he'd leave our names with you."

The security guard stuck the cigarette in his mouth, freeing his hands to pick up the clipboard from his desk. He flipped through the pages. "Yeah, here you are." He looked up, eyes narrowed suspiciously. "I'll still need to see some ID."

Cliff and Lily provided driver's licenses. The guard scrutinized the tiny photos, then Lily's and Cliff's faces. He went back and forth a couple of times. Finally satisfied, he handed them back. His tone was suddenly friendlier. "Sorry about the hassle, but so many folks have started working late that I gotta be especially sharp."

Cliff looked at the cigarette, which was back in the man's hand. It had burned down so far it was about to scorch his fingers.

The guard followed Cliff's gaze to the cigarette and immediately stubbed it out on the *Sports Illustrated* he'd been reading. Then he picked up the magazine and funneled the butt and ashes into the wastepaper can under his desk. "I quit smoking a few weeks ago," he explained. "I'm down to only three a day."

Lily finished signing the log book and handed the pen to Cliff. He signed under her name and jotted in the time: 10:23 p.m. They started toward the elevators.

"Sixth floor," the guard hollered after them. "And only the middle elevator is operating at night."

Cliff waved thanks and punched the button. The doors to the middle elevator immediately shushed open and Cliff and Lily entered.

THE SECURITY GUARD unsnapped the holster strap that kept his .38 secure. He drew out the gun with a smooth fast movement and checked the cylinder, though he'd done so twenty minutes ago. But that was then and this was now. His reputation was for efficiency and accuracy. When someone hired Charon to do a job, they knew it would be done.

Charon stuffed the gun back into his holster and walked down the hallway toward the stairwell. On second thought, he pulled out his gun, held it high near his face so it would be ready and began his slow, silent climb to the sixth floor.

"IS THIS IT?" Lily asked. They both stared at the polished oak door with the black lettering: FANDANGO VIDEO CORPORATION.

"It's suite 609," Cliff said, "so this must be it."

"Fandango," she mused. "Somehow that doesn't sound like Francis Cromwell. Too frivolous."

"Maybe it was his wife's idea."

"Yeah, maybe." Lily took out the square piece of plastic with a Swiss cheese pattern of holes that was the office key. Cromwell had explained the lock was the same kind used in certain hotels and enabled them to change the combination daily.

"From a security viewpoint, that's a good idea," Cliff had told Cromwell earlier that day when he'd come by their office to deliver the keys and passes. "However, the plastic keys tend to bend at the edges after a little use and become difficult to use. Am I right?"

"Yes," Cromwell admitted, looking embarrassed. "We've had a few minor problems."

"Also, there are a few ways around them. I think you might be better off with the magnetic strip ID card that logs in the time the card is used and whose card it is. It's a little more expensive, but worth it."

Francis Cromwell straightened his already impeccably straight tie and tugged at the razor crease in his pants. He allowed himself a faint smile of satisfaction. "It seems you're already earning your money, Mr. Remington."

Cromwell wrote out a deposit for services, and Lily had it in the bank within the hour. She was very strict about business finances. Every dollar had to do the work of two.

"No one should be there tonight," Cromwell had told them. "I purposely arranged for a nice dinner at the Cannery in Newport Beach tonight. Me, and my wife and the nephew. The video should be safe."

"What time will dinner be over?" Lily had asked.

"Oh, I don't know." He'd run his fingertips over the stitched duck flying across his tie. "Say, eleven?"

"Fine. That'll give us a chance to go in, check out your current security system and hang around a bit in case someone tries to come in and steal anything."

Francis Cromwell had stood up, his thin sunken face flexed into a faint smile. "I can't tell you how much I appreciate this."

"That's our job," Lily had said, drenching him in one of her huge toothy smiles. When Cromwell finally left, Lily had beamed at Cliff. "In a couple of weeks we'll be doing half a dozen corporations. Word gets around fast in Orange County."

Now they stood in the dim hallway outside Fandango Video. The overhead lights were large squares in the ceiling, but only every other one was lit, the usual nighttime procedure. Down the hall, they heard the clacking of a printer. Cliff smelled fresh coffee and his stomach knotted slightly. Apparently there were others on this floor also working late.

Lily rapped her walnut knuckles on the door of Fandango Video. "Hear that, Cliff? That's opportunity knocking, bro. We have arrived."

Cliff laughed. "Yeah, and now let's get to work."

Lily shoved the plastic card into the brass slot below the door handle.

yyyeeyyyeeyyyeeyyyeeeeeeeeeeee . . .

The alarm screamed. The screeching was loud and unnerving, a high-pitched electronic warble. Lily kept fidgeting with the key in the lock, but it was stuck. She slammed her shoulder into the door, rattling the door and frame, but not jarring the lock free. She stepped back and covered her ears. "That stupid sonofabitch gave us the wrong key."

Cliff stood for a moment. No, less than that. A fraction of a moment. The time it would take a hummingbird's heart to beat once. No more. It was as if a giant crude ax had hacked a gash in time and he was looking into the bloody ruptured wound and seeing the future.

The patch at the back of his neck burned as if acid had been splashed on him. His eyes felt large in his head, too large for their sockets, almost painful. Everything was happening at once and he seemed to know what would happen before it did, yet he was powerless to prevent anything.

Lily stepped back from the door, her hands clamped over her ears, cussing loudly at the absent Francis Cromwell. At the same time, the door to one of the offices down the hall opened, and two men in loosened ties with their shirtsleeves rolled up launched themselves into the hallway. The first man was tall and handsome, in his late twenties, with horn-rimmed glasses pushed on top of his head. He was running toward them, shouting. ''What the fuck are you doing? That's my office!''

Lily looked confused, her brown face tight and wrinkled. Then she realized what Cliff had already realized, and her face relaxed into a smooth mask of resignation.

Cliff grabbed her by the arm and jerked her after him. Assessing the two men in front of him, he decided they were a lesser danger than what he was certain was waiting for them at the other end of the hall behind the door to the stairs. If they could make it into the open office door, they'd have a chance, depending on how many assassins had been sent. As they ran, he tore Lily's handbag from over her shoulder and plunged his hand inside, fingers clutching at the heavy grip of the Browning 9 mm.

The wailing alarm drowned the sound of the first shot, but Cliff knew it had been fired. Knew where it had hit. Lily fell to the floor, her deadweight prying open his fingers and forcing him to release her. Cliff dived to the ground as the second bullet flew over his shoulder and punched a softball-size hole into the wall. He was still diving and rolling across the carpet when the third bullet tore through his side, splintered the tip of the floating rib, and ripped out the front of his shirt. The impact sent him crashing into the wall, the Browning flying out of his hand. He was dizzy and half conscious, having no idea where the gun landed. Through dreamy eyes he watched the rest as if gazing into a murky aquarium. The security guard from downstairs was crouching and lazily aiming his gun at the two executives who were now running back toward their office door. He fired two quick shots, and Cliff saw the handsome man lurch forward into his partner, knocking him off his feet. The dead man's limp body smothered his living friend's legs, pinning them to the floor. The man furiously kicked his dead partner away, freeing his legs, clambering to his feet to dash the final five feet to the open doorway. He never made it. The security guard, seeming almost bored with the simplicity of it all, fired a final round into the man's lower back and his target folded backward at an angle where people's backs don't normally fold.

Cliff looked down the hall at Lily, his eyes even with her sprawled body. He couldn't see her face and was glad. He saw the back of her head, most of which had been blown away. Amid the long black hair, an oozing red volcanic crater spilled the contents of her head onto the blue carpet.

Sometime during it all, the alarm had stopped wailing. The security guard surveyed the scene with a practiced eye. Cliff expected him to pump another round into him, finish the job. But he didn't. The assassin grasped the grip tightly and twisted, smudging any fingerprints. Then he tossed the gun onto the floor. Smiling, he made his finger and thumb into a mock gun, pointing it at Cliff. "Pow," he said, and blew at the tip of his finger. "You're dead." Then he spun around and disappeared through the door to the stairs.

Cliff did not pass out. He wouldn't let himself. He dug his heels into the carpet and pushed his body against the wall until he was sitting upright. He spotted the Browning a few feet behind him near the elevators. He crawled along the wall on hands and knees, his right hand clutched to his bleeding rib. When his hands were finally around the gun, he pressed his face against the wall and clawed himself to his feet. The pain in his side made the wound feel as large as a tunnel, but he staggered down the hallway, shoulder leaning against the wall for support, stepping over the crumpled dead executives, stumbling toward the elevators. He jabbed the button with the barrel of the Browning. The arrow on the button lit up. He could hear the huge machine whooshing toward him. He blinked rapidly, thinking that the effort would somehow help keep him conscious. The elevator rumbled closer and closer and Cliff felt his hand tighten around the gun. Finally it thumped to a halt. Cliff pushed himself away from the wall, waiting for the door to open.

The elevator doors slid open and four uniformed cops rushed out, guns drawn and pointing at Cliff.

"Drop it, asshole!" one of them shouted. "Drop it or die!"

10

"CAVANAUGH! Jesus, is that you?"

Cavanaugh spun around so quickly some of the red punch rocked out of his plastic cup onto his hand. Two men with slightly drunken grins were pushing their way through the crowd toward him.

"My God, Cavanaugh!" one of them said as he slapped him on the back. "We heard you were dead."

"He just smells that way," the other one said, chuckling.

Cavanaugh had a smile pasted on while he tried to remember their faces. Most of the people here wore name tags, but quite a few refused, these two among them. Cavanaugh wasn't wearing his either. In fact, he hadn't even checked in at the front desk. He'd merely slipped in the side door and wandered over to the punch bowl, nibbled a few deviled eggs and scolded himself for taking this kind of risk without a good reason.

"He looks a little stoned, Chuck." One of them winked at the other.

"Stoned? Are you shitting me? Cavanaugh's the guy who took the whole swim team's kitty and bought four ounces of oregano." Chuck frowned. "You haven't gotten into drugs or anything, have you, Cavanaugh?"

"No."

"Hey, buddy, you okay?"

"Chuck Darrow?" Cavanaugh asked, placing them at last. Then he turned to the shorter man. "Larry Bodine?"

"Who the fuck else?" Chuck said.

Cavanaugh stuck out his hand and vigorously shook both of theirs. "Man, I can't believe it. Jesus!"

"*You* can't believe it?" Larry said. "*We* thought *you* were dead."

Chuck nodded. "That's what we'd heard, man. You were killed in Nam. Of course, we heard the same thing about Jerry Mathers, you know, the Beaver. He's still around too."

Cavanaugh looked around the gym. Tacky papier-mâché decorations were hanging from the rafters: bright paper bells and twisted ribbons, intertwining the school colors of gold and black. A giant banner drooped between two of the basketball hoops: Welcome! Gladfield High School Fifteen-Year Reunion!

"Quite a turnout," Chuck said, looking around.

"Yeah," Cavanaugh nodded.

"Jesus, it's really Cavanaugh." Larry shook his head. "All this time we thought you were dead. Killed in Nam. God, back in the seventies. Heard that at the fifth reunion from Trixie Lendal. Then again at the tenth. Everyone said you were dead."

Cavanaugh half smiled. "They were right."

He walked away from Chuck and Larry. He was glad to see them, but it wasn't them he'd come here to see. They'd been in German class together a couple of years, but they'd never really been friends. He worked his way through the crowd of laughing people, not slowing to read name tags or study faces or have his own studied. This was a mistake, he thought. You should never have come here. It was stupid. Christ, where were your brains, man?

A hand hooked his arm. "Where the fuck you going, Cavanaugh?"

Cavanaugh started reacting before the sentence was even finished, before he knew who'd said it, before anything. He clamped onto the hand holding him and twisted until the person who had accosted him dropped to the floor.

"God, Cavanaugh!" the voice rasped.

Cavanaugh looked down. The man's face wore an expression of pain. He had bright blue eyes, balding blond hair, ears that stuck out like Gable's. Immediately Cavanaugh released his grasp. "Eric!" He helped the man to his feet. Those who'd stopped to watch started chattering again, trying to be heard above the rock 'n' roll oldies played by the band on the makeshift stage.

"You lint fucker, Cavanaugh," Eric said, but not angrily.

"Sorry, Eric. Didn't recognize you at first."

Eric grinned and ran his hand over his hair. "Yeah, I lost a little of the mop. My dad claims it's God's punishment for all the fights we used to have about me getting my hair cut."

"I was hoping to find you here," Cavanaugh said.

"Yeah, well, I'm surprised to find you. I heard you were dead."

"They tried."

Eric laughed, patted Cavanaugh's stomach. "Fuck, man, hard as a refrigerator. You belong to a gym or something?"

"No."

"Tell me your secret." He patted his own sagging gut. "I've been trying to lose ten pounds for the past fifteen years."

Cavanaugh smiled. "You look good, Eric."

"Christ, you're not gay, are you? You're not going to come out of the closet tonight? I mean it, man. Tonight alone I found out three guys and one girl in our class were gay. Sally Dieter, for Chrissake. Best fucking ass and legs on the whole cheerleader squad. I used to get blue balls watching her do splits at the football game. I could hardly play."

"You could hardly play anyway. That's why the coach never sent you in."

Eric smiled. "You may be on to something there."

Cavanaugh sipped the last of his punch. Eric pulled him through the crowd toward the refreshment table. Over a hundred graduates and their spouses were milling around the gym. Some were overdressed, with fashionable clothing, too much jewelry—gaudy status symbols to show how far they'd come since graduating from Gladfield, Kansas. Most though, still lived in Gladfield, and they dressed and looked it.

A hand pinched Cavanaugh on the buttock, but he could tell from the location and pressure who it was. "Audrey," he said and turned around.

"Nice butt," she said.

"Uh-oh," Eric said. "I see a minireunion unfolding here. I'll circulate and see if I can hit on any old flames. Be back in a flash." He wandered off.

Cavanaugh turned and looked at her. He said nothing.

"Hey, quit staring," she told him. "Fifteen years make some changes on a girl."

"For the better."

"Hmm, nice line. You sure talk better, Tim. Of course, *any* talking would be an improvement. You were into being the strong silent type back then."

"I just didn't have anything to say."

"You said enough," she smiled. "Remember?"

He did. Two years they'd dated. She had been a grade behind him, pert and leggy and smart. He'd never figured out what she saw in him. Still, she'd come to every dance and party he and his rock group played at. Then came graduation, college, the draft lottery, the Marines. Vietnam. A few letters.

Then the Junkyard Dogs.

"I didn't expect to see you here," she said.

"You heard I'd been killed."

"No, I didn't. I heard your dad was."

"That's true." Cavanaugh's mother had died when he was ten. His father had died in a tractor accident six months after Cavanaugh went to Vietnam.

"Actually, I haven't kept up with the old gang. I live in San Francisco now."

"What do you do?" Married? he wondered. Kids?

"You'd never guess."

"Governor?"

"Gynecologist."

"Thought you were going to be a cowgirl."

"At least I've got the stirrups."

Cavanaugh laughed.

"What about you, Tim? Married?"

"Once."

"Kids?"

He shook his head.

"Do I have to pull every word out of you? Give me a break, huh?"

Cavanaugh shrugged. "Not much to tell. I move around a lot."

"That surprises me. You were never the restless type. Used to talk about coming back here after the Marines and working your daddy's farm. I thought that was kinda cute."

"Things happen," he said.

They were silent a minute, looking at each other.

"I'm not married either," she said. "I'm in the middle of an amicable divorce right now. What we in California call no-fault divorce. No fault—that phrase appeals to me."

"Kids?"

"A son. Eight." She looked down into her cup of punch. "I don't know. Maybe that's why I decided to come to the reunion this time. Maybe I hoped you'd be here."

Cavanaugh's eyes tingled, and he fought to keep tears from forming. He didn't know why he'd come. All these years he'd avoided any contact with relatives, with anyone he'd known. He never used his real name, hadn't since his release. Officially, Tim Cavanaugh was dead. MIA. Along with all the other Junkyard Dogs.

He'd tried to make it impossible to be found by those who knew he existed. Even though they'd promised him and the others that their past would be buried, even though Vatican Towne himself had shaken their hands on it, Cavanaugh knew

enough about the military to know they'd never let an opportunity like this go forever. Sooner or later someone would get
to thinking. Then the horror of the past would be forgotten,
the promises ignored.

But looking at Audrey now, Cavanaugh dreamed of possibilities. Why not go to San Francisco, start seeing her? See
what happens. A normal life.

"What's wrong, Tim?" she asked, touching a finger to his
cheek. When she brought the finger away, it was wet. "You
okay?"

"Fine. Guess I missed you more than I realized."

Her smile was the only genuine thing he'd seen in fifteen
years. He wanted to kiss her right then.

"Attention, bug-fuckers!" Eric's voice boomed over the
loudspeakers. "Oops. Guess that's the kind of language that
always got me in trouble with Principal Kingsley."

That got a big laugh and some scattered applause. Cavanaugh and Audrey turned to face the stage. Cavanaugh felt Audrey's arm slip around his waist. He curled his arm around her
shoulder. He felt giddy, as if he ought to give her a letter
sweater or a friendship ring or something. He couldn't stop
grinning.

Eric continued: "I don't know about the rest of you, but I
think music has gone to hell since we left this place. Rapping?
Shit, man, Dylan did that long time ago. Only he had something to rap about!"

More applause, some shouts of agreement.

"So, as a little treat, I've managed, through great personal
sacrifice and expense, to locate three of the members of Hard
Knocks and jet them right here to Gladfield Kansas, to play
for you."

Whistles, shouts and applause.

"So here they are, playing the hits just like they used to when
we were the best fucking rock 'n' roll band in Kansas. Jimmy
Lawrence, come on down."

A skinny man in a red bowtie ran onto the stage to the enthusiastic shouting of the crowd.

"My God!" Cavanaugh said. "Jimmy's lost fifty pounds."

"Where's the ponytail, Jimmy?" someone from the audience yelled. The ponytail tied with a black ribbon to protest the Vietnam War had been his trademark.

"And as a special treat," Eric said. "Not really dead but just resting his eyes, Timothy Cavanaugh!"

The crowd whistled even louder. They all turned, followed Eric's pointed finger to see Cavanaugh. He froze under their gaze.

"Still trying to get into Audrey's pants, eh, Tim?"

Audrey nudged Cavanaugh. "Go ahead. Go on up and play."

Cavanaugh walked slowly at first, then faster, then trotted up to the stage. The young musicians who had been playing were good-natured, offering the old graduates their instruments, but handing them over with a little trepidation, like adults teaching children how to shoot guns.

Cavanaugh hung the fancy red Fender electric guitar over his shoulder. His fingers flexed into a dozen different chords, testing the play of the strings on the frets. The one thing he had kept up on was his guitar. That was how he'd made his living these past years on the run.

"How ya doin', Tim?" Jimmy asked as he sat behind the drums.

"You look great, man," Cavanaugh replied. "You okay?"

Jimmy laughed. "I went on a diet, man, I didn't get cancer."

Cavanaugh smiled. "Ready to play?"

"You kidding? I been waiting to do this for twenty years."

Eric turned to Jimmy and Cavanaugh. He dangled a big electric bass guitar from his neck. He was tuning it as he spoke. "You guys remember any of the old sets?"

"Some," Cavanaugh said.

"Let's start with 'Kicks' then do 'Magic Carpet Ride.' Okay?"

Cavanaugh looked over at Audrey. She was smiling encouragingly, just as she used to. Maybe certain feelings couldn't survive in the reality of the morning after a reunion. Maybe her being a doctor, having a child, his being a traveling musician, having a past he could never tell her but would live in fear of her discovering—maybe all that would prove too much for them tomorrow. But for tonight, everything was perfect. This was what he'd come here for. To see people who remembered him the way he used to be... before what had happened to him, before the terrible things he'd done. Before the Junkyard Dogs.

"Ladies and gentlemen," Eric announced. "Here's a little something by Paul Revere and the Raiders."

And they played.

There were whistles, applause. Several in the audience began to dance to the music.

After the old-timers played a few more songs, the members of the band that had been hired to play started looking impatient. Eric kept announcing just one more song, and then another. Cavanaugh was glad. He and Jimmy and Eric kept singing and playing until the younger musicians finally climbed on the stage and stood next to their instruments, glowering.

Eventually, Cavanaugh, Jimmy and Eric climbed down, to the uproarious shouts and wild applause of everyone there. Jimmy and Eric were approached by some classmates and stopped to chat with them. Cavanaugh politely excused himself and went to rejoin Audrey. She picked up a napkin from the table and wiped the sweat from his face.

"You're still good," she said.

"I enjoyed it."

His heart was still pounding from the music, but now it shifted into another rhythm as he felt her hands taking both of his.

"I have to go to the bathroom," she said. "I'll be back in a few minutes for a dance. Okay?"

"Okay."

"Don't go off with one of the other sluts around here."

"You're the only slut for me."

She laughed and hurried off.

People came up to Cavanaugh, congratulated him on his playing, asked him personal questions, told him about their lives, their victories and defeats. He listened, spoke little. Finally, to avoid them, he went out into the hallway where the rest rooms were. He didn't want Audrey to see him waiting for her like a puppy dog, so he walked outside to the parking lot. He could wait there all alone and still keep an eye on the rest rooms through the glass doors.

He'd been waiting for about three minutes when he felt the sudden pressure of a gun in his back.

"Stupid, Cavanaugh," a voice said. "Very stupid."

They were taking him toward the dark blue car with the tinted glass. He looked over his shoulder, through the glass doors. Audrey was coming out of the rest room, straightening her dress, smiling happily as she hurried back toward the gym to dance with him.

"YOUR STORY is shit, Remington."

Cliff pushed himself up to a sitting position in the narrow hospital bed. The detective who had spoken grabbed a fistful of the yellow curtain next to the bed and yanked it along its horseshoe runner until they were both enclosed like boys in a tent.

The detective was a big man, well over two hundred pounds, with woolly gray hair and a crow-black mustache. The combination of gray hair and black mustache gave him an unbalanced look, as if one or the other was a disguise, and not a particularly clever one. He hooked his square thumbs under his suspenders like some old-time Southern lawyer and glowered at Cliff.

"You hear me, Remington? I checked out your story. It's shit." His voice was brittle, like cracking knuckles. "You got anything to add?"

Cliff showed no expression. "I'd like to use the phone now."

"No lawyer's gonna make this turkey fly."

"I want to call my wife."

The detective studied Cliff a minute while he thought. His thick meaty hand swept open the curtain and he stuck his head out. "Hey, Bastion, get me a phone in here."

"Sure thing, Lieutenant," someone answered. Rubber soles squeaked down the hospital corridor.

Cliff touched the bandage wrapped around his chest. It was so tight he could only take shallow breaths. Medication had dulled the edge of the pain, but he still felt the pulsing pressure, like some small animal under the skin trying to claw its way out. The Korean doctor in the emergency room had told him the bullet had nicked the floating rib, but the entry and exit wounds were clean and he'd be fine in a week or two.

Four hours had passed since the shooting. Cliff had recounted the events for several different detectives, finally repeating it all once more for the burly cop in front of him, Lt. Slew Godfrey.

Lieutenant Godfrey leaned against Cliff's bed, and the mattress sagged dramatically. He kept staring at Cliff, flexing his suspenders, occasionally brushing an imaginary strand of hair from his forehead or wiping some unseen crumbs from the bed. He seemed to see dirt and disorder everywhere.

"You're not jerking me off, are you, man?" Lieutenant Godfrey asked.

Cliff lay back against his pillow and closed his eyes.

"I mean, this cock-and-bull story about Francis Cromwell and the 'Baby-sitter' videos and the maniac security guard." He shook his head disgustedly. "There is no Francis fucking Cromwell. We checked. And the Fandango Video Corporation is a subsidiary of Carleton Enterprises, whose offices are down the hall from Fandango. The young gentleman with the glasses was Bradley Carleton, owner and self-made millionaire. The other lad, the one with the shattered spine, was his CEO, Phillip DeSoto. You can see my problem with your story, can't you?"

Cliff nodded. "I have security keys that I shouldn't have that a man who doesn't exist gave to me. Three people are shot to death. You've got the murder weapon, but no readable fingerprints. One person is alive. Naturally he's your suspect."

"Bingo!" Lieutenant Godfrey found a stray hair on Cliff's blanket and plucked it off, tossing it to the floor. "It doesn't fit perfectly yet, but I think with some creative police work, we might be able to pin the whole thing on you."

"There's a problem of motive."

"Well, let's say you and your partner were trying to steal the videotapes for illegal duplication. Just what you claimed you were preventing."

"Why'd I kill my own partner?"

"Maybe Carleton caught you two breaking in, shot both of you. You pulled the Browning, got him to drop his gun, then turned his gun on the two of them? How's that sound? Not bad, huh? If I add a nude scene I can sell it to the movies."

Cliff stared at the ceiling. None of this mattered. What did matter was who had pulled the trigger, and who had sent him to do it.

The lieutenant leaned back even farther on the bed, supporting his bulk on his elbows. "Thing is, we found the body of the security guard. Skinny kid about twenty-five, blond hair and acne scars. Stuffed in a garbage Dumpster behind the building."

"The guy who did the shooting must have killed him first."

"Conventional wisdom suggests you and your partner did away with him."

A uniformed cop poked his head through the curtain. "Got the phone, Lieutenant. Where do you want it?"

Godfrey gestured toward the phone jack next to the nightstand. Officer Bastion's knees cracked when he stooped. He clicked the plug into the jack and stood up, his knees cracking again. He handed the phone to Lieutenant Godfrey.

"Thanks," Godfrey said and jerked his head. Officer Bastion nodded and left. Godfrey set the phone on Cliff's lap, but kept his heavy hand on top, pinning down the receiver. Cliff made no move toward it. He waited quietly.

"Thing is," the lieutenant said, "I know all about you being some kind of former spook. Some government hotshot. Word's out on you, Remington."

"What word is that, Lieutenant?"

"Two years ago. Some people got killed, and you were involved."

"I was the one they were trying to kill."

"Hey, I'm no conspiracy nut but I got an open mind. Maybe Bobby Kennedy did have Marilyn Monroe killed, I don't know. Maybe Wall Street snuffed Martin Luther King, Jr. Go figure. Thing is, this whole thing doesn't add up right. Cop logic says you're dirty. But something doesn't feel right here."

Cliff watched Godfrey wet his thumb and erase a smudge of dirt from the phone receiver. The man wasn't stupid, nor was he lazy, willing to accept easy answers. He was conscientious, treated his job as if it mattered. Cliff could tell he was very good at his job.

The lieutenant removed his hand from the phone and walked away from the bed, turning his back to afford at least a little privacy. The privacy of facial expressions.

Cliff dialed.

THE CHIME of the doorbell was followed by loud knocking. Then the doorbell again.

Ginger sleepily reached across the bed for Cliff. When her hand found nothing but empty space, she was suddenly awake. The digital clock beamed its time: 3:36 a.m. A cold shiver crawled across her back as if someone had just ripped a hunk of tape from her skin. He'd warned her he might be late, that he and Lily might stake out the place the whole night. Still, the room seemed empty without him, the shadows more threatening.

Heavy knocking again.

Ginger snapped on the bedside light. Adrenaline chilled her stomach and dried her throat. She jumped up, naked, and rummaged through the three days' worth of dirty laundry next to the bed she hadn't yet gotten around to stuffing in the hamper. She found a pair of black sweatpants covered with white cat hair and a white sweatshirt crusted with patches of dried food. Her cooking sweatshirt. Cliff teased her because every meal she cooked was a battle, a test of will between her and the stove. She usually emerged victorious with a hot meal, but she always looked as if she'd been through a children's food fight.

Ginger walked briskly down the corridor toward the living room. Liza's bedroom door opened and she stood there in her flannel nightgown, knuckling her eyes. "What's going on? Cliff forget his keys?"

"I don't know. Go back to bed." She kissed her cheek in passing, and Liza nodded sleepily and shuffled back into her room.

Ginger screwed one eye to the peephole in the front door and saw the policewoman standing outside. "Oh, Christ!" she said and quickly unfastened the locks and pulled open the door. "What's wrong, Officer?"

The woman looked at her notes on the clipboard. "You Mrs. Remington?"

"Yes."

"Your husband was involved in an exchange of gunfire this evening—"

"Is he okay?" Ginger interrupted.

"He sustained a slight wound, nothing serious. Lieutenant Godfrey thought you might want to come to the hospital to visit him."

"Yes, of course." Ginger stepped back, ran her hand through her hair, trying to organize her thoughts. "I'll get some shoes on, grab my purse. Come in."

The policewoman shook her head. "Thank you, ma'am, I'll wait out here. Keep my ear on the car radio."

"Okay," Ginger said absently. She left the front door open. It seemed rude to shut it in the police officer's face. One of the things she liked about living in Irvine was the large number of women on their police force. Seeing one patrolling in a cruiser always cheered Ginger. It was a sign, an indication that things would be better for Liza when she wanted to pick a career. Not so many sexual roadblocks and taboos. But right now, Ginger felt nothing, just a deep relief that Cliff hadn't been injured seriously, and a dull dread that this might not be the last time she'd have such a knock on her door and waken to an empty bed and a cold fear that while she'd been sleeping, her life was being rearranged.

Ginger was walking toward the bedroom when the phone rang. She hurried to the bedroom phone and snagged it on the third ring. "Hello?"

"Hi, sweetheart."

"Cliff! For God's sake, what happened?"

"You know?"

"Yes. A policewoman sent by some Lieutenant Godfrey showed up here and said you'd been wounded. I was just getting ready to come over to the hospital."

"Really, I'm okay. I'll be out by morning."

"What happened? The officer said there was gunfire."

There was a long silence and for a moment Ginger thought they'd been disconnected. "Cliff?"

"Yeah, I'm here. I'll tell you about it when you get here, okay?"

Ginger's eyes blurred with tears. "Cliff, what about Lily?"

Cliff sighed. "She's dead."

"Oh, Jesus!"

"Look, I'll explain it when you get here."

Ginger nodded, then realized he couldn't see her. "I'll be right down. But, Cliff?"

"Yes?"

"This ends the six-month trial period, okay?"

"Yes."

Ginger breathed deeply with relief. "I'll be there in a few minutes. I love you."

"Me too."

Ginger sat on the edge of the bed and began lacing her shoes. Suddenly she heard the front door close and she looked up, startled.

CLIFF SWUNG HIS LEGS over the side of the bed. "Where are my clothes?"

Lieutenant Godfrey frowned. "You haven't been released yet. Either by the doctor or by me."

Cliff hopped out of bed and opened the cabinet against the wall. His jeans and sweater were hanging there. In the drawer, he found his underpants and socks discreetly folded. He began dressing.

"God, you're cocky," Godfrey said. "I ought to throw you in jail just for being a smartass."

Cliff buttoned up his 501 Levi's. "Lieutenant, if you had real evidence, I'd be in the prison ward of this hospital right now. If I knew anything more, I'd tell you. I want that bastard caught too."

"You're not going to do anything heroic, are you? You're not going to fuck up my case?"

"I'm no vigilante, if that's what you mean. I'm a landscaper, Lieutenant, a fact that has never been clearer to me than it is tonight." Cliff eased into his sweater, wincing at the pain in his side as he lifted his arms. "Now, I just want to wait for my wife and go home with her."

"Okay," the lieutenant nodded. "For now."

"Right," Cliff said. "And thanks for sending an officer to pick her up. I appreciate that."

Godfrey's face stiffened. "I didn't send any officer to your house."

Cliff didn't bother with his shoes. Bare feet slapping cold linoleum, he pushed past the burly detective, swiped open the curtain and dashed down the hallway. Two uniformed cops started for him. Lieutenant Godfrey, running a few feet behind Cliff, waved for them to follow them both.

The house was dark, as were most of the others in the neighborhood. It was barely four in the morning when Cliff and Lieutenant Godfrey pulled up to the curb in Godfrey's unmarked Chevy. The two uniforms in the patrol car glided up behind them, radio chatter crackling rudely in the quiet neighborhood.

Godfrey had already radioed for the dispatcher to try phoning Ginger. No one had answered the phone. Other than that, there had been no conversation on the ride over. Cliff had stared out the window battling the horrid thoughts trying to enter his mind. It was a losing battle.

Godfrey's Chevy was coasting to the curb, not yet stopped, when Cliff flung open the door and leaped out. He hit the ground running. The grass was still wet and slippery from the sprinklers. He grasped the front doorknob and turned. It was unlocked. A bad sign.

Cliff clamped his teeth down hard, locking his jaw. He didn't know what he would find, but he tried to prepare himself. He threw open the door and dived into the living room, skidding across the thick gray carpet. Glancing around the room, he identified every shadow before climbing to one knee.

"Ginger!" he called. "Liza! Bogie!"

No answer.

Behind him, the lieutenant led the two uniformed cops through the front door. They all had their guns drawn. One of the uniforms flipped on the light switch.

"If a gunman's hiding behind that sofa," Cliff said, "you three are now perfectly illuminated targets."

The two cops swung their guns toward the sofa. Godfrey made a sour face at them. "Knock it off. There's no one there."

Cliff was already on his feet and rushing down the hall. This was his home, really the first place he had ever lived that he considered a home. He never felt safer, more relaxed, more a part of humanity than when he was here. But now, as he tore down the hallway, the house was at once the same, yet sinisterly unfamiliar, as if reflected in a funhouse mirror.

He stopped at his and Ginger's bedroom first. The bed was mussed, the sheets twisted into long braided knots, strangled during the night by Ginger's restless movements. How many times had Cliff awakened shivering, only to find Ginger wrestling the blankets into submission while she slept. He searched the room quickly. Each door he opened—bathroom, closet—squeezed his heart with sharp pain. Never had he been so afraid of what he might find.

Cliff emerged from the bathroom to find Godfrey on his knees checking under the bed. Cliff had already checked there, but he said nothing, stepping around the big man and hurrying toward the children's bedrooms. The two uniforms stayed with the lieutenant as if standing guard over him.

Cliff eased open Beau's door. Light from the hallway sliced through the dark room straight to Beau's bed. Empty. Cliff reached inside, brushed his hand along the wall until he caught the light switch and flicked it on. The room, suddenly bright with the 150-watt bulbs that Beau preferred, was oddly neat for a thirteen-year-old boy. But Bogie liked things orderly and organized. He was not a spontaneous child, but inclined toward planning even the simplest trip to the grocery store. Ginger was well-known for making shopping lists and then losing them on the way to the market. Beau not only made lists, he typed them and kept carbons.

It didn't take long to search the room. Empty.

Godfrey and the two uniforms were waiting for Cliff outside Liza's room. The cops were grim faced and didn't look at him. Godfrey's face was pasty white, with pinpricks of sweat dotting his forehead. Cliff reached for the doorknob and the lieutenant shoved himself in front of the door. "You don't want to go in there, Cliff."

Cliff felt the air cut off in his throat, like a valve suddenly wrenched closed. He tried to take a deep breath, but couldn't quite get enough air. He knew from the words, from their expressions his worst fears were true. He tried another deep breath and coughed. Air would not squeeze by that lump in his throat. What was it in there lodged like a rock? Hope?

Cliff stepped around the detective and reached again for the door. Lieutenant Godfrey sighed, shook his woolly gray head and moved aside. Cliff entered.

The lights were already on. Liza's room was as it always was, a messy collection of piles. Piles of schoolbooks, piles of dirty clothes, piles of clean clothes, piles of shoes, piles of *People*, *Glamour* and *Cosmopolitan* magazines. Two long foam bolster pillows that Ginger had covered with fabric to match the curtains were leaning against her desk. The bolsters were meant to transform the bed into a sofa during the day, but since Liza rarely made her bed without prompting from Ginger, the bolsters never moved from that spot.

The bed was still unmade.

But, unlike the others, not empty.

Ginger was in the middle, Liza and Bogie propped up on either side of her like drunks. They were sitting, their backs against the wall. Ginger's arms were around the kids, obviously arranged that way.

Their throats had been cut.

Blood soaked the front of Ginger's sweatshirt, Liza's flannel nightgown, Bogie's bare chest. He wore only pajama bottoms. His smooth hairless chest sent the thin streams of blood in crazy patterns across his pale skin.

A long sign made from pieces of notebook paper taped together was strewn festively across the bodies. The ends were clutched under the children's rigored hands. The lettering was in purple marker.

The sign said: *Happy Father's Day!*

Cliff didn't know how he managed to stay on his feet. He couldn't feel his legs under him. Couldn't feel the floor. He thought for a moment he might be floating weightless in this oxygenless room.

Suddenly he felt the heavy hand of the lieutenant on his shoulder. "Come on, Cliff. Come on out of here."

IT WAS like a party. Uniformed police, ambulance attendants, people from the coroner's office, detectives, photographers, forensics.

Cliff made coffee. No one asked him questions, Lieutenant Godfrey saw to that. The lieutenant also answered the phone, which seemed to ring every five minutes. Cliff didn't mind all the people, the chattering, the activity. Once he heard a couple of cops laugh, and he didn't even mind that. Every person there was staring at death and tragedy and trying to find his own place in it. Cliff and Drew used to do the same thing.

Once in Tampa, Florida, they'd been sent to kill a Navy man on leave from his ship. The sailor had been passing classified ship documents to the Soviets for three years. Someone at Graceland had hoped to feed him some bogus documents, but that plan hadn't worked and they decided to just plug the leak for good. They sent Cliff and Drew.

Cliff found the sailor in his motel room in his boxer shorts, splashing on Old Spice after-shave, whistling happily. They'd killed him quickly, Drew grabbing him from behind and snapping his neck. Cliff made it look like a fall. Only after they'd finished arranging everything did they actually look at the sailor's face. He couldn't have been more than twenty-two. His shaving had been more a ritual than a necessity. A note next to the phone indicated he had a date that night. They found letters from his girlfriend in his jacket. His high school sweetheart.

While they arranged everything to look like an accident, they made jokes about the guy, about his girl. "She'll sell the rights to the *National Enquirer*," Drew said.

" 'The Spy Who Loved Me,' " Cliff said.

And so on. They'd laughed, chuckled, poked fun. When they were finished and about to leave, they'd looked at each other and Cliff could tell Drew was thinking the same thing. They were both picturing the poor girl, all dressed up and waiting for her handsome Navy man in uniform to pick her up after all these months. They could see her watching the clock, worrying as the night wore on, calling the motel but getting no answer, phoning hospitals, finally the police, sobbing hysterically into the phone.

Drew had picked up the receiver and handed it to Cliff. Drew punched in the phone number. Cliff spoke: "Hello, Dinah? I'm calling for Gerald. He was called back to the ship on an emergency and won't be able to make it tonight. He'll call you later."

Drew and Cliff had exchanged glances and left. Later, when their report was read, they had been reprimanded for the breach in security that call represented.

Tonight, Cliff brewed and poured coffee. Pot after pot. Cup after cup. Everyone thanked him politely but kept a certain distance. After all, he was on the other side of the line tonight. Among the victims, those wretched people whose luck had run out. Mustn't get too close; bad luck could be catching.

Godfrey had just hung up the phone. He shambled over to Cliff. "They found a body washed up in Laguna Beach. Throat cut." He described the body.

"That's Cromwell," Cliff said, showing no surprise.

"We also have a little more information on Carleton, the whiz kid who was gunned down tonight. Apparently he has a very famous father."

Cliff waited.

"Vatican Towne."

Cliff turned toward Godfrey. "Are you sure?"

"Yup. He took his mother's maiden name because he wanted to make it on his own, you know, without his father's name opening all the doors. Guess he had something to prove."

Cliff went back to making coffee.

After it was all over and everyone else had gone, Godfrey tried to coax Cliff to leave the house too. It was an official police crime site, he said, pointing to the yellow tape across the front door to keep onlookers out. I'm staying, Cliff told him. Lieutenant Godfrey threatened him, pleaded with him, even offered to put him up at his own house. Cliff refused. This was his house. This was where he would stay.

"It's not healthy," the lieutenant said, relenting.

Cliff smiled.

Alone now, Cliff washed the cups and put them away. He wiped the counter and swept the floor. He turned off all the lights. Early-morning sunlight stabbed in from every angle, so he pulled all the blinds and curtains and sat on the living room sofa. After a few minutes he went to the stereo and began looking through the record albums. Some were his, but most were Ginger's. Slowly his fingers flipped the albums.

There were questions. Questions about how this happened, who was responsible, what would be done? Those weren't the questions that he thought about now. Instead, he wondered what Bogie would have done about his gay friend. Would he ever have called Cliff Dad? Would Liza's shallow boyfriends have turned out to be okay after all? What kind of husband and father would Cliff have made in the long run, when the kids were older, when Ginger was older? Would they have had the baby they'd been discussing all these months?

Ginger had taught him the essence of parenting the first time the four of them had gone to the movies. Bogie, always a little small for his age, had been sitting next to Cliff. Liza had been next to Bogie, and Ginger had been at the other end. When the movie was about to start, Ginger had said to Liza, "Change seats with your brother." Cliff had taken it as some kind of slight, not understanding the reason for the sudden shifting of seats. Had he offended the boy somehow? Ginger noticed the perplexity on his face and smiled. "He can't see over the man in front of him," she explained. It was true—there was a couple in front of them that blocked Bogie's view of the screen. The boy hadn't said anything, but Ginger had noticed and moved him where an empty seat was in front of him. She had known without Bogie telling her. She had looked out for him. That was what being a parent was.

And Cliff had failed at doing that. They were all dead. All because of Cliff. He hadn't looked out for them.

The house no longer seemed familiar. The air smelled sour, decayed. Cliff felt as if he were standing in the smoldering blackened husk of a bombed-out building.

For some reason, he selected a record and placed it on the turntable. It was Ginger's favorite album. *Camelot*. He sat back on the sofa and listened to Richard Harris and Vanessa Redgrave sing. Somewhere along the line, he stopped hearing the music, and he thought everything through, replayed the past twenty-four hours, over and over, until he understood what had happened to destroy his life this way. When he snapped out of his thoughts again, Richard and Vanessa were singing, "What Do Simple Folk Do?" The queen wanted to know what the common folk did to chase away the blues. King Arthur explained that they whistled, and proceeded to gaily whistle a tune for her.

Cliff felt the heavy tears roll down his cheeks. He laid his head back, closed his eyes and puckered his lips to whistle. He puffed air through rigid lips. But there was no sound, no whistling notes. Just the rush of dry air like a lost desert wind.

PART THREE:

TROUBLES

CLIFF CRUMPLED another pink while-you-were-out note and fired it across the office at the metal waste can. The wad caught the rim and bounced away from the can. He tore off another sheet, crumpled, fired. He didn't notice whether they fell in or missed. He was just mindlessly occupying his hands.

Cliff wasn't sure what had brought him to Lily's office. He'd already gone by the landscaping business and given Denise and Jesus the week off, with pay. He wasn't sure what he would do with the business after that week—maybe go back to working it, maybe sell it. Right now, he didn't care enough to think about it.

All night he'd sat in the dark living room, playing musicals, ignoring the phone. *Fiddler on the Roof*, *Man of La Mancha*, *Little Shop of Horrors*, *Grease*, *Paint Your Wagon*, *South Pacific*. Dozens of albums, hundreds of songs, mostly happy songs about the joys of living overcoming the minor inconvenience of tragedy. The loss of the kids felt like a cold, numb spot at the back of his brain, some frozen chunk that ached and wouldn't thaw. The loss of Ginger was like something reaching into his stomach and starting to disembowel him, slowly yanking the intestines out inch by painful inch. The pain never ebbed. His face felt inflated and stung. But except for a few tears that welled and drifted down his face on their own, he just sat and listened.

Now, sitting behind Lily's desk, balling paper and tossing baskets, he remembered the song from *West Side Story*, the one Anita sings to Maria. He and Ginger used to do a comic duet to that song. "A boy like tat, he keel yo brudda," she'd sing. Then he'd come in with, "Forget tat boy an' find anodda."

She: "One of yo own kind." He: "Stick to yo own kind." Together: "Just wait an' see, just wait, Maria, just wait an' see."

He smiled at the memory, and the flexing of cheek muscles squeezed tears out of his eyes. They sluiced down his cheeks, burning the skin like battery acid.

Cliff knew he should do something. Get up. Make calls. Find the sick bastard responsible. That security guard. Then Vatican Towne. Then Standish Ford. Then Aaron Leland. Killing them would be good therapy.

He crumpled another pink phone message slip and lobbed it toward the can.

Polite rapping on the door interrupted him.

"Yeah?" Cliff shouted.

"It's me. Fender."

"Door's locked."

Suddenly the door swung open. Fender stood there, holding a key. "That's okay, I've got a key."

Cliff crumpled another piece of paper. "I didn't know elevator operators carried keys to the offices."

"They don't," Fender said. "But building owners do."

With no surprise registering on his face, Cliff looked Fender over. Same short old man, same plaid sports cap, same jaunty walk and mischievous eyes. Cliff hooked the ball of paper at the can. Missed. "You own this building?"

"Yup. The whole thing. And seven more besides."

Cliff closed his eyes. Any new information seemed to hurt his brain.

"Yeah, I know it's hard to believe," Fender said. "But I'm rich. Very rich." He sat down where Francis Cromwell, or whoever he was, had sat two days ago. Slowly he removed his cap and hooked it over one bony knee. "The Carpathia Building. You know what I named it after?"

Cliff sighed to show he did not care.

That didn't stop Fender. "Most people would have guessed the Carpathian Mountains in Eastern Europe. You are familiar with them?"

Cliff balled another pink slip and tossed it. "I've seen them, at least the part that runs through Czechoslovakia."

"Ah, a world traveler. I thought so. Nevertheless, you'd be wrong. I didn't name it after the mountains. I named it after the Cunard ocean liner, *Carpathia*. Ever hear of it?"

"No."

"It was the first ship on the scene after the *Titanic* sank. One hour and twenty minutes after the ship went down at 2:20 a.m. on April 15, 1912, the *Carpathia* arrived. Over 1500 lives had already been lost, but when she sailed into view through the heavy fog, my God, it was like the archangel floating down from heaven."

Cliff stopped crushing the wad of paper in his hand and looked at Fender. "You were aboard the *Titanic*?"

"I was eleven years old. My father drowned, my mother died a month later of pneumonia." He smiled sadly. "I could never get the vision of the *Carpathia* out of my mind, steaming toward us. I was never so happy or sad ever again. It was like once you've experienced that intense of an emotion, nothing in life ever equals it again."

He leaned back, turned the cap on his knees. The top of his head was bald with a few wisps of white hair curling crazily. "You think I'm nuts to do this, work in an elevator that doesn't need an operator, stand around here all day taking people up and down. Let me tell you, son, I've never felt more useful in my life. Maybe there's some complicated psychological reason. I don't know. But the sensation of taking people up in that elevator is the closest I've ever come to matching that feeling when they hauled me up the side of the *Carpathia*. It was like they were pulling me up to heaven, I swear. And somehow I get just a fraction of that same glorious feeling hauling people up and down my building. Crazy, maybe, but I can afford to be crazy.''

Cliff stared at the little man. ''What about Dr. Grundel? The petition?''

''Oh, there's nothing wrong with Bob that a little threat of a rent increase won't solve. Tell you the truth, I even like taking him up.'' He wagged a finger at Cliff. ''You're sad now, son. You've lost your family, your friend. You feel adrift and cold. Maybe you can't see through the fog, but I'm telling you true, son, there's a rescue ship somewhere out there. Maybe you gotta swim for her, but she's there.''

''You've seen too many movies.''

Fender leaned forward, his face angry. ''You don't god-damn know everything, son. You think you do—that's your problem. For instance, I bet you didn't know that Lily and I dated.''

''What?''

''Yeah, that's right. Not anything serious. But once a month she and I would go out to a fancy dinner, maybe dance a little, go back to my home, make love. Yeah, we made love. Some picture, huh? Big shapely woman like her, old scrap of a man like me. Of course, this started long before I told her I was rich, so it didn't have anything to do with that. Maybe she did it out of pity, but I don't think so. I think she did it out of friendship. Because she liked me.''

Cliff thought it over, nodded. ''I think so too.''

Fender's eyes were watery, but his voice was firm. ''Like I said, you don't know everything.'' He stood up, walked slowly toward the door. ''Maybe if you did, you'd be able to live with what's happened.''

Fender put on his plaid cap, adjusted it perfectly and walked out.

Cliff sat, stunned. He hadn't really known Lily at all, though he'd liked her. And maybe Ginger hadn't really known him, though she'd loved him. There were secrets everywhere—who did what to whom and why. Those were the questions Bogie had asked Cliff while trying to grapple with the problem of his friendship with Todd. Those were the same questions Cliff asked now about what had happened to his life.

Last night, sitting in the dark on the living room sofa and listening to musicals, Cliff had begun to pick unconsciously at a loose thread on the sofa's cotton covering. He'd pulled hard enough that the thread had skipped *tidatidatida* across the cushion, then broke, leaving tiny train tracks in the fabric. Fascinated, Cliff found another loose thread and pulled, then another and yet another. He piled the broken threads on the carpet. When he couldn't find any more loose threads he made fresh ones, digging them out with his fingernails, even his teeth, gnawing the thread into a tiny blossom of frayed cotton. He became obsessed with tugging threads, with unraveling. He continued through dawn and early morning, through *Oklahoma*, *Guys and Dolls*, *The Fantastiks*, until he'd finally stripped the sofa of its skin and laid bare the plain white patternless fabric that resembled some ice planet's barren surface. The sofa itself looked bony, undernourished, embarrassed. It was an odd and lunatic thing to do. But he had done it because he'd been convinced the act would make him feel better.

It had not.

He poked his key into the bottom desk drawer, unlocked it and pulled out the .45 Colt 1911 A1 pistol Lily kept as a backup piece. The seven-shot clip was fully loaded. He hefted it in his hand, squeezed the checkered walnut grip. He knew something was going on around him right now about which he knew nothing. He probably never would. He knew that important people were making plans, executing moves, lying, tricking, deceiving, and that he was at one end of this long line of deception. No, not at the end. At the end was Bradley Carleton. Phillip DeSoto. Francis Cromwell. Lily. And Ginger, Liza and Bogie.

Cliff lifted his sweater and stuck the gun in the waistband of his jeans. He started for the door, knowing exactly where he was going, what he would do. It was another odd and lunatic thing to do. He hoped it would make him feel better.

He was tired of the same old questions. Now he wanted some answers.

Even lies would do.

• 13 •

"BASTARDS!" Stan banged the door of the conference room behind him. "You set me up. The three of you."

The three men sat at the polished mahogany table in the same positions as when he'd last seen them. There was even a pot of steaming coffee on the table and an empty silver platter dusted with the crumbs of eaten doughnuts. Somehow seeing that empty platter, picturing them wolfing down pastry, angered Stan even more. "You fucking bastards."

Dubus's dark skin became mottled with even darker spots, like two shades of chocolate pudding marbled together. He removed his glasses as the warbles of a strangling finch gargled in his throat.

"Come on now, Stan," Collins said, but his voice too trailed off and his eyes shifted downward in embarrassment.

Only Aaron Leland remained in control, his back straight, shoulders square, facial muscles rigid with purpose. "Let us explain, Stan," he urged in his soft voice. "You'll see why we were forced to do this."

Stan threw the morning newspaper on the table, knocking over Leland's cup. A small puddle of coffee spilled onto the table but was absorbed by the edge of the paper, the brown stain blooming like a tumor across the newsprint. Stan swept the cup onto the floor with his left hand and slammed his hook down on the front-page article. The tip of his hook gouged through the paper and into the mahogany tabletop, pocking the wood. The headline read "Son of CIA founder murdered in slaying spree."

Leaning over the paper, Stan used his hook to skim down the page to the passage he was looking for. When he found it, he read aloud. " 'The sole survivor of the killing spree, Clifford Halsey Remington, later suffered an even greater tragedy when it was discovered that his house had been broken into and his wife and two stepchildren slain. Police refuse to release certain details of the slaying, but they have not ruled out a connection between the two murder sites.' "

Stan glared at each of them in turn, finally fixing on Aaron Leland. "You had them killed. All of them. And you sent me there to set Remington up. That whole planning session Collins, Dubus and I went through was just bullshit. Smoke. The three of you had already met and decided to send me. Right?"

Dubus and Collins looked at each other but not at Stan.

"You're upset, Stan," Leland said. "And with good cause. But things aren't what they seem."

"Then tell me just what things are, Aaron. Make me see the goddamned light."

Leland pushed the sleeves of his sweater high on his forearms. He wore a simple watch, white face and black hands, no numbers. He looked at it, then turned to Collins and Dubus. "Leave us alone, would you, gentlemen?"

Collins and Dubus quickly rose, relief relaxing the frowns on their faces. Dubus stopped by Stan's side, opened his mouth as if to say something, didn't, closed his mouth and followed Collins out the door.

Stan sat down, suddenly exhausted. His rage and guilt had drained him. He couldn't get the image of Remington out of his mind, that picture of him perched on the bar stool in that beach house, a happy man filled with confidence and strength. What had they done to him? What had they done to his family?

"We haven't made any progress in stopping the shutdown of Fat Boy," Leland said.

"Right now, Aaron, I don't give a fuck."

"Vatican Towne has closed off one of the PAWS."

Stan looked up. "Damn."

PAWS were the Pre-Alert Warning Satellites that signaled the United States when a missile was heading toward it. They gave the military plenty of time to launch interceptors as well as counterattack missiles. They also doubled as spy satellites, so they were hooked into Fat Boy as well as military computers. "What about the Pentagon computer?"

"Locked out too. Once the satellite is closed, it can only be accessed through the same channels that closed it. Which means unless we get Towne to reverse it, this country is now a sitting duck for a missile offensive from the Soviets or China or even Liechtenstein. There's not a damn thing we can do about it?"

"Who knows?"

"Me and General Fleischmann. Now you."

"Dubus and Collins?"

Leland shook his head. "Just the three of us. And Vatican Towne."

Stan pressed his hook against his forehead. The metal felt cool. "Why'd you do it, Aaron? You didn't have to kill them, for Christ's sake."

Aaron Leland leaned back in his chair and closed his eyes as if to shut out the world and its earthly concerns. He pinched the bridge of his nose, massaged the skin. "No one was supposed to die. It's all gotten out of hand."

"What's gotten out of hand. What *exactly*?"

"The first part of the plan was for you to go to L.A. and bait Remington. Just as you did. We couldn't tell you the rest of the plan because I wanted you to be sincere. Cliff may be rusty, but he was never a fool. He might have picked up on any hesitation on your part."

"So I was the second whipping boy?"

"Yes. I didn't really expect him to take you up on your offer. I just wanted him to know who the players were and what the score was. Then we brought in an agent pretending to hire Cliff and his partner for a simple security job. We sent him to an office, which happened to belong to Bradley Carleton, Vatican's son, forming a link between Cliff and Towne. I hired a free-lancer to close the trap."

"By killing everyone."

Leland's face sagged. "That wasn't supposed to happen, Stan. Our free-lancer was told to wound Carleton, make it look like he was part of Remington's burglary attempt. Then Cliff would have to help us or rot in jail. All we wanted was a little blackmail leverage against Remington."

"What the hell happened? What went wrong?"

"I don't know. The free-lancer went nuts, killed everybody. Maybe one of them pulled a gun and he had to kill them. I haven't spoken to him yet."

Stan pulled the coffeepot and a clean cup closer to him and poured. "And Remington's family?"

"That wasn't us, Stan."

"Then who was it?"

"Vatican Towne. I read the police report. The way the bodies were arranged, the sick sign that was left. Towne got his revenge quickly. I didn't think he'd move that fast."

"That just doesn't sound like him. He never went in for that kind of thing."

"He never went in for dismantling his country's defense system either. But he's doing it."

Stan had to admit it made sense. Vatican Towne had found out about his son's murder. Probably was told that Cliff Remington was a suspect. A quick check would have revealed who Remington's former employers were, and Vatican would have assumed Remington was being reactivated because of what had happened to Fat Boy. Perhaps he thought it was a botched kidnap attempt, or even a straight assassination. Either way, Towne reacted swiftly and wickedly, wiping out Remington's family.

"What now?" Stan asked wearily.

Leland looked up at the ceiling at the air-conditioning vent. Cold air blasted through the grille with the steady hum of a Gregorian chant. Leland pulled the shawl collar of his sweater high around his neck. "I don't know. Pray, I guess, for that miracle you were talking about."

"Who was the free-lancer?"

"You don't know him."

"I know everyone on the approved list, Aaron." The Agency kept a list of approved free-lancers for hiring for situations where they didn't want anything traced back through their own agents.

"He's not on the list, Stan."

Stan looked at Leland. "That's not only against policy, that's dangerous."

"I couldn't take the chance that Towne might be hooked into that list. I needed someone Towne wouldn't know, someone outside. Way outside."

"Like who? Palestinian?"

"No. Believe me, you don't know him. Only a handful of top intelligence people in the world do, and even they don't want to. He's the most efficient agent I've ever seen."

"Then why isn't he on the list?"

Leland stirred the patch of white hair at his temple with his fingers. "He's unpredictable. Oh, he'll complete an assignment all right, but if there's a way for him to run a scam at the same time, he'll do so. His name is Charon."

"Karen?"

Leland spelled it.

"Christ, to be a spy today you have to know as much about Greek mythology as you do about guns."

"You have to remember the kind of men who started our organization. Guys like Vatican Towne, Ivy League-educated and boyishly adventurous, looking to add a little glamour and romance to the ugly business of spying."

"Let's see, Charon was the ferryman, took the shades of the dead in his boat across the river Styx into Hades. Each passenger had to pay for his fare, which is why the ancient Greeks always put a small coin in the mouth of the deceased before burial."

"Believe me, our Charon has ferried his share of souls into the shadow land of the dead. He is completely ruthless. Truly evil."

"Is he smart?"

"He's been doing this for fifteen years and we still don't know anything about his past. Not his real name, where he came from, who his parents are."

Stan sighed and nodded. "He's smart."

"All we know is that he is a genuine hermaphrodite."

Stan laughed. "You mean a cross-dresser? High heels and garter belts?"

"No, I mean he possesses both testicular and ovarian tissue. He is both male and female."

"There are surgical procedures to cure that situation."

"As far as we know, he doesn't want to change."

A dry silence settled between them.

Finally, Stan spoke. "This is the kind of guy you hire to set the trap for Vatican Towne? An unstable, unreliable, ruthless hermaphrodite?"

"He has never failed in a mission in fifteen years."

"He sure as hell failed on this one. Look at the carnage, Aaron."

"True, and I'm as angry about that as you are, Stan. But let's look at it objectively for a moment. He did what he was assigned to do: set up Remington to draw Vatican Towne out of hiding. Towne thought Remington killed his son, so he went after Remington's family. I know Cliff—he will avenge the slaughter of his family. He has no choice."

"That doesn't mean he'll work with us."

"Doesn't matter. We'll put Charon on him. Sooner or later, Towne and Remington will meet. When they do, Charon will be there."

Stan studied the pattern on his coffee cup. Pink cherry blossoms and a single hovering bee frozen at life's most precious moment, the instant prior to fulfillment. "I don't like what happened back there, Aaron. I don't like what you did to me. You used up some serious favors."

"Believe me, Stan, there was no way. If we—"

The phone in front of Leland buzzed and he snatched up the receiver. He gave his name, then listened. Stan watched his face stiffen and grow grave. When he hung up he turned to Stan. "All PAWS are unresponsive now. Shut down. The whole country is a sitting duck. If the Soviets attacked right now, they'd conquer us in twenty minutes."

"Then we have no choice."

"That's what I've been telling you, Stan. None of us does. Not you, not me, not Cliff Remington."

Stan nodded. Aaron Leland had been right all along. The situation with Fat Boy was getting more serious. The only hope now was to find Towne. And as much as Stan hated the way everything had happened, at least they were a lot closer now to that goal. "I guess you want me to fly back to California and act as liaison with Remington, right?"

"Right. Be careful, Stan. No matter what you tell him, he's going to blame you for the death of his family. After he's found Vatican Towne, he may even try to kill you."

"I wouldn't blame him for trying," Stan said. "But I sure as hell won't let him succeed."

"Good man."

"One condition, Aaron."

"Condition? This isn't a favor I'm asking, Stan, this is national security. Your damned duty."

"You've pushed the limits of duty, Aaron. Now I want something back."

"What, Stan? What is it you want?"

"When it's over, however it ends, I want this Charon person terminated with extreme prejudice. Dead."

Leland sighed. "Agreed. Anything else?"

"I'll let you know." He stood up, headed for the door. "What time do I leave? I assume you've already had my flight reservations booked."

Aaron Leland smiled. "You're starting to get the hang of this job, Stan. You may just take my place yet."

COL. YURI HWAN DANZIGKOV rolled the thin tungsten dart between his fingertips as carefully and passionately as if it were a fine Cuban cigar. When the metal had warmed properly to his touch, he lifted the dart to its ready position next to his ear and stared at the target on the wall.

"Careful, Yuri," Gen. Sergei Lvov warned. "This is your last chance."

Yuri Danzigkov felt the edge of the adhesive tape on the dart shaft that let him know his fingers were in the right place. His eyes focused on the target, expanding it in his mind until the target seemed as big as the wall, impossible to miss.

"One of my men confiscated a truckload of goodies yesterday," General Lvov said. "Madonna albums, videotape movies—VHS and Beta—Reebok shoes, Swatches. Anything you'd like, Yuri?"

"Thank you, no, sir." Yuri knew General Lvov was merely trying to distract him, not entrap. The general was always most generous with goods from the West, dispensing them to his favorites. But Yuri, who admired all of the items the general had mentioned, didn't think it right to enjoy them unless they were available to everyone. A matter of conscience. Conscience was what dictated Yuri's actions, not comfort or convenience or ambition. Sometimes he was ridiculed for his principles, though never to his face. His superiors accepted his naive dedication because they appreciated his other talents too. Yuri Danzigkov was the best political/military analyst in the KGB. His analyses of events and trends were uncannily accurate.

"Calvin Klein underwear, Yuri," the general chuckled. "Very soft. I wear it myself." He reached down into his pants and pulled up the white elastic band, revealing the stenciled brand name, Calvin Klein.

Yuri launched the dart. It arced through the office toward the back of the door, where the target hung. The red plastic flights twirled like a paddle wheel. When the point thumped into the thick bristol board, it stuck straight out of the magazine page they'd tacked to the target. The metal point had pierced the head, no bigger than a thumbnail, of Sylvester Stallone, bare chested and snarling in his Rambo pose. "That's three dinners you owe me, General," Yuri said, plucking his dart out of Stallone's face, and the general's dart out of Stallone's neck. "But you're getting closer."

The general laughed. "A wiser man might have let me win once, Yuri."

"Perhaps. But I would not insult you that way."

The buzzer on Yuri's desk sounded. He picked up the phone, listened, nodded, then hung up. He turned to the general and shrugged. "Sorry, General. Business."

"No need to apologize, Yuri. I suppose I should get back to work myself. I have a thousand Madonna records to give away."

Yuri shook the general's hand and ushered him to the door. At least two-thirds of those records would be sold to the black market, and the general would make a nice profit. That didn't bother Yuri. That kind of thing went on all the time, just as it did everywhere else in the world. It was neither his job nor his inclination to police everyone. The fact that he didn't indulge in such schemes himself was his personal choice. That others did was their choice. Harmless diversions.

Once the general had gone, Yuri slipped back into his stiff military jacket. He marched out of the office and down the hall and ran down the five flights of stairs to the office he wanted. The elevators worked fine, but his job restricted the amount of exercise he was able to squeeze in, and last week he'd noticed a little tightness to his pants.

He was met at the stairway door by two uniformed guards who knew him well, had seen him every day for the past three years. Nevertheless, they demanded to see his identification card, which they scrutinized suspiciously. When they were through, Yuri entered the security wing and hurried to the office from which he'd received the phone call.

Yuri was the best at what he did, but he had to be the best. Yuri Hwan Danzigkov. The Hwan came from his biological father, a South Korean importer. He had met Yuri's Soviet Georgian mother, a circus acrobat, in San Francisco—two foreigners whose only common language, English, was also foreign. The Soviet circus performed for two months in the United States, traveling from city to city. Park Kuo Hwan had followed the circus for two months, seeing Sasha whenever they could sneak away together. At the end of the second month, they were married by a nondenominational minister who wasn't at all certain of the legality of the ceremony but was certain that the two were in love and paid in cash. They were discovered by the KGB. Park Kuo Hwan was beaten and Sasha was taken back to the circus, guarded every minute she wasn't performing. When the circus returned to the Soviet Union, she was never allowed to leave the country again.

Sasha finally married again, a soldier named Danzigkov, who adopted little Yuri and treated him politely, if never warmly. Yuri had the darker skin, the oriental eyes of his father. Soviet prejudice against Koreans caused him much pain, but he endured. It was a tribute to his intelligence and character that he managed to rise so high in the KGB, despite his Korean heritage.

Yuri found the door with no markings on it, no nameplate, no numbers or letters or titles. He entered.

It took a moment for his eyes to adjust to the dim light. The room was small, no larger than his own office upstairs, but every inch was crammed with computer equipment, monitors, printers, modems. The monitor screens all displayed green lettering, so the room had a slight greenish haze to it. "What have you got, Georgi?"

The man in front of one of the screens turned his head and smiled. Clamped between his teeth was a long pencillike pointer. He needed the pointer to enter commands in the computer, for he had no arms, and only thighs for legs. He was held in his wheelchair by thick nylon straps that crisscrossed his chest like a banditto's cartridge belts. Even with no limbs, he was a big man, barrel chested, his thighs thick. The empty sleeves were pinned to his military shirt. He held the rank of major.

Georgi spoke around the pointer. "See for yourself, Yuri." He bent his head and pecked away at several keys on the keyboard. The monitor lit up with a report from the space-tracking branch.

Yuri scanned the report. "Is this possible?"

Georgi dipped his head, placing the pointer in its holder on the arm of his wheelchair. He fitted his chin into the metal cup that controlled the electric wheelchair, shifted his jaw and the chair spun around to face Yuri. "It's possible, but I don't know how. Somehow, the American PAWS are not emitting the usual amounts of energy, nor are they receiving the usual signals, nor are they shifting to photograph us. They remain in orbit, but that's all."

"This is true of all of them?"

"Apparently."

"That is strange. One might become nonfunctioning, but not all eight. Perhaps they are running tests?"

"Possible. But what kind?"

"A trap maybe?"

Georgi shrugged. "A little like a bully sticking his face out and daring someone to hit it."

Yuri pulled up the only other chair in the room and sat down. "It doesn't make sense. What are they up to?" He studied the screen again.

Georgi used his chin to scratch an itch on his shoulder. "There's something else. I don't know whether it's related or not."

"Punch it up."

Georgi bit the rubber end of his pointer and began tapping on the keys like a woodpecker. When the display he wanted appeared, he sat back, replaced the pointer. "See what I mean? Ex-CIA agent, Clifford Halsey Remington, and the son of Vatican Towne mixed up in some kind of murder."

"Yes, I saw the report this morning. What possible connection could there be?"

"I don't know. But I do know that one of our moles revealed that Standish Ford flew to Los Angeles the day before all this happened."

"What about Aaron Leland?"

"He remains in Washington."

Yuri sighed. "Is there any indication how long the PAW satellites will be incapacitated?"

"None."

Yuri didn't move. His stare was as focused as when he'd thrown his dart. His mind expanded the information until he could walk among each bit of intelligence freely, explore it as if with his fingers, feel its texture. See how it all fitted together. After a few minutes he reached for the telephone, punched the appropriate numbers, waited for the call to be transferred to General Kerensky, his direct superior.

"General," Yuri said flatly, "we now have a first-strike window on the United States. We have a twenty-second advantage that makes winning a limited nuclear war with minimal losses an eighty-percent certainty."

14

CREEP.

"What?" he asked, turning toward her.

"I didn't say anything," Tory Fawley said.

"I thought you did."

"No, I didn't." She quickly looked away. Jesus, what was going on? Was she starting to talk aloud to herself? "Watch the bricks," she warned him as they walked toward her front door. "The moss gets kind of slippery at night."

"Boy, I'll say." His body contorted into exaggerated gestures, legs wobbly, arms windmilling for balance. He grinned at his own antics.

She gave him a laugh, but not much of one. Not a creep, she corrected herself, just another loser. She didn't know why she was being so hard on him. They'd just finished dinner at a semiexpensive restaurant. The conversation had been pleasant, the food good. He'd been attentive, amusing, considerate. And a good tipper. Important sign, tipping. Her ex, Ed, had been a strict ten-percent tipper, and then only if the waitress had enormous tits and crawled across the floor, balancing the tray on her nose. Bad tipper, cheap husband. Simple equation. Not that she was looking for another husband, God forbid, and certainly not this guy. Kenny Hanes. How could you take a full grown man named Kenny seriously? Hey, Mrs. Hanes, can Kenny come out and play? And his last name, Hanes, wasn't that a brand of underwear?

Men. Jesus, the pickings seemed to get slimmer every year. But no more married men. She'd made that resolution after her affair with Dr. Frank Polking, plastic surgeon, nip-and-tuck specialist to the sagging wealthy. Their affair had lasted three months, one full season, spring. Thirteen weeks of what she called nip-and-fuck. He came over afternoons from his Beverly Hills office, had a nip of cognac and hopped on her bones like a wild coyote.

Kenny Hanes cupped his hand under her elbow as they climbed the three steps to her front door. Sweet guy, not really a creep. She'd just gotten too hard. Seeing Ed again, having him in the house ranting about the furniture, made her wary of all men. At least Kenny was a lawyer, so they had something in common that wasn't clandestine or sinister. Something they could talk about out loud in restaurants. True, his specialty was workmen's compensation cases, but it was still law. Not spying.

They stood before the front door and she could feel the waves of nervous heat pulsing from his body. He even tugged at the knot of his silk tie and cleared his throat.

"Well," he said.

"Yeah," she nodded.

Then he reached for her, pulled her close and kissed her, catching only the edge of her lips in his hurry, then sliding his mouth a little to the left until they were smashed tight, his tongue lunging into her mouth. She let him press closer, bump his hips against hers until she felt the urgent erection she'd already noticed in the car. He smelled good, she had to give him that. Tangy after-shave. Not a bad kisser either, though a little too sloppy. He was moving his tongue around as if he was swabbing her mouth. Still, she had to admit, she did enjoy the sensation, the warmth spreading deep inside her.

"Come on in," she said, knowing she'd regret it.

An hour later, thinking he was asleep, Tory hopped out of bed.

"Where you going?" he asked, reaching across the bed.

Tory patted his hand. "To feed the dog."

"Jesus, now?"

"He's hungry."

Kenny grinned, nodded at his crotch. "So's he."

She didn't say anything. She thought about rooting through the closet for her Japanese robe, but she didn't want to stand there naked in front of him longer than absolutely necessary. She hurried out of the bedroom, still naked. "Coffee?" she called back to him, hoping a strong cup would jolt him awake enough to get in his car and drive home. She did not want him sleeping over.

"If it's not any trouble," he said. "Cream and sugar."

Tory sighed. At the office, he'd been bringing her coffee for almost a year. One hump in the night and he expected room service. Tory walked down the corridor, stepping carefully where the carpet had been peeled back. The sweet-and-sour smell of paint reminded her of Chinese food, and she was suddenly famished. As soon as she got Mr. Kenny Hanes the hell out of there, she could raid the refrigerator in peace, gobble down a frozen pizza in bed and watch David Letterman.

"Mike," she called. "Here, boy. Come on, Mike, where are you?"

No sign of him.

She checked the spare bedroom, the one that used to be Karen's. Now it was Mike's room, where he brought all the stolen socks, tennis balls, magazines, lipsticks that he got hold of. If anything in this house was ever lost, it always turned up in Mike's room. Tory stuck her head in the doorway, flipped the light. No Mike.

This whole night had been a big mistake. She'd worked in the same office with Kenny for almost a year now. He'd asked her out a dozen times before, and she'd always refused, adamant about not mixing work and social life. But tonight, as they rode the elevator down, he'd asked again. Impulsively, Tory had said yes. Kenny had looked stunned at first, but quickly recovered, hustling her off to a restaurant before she changed her mind.

In bed he'd been good. Too good. He turned it into an Olympic event, coming at her from all directions, trying to make it last. He'd been inside her for forty-two minutes; she'd clocked him on the bedside Sony. All the time he'd moaned and groaned louder than she. Actually, the moans she'd given were either obligatory, to make him feel better, or moans of pain because he just wouldn't stop and she was getting sore. Finally she'd had to fake an orgasm just to get him to come. She resented having to resort to that, but Kenny had too much to prove. She didn't know why she'd accepted his dinner invitation in the first place.

That's a lie, Tory.

"Mikie? Dinnertime." She passed the bedroom next to hers. The door was closed, as always, so there was no reason to look in there. It was her home office and Mike was forbidden access to that room.

In the kitchen she poured Gaines Dog Chow into Mike's metal bowl. The hard kernels clattered like machine gun fire. She hoped the sound would bring Mike running. Tory looked at the bag. Gaines. Sounded too much like Hanes, another reason she couldn't take Kenny seriously.

She stared at the coffee brewer a moment, considered making Kenny some fresh coffee. Instead she filled a ceramic mug with tap water, stuck it in the microwave and waited for the waves to nuke the water.

You know damned well why you went out with him, she scolded herself. The goddamned newspaper. She'd read the article that morning about Clifford Halsey Remington. The murder of his partner and his entire family. She didn't know how exactly, but she knew she was mixed up in it—that the favor she'd done for Ed was somehow connected. The thought of spending the rest of the evening alone with her guilt had made her accept Kenny's invitation, had made her let him into her bed. She'd wanted the company, the distraction. It hadn't worked. She still couldn't stop thinking about the article, about Clifford Remington.

The microwave timer pinged and she quickly stirred instant coffee granules into the steaming water. The hell with cream and sugar. She wanted it strong enough to send him on his way.

"Okay, Mike, sulk if you want." She marched back up the corridor balancing the coffee.

As she passed her study, she thought she heard a huffing noise, Mike's steam-engine snorting. "Jesus, Mike," she said, imagining the damage he'd probably done to her papers in there, eating half of them, scattering the rest on the floor. She switched the coffee to her left hand and turned the doorknob with her right. When she flipped on the light, she gasped.

Clifford Remington sat on the sofa next to her desk, Mike resting in his lap, nipping playfully at his hand, making his chuffing noise. Cliff looked up at her, not at all intimidated by being discovered. His eyes were red rimmed, his face swollen with grief. Or maybe she was imagining that. He continued to scratch Mike behind the ears.

"My God, what are you—?" she started to say.

Cliff put a finger to his lips and nodded over his shoulder at her bedroom next door.

She lowered her voice to a whisper, though a gruff forceful whisper. "What the fuck are you doing here?"

"You sure you want to talk now?"

Tory suddenly realized she was naked, not just naked, but after-sex naked. She started to cover herself with the coffee mug, slopping some onto her hand, burning herself. She gave up. "All I have to do is holler and he'll come running in here."

"If he's got the strength." Cliff looked at his watch. "More than forty minutes of sexual activity can be quite exhausting. Especially with all his moaning. Most people don't realize, but moaning takes a lot of energy too."

Tory glared as she felt her face flush. "You listened? You goddamned pervert."

Kenny interrupted. "Hey, Tory, you need any help? Sounds like the dog did something pretty awful."

"He messed on the floor!" Tory hollered back, her eyes fixed on Cliff's.

She turned and left the study, closing the door behind her, relieved to be away from his eyes. He hadn't stared at her body, hadn't even glanced at it. His green eyes had burned into hers like bronze shields tilted in the sun. He wasn't any more interested in her physical beauty now than he had been that day at the racquet club. Ed had convinced her that all she had to do was wear tight shorts and Remington would follow her out to the car. But Ed thought every man was like him, or should be. Still, she had been pissed at how easily he had ignored her. She was always going on how she wanted men to disregard her looks and respond to her as a person. Then this bastard came along and actually did it. She smiled, sipped the coffee, walked back to the bedroom.

"You gotta go," she told Kenny, not even handing him the coffee. She set the mug on the dresser, pulled open the drawer for some sweatpants and a sweatshirt.

"Go?" Kenny asked, sitting up.

"My dog's sick."

"I'll drive you to the vet."

"Thanks, no. I'll take care of him."

"Really, I don't mind. We'll drive him over, come back, finish up what we started."

Tory tied the drawstring of her red sweatpants around her waist. Then she pulled the white sweatshirt over her head. "Get dressed, Kenny," she said, tossing him his underpants. She looked at the label. Hanes. "See you tomorrow at the office."

Kenny dressed quickly, mismatching buttons and holes on his shirt, looping his silk tie around his neck like a scarf. "How about tomorrow night? Dinner and a movie?"

"No."

"Disneyland? Bet you haven't been there in a while. It'll be great."

Tory cupped her hand under his elbow, just as he had done to her when walking her home. She led him to the front door, kissed him on the cheek and nudged him out. "Thanks for dinner, Kenny."

He stood in the doorway, shoes in hand, socks stuffed into the shoes. "I know this great Italian restaurant—"

"We'll talk," she said, and closed the door.

Back in the study, she found Cliff and Mike in the same position. Mike was gnawing gently on Cliff's hand, just getting the taste of him. Cliff didn't seem to mind.

"Now tell me what the hell you're doing here?"

Cliff stood up, gave Mike a final pat on the head, then led Tory back into the hall, closing the door behind him.

"You afraid the dog will overhear?" she asked. "Jeez, you've been spying too long."

"I just don't want him interfering," Cliff said softly, his voice barely audible. "When I do this." He shoved her roughly against the wall, pulled out Lily's Colt .45 semiautomatic. He jammed the barrel under her chin, lifting her onto her toes. "You set me up, Mrs. Fawley. You, your macho ex-husband and his redheaded buddy. The three of you and Standish Ford."

"I don't know anything about that. Honest." The gun twisted deeper into the soft skin under her chin. She felt the air being choked off in her throat. "Is this all you ever do, choke people?"

He thumbed back the Colt's hammer. "No."

Tory leaned back, pressing her shoulders even harder against the wall. Behind her, she could hear Mike pawing at the door. "I don't know anything. Ed asked me to help him out."

"And you did. Just like that."

"No, not just like that." Tory looked into his face. His expression was hard, solemn. And angry. She could see now that his green eyes were flecked with brown wedges, like arrowheads. His hair was sandy brown peppered with a few gray strands. His features might have been sculpted by a classical artist who abandoned the piece before polishing the roughness out of the stone. With him leaning up against her now, she could feel the rocky hardness of his muscles, smell his scent, not cologne like Kenny, but something rich and moist. A smell unearthed but pleasant.

"You aren't CIA?" he said, not believing her.

"No. Not anymore."

"Then why'd you help them? Old times?"

"None of your business!" she snapped, pushing against him. She knew her own strength and should have been able to shove him backward at least a couple of steps. He didn't budge.

"Everything's my business now. Look at me, Mrs. Fawley. Look close. You know I'll pull this trigger, don't you?"

Tory looked deep into his eyes again. She nodded. "I did it for Karen."

"Who's Karen?"

"My stepdaughter. Ex-stepdaughter. Ed's daughter from his first wife. Karen lived with us while Ed and I were married. We were very close, still are. But Ed doesn't want me to see her. He's got her stashed at his mother's house in Pasadena. She's only thirteen, for God's sake. He said if I helped him rope you, I could have her one weekend a month."

Cliff didn't move. The gun didn't move. The only sound was Mike's labored breathing and his heavy paws scratching at the study door. Finally, Cliff turned away from her, shoved the

Colt into his jeans pocket and pulled his sweater over the checkered walnut grip.

"Got any more of that Poland water?" Cliff asked, walking toward the kitchen.

Tory rubbed under her chin, tried to massage away the feeling of the gun barrel against her skin. She could still feel the cold hard pressure branded there. "You finished it off, thank you. I haven't had time to get to the supermarket."

He didn't answer. She heard the refrigerator door open. Tory let Mike out of the study. He followed her down the hall to the kitchen, where she found Cliff leaning against the counter, drinking V-8 juice from the can.

"Last one," he told her. "Better go shopping soon."

For the first time she noticed that the tip of his left thumb was missing. She nodded at it. "What happened?"

"Bullet."

"Then you get government disability."

He laughed, shook his head. "Happened after I left Grace-land. What about you?" He touched his own lip approximating her checkmark scar.

"Domestic dispute. Just another sad statistic."

"You don't look like the type."

"What type?"

"To take a beating."

She shrugged. "Who's to say? We'd been married a year before he hit me the first time. He swore it wouldn't happen again. Another year before the second time. Same begging for forgiveness. Third time I called the cops. That was that." She smiled sadly at Cliff. "Love, right?"

Cliff finished the V-8 and tossed the can in the garbage under the sink. "Let's go."

"Where?"

"Your ex-hubby."

"What the hell for?"

"Answers."

"No way, Remington. Look, I'm sorry about what happened to your family. But I swear I don't know anything more than I've told you."

"Maybe. That's why I have to talk to Ed."

"You don't need me for that."

"No, but I can't be sure you won't try to warn him, or place a phone call to Langley."

"Hey, I quit that madness years ago."

"Yeah," Cliff said. "Me too."

She watched Mike bury his face in his bowl, his teeth crunching away like a trash compactor.

"I could tie you up," Cliff suggested. "But I'd have to do it real tight to make sure you couldn't escape. And, of course, if something happened to me while I was gone, who knows how long it would be before someone found you."

"Bastard," she said.

"Yup."

15

"YOU GOING TO bust it down?" Tory asked when they arrived at Ed Fawley's apartment door.

Cliff frowned at her. "How much field experience do you have?"

"Field experience? Like undercover work?"

"Yes."

"Actual hands-on experience?"

"Yes. Hands-on."

"None. I took over recruiting from Ed. Turns out they'd assigned him to recruitment as punishment for some screw-up he did in the field. He never told me exactly what happened, but a couple of our people were arrested in Nicaragua because of it. After I joined recruitment, they let Ed go back to field work again."

"What a prince."

"He can seem that way. At first."

"Well, we don't bust open doors in the field. That's strictly movies." Cliff tugged his Colt out from under his sweater and flattened himself to the right of the door. "Just get him to open the door."

"Me?"

"You." Cliff cocked the gun's hammer. He had to force himself to breathe, dragging the air into his nostrils, forcing it back out his mouth. He wasn't scared. He couldn't imagine anything ever frightening him again, not after walking into Liza's bedroom, seeing them lined up like dolls, the ludicrous sign draped across their dead bodies. His deep breathing wasn't from fear, it was to relieve the constant ache in his stomach, the fist inside him that was crushing each organ in turn, then starting all over again.

Tory pounded the door frantically. "Ed! Ed, it's Tory! Open up!"

Less than five seconds of silence. Ed was well trained. "Tory? What the fuck?"

"Ed, open the door. Hurry!" Tory rapped her knuckles against the wood. Cliff nodded at her, encouraging. She knocked harder. "Ed!"

Ed opened the door a few inches. Cliff could hear the door chain rattle as it went taut. "What do you want?"

"That guy. He's after me."

"What guy?"

"Remington. The guy we set up the other day. He called me."

"He called you?"

"For God's sake, Ed, let me in."

Ed was silent a moment. "I've got company."

"I don't care if you're fucking a goddamned mule, Ed. He threatened to kill me."

"He's bluffing. Go back home."

"Jesus, Ed! He said he'd kill me."

"I tell you he's bluffing."

"What if he's not?"

"You don't know anything. He's got no reason to kill you."

"You son of a bitch. You'd let him get me, wouldn't you?"

"Hey, we're divorced, remember? Go beg your hot shit lawyers for help. Maybe they can slap him with an injunction." He chuckled.

Cliff realized Ed wasn't going to let her in. He was either a better agent than Cliff had given him credit for, or he was a worse bastard than Tory thought. Either way, Cliff was still going through that door. He clutched the gun to his chest to keep it out of the way, and swung his body weight around, crashing into the door. At impact, pain skewered his injured side, where last night a bullet had eaten away his flesh. He felt his bandage quickly become soaked with fresh blood. The chain ripped from the wall and Ed went sprawling backward onto the floor. He was wearing only blue skivvies and his glasses. Cliff aimed the Colt at Ed Fawley's face. "By the way, Ed, Tory wants her Meat Loaf album back."

"You asshole," Ed sputtered, straightening his glasses. "You're dead, Jack. You know that? You're guaranteed dead, fucking with an active operative. You know standard procedure. Someone's gonna come around and start feeding your parts to a blender. By tomorrow night you're gonna be a tropical drink, man."

"Won't be you, though, Ed. Will it?"

Ed looked at the big blue-steel Colt and calmed down. He even smiled, the smile that had charmed a hundred cheerleaders. "Okay, Remington, you want to chat. Go ahead." He glanced over at Tory, his smile still intact, but his eyes murderous, promising painful retribution. He twisted the lumpy ring on his finger.

Cliff turned to Tory. She looked edgy, still frightened of her ex-husband, but determined to fight it. "Go check the bedroom," Cliff told her.

"God, no. I don't want to see some naked bimbo."

"Do it."

She hesitated, but went. She returned with a condescending smile and a handful of magazines. "Here's his 'company.'"

She threw the magazines onto the floor. Well-used issues of *Hustler*, *Penthouse*, *Beaver* and others scattered across the mustard-colored shag carpeting, thudding against the leg of the cheap coffee table.

Ed's grin widened. "Hell of a lot better company than some bitch with a headache."

"Or a brain."

"Brains and broads don't go together. Like drinking and driving."

Cliff nudged Ed with his foot. "Get up."

"Make up your mind. First you knock me down, then you want me up." He climbed slowly to his feet, adjusting the waistband of his skivvies to accentuate his impressive body. The solid bumps and ridges of his massively muscled chest and stomach looked like tough terrain even for a tank. He bounced happily on his toes, rocking back onto his heels. "So who brought the cards?"

"Stick your hands down your pants," Cliff ordered.

Ed's face darkened. "Fuck you, man."

"All the way down so your hands come out the pant legs. I want to see those hands grabbing your thighs."

"You're loony, man. What do you think Aaron Leland's gonna do when he finds out you been fucking with one of his men?"

"Do it, Ed, or he won't be hearing about it from you."

Ed reluctantly jammed his hands under the elastic waistband of his underpants, hugging each arm to the hip. A hand appeared out of each pant leg. Cliff relaxed. It would be difficult for Ed to reach for anything too quickly now, and it saved Cliff the time and trouble of having to tie him up.

"Now, Ed," Cliff said, standing in front of him. "I want to know where Standish Ford is."

"Washington. He went back the same day we picked you up."

"Who else did he see while he was out here?"

"No one I know of. He stayed in his hotel room until we took you to Tory's house. Afterward we took him back."

Cliff studied Ed Fawley. Despite the belligerent expression, Ed looked uneasy, anxious for the interrogation to be over. Standing there like that, arms at his sides like a little boy, hands sticking out of his underpants, compromised his sexuality. He wanted it over and the fastest way to end it was to tell the truth. Cliff believed him, but so far he hadn't learned anything useful.

"What about the shooter?"

Ed frowned. "What shooter?"

"The one who did my family? A woman posing as a cop."

"I don't know anything about that. From what I heard, that was personal." His smile decayed into something malevolent. "I can see why."

Cliff forced his finger not to squeeze the trigger. "What about Bradley Carleton and Phillip DeSoto? What about my partner? Who was the shooter there? Guy about forty, five foot ten, slender, dark hair. You hear anything?"

"Fuck, no. We're not even looking into it, man. That's local cops."

"You don't know of any free-lancer who fits that description?"

"Yeah, maybe a coupla dozen and a coupla dozen more who could make themselves up to fit that description."

Cliff could see this wasn't getting him any closer to either Lily's killer or his family's killer. He'd gone to Tory Fawley because she was the only link he had to Ed Fawley. Now Ed Fawley didn't know anything.

Cliff glanced over at Tory, who stood quietly to the side, not saying anything, not even gloating over Ed's embarrassing stance. Cliff was about to tell her they were leaving, when he felt the sudden impact of a battering ram slamming into his chest, toppling him backward.

Ed had lowered his shoulder and plowed right into Cliff, knocking the wind out of him and sending him reeling. If the Samoan could see him, she'd have shaken her head sadly and said, "Reflexes shot, man. Rusty as hell." She'd have been right.

Cliff did two things right this time. He didn't lose his balance and he didn't lose the gun. He did stagger back, legs rubbery, the pain at his side bringing tears to his eyes. Ed, his hands now free and grabbing for Cliff's gun, lunged at Cliff with his mouth open, teeth flashing, as if killing him wouldn't be enough, only eating the body would do.

Cliff felt the backs of his legs hit the sofa, which braced him enough to keep from falling. Using this leverage, he swung the gun around in a heavy arc, raking the barrel across Ed's cheek. The solid impact against bone almost jarred the gun loose from his hand. At the moment of contact came a crack, like someone snapping a branch from a dead tree. Ed's glasses flew from his face. He dropped to his knees, the left side of his face caved in, a long gash spilling blood down his jaw and neck. He clamped a hand on the wound, then winced at the painful contact.

Cliff pointed the Colt at Ed's forehead. "Feel better?"

Ed tried to smile, but the crushed cheekbone wouldn't oblige him. Only half of his face moved. "I will. Next time we meet."

"Well, then I guess I'd be pretty stupid to leave you alive." Cliff cocked the hammer and shoved the barrel of the Colt against Ed's forehead. "Bye, Ed."

Ed's eyes went wide with terror and he fell back to the floor. He held one hand palm out as if to deflect the bullet.

Tory ran to Cliff's side. "No! Don't!"

Cliff backed up toward the door. "A little lesson in spymanship, Ed. Never make threats you can't follow through on the spot." He looked at Tory. "You coming?"

She hesitated, glanced at Ed Fawley's crumpled form, his bleeding face. She walked over to the stereo next to the TV, flipped the dust cover and pushed the record on the turntable into the album jacket. Meat Loaf. She marched straight out the door without looking back. Cliff backed out after her, closing the door.

They walked down the brightly painted corridor toward the elevator without speaking. Ed's apartment building smelled of strong perfume and stronger after-shave, one of those ul-

tramodern singles complexes that Cliff saw advertised in the
Los Angeles Times. Pool, tennis courts, available partners. The
Good Life.

It occurred to Cliff for the first time that he was technically
single. He didn't think of himself that way. He still thought
of himself as a husband, a father, a household handyman. He
stepped closer to Tory while they waited for the elevator, because he could still smell the faint sweetness of baby powder
on her and that scent reminded him of home more than the
desperate floral and musk smells of this building's residents.
He took a deep breath and the familiar scent swirled in his
head, each white grain forming a bleached picture of Ginger
in the supermarket, sneaking up behind him and sprinkling
baby powder on his shoulder. "Get used to the smell," she'd
said. " 'Cause if we have a kid, pal, this is the major smell in
your life."

"Hey!" Tory said, frowning at Cliff. "What are you sniffing? Do I smell funny?"

The elevator door opened and Cliff entered without saying
anything. Tory followed.

They'd driven Tory's Porsche from her place to Ed's. Now,
as they approached the car in the apartment's parking lot, they
saw someone sitting behind the wheel reading a paperback
novel. Don Delillo's *White Noise*. He looked up only when
Cliff and Tory were standing next to the car door.

"I locked it," Tory said.

"I know."

Stan Ford closed his novel, opened the car door and climbed
out. "You didn't kill him, did you? Poor Ed, I mean."

"Does it matter?"

Stan shrugged. "It would complicate things."

"But you'd fix it."

"I'd fix it."

Cliff's mouth stretched into an expression that no one would
mistake for a smile. "If I help you find Vatican Towne."

Stan didn't answer. He met Cliff's flat stare.

"I didn't kill Ed." Cliff snatched the Colt from under his sweater and nudged it against Stan's stomach. "I haven't yet decided about you, though."

Tory spoke up. "Look, you two don't need me here. I'm just the kidnap victim. I don't want to know what the questions are and I certainly don't want to know the answers."

"He's the one with the gun," Stan said.

Cliff looked at her. Under the harsh parking lot lights he could see the dark shadow of the scab on her scalp where he'd smacked her with his racquet. He reached into his pocket, found her car keys and handed them to her. "Go."

Tory immediately slid behind the wheel, threw the record album on the passenger seat and started the engine. She jammed the shift into reverse, started backing out, then braked with a squeal. "Hey," she said to Cliff. "I'm sorry about your wife and kids. I'm . . ." She hesitated, as if she wanted to say more, but finally just repeated, "Sorry." She wheeled the Porsche around and roared away.

Stan gestured at the white Chevy Celebrity parked a few rows away. "That's my rental," he said. "We can go somewhere and talk."

"We can go somewhere," Cliff said. "And you can talk."

"Can you keep a secret?" Stan asked.

"No," Cliff answered.

Stan smiled, looked up at the stars.

They were sitting side by side on the sand of Malibu Beach. The sky was unusually dark despite a half-moon suspended above them. Except for a few patches of reflected moonlight, Cliff couldn't tell where the ocean ended and the sky began. Behind them, homes that looked patched together but cost well over a million dollars each lined the beachfront.

Whoever owned one of them had had a wall of sandbags erected in preparation for a big storm, though none had been announced. Cliff knew the house from a tour of Hollywood stars' homes he and Drew had once gone on when they had a day to kill waiting for a flight to Tokyo. They'd bought a map on Sunset Boulevard from this kid with coked-out eyes and had driven around the whole day, hunting out each home. For more than three hours they'd hung around at the house that was supposed to be Priscilla Presley's just so Drew could catch a glimpse of the King's former wife. In three hours, no one had come out or gone in. "She must be lonely," Drew had concluded as they left.

"Are you going to kill me?" Stan asked with casual curiosity.

"I don't know yet."

"Depends on what I tell you?"

Cliff looked directly into Stan's eyes. "Not necessarily."

"Your mood, then."

Cliff shrugged.

Stan picked up a rock and threw it at the ocean. It plopped into a baby wave that was bellying up the sand. "You think I set you up."

"Didn't you?"

"Yeah, I guess I did. But that wasn't my intention."

Cliff rested his hands on his knees, his gun dangling loosely from one finger between his legs. The sand they were sitting on was moist and he could feel the dampness seeping through his jeans.

"Here's what happened," Stan said. "Aaron Leland sent me out here to get your help to track down Vatican Towne. We needed a free-lancer, one who wasn't active so Towne wouldn't suspect."

"I'm still not sure I believe that Vatican Towne is sabotaging Fat Boy."

"Don't bullshit me, Remington. You know goddamn well I wouldn't be telling you that if it wasn't true. You know how vulnerable we are even to a rumor about Fat Boy. You believe me. And you believe me when I tell you that things have gotten even worse. The PAW satellites are off."

Cliff raised an eyebrow. "That is bad."

"Bet your ass it's bad. That reduces our response time to a missile invasion by eighteen seconds. A lifetime." Stan shifted, dug his hook into the sand, plowing a deep rut. "Every day Vatican Towne shuts down more of Fat Boy. Well, not shut down exactly. We can still feed it info, but we just can't access it again."

"Can Towne?"

"No."

"Then why's he doing it? Not just for Leland's head. Towne knows you guys wouldn't agree to that."

"That's what makes this so hard. We don't *know* why."

"Crap."

"All right, *I* don't know. And if Leland knows, he isn't telling." Stan shifted to face Cliff. "Here's the whole damn story as best as I can piece it together. Leland sent me out here to recruit you. When that didn't work, he hired a free-lancer named Charon. Ever hear the name?"

"No."

"Good—you're not supposed to have. Top-level assassin known only to a few. Unstable, but never misses. There's more, but that can keep. Anyway, Leland hires this Charon to implicate you in an attack on Vatican Towne's son. Charon's orders were to wound Bradley Carleton, not kill him. Not kill anyone."

"That's what Leland said."

"Yes."

"And you believe him?"

"Yes, I do."

Cliff said, "Go on."

"The idea was that if you were implicated, it would bring Vatican Towne out after you. No one even considered he'd go after your family. It isn't like him at all."

"Neither is shutting down Fat Boy, but Leland was willing to risk being wrong."

"He had no choice."

"You believe that?"

Stan didn't answer. He tossed a broken shell into the surf. "The point is, we both want Vatican Towne. You want him for killing your family. We want to stop him before he makes attacking this country too attractive to the Soviets. He could be anywhere in the world. Singapore or Salt Lake City. We have some leads. You don't. You can't find him without us. We can find him without you, but it might be too late."

"So you want me to paint a target on my back and go after him. When he pops out of the bush to take a shot at me, that's when you nail him."

"Right."

"Before or after he pulls the trigger?"

"Before, if possible."

"What about Lily Vaiala? Who pays for that?"

"Charon. Leland promises to give him to you after it's all over. If you want him."

Cliff ignored that. "And Leland?"

Stan's face hardened. "Don't be stupid."

"What happens when I find Towne? Provided he doesn't find me first. Terminate?"

"No. Merely identify. We have an interrogation team ready to go and find out how to reverse the process in Fat Boy."

Cliff didn't say anything. He looked out at the black ocean rolling toward him. The air was surprisingly warm and the dark water looked even warmer. He felt like a swim, a long swim. Fully clothed, gun tucked in belt, sweater as heavy as a bulletproof jacket from soaking up saltwater. Swim across the black sea into the black night until both blacknesses became one swirling union. Indistinguishable. Sweeping him out into that great endless flowing. The thought made him un-

PLAY THE

LUCKY CARNIVAL WHEEL

scratch-off game
and get as many as

THREE FREE GIFTS...

HOW TO PLAY:

1. With a coin, carefully scratch off the silver area at right. Then check your number against the chart below to see which gifts you can get. If you're lucky, you'll instantly be entitled to receive one or more books and possibly another gift, ABSOLUTELY FREE!

2. Send back this card and we'll promptly send you any Free Gifts you're entitled to. You may get first time in paperback novels from the Mystery Library and an exciting Surprise Gift!

3. We're betting you'll want more of these page-turning stories, so we'll send you two more intriguing books every month to preview. Always delivered right to your home and before they're available in stores.

4. Your satisfaction is guaranteed! You may return any shipment of books and cancel any time. The Free Books and Gift remain yours to keep!

NO COST! NO RISK!
NO OBLIGATION TO BUY!

FREE SURPRISE GIFT!

We can't tell you what it is—that would spoil the surprise—but it could be yours FREE when you play the "**LUCKY CARNIVAL WHEEL**" scratch-off game!

Mystery, Intrigue, Suspense!

The plot thickens with every page…the clues seem crystal-clear, yet the outcome is always a surprise! That's the suspense and drama you'll find in every novel from The Mystery Library—each a thrilling read just like the one you're reading! So treat yourself to hours of riveting, thoroughly enjoyable reading with each and every Mystery Library story!

If offer card is missing, write to: The Mystery Library, 901 Fuhrmann Blvd., P.O. Box 1867, Buffalo, NY 14269-1867 expectedly happy, joyous. At that moment Cliff knew for certain if he didn't accept Standish Ford's offer, he would indeed walk into the ocean and swim away forever.

16

CLIFF DUCKED UNDER the yellow police tape strapped across the front doorway and found Lieutenant Godfrey waiting for him inside the house. The big cop had one of Bogie's "Star Trek" glasses in his fist, sipping mud-colored bourbon he'd found in the liquor cabinet above the microwave. The liquor cabinet consisted of one bottle each of vodka, bourbon and gin, all less than half full, left over from a Halloween costume party a year ago. Ginger had dressed as Ado Annie from *Oklahoma* and after a few drinks began singing "I'm Just a Girl Who Can't Say No."

"I've been told," Godfrey said angrily.

"Told what?" Cliff asked.

Godfrey snorted. "Sure, play dumb."

Cliff stood in front of the lieutenant, well aware that the heavy Colt tucked under his sweater was illegal. "What have you been told?"

"Told to lay off. Back off. Ease off. Fuck off."

Cliff nodded. Standish Ford was already pulling strings. The cops would leave Cliff alone now. No more questions.

"I don't like it, Remington," Godfrey said. "I don't like being told how to handle my cases."

"You've been a cop a long time. You should be used to it by now."

Godfrey frowned and his straggly black mustache shifted. "Some things you shouldn't get used to. Once you do, you're finished. No good for nothin'."

Cliff didn't want to debate. He wanted to pack. He didn't know for where yet. Stan Ford would tell him that soon enough. Meanwhile, he would throw some clothes together and sit and wait. If he got tired of waiting, there was always the long swim out into the ocean. Or the Colt. He'd thought agreeing to hunt down Vatican Towne would make him feel better, like unraveling the sofa. It hadn't. No matter. He had a few hours to decide what to do with his life. At the end of that time he would either be alive or dead. Right now he didn't care which.

"Where's the cat?" Lieutenant Godfrey asked, gesturing at the food bowl on the kitchen floor.

"Neighbors."

"You move fast—I'll give you that."

Cliff had moved fast. Closed the business, boarded the cat, tried to tidy the loose ends as if he really had some control over his life. He'd phoned Ginger's parents in Montana, listened to the sobs of her mother, the choked whisper of her father, their voices as frail as their understanding. "Why, Cliff?" each had asked separately and Cliff had mumbled soothing words he couldn't now remember. He hoped he'd been some comfort but doubted it.

Ginger's ex-husband, the children's father, had already heard the news when Cliff phoned him and wasn't accepting any calls. Cliff had driven over to his house, only to be told by his Salvadorian housekeeper that Dr. Kendall had left town.

Now Cliff walked around the lieutenant's wide girth to the kitchen telephone and poked the Play button of the answering machine.

"Cliff, it's me."

The message was from Aaron Leland.

Cliff stiffened, heat radiating from the patch at the back of his neck. His fingers curled into fists.

"I know you wouldn't talk to me in person. I just want you to know I'm sorry about what happened. Everything's screwed up. I swear to God, I'd do anything to change it. I can't. St. Francis of Assisi once said, 'Lord, make me an instrument of Your peace.' That's what we both are, Cliff. Instruments of peace. Like it or not.''

A loud beep signaled the end of message and Cliff shut off the machine. He could feel the lieutenant's intense gaze on him.

"If I was still pursuing this case," Godfrey said, "I might ask you what that was all about."

"But you're not."

"Right, I'm not." He gulped down the rest of his drink. "But if I were, I'd say that man sounded sincerely sorry. Now just what does he have to sound sorry about?"

Cliff turned on the cold water and bent over the kitchen sink. He splashed water on his eyes, patted some on the back of his neck.

"One of your old spook buddies from Washington?"

"The one who's got his foot planted smack on your neck, Lieutenant."

Godfrey reddened, plucked at his suspenders. "Don't fuck with me too much, Remington. I've been known to hold a grudge."

"Yeah, well, you mind holding it over at your own home? I'm busy."

"Yeah, I saw the sofa. Quite an upholstering job."

"I'm looking for new hobbies."

Godfrey filled his glass with some more bourbon and walked into the living room. Cliff followed him. The lieutenant poked his finger into the tangled mound of string Cliff had unraveled from the sofa. "When my dad died a couple of years ago, I went into the garage for three days and built a bird feeder. A big goddamn bird feeder with a pedestal and little carved blue jays. I mean, we live in a condo and don't even have anyplace to put it. So why'd I do it? For my old man's sake? He didn't particularly like birds. Didn't hate them, understand? Just didn't notice them. But I went three days without eating or sleeping or going to work so I could build a fucking bird feeder that nobody wanted. Finally sold it at a neighbor's garage sale for four bucks. Hell, the lumber was worth more than that.''

Cliff sat on the overstuffed chair that matched, or used to match, the sofa. ''We all mourn differently. Some people build, some destroy.''

''It's not that simple.''

''Isn't it?''

''I'm a cop—some would say that's a destructive job. You're a landscaper, that's building.''

Cliff smiled. ''Who're you kidding, Lieutenant? You know exactly what I am.''

''Retired.''

Cliff didn't answer.

Godfrey offered him the bottle of bourbon. Cliff didn't drink alcohol, except for the occasional glass of wine. While he'd been on the active list, not drinking had been a matter of survival. Later, it was just habit. But he accepted the bottle and took a swig.

One swig led to another, and soon the two men had finished off two of the bottles of booze and were sharing the bottle of vodka. Cliff wasn't drunk, but he allowed himself to act a little tipsy for Godfrey's sake. The lieutenant staggered slightly and had trouble with his tongue, but otherwise was perfectly lucid. Cliff couldn't decide how much of it was an act, how much real. He sensed, though, that Godfrey wanted to talk, honestly and openly, and that two grown men such as they could never do so sober. They needed at least the pretense of drunkenness so that anything revealed that was too personal could later be denied or ignored. A complicated ritual, but one Cliff understood.

Godfrey sat on the floor, leaning against the savaged sofa, his eyelids heavy. Cliff had put *Porgy and Bess* on the stereo. They'd been sitting listening for twenty minutes. Whatever the lieutenant wanted to say, he hadn't gotten around to it yet.

''Gershwin, huh?'' he asked.

Cliff nodded.

"Yeah, I thought so. Saw the movie when it first came out. I was a teenager. Asked a girl to go with me. Diane Klempner. We were both seniors and I'd had the hots for her since junior high school. I used to lie awake in my bed planning and scheming how to get my hand under her sweater. I would have traded my left foot to touch those nipples. When I finally worked up the nerve to ask her out, she looked at me with the most puzzled expression and said, 'Why on earth would I want to see a movie about a bunch of coloreds?' Can you believe that?"

"Did you go out with her?"

"Damn right. We went to another movie. Can't remember which one, I was so busy working my fingers under her bra. At that age hormones always beat out social conscience."

Cliff laughed.

Godfrey had a sloppy grin on his face. He handed Cliff the bottle; Cliff drank, handed it back. While reaching for the bottle, Godfrey noticed a loose thread in the chair's covering. He flicked at it with his finger.

"Go ahead," Cliff said.

Godfrey shook his head. But his finger kept tickling the stray thread.

"It's easy," Cliff said. "Do it."

The cop's grin widened mischievously as he grasped the loose thread and yanked. It zippered across the fabric.

An hour and a half later they had completely unraveled the fabric of the chair. They were both sitting on the floor now, the pile of loose thread between them.

"Beats building a birdbath," the lieutenant said.

"Bird feeder."

"Whatever."

They sat quietly for a few minutes. Cliff put *Dreamgirls* on the stereo.

"I saw that show with my wife," Godfrey said. "At the Schubert. Our seats were forty dollars apiece, but they had us so far up in the balcony I got a nosebleed." His thoughts seemed to drift away a moment. "My wife liked it though."

Silence settled between them again. Cliff leaned his head back, closed his eyes and listened to the music. He would never admit it to the lieutenant, but he was enjoying his company, was in fact happy to have it. During the silences his mind wandered back to Ginger and the kids until Godfrey spoke again, banishing the painful thoughts.

"It isn't easy," the cop said, his voice curiously sober now. "It isn't easy being us. We're trained to hold back so much of ourselves. And that's a good thing because that's how we survive the constant human misery that we try to alleviate. Trouble is, for every person you help, you harm someone else. I arrested this guy, a little runt of a man, who'd stabbed his daughter's boyfriend because he didn't like him. The boyfriend's parents were so happy when we arrested the guy. The only relief to their sorrow would be to see this guy punished. But the killer's family was in hysterics when we took him away. Even his daughter. God, it's hard to feel like a hero anymore." The lieutenant shifted awkwardly until he was looking into Cliff's eyes. "A couple years ago my wife had a radical mastectomy. Lost her breast and a large chunk of muscle all the way under here." He tapped the muscles under his arm. "It was horrible. She was only thirty-seven. We went through a lot of shit together. But, you know, at the back of my mind, I had this strange thought. I've never told it to anyone before because it's too embarrassing. I'm not sure I even admitted it to myself."

Cliff watched the lieutenant's eyes glisten.

"A part of me, somewhere down deep, was glad she was sick. Glad because it gave me a chance to show her how much I loved her. A chance to be there for her. You understand?"

Cliff nodded.

"The cancer's gone now. She's fine. But right before her operation, I found I was taking more chances on the job. Pulling my gun more than I had to, not waiting for backup." He shrugged. "Maybe I was trying to punish myself because I couldn't protect my wife better. Or maybe I felt guilty because it wasn't me. I know I wasn't afraid to die. Not just that—I almost welcomed it. Who knows why? I don't think too much about such things. Luckily, the feeling passed away before I did."

He stood up and walked unsteadily toward the front door. Cliff followed him, also putting a little wobble in his walk, though he was certain either of them could have walked two miles of railroad track without losing their balance if they'd had to.

Lieutenant Godfrey opened the door and ducked under the yellow tape. He looked at his watch. "In a few hours I'll be investigating this case again." He nodded at Cliff's sweater, the part that covered the Colt. "I'd hate any more complications."

Cliff shook Godfrey's hand and watched him walk to his car, his gait steadying with each step. Cliff closed the front door and pulled out the Colt. He stared at it for a long time before he reached his decision.

17

THE SUDDEN SOUND woke Tory.

"Mike?" she called.

Silence.

She didn't hear Mike's heavy footsteps or the chuffing of his breath as was usual when she called him. She flung the covers off her legs, but didn't hurry out of bed. She tried to remember what the exact sound had been that woke her. A scraping sound, like a washboard in a hillbilly band. Maybe just someone stumbling home late after a party.

Tory silently opened the nightstand drawer and removed the little .22 Beretta Minx M2. The barrel was only two and a half inches long, but it fired at a semiautomatic rate and carried seven shots. Enough to stop an intruder.

"Mikie?" she called again. Still no response. Goddamn it, she thought, if it's that Remington guy playing games again, I'll... Well, she wasn't exactly sure what she would do. Not shoot him, probably, but scare the crap out of him.

Quietly she slid out of bed, put on her short Japanese robe and tiptoed out of the bedroom. She hugged the wall, the Beretta close to her chest and ready to swing around into a proper shooting stance. Just the way they'd taught her. Of course, that was on a target range. She'd never actually fired at anyone.

She'd never actually done anything in the Agency except recruitment work. The recruiting supervisor, Ed's boss at the time, had explained to her how important it was to have someone like her traveling around to college campuses. "We need women," he'd said with a smile. The smile had revealed a gap between his front teeth that reminded Tory of David

Letterman. She'd thought of David Letterman as a CIA recruiting officer and had almost laughed in the man's face. "We send someone like you to talk to these women, and they realize that all the women in the Agency aren't fat bulldogs with no brains."

"You mean dykes. I'm proof that we aren't all dykes."

"Well, there's that too."

"What makes you think I'm not? A dyke."

He looked down in embarrassment, his face reddening. "I just assumed... from what Ed Fawley said, I assumed you weren't."

Ed. He'd undoubtedly bragged about what had been going on between them. They'd had a fight about it that night. Ed had stormed out of the house, returning with a bunch of flowers from God knows where and a boyish apology. They'd made love and Tory had thought all their arguments would be settled that easily.

Tory tightened her grip on the Beretta. She flattened her back against the wall, and for some reason she felt her heart contract with fear. It actually hurt. Her breaths puffed out in choppy spurts. Her legs erupted in goose bumps and refused to move. Sweat chilled her breasts.

She had been so busy feeling sorry for Remington, she hadn't stopped to think things through. Someone had killed Remington's partner and a couple of others at some office building last night. Then Remington's family got wiped out. The killing of his partner might have had something to do with whatever the Agency was involved in. But slaughtering his family was an act of retribution. And where else had Remington been? Here! What if someone saw him, she thought, saw me drive him away? They might have concluded I'm working with him, or romantically involved with him. They might want to kill me too!

She had been so careful to avoid overhearing any information, to keep her distance, as if ignorance were a shield, like painting a red cross on her forehead and walking through a battlefield.

She started back for her bedroom, deciding to call the police first, then try to hide out until they came. If they found no one in the house, she could smile charmingly at them and act the dumb broad, and they could leave, flipping closed their notebooks and shaking their heads. Whatever worked.

Once in the bedroom, she locked the door behind her, then hurried to the telephone. When she picked up the phone she was surprised to find that it worked. The dial tone hummed at her as steadily as a healthy pulse. For some paranoid reason, she'd expected the line to be dead, the wires cut by whoever made the noise that had awakened her.

Suddenly she felt silly, hunched over the phone, holding a gun, her finger poised to punch 911. Just go back to sleep, she told herself.

Then her bedroom door exploded inward, slamming open with a wicked crash, and a large figure, shapeless in the dark, stood in the doorway. Tory swung the Beretta around toward him, but he was on her too quickly, powerful hands locked around her wrist, twisting and bending and hurting.

"I JUST came from the president," Aaron Leland said.

Stan's grip on the telephone tightened. If the president found out what had been going on behind his back, they were all in deep shit. But Aaron's voice reflected no concern, so Stan didn't allow his to either. "And?" Stan said. "His reaction?"

"He wanted to know about my progress on this terrorism project. Terrorists. That's the only thing on his mind lately. Talks about it all the time."

"Everybody talks about it, Aaron. People are getting blown up every day."

"He's obsessed."

"He's running for reelection."

"Here's the latest wrinkle. The FBI's been investigating these radio interference incidents at the Phoenix Sky Harbor Airport. Someone jams out the air traffic controller, then gives false flight instructions to the planes. They've had one crash already and a near miss the other day."

"Who's behind it?"

"The president thinks it's—what else—terrorists. KGB-backed goons holed up in an apartment eating borscht, on a sacred mission to make him look bad, stop him from being reelected." A short tinny silence followed. "Thing is, preliminary investigations prove he may be right."

Stan understood the president's obsession with terrorists. He had been an unusually popular president until last year's hijacking of a TWA jet in Berlin. The president, ignoring CIA advice and acting on the urging of his personal friends, had authorized a hit squad to rescue the twenty-eight American hostages. The German officials had warned against such an operation, had insisted that negotiating was the best policy. The longer it dragged out, the better the odds for the hostages. But the president, mindful of Carter's botched Iranian rescue attempt and the flap over Reagan's ransoming hostages with military parts to Iran, was adamant. He would demonstrate the power of strong leadership. He ordered the squad to go. Almost immediately the terrorists blew up the plane, killing themselves, the twenty-eight hostages and six American soldiers. No matter how often they read about it or even saw it happen, Stan realized, Americans could never understand the terrorist mentality, the willingness to kill oneself for a holy cause.

Naturally the president had been condemned by the world press and hadn't fared much better at home. His popularity sank miserably. Trying to reduce the heat on himself, he'd blamed faulty intelligence reports from the CIA. Aaron Leland had seen his opportunity then, had convinced the president that he could do much better in the war against terrorists. The president fired the CIA director and put Leland in his place. Terrorists had made the president look bad; he would use them to make him look good again. Simple justice.

The parking lot light above Stan's phone booth flickered suddenly as if it were about to wink out. Instead, it merely dimmed, then brightened back to normal. Stan had pulled off the freeway on his way back to his hotel from his Malibu meeting with Cliff Remington. He'd driven into one of the tiny shopping centers, looking for a phone. Now that he had made his connection, he noticed for the first time that all the stores around him, though closed, had Vietnamese signs. Nothing was in English. Stan suddenly felt like a lost tourist in a foreign country.

"First thing the president says," Leland continued. "'How's our war against terrorism coming, Aaron?'"

"What did you tell him?"

"I said, 'It's coming along nicely, Mr. President. Way ahead of schedule.' He wanted to know exactly when we'd see some concrete results."

"Something newsworthy."

"Exactly."

"What did you tell him?"

There was a pause, then, "Within the week."

"Jesus, Aaron!"

"Then he shook my hand and thanked me. Doesn't want to know any details."

"Aaron," Stan said softly, "do you really have any kind of plan, any program?"

During the silence, the phone emitted a hushed echo, like the sound one hears listening to a seashell. When Leland finally spoke, his voice was firm. "Yes, Stan, I do. I have a plan."

"It has something to do with this Vatican Towne thing, doesn't it?"

"I'm impressed, Stan. You're getting better."

"Are you going to tell me about it?"

"Tell you what?" Leland's voice was suddenly grim, sad. "Some things are best left unknown for now, Stan. It could all blow up in our faces. The less you know, the safer you'll be."

"For Christ's sake, Aaron, it's already blown up. The whole country's defense is compromised. We're hanging by a thread right now."

"If it hadn't happened now, it would have happened eventually. This country can't exist being blackmailed by another country, and certainly not by any individual like Vatican Towne. We have to end it now, Stan. Find the man and end it."

"What does he really want, Aaron?"

"You mean besides my head?"

"Yes."

Aaron Leland laughed. "Isn't that enough for you?"

Stan pressed his forehead against the glass. He couldn't read Vietnamese, but he liked the way the letters looked in the clean windows. He liked the handmade signs, cardboard flaps cut crookedly from boxes, then lettered with thick black markers. Certain words underlined several times, implying great bargains. These were the mom-and-pop stores of the eighties. In the morning, refugee families wearing long white bib aprons, the traditional uniform of emigrant store owners from Italians to Jews, would stand behind these Formica counters and sell their wares to their friends and neighbors. All speaking in a tongue that did not make them feel foolish.

The light above the booth crackled and dimmed and brightened again. Before phoning Aaron Leland, Stan had first called Lanie, waking her from an erotic dream she'd immediately told Stan about. He wasn't convinced she'd really had this dream, but she enjoyed telling it and he enjoyed hearing it. Lanie was a former beauty queen, Miss Rhode Island, who'd had her title taken away when she'd been photographed among a crowd protesting the Vietnam War. The pageant promoters had offered to let her retain her crown if she would publicly attest that she had only been there by accident. She had refused.

"So what do you think of my dream, Stan?" she'd asked.

"It made me horny."

"Which part?"

"All of me."

"No, which part of the dream?"

"All of it."

She'd laughed. "But what does the dream mean?"

"That you're horny."

"You just want me to talk dirty."

"I just want to hear your voice."

She was silent and Stan sensed her tension.

"You're going away." It was a statement of fact.

"Probably. I haven't talked to Aaron yet."

She knew better than to ask for details. "I've been thinking about Aaron. About why he left the Jesuits." This was a topic they speculated on sometimes while waiting in restaurants or in line at the movies. Idle chatter. "You think maybe he's gay and they caught him diddling one of the other priests?"

"For God's sake, Lanie. Why would you think that?"

"Well, they're all a little gay, don't you think?"

"Are you serious, or just waiting around for the next Age of Enlightenment?"

She laughed. "You're so easy to tease."

Stan laughed too. "That's just my cover."

When they'd said goodbye, their voices were hollow parodies of good cheer, each not wanting to sadden the other. But at the very moment he hung up, his wife's voice still echoing faintly in his ears, Stan had thought of Cliff Remington and his wife. An icy chill had shriveled his scalp.

Now Aaron Leland's crisp voice brought Stan back to his present conversation. "How's Cliff doing?"

"He said he'd cooperate."

"No, I mean how's he *doing*? How's he holding up?"

Stan hesitated. Aaron sounded genuinely concerned, not about the mission, but about the man. Like an old friend. "Not great. He's a little shaky. I'm not sure how much we can trust him."

"We can trust him. That's the one thing about him I'm sure of. With the right supervision."

"Meaning I'm going with him."

"Correct."

Stan sighed. His breath fogged up the glass of the phone booth. "Have we been able to come up with a location to start?"

"We're still working on that. We have one likely prospect. Flight arrangements have already been made."

"So you want me to take Remington to this place and parade him around until Vatican Towne pops out to kill him."

Aaron Leland's voice tightened, taut as a piano wire. "Listen, Stan, I appreciate your feelings about the way we're doing things here. I don't like it any more than you do. But unless you have any better suggestions, keep your attitude to yourself and follow orders. You think you can run this show? Say so right now and I'll step down. I mean it, Stan. You want the responsibility for everything that's happening? You want to make humane decisions yet protect this country's existence? I'm willing to learn. Fly back here tonight and I'll set up a meeting with the president and convince him that you should take over for me. Health reasons. I mean it, Stan. I goddamn mean it."

Stan knew he did mean it.

"Well, Stan?"

I should do it, Stan thought. Climb on the next plane to Washington, tell the president about Fat Boy, about Towne, about everything. But what would that accomplish? There would be emergency meetings all over Washington. If the Soviets didn't know about Fat Boy and the PAW satellites by now, they would certainly know by morning. Their guesses would be confirmed. Then things would really heat up.

Stan would still be no closer to Vatican Towne or solving the problem. Worse off, actually. And what if he made the wrong decision and there was an attack? A nuclear fucking war! It would be his own damn fault. Could he live with that? Did he have the balls to march into Washington, boot out Aaron Leland, one of the smartest and shrewdest minds Stan had ever known? Stan never thought of himself as the guy in charge. In the movie of his life, he was always the co-star. The strong sidekick, the second in command. Mr. Spock to someone else's Captain Kirk.

Stan took out his pen and pad. "What airline and where are we going?"

19

TORY STRUGGLED against the intruder's grip. Her own strength was considerable, and she felt his fingers give way as she pried them open from around her wrist.

"Dumb cunt!" he barked and slapped her hard. His palm was rough and leathery and hard. Tory's cheek ignited with pain. He slapped her again, and she felt the bone in her cheek shift slightly away from the jaw as her head swiveled around from the force. He released his grip on her wrist and she flopped back on the bed, dazed.

Tory lay there, groggy. Blood oiled her teeth where the inside of her cheek had shredded on her incisors. She looked up at the figure leaning over her, his face still indistinguishable, a clump of unformed darkness. "What do you want, Ed?" she said, her voice calm, emotionless. She wouldn't give him the satisfaction of anger, fear, helplessness, hate.

"How's it feel?" he said. It was his voice, but the words came out a little lumpy, slurred. "Not so good, huh? Well, now you know how I feel. Your shithead boyfriend Remington broke my fucking face. Broke the goddamn cheekbone!"

Tory looked over her shoulder for the Beretta. It must have fallen somewhere on the bed in the struggle, but she couldn't see it. There was a small pocket of dark near the edge of the covers, so she let her hand slowly slide toward it.

Suddenly Ed's open palm glanced off the side of her face again, and he followed the blow with a backhand. The backhand scraped his bulbous class ring across her chin. "Don't you fucking move unless I tell you!" He jumped on the bed, his knees straddling her ribs. He rocked backward, resting his buttocks on her stomach, sinking more and more of his weight against her. Tory's breath rushed out, her organs shifted about for comfort. She couldn't breathe.

"What do you want, Ed?" she rasped.

He rocked forward and took the weight off her stomach. "Want?" Yanking open her robe, he revealed her naked body. He picked up the Beretta from the bed as if all the lights were on and he could see everything clearly. Slowly, with great precision, he lowered the mouth of the barrel to her right breast, screwing the metal against her nipple. "I'd have gone over and killed Remington but apparently we need him for something. So I'll have to wait until we're done with him before I pay a little visit. Too bad somebody already goosed his family, otherwise I might be doing this to his wife instead of you."

Tory remained rigid. If she didn't antagonize him, didn't respond with any of the emotions he was trying to elicit, she could ride this out. He would hit her, but he wouldn't kill her. He couldn't afford what that would do to his career.

Ed Fawley poked at her other nipple with the gun. "Don't these things ever get hard? Maybe if you rubbed them." He chuckled. "Go ahead, rub them for me. Pinch them. Make them stand up and salute, and maybe I'll go away."

There was a sound at the bedroom doorway. Tory looked around Ed and saw the tall man standing there.

"Christ, Ed," his redheaded associate said, "get it over with and let's get the hell out of here."

"Shut up, Onan."

"Fuck you, Ed."

Ed laughed. "He hates that name, dontcha, Onan. That's what we call him though. You know why?"

Tory didn't answer and Ed slapped her face.

"You know why?" he repeated.

"No," she said.

"Fuck you, Ed," the redhead said. "I'm your partner, so I went along on this bullshit. But I don't have to take any shit from you."

Ed snarled at him. "You came because you knew I'd break your fucking nuts if you didn't. Now shut up." Then Ed turned back to Tory. "His first undercover stakeout over in Frankfurt—following a courier going to meet some East German embassy official. Only the courier's about an hour early, so the dumb kraut goes over to some whorehouse and gets his ashes hauled. Poor Onan here and his buddy watch the whole thing through binoculars. Our redheaded boy excuses himself, goes to the bathroom. But while he's gone, the courier takes off and Onan's partner runs into the bathroom to get him. Finds him beating off in the urinal. Ever since, he's been called Onan. Something biblical suits his personality, don't you think?"

"I'm getting the fuck out of here." The redhead started back up the hall.

"Gee, I think I hurt his feelings," Ed said. "What do you think?"

Tory was about to respond, but Ed's hard slap knocked the word loose in her throat.

"Answer when I ask you a question."

"Give me a chance to."

He laid his callused palm on her burning cheek and stroked. "Sorry, baby. But you shouldn't have brought that Remington bastard to my home. That was stupid."

"He forced me. He had a gun, for Christ's sake."

"Maybe he did. But you were enjoying yourself just a little too much, throwing my magazines, strutting around like a fucking bitch-cunt."

"I didn't, Ed. I just did what I was told."

"I'm the only one who tells you what to do. Understand?"

"Yes," Tory said quickly. She felt the Beretta tapping against her breast.

"Now, are you going to make that nipple hard for me, Tory? Gonna do as I ask?"

"Listen, Ed—"

His hand slammed her cheek, clipping her nose. The pain flooded her eyes with tears, making it even harder to see. She tilted her head to drain the tears.

"I don't want to listen, Tory. I want you to do what I tell you. I want you to make those nipples hard. I want you to convince me that you can still get them up. I'll even help."

Tory felt the barrel of the gun pressing at her crotch. He rubbed the metal over her pubic hair, then lowered it, nudging it into the folds of flesh.

"There," he said. "Doesn't that help? Don't you feel sexy now, feel like a woman? Answer me, goddamn it!"

Tory knew she should agree, should let him play his filthy game because that was what it would take to get him to leave. He'd been humiliated in front of her, and now he was going to humiliate her to make them even. If she just did as he asked, he would soon leave, swaggering away as usual. All she had to do was say yes.

Instead, she bucked her hips high off the bed, catching him unexpectedly and launching him over the side of the bed onto the floor. She didn't know if he still had the gun or not. She didn't care. She leaped off the bed on top of him, grabbed the telephone from the nightstand and rammed it straight into his nose. She felt a spurt of greasy blood splash onto her wrist. She rammed the phone again. And again.

Her strength had surprised him, she realized, not just the new power in her muscles, but the strength of will to actually confront him. The will part surprised Tory too. She'd been running and lifting weights and playing racquetball since they split up, building her body and confidence. But when he smacked her it was as if he'd dislodged her willpower. She'd felt as if she'd tumbled back through time to the way she was before with him. Enduring.

Ed Fawley reached up and grabbed a handful of her hair, yanked her head around at a painful angle. Blindly, she slammed the phone into his forehead. His grip only tightened. She tried to bring the phone back down again but his huge hand snagged her wrist and shook it until the phone flew off across the floor. Its wire draped over the nightstand went taut and swept a half-filled tumbler of Diet Apple Slice against the wall. The glass shattered into sharp fragments and warm drops of the soft drink showered Tory.

"You stupid cunt," Ed growled, forcing her head back while at the same time twisting her wrist. "You didn't think a few aerobics classes would change things between us, did you? I'm still the man. No, make that god. In your case, I'm your god, with the power of life and death." He emphasized the word *death* with a powerful jerk on her hair. She felt a vertebra crack and a hot wire of pain at the base of her head.

With a final hard tug, he rolled her off him onto her back on the floor. Instantly, with an agile move he was astride her again. He released her hair and grabbed one of her nipples. "I told you we'd make this hard, and we will." He pinched it hard, grinding his thumb against his finger until Tory arched with pain, though she did not scream out. "Oh, yes, that's better, sweetheart. Much better."

He pinched again, even harder.

The pain was sharp, as if he'd stuck a finger into her eye. Worse was the humiliation. She knew him. He wasn't about to stop here. He would continue this all night. She looked up into his face. Her eyes were accustomed to the dark and could recognize his features as splotches of shadow. His nose was bent slightly and dark blood oozed out, a few drops falling on her chest. A long gash stretched across his forehead. The cheek that Remington had bludgeoned earlier was still collapsed, flattening half of his face.

Tory's free hand crabbed along the carpet. She hoped to find the phone cord, haul in the phone and bash him in the face again. Instead, her finger was stabbed by a shard of glass. Her fingers gently slid over the glass, checking its size and heft. It was a spiraling curved hunk about four inches long and three inches wide. She grasped it tightly.

"By the way, Mike the canine torpedo is sleeping it off in the kitchen. Onan gave him a tap on the head when he came in. Personally, I was for shooting the mutt." Again he twisted her nipple hard and she gasped, her eyes watering from the pain. "Admit it, Tory, you like it this way. You always have."

Tory swung her hand around, the sharp edge of the broken glass catching Ed on the cheek and plowing a deep furrow all the way to his open mouth. She could feel the glass penetrate all the way through the skin and into his mouth, slitting the cheek into two separate flaps, making his mouth two inches wider. He howled with pain.

Tory pushed at him, trying to topple him again, when she heard heavy footsteps running up the hallway. Ed's redhead partner was coming back to help. She had to work fast. With all her strength, Tory shoved Ed backward, rolling him off her. She scooted her legs free and was scrambling to her feet when Ed's hands encircled her neck from behind. He snapped her head back, reeling her backward as if she were a fish. His fingers tightened around her throat.

"Bitchhh!" he screamed, but the word was garbled in flapping skin and frothing blood.

Tory clawed at his fingers, tried to peel them back. She couldn't. His anger had given him new strength. Her eyes started to float in a blacker darkness than the room. Her body felt limp and light. She couldn't remember what she was frightened about.

Then the fingers were gone. She collapsed on the floor, air scratching its way down her throat. Her eyes finally focused. She looked around.

Cliff Remington had his arm wrapped around Ed's neck and was pulling him backward, Ed still on his knees. Ed's face was a horrible mask of ridges and bumps, the two burning eyes like openings to steaming red volcanoes.

Ed managed to get his feet under him and pushed back with a mighty roar, catapulting himself and Cliff into the wall. A framed poster of quirky sailboats by Richard Lyon Clark dropped to the carpet without breaking. Ed backed Cliff into the wall again and again, and each time Cliff's grip around Ed's neck weakened.

Tory staggered to her feet, stumbled across the room to help. She kicked at Ed's crotch, but he brought up a knee to block her kick, then snapped out his leg, striking her sharply in the thigh. The impact knocked her leg out from under her and she collapsed to the floor.

She struggled back to her feet, limping slightly, looking for a weapon. Meanwhile, Ed had managed to flip Cliff Remington over his shoulder. Cliff had held on, pulling the big man down with him. The two were locked in a death grip, rolling across the floor.

Tory flung open the closet door, grabbed a spike-heeled shoe she hadn't worn for three years and leaped on top of both men, straddling them as if they were one wild beast. Grabbing a handful of Ed's hair, she hammered the spiked heel into his scalp as if she were driving a stubborn nail.

Suddenly a fist shot straight out of the tangle of arms and legs, glancing off her jaw. The powerful blow knocked her off the men. She lay dazed a moment, cupping her jaw. By the time she was ready to jump back in, Cliff had Ed in a headlock. He brought up his other hand, placed it carefully, almost tenderly, against the side of Ed's face, then shoved with his hand while pulling with his arm. Ed's head pivoted around to the sound of grinding bones.

Cliff released Ed.

Ed's body slumped to the floor, dead.

"Jesus," Tory said. "Jesus."

Cliff leaned against the bed, sucking in ragged breaths. "You okay?"

"Jesus," Tory said.

"NOT A VERY GOOD START, Cliff," Stan said. He stepped over Ed Fawley's contorted body and sat on the edge of Tory's bed.

Cliff leaned against the antique oak dresser. "Not much choice."

"That's bullshit. You're a trained operative. You know how to disable without killing."

"I'm rusty."

Tory, dressed in jeans and sweatshirt, came in carrying gauze, adhesive tape and scissors. Cliff watched her walk, her movements a little stiff. She was trying to look and sound nonchalant, in total control of herself. "Ed's partner will be okay," she said. "He just hit his head when Cliff choked him out. The inside of his mouth's a little raw from where his braces cut him. I gave him some saltwater to rinse with."

"Thank you, Mrs. Fawley," Stan said.

"Call me Tory. I kept the last name because it was easy. All my friends knew me as Tory Fawley, not Victoria Meyer. First thing I do today is change it back."

Stan looked around at the mess. "First thing we do is call the Agency's disposal squad to haul Ed out of here. We don't want anybody knowing about this."

"You're too late," Lieutenant Godfrey said. He walked into the bedroom leading the redhead, who was handcuffed and wore a large bandage on his forehead.

"This is Lieutenant Godfrey," Cliff said to Stan.

"I'm a little disappointed," Godfrey said. "All you trained spies standing around in here while a slightly overweight common flatfoot waltzes in and surprises you."

Cliff picked up an atomizer from the dresser, sprayed the air, sniffed. It smelled slightly of cinnamon. "You followed me from my house over here, parked down the street behind the

Dodge van, the one with the surfer painted on the side. You entered the house about six minutes ago, waited for Tory to come in here, then cuffed Lucky here about three minutes ago. You've been listening outside the door for about two minutes." He picked up a different bottle and sniffed it.

"My, my," Godfrey said, smiling.

Stan turned on Cliff. "You knew he was out there the whole time? You called me in here without telling me security had been breached?"

"Whose security, Stan?" Cliff asked. "Ed's?"

"Knock it off, Remington."

"You forget, Stan, I have no more reason to trust you than I had to trust old Ed here. I figure the more witnesses, the better my chances of staying alive. Besides, Aaron will see to it that the lieutenant keeps his mouth shut. This is obviously a case of self-defense. But if something suddenly happened to me, well, maybe Lieutenant Godfrey might find it lucrative to call Mike Wallace at *60 Minutes*."

"Hey," the lieutenant beamed. "Me and Mike Wallace. Gee, you think?"

Stan looked back and forth at both men, his face grim. "I have a phone call to make." He stalked out of the room.

Godfrey shoved the lanky redhead out the door. "Why don't you go wait in the living room, son? Ponder your evil ways."

The redhead stumbled down the hall.

Godfrey leaned over Ed's body. "Nasty bit of work."

"He was even worse alive," Tory said.

Godfrey glanced up at Cliff. "What the hell was all the *60 Minutes* nonsense?"

"You wanted into this case. Now you're in."

The lieutenant rubbed his jaw thoughtfully. "Yeah, but what do I do now?"

"You write an account of everything you saw and heard, you sign it and leave copies with several people to be opened in event of your death. You make sure Aaron Leland knows about it."

"My God," Tory said. "You're even more paranoid than Ed was."

"Just do it, Lieutenant. I warned you to stay out of this."

"I guess I have no choice," Godfrey said.

"There's a lot of that going around."

20

CLIFF STUDIED Stan's walk as he returned from making his phone call followed by a quick stopover at the bathroom. The stance was a little hunched. Otherwise his stride was confident. Others Cliff had observed who had lost a hand or arm tended to list a little, favoring the damaged side protectively. Not Stan. Having a mechanical hook for a hand didn't seem to bother him. Cliff hadn't yet decided how much he could be trusted. Or was he just Aaron Leland's oracle?

Stan looked around the room. "Where's the detective?"

"Paperwork," Cliff said.

"I see. At your suggestion?"

Cliff shrugged.

"Your attitude is making this difficult, Cliff. None of what happened here tonight is the least bit important. Not compared to what's going on in Washington. And maybe Moscow."

Tory held up her hands. "Before you say anything else, what happens to me? I mean right now, tonight?"

"We'll send you away somewhere safe," Stan said.

Cliff laughed. Safe. The word itself made him laugh. Safe. He pictured himself playing baseball, rounding third base and heading for home as the ball spun over his head toward the catcher, a rotating globe orbiting the earth like a tiny moon, about to be stopped by a padded lump of leather and a man wearing a cage over his face. And Cliff was running, running, arms pumping, flying now as he started his dive toward home, arms outstretched, teeth clenched, eyes locked on the dusty white diamond, fingers reaching. Sliding facefirst, dust puffing up his nostrils as the catcher's glove thumped him in the back. Waiting for the umpire's call. Safe?

Earlier that evening, Cliff had stood in his house after Lieutenant Godfrey had gone and stared at the Colt. For a moment he had considered shoving the gun into his mouth and pulling the trigger. Eating the gun, they called it. The only sure way to make it home safe. The amount of revulsion and hate he felt wasn't directed at Aaron Leland or Vatican Towne or even at the mysterious security guard at the Carpathia Building. It was aimed at himself. Clifford Halsey Remington. Hotshot spy. Trained to protect, to defend, to kill when necessary. Within a few hours everyone he cared about had been killed and he had been helpless to prevent any of it. His uselessness, his inadequacy were too evident.

Then he had remembered Tory. He had forced her to help him track down her ex-husband. Perhaps Vatican Towne would think she was a friend of his and kill her too. Cliff saw his chance, one more time up at bat, one more opportunity to run for home. Arriving here, he had been surprised to find Ed Fawley, but also relieved. What if there had been no one? No threat. No opportunity.

"There is no safe place," Cliff said to Stan.

"Not so fast," Tory said. "I want to hear him out."

"Forget safe," Cliff said. "You're involved. It's too bad. You didn't know what you were getting into. Even Ed didn't know how big this was. But you're in now."

Tory flopped down on the bed. "Christ, I only wanted to see more of Karen. My God, what about Karen? I should tell her something. Say something about her father."

"We'll send someone," Stan said. "Give the family the killed-in-the-line-of-duty speech. Insurance money, pension until she's of age." Stan glared at Cliff. "Meantime, we've got plane reservations, Remington. Four hours from now we're in the air. Fawley and Dysert were supposed to go with us for backup. I'll have to arrange something on the way."

"No need," Cliff said. "Tory here is going along."

"Like hell I am!"

Stan shook his head. "Impossible."

Cliff walked over to Tory. He stood directly in front of her. She looked up into his eyes. "You won't be safe anywhere they send you. The man we're up against can find you. Believe me. You're safer with me."

Tory glanced down at the floor as if she couldn't face him. Her voice was faint. "No offense, Cliff. I mean, you did save my life tonight and all. It's just that, well, I wouldn't feel very safe around you. I mean, look what's happened to everyone you know."

"The same will happen to you if you stay behind." Cliff wasn't sure anymore if he even cared. He had saved her once, he had proved himself. But part of him thought about Tory and Ed's daughter, Karen. The possibility of the two of them being a family again. He would create what he had allowed to be destroyed. A family for a family. Balance the cosmic books.

Tory was staring up at him, her eyes shifting back and forth as she studied his face. She was looking for an answer, hoping to discover it in his eyes. Cliff knew the expression she wanted to see, the sincere look, the firm but liquid eyes. Undercover agents were mostly actors anyway. He adopted the look he knew she wanted.

"Okay," she said finally. "I'll go."

Cliff turned back to Stan. "We're ready."

Stan puffed up his chest as if he were about to argue, then let it all out in a deep sigh. "Okay, okay. There's no time for argument." He pulled out a small notebook and jotted something down. He tore the paper from the notebook and handed it to Cliff.

"Flight number and time of departure. I'll meet you there." He gestured at the room with his hook. "Meantime, get out of here so the disposal people can come in and do their work."

CLIFF POPPED A CAN of Hires Root Beer and set it on the nightstand. It was the only soft drink that the machine down the hall wasn't out of. He could smell the bubbles fizzing. His thoughts slid back to his boyhood when he and Tommy Springman used to peel the bark from birch trees and gnaw the juice from it. Same taste. Tommy was going to be an astronaut when he grew up. Cliff was going to be a doctor and be flown all over the world to perform operations no one else would do. Each time the operation would be successful and the patient's life would be saved. Later they'd thank him with tears in their eyes. When adults asked him what kind of doctor he wanted to be he would always answer, "A specialist."

"Just two hours of sleep. Please, God, that's all I ask," Tory said, coming out of the bathroom. She sat on the other twin bed, set the alarm and stretched out with a big yawn.

They'd driven up to L.A. and checked into the Travelodge near the airport. Tory had wanted a couple of hours' rest before the flight. Cliff had wanted to keep out of sight.

"What time should I set the alarm for?" she asked. "I mean, you want to have breakfast first, or go straight to the airport?"

"Airport," Cliff said.

"Okay."

Cliff lay back on top of the bedspread, his fingers laced behind his head. He stared at the Harvey Edwards dance poster on the wall. A pair of worn ballet slippers, tattered from use, stained with the sweat of dedication. Cliff had once felt that way about working for Graceland. Then he'd felt that way about Ginger and the kids. Now he felt nothing.

Almost an hour passed. He didn't look over, but he knew Tory was awake. "Why'd you do it?"

There was a long silence. Then, "Do what?"

"Agree to come along? You don't trust me to protect you, do you?"

"No."

"Then why come?"

"I don't know. I guess I owe you that much. You did save my life."

"That doesn't mean you owe me your life."

"In some cultures it does."

"Not this one. Definitely not this one."

"I guess not," Tory said. "Maybe I made a mistake."

"It's not too late to back out," Cliff told her. "Just walk out that door. You'll probably be better off." He frowned. "You'll definitely be better off."

Tory stood up, tugged her sweatshirt in place. She walked around her bed and sat on Cliff's bed, just inches away from him. "We made a contract."

"An oral contract."

"Still binding."

Cliff shook his head. "You were conned."

She stretched out next to him. "I know." Her arm rested on his chest.

For the first time since they'd been in the room, he looked at her. "I couldn't do anything now, not sexual. It's too soon. I think maybe it will always be too soon."

Tory tightened her grip on his chest. "This isn't sex, Cliff. It's human companionship. Sometimes there's a difference." She looked up at him. "You mind?"

He shook his head.

She smiled. "Good." She closed her eyes.

Cliff closed his eyes.

They lay there like that for two hours, each with closed eyes, each knowing the other was not asleep.

21

AARON LELAND watched the handsome, elegantly dressed man light the beautiful woman's cigarette. The lighter was gold, the cigarette was a thin dark brown stick, something European. She puffed, tilting her head back as she exhaled the gray smoke.

Like an old movie, Leland thought. A black-and-white movie—a *film noir*. All they needed was zither music.

Leland was sitting at the bar, a curved block of black wood that had the faces of all the presidents carved into its surface, which was then covered by thick glass. Each face was only the size of a fist, its likeness to the original was remarkable, though there was some debate whether Teddy Roosevelt looked more like Eleanor Roosevelt.

Leland sipped his Perrier with a wedge of lime, keeping his eye on the couple dining. They sat at a table large enough for four, but had chosen to sit next to each other at a corner rather than across. They leaned into each other, whispering, laughing. Leland watched the woman's hand slip under the white tablecloth. From the wicked look on her face, he knew where her hand had landed. The man, however, continued to smile without any noticeable reaction.

The woman was an actress, famous for her continuing role as an indefatigable bitch on an afternoon soap opera with a medical setting. Leland had never seen the show, but her face stared at him from supermarket tabloids all the time. She had black hair and full black eyebrows. Her low-cut dress was also black. Her skin was surprisingly pale, as if powdered with flour. Her only color came from the bright red lipstick, thick as paste, on her full lips. Even in a restaurant renowned for its famous patrons, she had the other diners staring.

"Another, sir?" the young bartender asked. His accent was stiffly British, though Leland suspected it was phony, affected to add atmosphere and to elicit bigger tips. Leland had spent enough time in London with Cliff and Drew to recognize the real thing.

"Yes, another," he said. He looked at his watch. The phone message had said to be here at 11:30 p.m. That had been half an hour ago.

Leland realized his shawl cardigan sweater and penny loafers looked a little out of place here amid the expensive suits and silk ties. Some thought he affected this look just as the bartender affected his British accent. For effect. The cool casual head in a sea of political ulcers. The truth was, he reflected, that he'd been wearing the same style of clothing since the seminary. The penny loafers had been cheap to buy and a convenient place to keep two dimes in case he needed to make emergency phone calls. The shawl-collared cardigan had just as practical an origin: with icy regularity a chill breeze had swept through his study cubicle on the second floor of the library. Turning up the collar on the sweater had kept his neck warm.

"Waiting long?"

Leland turned. The elegantly dressed man he'd been watching leaned against the bar next to him. Beneath the glass surface the carved face of Grover Cleveland stared up at them through a Perrier and lime monocle. Leland looked over his shoulder, saw the actress walking toward the rest rooms. Even her walk was a performance. He turned his attention back to the man. "Doesn't it ever get confusing?"

"What do you mean?"

"Out as a man one night, a woman the next."

"It's a living."

Leland was surprised. "She's an assignment?"

Charon laughed. "Constance? No, she's a cover. I can use her to get into certain parties. Washington parties—that's where I do most of my work."

"You hear about Eli Schwartz?"

"The industrialist?"

Leland frowned at him. "Yes, the 'industrialist.' Murdered. In a hotel room bed."

Charon shrugged. "Police will catch the killer. I have faith in D.C.'s law enforcement."

"Why are we meeting here?" Leland asked impatiently. "This isn't exactly private."

"That's the point. I didn't want to meet someplace your spooks might try to mess up my suit."

"For God's sake, Charon, you're working for me now. Why would I jeopardize your safety?"

"Why indeed."

Aaron Leland fished the lime wedge from his drink and, though it had been squeezed already, squeezed it again, grinding wet green pulp onto the ice cubes. "Perhaps this is not the best time to discuss business. You have a guest."

"I have insurance. Nothing messy while I'm with her or there'll be newspeople sniffing up your shorts."

"There is no insurance in this business, Charon. You know that."

Charon smiled, his face so open and charming and handsome that people often wondered if he too was a movie star whose name they couldn't remember. "You're angry about Los Angeles."

"You made quite a mess."

"I followed orders."

"Not exactly. You were to kill Remington's wife, not his entire family. And arranging them that way." He made a face. "That wasn't necessary."

"You didn't specify method, only results. You wanted Remington angry enough to agree to hunt down Vatican

Towne. Had I only killed his wife, he might have felt compelled to stay home and guard the children. Therefore, it was necessary to eliminate them also. Even then I couldn't be sure he'd go after Towne. Some men who lose their families fold, blame themselves and either commit suicide or vegetate. I had to make it a grotesque challenge." Charon's smile widened. "So you see, everything was planned. Professional. None of the sadistic improvising you thought."

"You're quite the psychologist."

"It worked, didn't it?"

"Remington has agreed to help."

"Then you owe me a bonus. As agreed."

"Already paid into your account."

Charon tapped the glass over Grover Cleveland's face. "You know, he lost the 1888 election to Benjamin Harrison, even though he had a larger popular vote? So much for democracy."

Leland looked toward the rest rooms.

"She won't be back for quite a while. She loves that demon white powder, loses all track of time when she snorts."

"You supply her?"

"Gratis. As a friend."

"For which you receive invitations to parties."

Charon still smiled, but his eyes narrowed angrily. "For which I receive nothing. You want to know if we sleep together, right?"

Leland shook his head. "I don't really care."

"Sure you do, Aaron. Everyone is curious how I do it. Yes, we do sleep together. We fuck like ... Well, I was going to say like you and everybody else. But I don't really know about you. Washington gossip never puts you with anyone, male or female. And you don't own any pets, so that can't be it."

"You're straying from business," Leland said casually.

"You don't rattle, Aaron. I like that about you."

"You can't imagine how much that means to me."

Charon laughed. "Okay, I'm listening."

"We have a lead on Vatican Towne. One of our field agents stumbled across it by accident."

"And you want me to do what?"

Leland shook his head. "Not here."

Charon studied Leland, sighed. He gestured for the bartender.

"Yes, sir?" the bartender asked.

Charon handed him two hundred-dollars bills. "When Constance Ryan returns to that table, I want you to tell her I was called away unexpectedly. I also want you to phone a limo to pick her up and take her home. A limo, pal, not a cab. Understand?"

"Yes, sir."

"Keep what's left over."

"Thank you, sir."

The two men walked out of the fancy restaurant and continued down the dark street. Leland was much taller, but he was surprised to notice how similar their build was, the way they walked, stiff-backed with correct posture.

"More wet work, right?"

"Yes," Leland nodded.

"Aside from Vatican Towne, who?"

Leland had just finished talking to Stan. Everything in Los Angeles was going to hell. Ed Fawley had been killed. No great loss—he had served his purpose in clearing his sector of the stray Junkyard Dogs that wouldn't be useful. Leland had only used him in the first place because he was a marginal agent with a record of foul-ups that could be used to prove he was acting on his own if it came to that. But now Cliff insisted on bringing along a former agent, Fawley's wife. Her records indicated she'd spent her brief tenure in recruitment, totally unsuited for the work Cliff had to do. A Lieutenant Godfrey was nosing around, despite his department's agreement to lay off the case. Here in Washington, Fat Boy was almost totally incapacitated. The experts admitted there was nothing they could do. Within three days, the computer would be totally shut down. He had to move now, move fast. He knew why Vatican Towne was doing this. The Junkyard Dog file. Vatican had never been able to see the importance of that group, the potential. He played according to some corny rule book that was completely unrealistic.

But that was about to change. Cavanaugh had been captured. That would make the rest of the Junkyard Dogs easier to handle when they went into action tomorrow. If the operation was successful, the president would finally get off his back. Also, a sharp agent had picked up on some rumors, and it looked like they'd found Vatican Towne's hideout. Cliff and Stan were on their way there now.

"Must be quite a list," Charon said during the silence.

"What?"

"Your death list. Checking it twice to see who's been naughty or nice?"

Leland didn't respond. They kept walking.

"Tell me about it, Aaron."

Leland looked at him. "What?"

"I don't know exactly what's going on, but I know it's got to be huge, tremendous. Vatican Towne was the best intelligence man ever. God, he was the last American hero. This Remington guy had a pretty good reputation too until he burned out. That London incident. You were involved in that, weren't you, Aaron?"

Leland stopped at the curb, pressed the button for the traffic light. No point in saying anything; Charon already knew the answer.

"Anyway," Charon continued, "the way I see it, you've got a hell of a problem on your hands. Something even your own guys don't know about. I've checked around a little. Your ass is hanging over the edge, Aaron. You've got everybody going in different directions. Only way to pull that off is to tell each person a different story. They can't all be true.'' Charon shrugged. ''What happens when they start comparing notes? You'd better have someone backing you up. Someone who knows the whole story.''

''Someone like you.''

''I'll leave that to your discretion.''

Leland watched the cars glide slowly by like sluggish over-fed slugs. Pedestrians walked with a clipped suspicious pace, fearful. That wasn't right. People should be able to walk slowly, enjoy the outdoors, the advantages of a city like Washington. Or even a small town in Ohio. But the world wasn't like that anymore. Americans feared the darkness, feared one another, feared themselves. It was up to someone to save them, redeem them from what they had become. The president was powerless, mired in politics. But Aaron Leland could make a difference. Truly make this country what it only dreamed of becoming. He never spoke to anyone about his personal vision. Once back in the seminary, he had mentioned to another novice that he intended to make a difference, make people feel safe again. The other boy, Martin Andrews, had suggested he become a cop. ''You've read *The Catcher in the Rye* too often,'' Martin had teased. That had been five months before the incident that caused Leland to resign.

Since then, he had kept his vision to himself. No one understood what this was all about. This was a Holy Crusade, the same as those of the eleventh and twelfth centuries. The capture of Cyprus and Acre, the sacking of Constantinople, the fall of Tripoli. But in the end, the crusaders had failed.

Aaron Leland would not.

He sensed Charon's anxiety next to him as they walked. Charon was the epitome of everything he despised. Worse than immoral, he was amoral. Though his physical malady was surgically correctable, he preferred to use it to entrap rather than to live a healthy normal life. The man, if he indeed could be called that, was as much the enemy as the Soviets and the Arabs. He was evil, satanic.

Leland liked the idea of using him to make his plan succeed. Perhaps he would confide in him, tell him all, knowing Charon would scheme for some way to use the information against him. By the time he figured out a scheme, the Junkyard Dogs would have acted, Vatican Towne would be destroyed and Charon too would be eliminated. Yes, the more he thought of it, the more he liked the idea of confiding in the man he most despised. It reminded him of the Book of Job. Leland as God, Charon as Satan. And Cliff as Job.

"You really want to know?" Leland asked.

"Isn't that Senator Baxter?"

A limo drove by, the licence plates familiar. "Yes."

"Only if you want to tell me."

"You're smooth."

"I'm what you want me to be, Aaron."

Leland told him everything.

Toward the end of the Vietnam War, Aaron Leland had been running a group of agents in Saigon. Reports had begun circulating about a squad of American Marines who were attacking their own troops, killing them, then mutilating the bodies in unspeakable ways. There was no proof, but panic was spreading through the forces. No one was sure whom to trust. Charles Devane, head of the whole Southeast Asia CIA operation, and Vatican Towne called Leland in. Towne had no official status, but everyone knew he had more power than the director of the CIA. He had the confidence of the president and the military. What he said went. He assigned Leland to find out the truth about this renegade Marine squad.

Leland had trekked through the jungles. His men had questioned villagers, and not always by the rulebook. Leland was never present at such interrogations, but before he left, he made sure any villager who'd been questioned had been generously rewarded, whether he'd talked or not. Sometimes

Leland had to use his own money. In some cases, only the relatives of the villager survived to receive the reward. Eventually, Leland found some answers.

He informed Vatican Towne of the location of the troops. Whether they were American soldiers, he didn't know. Why they were doing what they were doing, he also didn't know.

The location of the troops was just north of the DMZ. Towne, already in his sixties, accompanied the troops that raided the camp. Leland was there too.

What they found horrified them all.

Thirty-eight POWs. Kids no more than eighteen and nineteen who'd been captured, tortured and brainwashed. Not the usual military brainwashing procedures. Two specialists had been brought in from the Soviet Union who'd set up laboratories and mazelike huts whose purpose the liberators could only guess at.

When the troops had killed the guards and confronted the American boys, they did not receive cheers of gratitude. Each boy was naked, caged alone, eating the bugs he picked off his own body. Combat-hardened soldiers were afraid to open the cages to let these boys out.

It got worse.

Information was difficult to piece together from the POWs. This was a blitz maneuver and required that they all hurry back south of the DMZ. The caged boys were released, clothed as well as was possible, but chained together for the march back. After a few weeks in military prison hospital, a few of them responded to interrogation. Vatican Towne led the questioning. Charles Devane and Leland were the only observers.

Some of the boys had managed to kill themselves in the hospital. A few had killed each other. Three had jumped a guard and disemboweled him before escaping. They were shot during the escape.

By then they'd picked up the name the Junkyard Dogs.

The first of the group to become somewhat lucid was their leader, Timothy Cavanaugh. Drugged and bound, he told them what had happened as best he could, lapsing into incoherent mumblings at times, other times weeping uncontrollably.

He told how each of the members of the group had been hand-selected from other POW camps and sent to this special one. They were all young, healthy, strong. The first day they were lined up and the two Soviet doctors walked down the line, studying each man, conferring in Russian, making notes. Behind them walked a Vietcong officer with his gun drawn. Occasionally the Soviet doctors would agree that a particular prisoner was not suitable for reasons no one was sure of. They would point at him and the Vietcong officer would immediately shoot the boy in the head. Five Marines were shot that first day.

After that came the usual torture. They were deprived of sleep and food, locked in separate cages, naked, with not even a bucket for a toilet. Drugs were administered several times a day. Verbal and physical tests were given. They weren't allowed to communicate with each other. The first soldier who defied that order, Glenn Downing, had his tongue cut out. The tongue was fed to a camp dog while Glenn watched, screaming.

After that, no one spoke. A couple of boys used sign language. Their fingers were cut off, and they bled to death. After that, everyone did exactly as he was told. Still, things got worse. The Soviet doctors were trying to completely destroy any sense of personal identity, any loyalties. They wanted mindless zombies who would follow orders.

That was when they used The Cave.

Those who had survived the months of abuse were introduced to the final test. The doctors agreed that it was guaranteed to destroy any lingering shred of human decency, any sense of ego. Cavanaugh, speech slurred by the drugs, admitted to Vatican Towne that at the time he hadn't believed they could do anything worse. He was wrong.

The Cave was really a room. A small musty room with no windows, no furniture. After a week of no food or water, two boys were thrown inside, the door bolted behind them. There was no light. They were told they must remain inside for another week, without food or drink. After that, only one of them would leave. The survivor.

At this point in the interrogation, the men in the room all exchanged looks. Towne's voice was steady, but Leland could sense a softening in it toward Cavanaugh, but also a timbre of outrage.

Cavanaugh continued. The idea, he'd said, was to try to kill each other, then live off the dead man's carcass. The first two men into The Cave had not attacked each other. When their time was up, they crawled out into the sunlight and were beheaded. The next two went in. Corporal Singer managed to kill Private Pomada, but he couldn't bring himself to touch the dead body afterward. He too was beheaded. The next two were different. Sergeant Esterhaus killed Corporal Grimaldi, drank the blood and ate almost a whole leg before he was released. When he came out he was given cooked food, medical treatment, fresh water. It wasn't necessary. Stepping out into the sunlight that first moment, squinting up at the sun, he'd looked stronger and healthier than he had since it all started. After that, it had seemed easier for everyone. Almost a game. Who would survive?

Cavanaugh had strangled a Private Mengers and eaten a leg and buttock before being released.

The Soviet doctors had known their jobs. Following The Cave, the men had lost any sense of self. No one felt as if he could go back home. Most felt resentment and hatred that the United States had allowed this to happen to them. The rest was simple. Dress them in their old uniforms. Give them unloaded weapons. Dress some of the Cong in American uniforms with loaded weapons. Go in and kill some American troops, mutilate the bodies and send chaos through the whole American military.

Vatican Towne had sent the Cavanaugh boy back to the hospital. When the three of them were alone, he said, "You know what we face here?"

Devane nodded. "Hell of a publicity problem."

"What we just heard never leaves this room. Never. Am I clear?"

"There are files," Leland pointed out. "Records for each man."

"We confiscate them. I want these boys cared for. I want everything possible done for them to bring them back to whoever they were."

"It's too late for some of them," Devane said.

"Then we care for them for the rest of their lives. We split them all up, send them to different hospitals so no one sees a pattern. The doctors will receive explanations that will neutralize anything these boys might tell them. We'll emphasize the drugs they were given, hallucinogens. Their names will be changed, their locations known only to me. Everything gets fed into Fat Boy with a code word lock on it. Only that code word can access the file. Only I will have the code."

Leland had got up from his metal folding chair, walked over and sat down in the chair Cavanaugh had used. He felt Cavanaugh's body heat, the dampness of sweat that had soaked through Cavanaugh's hospital pajamas onto the chair. It was oddly thrilling. "You know the military will ask questions."

"That's true, Vatican," Devane said. "They'll insist on knowing what happened."

"We'll lie," Vatican said. "Anything else?"

There was silence. Finally Leland spoke. "We might as well say it now." Leland glanced over at Devane for support, but Devane quickly looked out the window. Leland faced Vatican Towne's grim face. "The thing is, however cruel and sadistic this whole operation has been, those Soviet scientists might have been on to something. Something of military value here."

Towne sat back in his chair, his hands steepled in front of him. "Go on, Aaron."

"Agreed they went to inhuman excess, but the principles are still sound. Methods of training the ultimate hit squad. Certainly it's worth studying. Perhaps keep these boys together for observation. Maybe even send them on a mission together, just to see what happens. These Junkyard Dogs are completely fearless, completely ruthless."

Vatican Towne stood slowly as if he had to lift the weight of each of those boys with him. "I don't ever want to hear that term used again. By anyone. And I don't want to hear even a rumor of what happened here today or with those boys." He glared at Aaron in such a way that Leland knew if word leaked out, Towne would not hesitate to have him or Devane assassinated.

Devane had died eight years later of stomach cancer. Leland had never told anyone. Until now.

It had taken all these years and special new cryptography computers that Vatican Towne could not foresee to break the code to that file. Once Leland had accessed the file, he began gathering the former Junkyard Dogs. Some were freed from sanitoriums, their departure made to look like escape. Some had been cured and released but were anxious to join up again. Others didn't want to come. They had had to be terminated. With the exception of Cavanaugh. He was needed to give the six men recruited some sense of order. They still trusted him. They could never truly trust anyone who hadn't been in The Cave.

Leland had arranged for them to be housed and trained on an Arizona military base. Separate from everyone else. They were drilled back into physical shape, taught to use the latest weapons, their ruthlessness encouraged. With the help of drugs and some civilized refinements on the Soviet doctors' theories, the Junkyard Dogs were the craziest, meanest bastards to ever carry a gun. And tomorrow, they would prove themselves.

"RATHER LIKE *Lord of the Flies*," Charon remarked. "Ever read *Lord of the Flies*, Aaron?"

"Tomorrow they attack and wipe out a nest of Libyan terrorists hiding out in this country."

"And if anything happens to them, they can't be traced back to you or the CIA or the government. Media will probably brand them as mercenaries and start interviewing G. Gordon Liddy to see if they work for him."

"I don't intend to lose them," Leland said sternly. "These men are getting a chance to set themselves straight and help their country at the same time. Redemption, Charon. It's the best medicine."

Charon stopped walking and looked Leland in the eye. "My God, I think you actually believe what you're saying. You're doing this genuinely out of patriotism, aren't you, Aaron?"

Leland looked away, embarrassed. "What difference does it make to you?"

"None. None at all. As long as I get paid."

They started walking again. Leland raised the collar of his sweater against the chilly night air.

"So once you accessed the file, you must have set off some kind of electronic alarm that Vatican Towne had programmed for certain files when the computer was first installed. Fat Boy probably called him right up on the damn telephone. That's how he knew what they were up to. Jesus, that's great." He laughed. "He had the computer electronically mined just in case someone got some fancy ideas about using those boys again. He probably had the same arrangement for all his supersensitive files. But now that he's out of the game, he doesn't have much influence in government, so he uses his home computer to close down the CIA. Boy, I'd hate to be having your nightmares right now, Aaron."

"The point is, we've located Towne. Remington will draw him out of hiding. You inform me of the exact location and I'll send in the Junkyard Dogs to mop it up. Stan should be able to get Towne to reverse the computer. If not, our experts will be able to do it from there easily enough."

"Which brings me back to your hit list. Who goes, who lives to share in the great reward of your success?"

Leland took out a folded piece of paper from his pocket. His fingers were cold, but not from the air. This was the part he loathed. But there was no choice. He had the whole country to think about, not just these individuals. He handed the list to Charon. "Here are the names."

Charon studied the list, grinning. "A cop, huh? Lieutenant Godfrey. Victoria Fawley. Cliff Remington—that should be fun. Oh, my goodness, even Standish Ford. That's a surprise."

Leland picked up his stride, but Charon kept pace. Stan was probably Aaron Leland's closest friend, though Stan might be surprised to hear that. Leland had truly hoped to make Stan his eventual successor. There was no one else he trusted or respected as much. Leland had no family, no lovers. He was not homosexual, as Charon had snidely implied. He was celibate. He had been since joining the seminary. Just because he'd left, he hadn't lost discipline or faith. He'd merely rechanneled his energy and focus to bring as much of heaven to earth as was possible. It was a sign of his deep commitment that he was willing to sacrifice Stan, his best friend, toward that goal.

Charon's hand on Leland's arm stopped him for a moment.

"I'll do this for you, Aaron. One, because you will pay me a lot of money, enough to retire on finally. And two, because I'm intrigued by the sordidness of it all. Perhaps in your evangelistic zeal you've made a convert out of me."

"This kind of talk is pointless."

Charon's eyes narrowed on Leland. "One small caveat, Aaron. Make sure my name does not end up on a list like this. You'd be surprised how hard it is to kill me."

"Of course."

Charon grabbed Leland's right hand and jerked him. Leland tried to pull back but Charon's strength was terrific. Leland could feel the elastic belt flattening the breast, but he could also feel the slight swell of flesh over the edge of the elastic. He cringed, but Charon pressed his hand hard against the breast.

"You have no one left to kill me, Aaron. Once they're all gone, who will do it? Perhaps another free-lancer? Takata from Japan? Luntz from Germany?"

Leland pulled at his hand. "Stop this."

Charon held firm. People passing by glanced nervously at them. "When they fail, and you know they will, I would have to come and kill you. Then what would happen to your holy cause, Aaron?"

He released the hand, which Leland immediately shoved into his pocket, scrubbing it against the pocket fabric. Leland had no intention of hiring someone to kill Charon. He would do that himself.

Charon cupped his hand under Leland's elbow and guided him down the sidewalk, two old friends chatting and strolling.

"I'll catch a flight tonight and be on Remington's tail by morning. As soon as I know anything I'll call you. Good luck tomorrow with your Junkyard Dogs." He smiled hugely. "After all, we're partners now. Right, Aaron?"

22

YURI DANZIGKOV dipped his handkerchief in the stream of water from the drinking fountain and tamped the wet cloth against his eyes. They still burned from all the cigar, cigarette and pipe smoke he'd been exposed to in the small room down the corridor. The room was filled with the most powerful men in the Soviet Union. Generals, party leaders, head of the KGB, politicos. Yuri had testified to the fact that the PAW satellites appeared dead in space and that there was some odd movement among top CIA officials, and had stated his own conclusion that there was indeed an opportunity to launch a limited attack on the United States immediately with a reasonable assurance of winning. Minimal damage and population loss, comparatively little radiation contamination. It would all be over so quickly, even the Chinese would be too late to interfere.

Yuri wet the handkerchief again and pressed it against his eyes, some of the water dripping from the cloth and running down the sides of his nose, over his lips and into his mouth. He licked his lips. Those were the facts, that was his professional analysis of the situation. But he hoped to the depths of his soul that they decided against attacking the United States. He pictured millions of burning bodies, smoking carcasses piled twenty feet high, thousands of survivors permanently blinded from the flash of the explosions running screaming into the streets, crying for their families. Yuri pressed the soggy handkerchief harder against his eyes until they ached.

The door down the corridor opened and the men began to slowly drift out, still arguing. Big lumpy bodies in drab, ill-fitting suits or military uniforms bumped against one another like billiard balls. General Kerensky, Yuri's direct superior, was among them, listening intently to Peter Mikhaylovich, General Secretary Gorbachev's most trusted adviser.

Yuri looked away. These men did not like to be stared at from a distance. It made them feel as if they were being watched. In Moscow, one adopted a bored, uninterested appearance when passing others, as if whatever they were doing or saying could be of no importance. Otherwise, one might find oneself being investigated because someone else suspected one was investigating him.

On the wall next to the drinking fountain was an old dark painting of Boris Godunov, who had had himself declared czar in 1598. Well-known for his chicanery, he'd cleverly married his sister off to Ivan the Terrible's idiot son. Ivan had murdered his eldest son in a fit of rage in 1581, so when Ivan died, power passed to the idiot son, Fyodor. Thanks to the arranged marriage, Godunov succeeded him. Despite his own ruthlessness, Godunov was not a bad leader and remained in control until the appearance of the False Dmitri, a defrocked monk who appeared in Poland and proclaimed himself the son of Ivan IV. The real Dmitri had died ten years earlier during an epileptic seizure. Gathering support among the Cossaks and the disaffected gentry, the imposter built a small army. Godunov's troops quickly defeated them, but ironically Godunov died a few weeks later. A coup overthrew Godunov's family and the False Dmitri ruled.

Yuri reached out and brushed his fingertips across the painting. All the colors were dark, the thick robes, the dismal background. The only brightness came from Godunov's face and eyes, as if he was Russia's only hope for light.

"It is nice they have permitted the old paintings again," General Kerensky said, clapping a hand on Yuri's shoulder. "Not as celebration of such men, of course. But as a warning."

Yuri nodded, pocketing his damp handkerchief. The False Dmitri was a defrocked monk who'd lied about his parentage, been defeated on the battlefield, but still had gone on to rule Russia. What lesson could one learn from that except that life was absurd?

The general guided Yuri farther down the corridor. They walked quickly, their military hard heels snapping a solemn cadence against the polished tile floor.

Yuri wanted to ask what decision had been reached, but he knew better. The general would not be rushed, certainly not until they were out of hearing range of the others.

Finally, in the stairwell, General Kerensky stopped walking long enough to light up his pipe. He puffed furiously until it was lit, then sucked in deep lungfuls of smoke, exhaling slowly and reluctantly. "It was a greater war in that room than any we might fight with the Americans."

"Who won?"

The general smiled sadly. "Won? What a curious notion, winning."

Yuri waited in silence.

"Naturally I spoke against the attack, as did General Mniszech and General Golitsyn. We pointed out that there might be an error in our readings of the PAW satellites."

"Doubtful, sir," Yuri said.

"Yes, I know, but possible. Even so, there are other explanations for our readings. The U.S. might be conducting tests, or they've switched to another power source we haven't located." He waved his pipe in the air to indicate other unmentioned possibilities. "But more important, even a limited strike would cause great devastation. We would have to send enough troops to secure the entire country. That would leave our own borders along Europe and China weakened. We would have to worry Europe and China might attack us then. So, should we attack them at the same time we attack the U.S.?

Where would we find enough troops to secure America, China and Europe?''

Yuri watched the general relight his pipe. The lingering smoke burned his eyes, but he did not take out his handkerchief.

''The politicos, however, advised that we attack immediately. They are war hungry, with visions of becoming provisional rulers of our newly conquered territories. They have no knowledge of the actual details of war. The stench of burning flesh as we incinerate the corpses to prevent diseases that will run rampant anyway. The civilian politicos think it is like a film. Declare war, then cut to a vision of them sitting in the White House signing orders.''

Yuri studied the general's face, the mixture of horror, disgust and compassion. Most citizens would have assumed the military men would most want a war, a chance to finally do combat. But in reality it was the military, those who had looked upon the face of war before, who advocated peace. ''What now?'' Yuri asked.

The general shrugged and started down the stairs. ''We wait. No decision has been reached. Gorbachev will decide, maybe today, maybe tomorrow.'' The general gave Yuri a sad smile. ''Perhaps by tomorrow we dine in Washington.''

PART FOUR:

THE DOGS IN THE YARD

23

"ALOHA KAKOU!" the young girl behind the car rental counter said cheerfully. "That means 'Greetings, everyone.'"

"Mahalo Nui," Cliff said.

Her smile brightened by a couple of hundred watts. "You speak Hawaiian?"

"Uuku," he said. "A little. Just tourist phrases."

"I'm just learning myself," she said. She was a pretty girl, hair so blond it was almost white, and skinny to the point of bony. Maybe twenty. "I've only been here two months. I came here to learn how to surf. You know, I grew up in Huntington Beach where just about everyone surfs. But I never learned. Then when I was ready, it was too embarrassing to go there and fall on my face in front of all my friends. So me and my girlfriend, Cheryl, came over here to Kauai, got an apartment in Lihue and got jobs."

"Get any surfing done?" Cliff asked.

She shrugged. "Not much. Not yet. But some."

Stan pushed ahead of Cliff and Tory, pulling the car reservations from his jacket. He was pale and looked miserable. He'd spent half the flight in the rest room, the other half strapped in his seat trying to doze. Tory and Cliff had secretly made a bet as to how many times he would go to the rest room before the flight was over. Once Stan had gotten up, hurried down the aisle, stopped halfway, then returned to his seat. Tory claimed that should be counted as a trip, but Cliff insisted it was merely a false alarm and since he did not actually enter the rest room, should not be counted. They'd argued about it to kill time until the movie started. Tory watched the film. Cliff had his headphones on, but listened to the classical music station because they had Wynton Marsalis playing "Eternal Source of Light Divine" from Handel's *Birthday Ode for Queen Anne*. Stan had lain back, eyes drowsy but staring at the movie, so that Cliff had been surprised to notice the earphones were set not on the movie channel, but on the same channel as Cliff's.

"If you'll wait right over there—" the young girl pointed with a chipped and gnawed fingernail "—the van will take you over to your car."

"It's not here?" Stan said miserably. He glanced in the direction of the airport bathroom.

"Just a short hop to our car barn," she smiled. "Less than two miles."

"You'll make it," Tory said, patting Stan's arm.

Stan nodded and the three of them, each carrying a small tote bag, trooped over to the waiting van.

"*Mahalo nui*." The blond girl waved.

"*Kipa mai*," Cliff said.

"Show-off," Tory said.

A helicopter lifted off a couple of hundred yards away. Tory shaded her eyes with her hand and watched it float upward, then dart off like a bee.

"Best way to see the island," Cliff said. "Take you down into Waimea Canyon. It's like the Land That Time Forgot."

"I don't like helicopters," Tory said. "I don't even like planes or jets. I barely tolerate elevators."

"There are parts of this island you can't see any other way."

"I'll buy postcards. When were you here last anyway?"

"His honeymoon," Stan said.

Cliff felt his neck get hot. He was angry, though not surprised, that Stan knew about that trip with Ginger. He'd been out of Graceland by then. Even Moonshadow was over. But they still kept tabs on him. He and Ginger had chosen Kauai for their honeymoon because it was so remote, the vegetation lush, the tourism minimal. It was the only island Cliff and

Drew had not been on during their one assignment in Hawaii. Ginger had gripped his arm in panic that entire bumpy twenty-five minute flight from Honolulu to Kauai, leaving five crescent fingernail marks in his arm when they'd landed. As Cliff thought of her now, his stomach clenched and knotted. He missed her.

Cliff and Tory squeezed into the van next to Stan, because all the other seats were taken.

"I think there's still a kidney you haven't crushed," he said grumpily to Tory.

Once at the car barn, Stan signed all the papers and they climbed into their compact Toyota. Stan tossed the keys to Cliff. "You drive."

Stan gave directions without consulting any maps or notes.

"You been here before?" Tory asked him.

"Never," he replied. Then he pointed and said, "Turn left there."

Cliff followed instructions and turned down Maluhia Road and knew they were heading toward the resort area of Poipu Beach. On either side of the car, huge ten-foot green plants dominated the fields, growing up and over knolls all the way to the base of the mountains.

"What's that," Tory asked.

"Sugarcane," Stan and Cliff said simultaneously.

"It's the island's main industry," Cliff continued.

"I thought tourism was."

"Not compared to Maui and Oahu. There's very little development on this island. Several fancy resorts and the usual tourist sight-seeing, but people come to Kauai to get away from it all. This is about as close as you're going to get to how Hawaii once looked."

Suddenly the road and the car were canopied by a mile-long tunnel formed by giant eucalyptus trees that stretched over the road, their branches intertwining like clasped fingers.

"My God," Tory said. "This is magnificent."

"You've been to Hawaii before," Stan said from the back seat. "You were sent here on recruitment assignment."

"Years ago. And I only stayed in Honolulu. To tell you the truth, I didn't know why everyone was always going on about Hawaii. Honolulu was pretty much like L.A. In fact, L.A. has nicer beaches. God, Honolulu beaches are about as wide as my hips. No jokes, thank you." She rolled down the window and stuck her head out. "But this is magnificent."

"You're letting the air conditioning out," Stan complained.

Tory rolled the window back up and glared at him with annoyance. "So this is what it's like to be on assignment with top agents. Jesus, what a thrill."

Stan sighed. "Sorry, I'm still fighting the Mexican terrorists in my stomach. They keep dynamiting my intestines."

"I know what'll help," Tory said. She leaned over the seat and, with great ceremonial flourish, clapped her hands together hard and rubbed them against each other as if she were scrubbing them. Then she quickly pressed them against Stan's stomach. At first Stan recoiled, reached to pull her hands away. But then he just sat back and relaxed. "That help?"

"Actually, it does feel better. What is that, some kind of chiropractic technique?"

"I don't know," she said, turning back in her seat. "I saw it in *The Karate Kid*. When the old man fixes the kid's leg."

Cliff laughed aloud. The sound startled him, coming from his own throat that way, an unexpected emotion. Out of the corner of his eye he could see Tory, and in the rearview mirror Stan, looking at him, just as startled. "Koloa Town ahead," he said.

Stan pointed. "Turn left on Koloa Road, then left on Poipu Road."

Tory gestured at the row of brightly painted wooden shops and restaurants. "Look at this place, will you. Like something out of the Old West."

"Except for the souvenir shops and pizza joints," Cliff said.

"I liked you better laughing," Tory said. "The buildings are so, I don't know, quaint. Like everyone's dream of the perfect small town. That's what this place looks like, a hometown. The hometown that people wish they were from and could go back to visit."

Stan stirred in the back seat. "This is where Hawaii's first sugar plantation was established in 1835. Koloa Plantation. This town grew up around that plantation."

"I thought you'd never been here," Tory said.

"I haven't. I read, I remember." He tapped his hook on Cliff's shoulder. "Pull over there."

Cliff followed Stan's instructions and wheeled the car into a parking lot in front of the wooden sidewalk of the row of buildings.

"Is this where we're staying?" Tory asked.

"No." Stan climbed out of the car and dashed into Lappert's Aloha Ice Cream Store. Cliff looked at Tory, she grinned and they followed him inside. Stan was already licking a cone. "Best medicine," he said, rubbing his tender stomach.

The three of them returned to the car, each clutching a cone.

"Here they come to save the world," Tory said, a smudge of Rocky Road on her chin. "Spybusters."

CLIFF WALKED ACROSS the living room to the glass sliding doors and pulled the drapes open.

"Incredible!" Tory said, staring.

Cliff and Tory gazed out through the glass across the half acre of perfectly manicured grass and patches of lush tropical garden near the other condominiums, straight to the sandy strip of white beach and beyond that, the turquoise ocean.

Stan ignored the view and went straight for the telephone. He spoke in quiet murmurs that Cliff didn't bother trying to overhear. He'd be told soon enough. Instead he gazed out at the ocean and wondered how much longer Ginger would be getting into her bikini and loading the camera. He loved it when they went snorkeling together. He was about to shout, "Hurry up, honey," when he caught himself just in time, turned, saw Tory staring enraptured at the view, saw Stan hunched secretively over the phone, his hook tapping on the phone stand.

Cliff sat on the sofa and looked up at the ceiling fan, the blades spinning lazily but methodically. He noticed when he glanced away quickly, the blades seemed to freeze in place and he could see each one separately. He continued testing his theory, darting his eyes back and forth while Stan mumbled into the phone and Tory raved about the view. He tuned both of them out, concentrating on the importance of his discovery, not permitting any thoughts of Ginger to creep back in. Perhaps this astute observation was one of those breakthroughs in science that would lead to greater things. Like discovering that mold was medicine.

Tory flopped on the sofa next to him. "I hope Mike's all right. That bump Ed gave him didn't look too good. Still, Kenny Hanes promised to check on him at the vet's every day."

"Kenny seemed like a reliable sort," Cliff said.

Tory gave him a sharp look. "He's not a bad man. And he's a hell of a lawyer."

"Don't forget stamina."

"Fuck off."

Cliff went back to his ceiling fan and Tory went to the bathroom.

Stan hung up the phone and sat in the chair next to the sofa.

"You bastards," Tory said, returning from the bathroom, scrubbing her chin with a wet washcloth. "Weren't either of you going to tell me I had ice cream on my face?"

"Not me." Cliff looked at Stan. "How about you?"

"Sit down," Stan said to Tory. "I just spoke to the agent who first picked up on Vatican Towne's location. We've got to see some local kid named Kyle Young. Apparently he's willing to sell us Towne's exact whereabouts."

"How much?" Cliff asked.

"Twenty-five thousand dollars."

"Cheap. He probably could've gotten a million."

"He thinks he negotiated us up."

Cliff stretched back, hands cupped behind his head, and stared up at the ceiling fan again. "Where do we find this Kyle Young?"

"That's my job."

"Don't you trust me, Stan?"

"You're going to parade around town a bit first. You're going to ask questions about Vatican Towne. You're going to be a nuisance. If Towne is on this island, he'll hear about you. That way if this Kyle Young guy is just blowing smoke, we'll have your allure as Towne's favorite target to fall back on."

"What about me?" Tory asked.

"You can stay here or go with Cliff. Doesn't matter to me."

"Which is safer?"

Stan stood up, headed for the bathroom. "Neither."

24

SHE FOUND HIM in the library, sitting in the middle of the floor. He was arranging paper patterns on swatches of white cloth. A plastic bag with wool batting sat in the leather chair behind him. A semicircle of implements—scissors, needles, thread—were arranged next to him like a surgeon's tools. The stereo was on much too loud. She could feel the vibrations throbbing from the speakers.

She stood in the doorway, closed her eyes and felt the rhythmic pattern poking at her body. She guessed at the composer. Wagner. Definitely. The notes pounded her skin insistently. Besides, he'd sneaked off into the library to work, which he did when he wanted to listen to Wagner because he detested the man personally and felt guilty for loving his music so.

She set her glass of iced tea on the small table behind him. The tea was made from the same family tea that he always drank, but she'd added a hint of cinnamon to cut through the woody taste. *I'll share it,* she signed.

"Did you add cinnamon?" he asked.

She nodded.

"No thanks."

Wagner? she asked, pointing at the speakers.

He nodded sheepishly. "No Nazi jokes, okay? I feel like a pervert every time I listen to him. I can't help myself. When I'm dead you can sell this secret to the *National Enquirer*, make a lot of money, go on Johnny Carson. Maybe Doc Severinsen will play a few notes from 'Siegfrieds Tod.'"

She sat on the wood floor next to him, watched for a few minutes as he continued the meticulous cutting of the red cloth

from the paper pattern. Quiltmaking was one of the arts Kauai
was famous for, and in moments like this, when he needed
some solitude, Vatican would pull out his cloths and work for
a few hours on the same quilt he'd been making for the past
five years. His expression was without emotion, but the creases
in his tan face were darker, deeper than usual. Thin black rivers of grief, she thought.

She tapped his shoulder so he would look up at her. *The funeral is tomorrow.*

"I know."

You should go.

He accidentally tore the paper pattern and swore. "I think
I made my design too difficult."

He was your son.

"I have work here."

What work? This?

"You know what work. Preparing for our guests." He began cutting a piece of cloth.

She grabbed the scissors from his hand. *This is stupid. Your
son is dead. His wife and son could use you at the funeral.*

"I spoke to them on the phone."

How compassionate of you. Her hands moved faster and with
choppier motions. *You sit here and plot, but you don't know if
these men will ever show up. There's very little chance that they will
find us here.*

Vatican Towne touched her cheek sadly. "They already
have."

Her eyes widened and she tensed. Cold fear chilled her skin.
How did they find us so soon?

"I told them. Not directly, of course. Through contacts and
informers. I made them pay for the information. That's the
only way they can believe it has value."

She tucked her knees to her chest and cupped her hands
around her bare feet. *You're crazy.*

"Perhaps. Perhaps I am."

They stared at each other for a minute. His eyes glistened. He let his hand rest on her knee. She laid her cheek on his mottled hand.

"I miss him, Dayna," he said. "I warned Bradley there might be trouble. I begged him to come here with his family, a little vacation until this was done. He refused. Had to prove to me he could handle himself, that he was as good as me at everything. Too damn stubborn." Vatican Towne leaned back against the chair behind him. "I never thought Aaron Leland would do it that way. Maybe question him, but not kill him. Not kill my son."

It's not too late to stop this. Before there's any more killing.

He smiled at her. "It is too late, Dayna. Their assassins are already here. Even if I stopped now, they would still come after me. Leland would see to it. Besides, I gave my word to a group of boys who'd seen more of hell than any eighteen-year-old ought to. I gave my word. I have no choice."

Dayna was about to argue when she felt a vibration on the floor. She turned toward the doorway as the Filipino man carrying a suitcase entered the room.

Hi, Kyle, she signed.

He winked at her, then turned to Vatican. "Hi, Dad."

"That it?" Vatican said.

"I paid cash like you said. I used the money your old CIA buddies paid me to tell them you were on this island."

"Good. Let's go to work." They started to leave the room with Dayna quickly falling in after them. Vatican stopped, placed his hands on her shoulders. "Perhaps you should stay here."

I'm coming.

He nodded, released her shoulders. She followed them out of the house into the two-car garage that Vatican had converted into a woodworking shed. He had all the tools, power and hand, that were necessary to build or repair just about anything on their land. He had built the house himself, from his own design, and built most of the furniture in it.

Kyle gently placed the suitcase on the workbench, unlocked it and opened the lid. "The guy in Honolulu who sold this to me said to tell you that this made you even. Don't ask again."

"Fine," Vatican said. He reached into the suitcase and picked up the cinder-block-size hunk of plastique explosive. He squeezed it in his fists till it oozed between his fingers. He smiled. "The rest of the stuff?"

"A little prestidigitation," Kyle grinned. He dug both hands into his pants pockets. When he brought them out again, the left hand held a knot of neatly wound black and red wires and the right hand held a new pocket calculator. "And presto chango, Bullwinkle finally pulls a rabbit out of his hat."

Vatican patted his son's broad shoulder appreciatively. "This should do the trick."

They were both so pleased with themselves that Dayna had to throw a screwdriver at the suitcase to get their attention. *What good will any of this do?*

Kyle looked at Vatican, whose face lost its momentary glee and returned to its former gray mask of grief. "I don't know what good will be done. Maybe none. Good rarely gets done at all, and never easily."

Are you sure you aren't enjoying this? The old warhorse hears the battle trumpets again.

"Dayna!" Kyle snapped.

Vatican held a hand up to Kyle, cutting him off. "I try not to ask myself hard questions anymore, Dayna. I try not to poke too deeply, turn over rocks in the mud. I take more things on faith now, especially concerning myself. I believe I'm doing this for a good reason, so I assume I am."

Is this Remington really responsible for your son's death?

"He's here, isn't he?"

Kyle nodded. "He's here. I saw him."

This doesn't seem right.

"Nothing is as it seems," Vatican said.

I speak in sign, but you speak in puzzles.

"Habit."

Bad habit.

"I'm afraid most of mine are."

Kyle touched her arm so she would face him. "You aren't being fair. You know how important this is to him."

I know I want you both to live. Hasn't Remington suffered enough already?

"He has come here to kill Vatican," Kyle said.

Because he thinks Vatican killed his family. He's being used. The way Vatican is using us.

Vatican placed his hand on her shoulder. She hadn't noticed that she'd been trembling until she felt his hand, warm and large, settle on her.

"Do you honestly believe that, Dayna? That I'm using you?"

Suddenly Dayna threw herself against Vatican, hugging him tightly. Her face pressed against his chest and she could smell the sweet soap on his body and in his clothes. She pulled back to sign. *I just want the killing to stop.*

"Soon," Vatican said. "Soon."

And he and Kyle busied themselves at the workbench making their bomb.

25

"SLOW DOWN. That's where they filmed *South Pacific*."

Cliff didn't slow down. He continued driving the rental car along narrow Highway 56 a little faster than was safe.

Tory rolled down her window and the cool air-conditioned air was sucked out and replaced with the sticky humidity of Kauai's north shore. "God, it's gorgeous. Slow down, will you?"

"We're not here for sight-seeing," Cliff reminded her.

"Oh, yeah, I forgot. We're here to save the world." She snorted. "A one-armed bureaucrat with weak bowels, an emotionally unstable ex-agent who vacillates between black guilt and white rage and a frightened lady lawyer trying to pretend she's on a free vacation so she doesn't wet her pants. If we're its saviors, the world's in some kind of trouble."

"Maybe," Cliff said. "But we're all it's got right now."

Tory rolled up the window and sat back with a weary sigh.

They drove in silence. Cliff had decided that they would drive around the perimeter of the island, stopping in all the towns, flashing Vatican Towne's photo, asking questions. Even if they didn't get any answers, which they hadn't so far, at least Vatican would know Cliff was here. Perhaps that would goad him into showing himself. Meanwhile, Stan was off somewhere supposedly meeting with this Kyle guy, buying Vatican's exact address. Things seemed to be progressing nicely. Before the day was over, Cliff knew he would be confronting Vatican Towne, the man who'd killed his family. Maybe it had been a mistake. Vatican, in a rage, punishing the man he thought responsible for murdering his son. It didn't matter. There were some rules to this game, a few. Most important, don't touch families. Vatican had helped establish that rule back in the OSS days. He'd broken it so Cliff would have to kill him. If for no other reason than it gave Cliff a goal, some reason to live.

Cliff had made this same drive before with Ginger. They'd stopped at every turnout on the road for what Ginger called, "Photo opportunities." They'd pull over, get out, and she'd snap a few pictures with her cheap one-button no-focus camera. At this same beach, she'd run along the sand proclaiming, "This is where Mitzi Gaynor washed that man right outta her hair. Remember, head full of lather. I wonder how they kept her head lathered that long. Stand over here, Cliff. Pretend you're lathering your head." She must have gone through a dozen rolls of film. They'd found one roll a couple of months ago in an old purse she'd stored in the closet. The newly developed pictures from it were still in the glove compartment of Ginger's car, along with a two-month-old empty yogurt carton, some torn panty hose and whatever else had accumulated over the three years she owned that car. How many times, in annoyance over the mess, had he suggested she clean it out, even offered to clean it out for her? She'd always looked surprised and laughed, "Whatever for?" He'd never had an answer to that. Remembering, he smiled.

They approached the small town of Hanalei. Many of the wooden stores were colorfully painted with elaborately designed signs.

"Looks like something out of the sixties," Tory said with delight. "Even the people have that give-peace-a-chance look."

"Those are the tourists."

"So this is where all the refugees from the love-ins went. I always wondered."

"You're too young to remember that time."

"I had an older sister. Wore beads and let the hair under her arms grow. She tried to let the hair on her legs grow too, but it was too gross even for her. Every time she shaved it was like a moral compromise for poor Maureen. I got some of her tie-dyed hand-me-downs. Still have a few splotchy T-shirts in my closet. Come the revolution, I'll have my uniform ready.''

Cliff laughed and Tory looked over at him. She smiled, holding her eyes on him long enough to make him uncomfortable. He kept staring straight ahead at the street, but aware of her gaze on him. He pulled into a parking space in front of a jewelry store.

''Lots of stores here,'' Cliff said. ''I'll start flashing Vatican's photo around. You can wait here if you want.''

''I think I'll bop over to that grocery store and pick up a soft drink. You want anything?''

''Reese's peanut butter cup.''

''You're kidding.''

''I have a craving.'' Cliff couldn't remember the last time he'd had one—maybe when he was a kid attending Saturday matinees at the movies when they showed cartoons, newsreels and Three Stooges shorts. He didn't know why he wanted one now; he hadn't eaten candy of any kind in years, especially chocolate. He'd read somewhere that chocolate produces the same chemical reaction in the body that falling in love produces. Perhaps it was withdrawal from losing Ginger. He shook his head at himself. He was losing his grip. ''Never mind. I was kidding.''

''Okay.''

''Meet you back here.''

''Fine.''

They split up. Cliff canvassed the stores just as he had done with the other towns on their tour: Lihue, Hanamaulu, Wailua, Kapaa, Princeville. The answers here were the same as in every other place. Some recognized Vatican Towne as being famous, though few could recall what he was famous for. No one recognized him as local. A few might have been lying. Despite the old photograph they could have recognized him.

They might even be contacting him right now. That was okay too. Either way, the meeting of the two men was inevitable.

When he got back to the car, Tory was standing in front of a kite store, snapping photos with a new camera. Multicolored wind socks in the shape of fish hung from poles like the catch of the day. Tory shot a couple different angles.

"Let's go," Cliff said.

"This is great, isn't it? I mean, I've seen the same damn wind thingamabobs in California, and here I am taking pictures of them just because they're in Hawaii."

"Where'd you get the camera?"

"Bought it. There was a little camera store near the grocer's. You don't have to do anything. Just point the sucker and it practically snaps the shot itself. It'll make great cover for us. Just a couple of shutterbug tourists."

Cliff climbed into the car. "We aren't supposed to be undercover, Tory. The whole point is for Towne to know we're here."

She pointed the camera at him and clicked the shutter. "Could you bare those teeth a little more? At a certain angle it might be mistaken for a smile."

Cliff snatched the camera away, popped open the lid and pulled the roll of film out. "We're not playing here. No pictures that might be used against us later." He dropped the camera on her lap.

"You can be a real shit sometimes."

"Most of the time."

Tory stuffed the camera in her purse. She reached into the purse and pulled out a Reese's peanut butter cup and tossed it on Cliff's lap. "Here." She opened a photo book about Kaui on her lap.

Cliff ate the cup. It was good, but not as good as he'd remembered. Certainly it didn't taste like love.

"HUNGRY?" Stan asked.

Cliff and Tory, each carrying a grocery bag, entered the

condo to find Stan sprawled out on the sofa watching television. *Route 66*. He was munching corn chips from a silver bag clamped in his hook.

"I never used to watch this show when I was a kid," he said, nodding at the TV set. "Couldn't relate to two guys who could afford a Corvette. If they'd driven that car into my neighborhood, they'd have driven out on a skateboard. The kids I grew up with were like those tiny piranha fish, travel in hordes and strip to the bone everything they see."

"What'd you find out?" Cliff asked.

"That wearing a hook in this climate is a sweaty business." He sat up, brushed a few corn chip crumbs from his shirt. "I got an address, if you can call it that. More like a map."

"From Kyle?"

"From our buddy Kyle. Wants to be as helpful as possible."

"For the right price."

"Naturally."

"You pay him?"

"Not until we check this out." Stan held up the piece of paper from Kyle. Cliff saw clumsily sketched lines of a map. "He put up a fuss, but he didn't have much choice. What about you?"

"I don't have much choice either."

"That's not what I meant. What happened with you today?"

Cliff set his bag on the counter and sat in the chair. He glanced up at the ceiling fan, caught the blades in freeze-frame again and was pleased to see his theory was still true. "I asked around but no one admitted recognizing him."

"You made yourself known though."

"Yeah. And I managed to let everyone know where I was staying."

"Good." He twisted the neck of the corn chip bag. "Anybody for dinner?"

Tory had wandered into the kitchenette and was unloading the two bags of groceries. Milk, eggs, beer, soft drinks. "We picked up a frozen pizza."

Stan made a face. "Frozen pizza."

"Cliff thinks it's safer if we stay in tonight."

"Safer? Not if we eat that crap." Stan patted his delicate stomach.

Cliff said, "We got some stuff for an omelet for you."

Stan went to the kitchenette, rummaged through the cabinets until he found a frying pan.

"I'll make it," Tory said.

"You don't have to," Stan said. "I can cook."

"Don't worry, I'm not taking this as sexual harassment. It'll give me something to do so I don't feel so nervous."

Stan went back to the sofa.

Cliff closed his eyes and laid his head back. The TV blared a commercial for an oldies album. When Connie Francis's voice warbled "Where the Boys Are," he opened his eyes and looked. The address they gave for ordering the album was the same building as his and Lily's office. Cliff smiled. So those guys really did sell those records.

The phone rang.

Stan ambled over to the wooden phone stand and answered it. He spoke in a low voice, secretively, his back to Cliff and Tory. Less than a minute later, he hung up.

"That was quick," Cliff said.

"Not much to report."

"Leland?"

Stan nodded. "He's concerned."

"He should be. He knows I'm alive."

"He's not concerned about you, Remington. In the scope of things, you're nothing but a fleck of dust."

"Ever get a fleck of dust in your eye?"

"Annoying. Nothing more."

"Ah, but it could be more. It could work its way in deep, infect the membrane, cause blindness. Maybe death."

"I hate metaphors," Stan said. He untwisted the bag of corn chips and threw a few in his mouth. "You don't have any idea what Aaron Leland's done for this country. The man has increased the efficiency of the CIA by twenty-three percent. That's from an impartial study. For the first time in years, the people who work there feel like they've got purpose. We're not just sticking our thumbs in the dam, we're building a new dam. We're creating something positive."

"According to Aaron Leland's master plan."

"It's worked so far."

"For you," Cliff said. "You got promoted. But for what? Leland never does anything without a purpose."

"So? What's so evil about that? We finally have some sense of ethics and morality in government. Isn't that what the country's been screaming for? Christ, I've never met anyone more sincerely devoted to his job than Aaron Leland."

"That's true. He's devoted, all right. He truly has a vision of the way the world should be."

"Is that so bad?"

Cliff sighed. "Depends on how you go about achieving that vision." Cliff leaned forward. Out of the corner of his eye he could see Tory slicing ham for Stan's omelet, her ear cocked toward them, listening. "You know what we used to call him? The Monk."

"They call him Reverend Father now. But affectionately."

"So did we. Affectionately. A friend of mine, Drew, used to say that Aaron always looked distracted, as if he kept seeing glimpses of another world. A better world. I think we admired him for that."

"You worked with Aaron?"

"More than worked, we were friends. Aaron, Drew and myself. We ran London for a while, years ago. It was our time, you know, like the best of times, the worst of times. During the best of times, I got married. Drew was my best man, Aaron was the minister. He wasn't a real priest or anything, and neither I nor my wife was religious. It was more like a party. We'd been married officially already. But we didn't consider it official until Aaron gave his blessing. Then came the worst of times.''

Cliff noticed Tory had stopped slicing the ham. She stood erect, knife poised, listening.

"Aaron had always been frustrated with Graceland. Nothing ever moved fast enough. He knew what needed to be done to make this world better and he was impatient that others didn't see it too. Or if they saw it, didn't give him the freedom to do what he knew was necessary. That's when he came upon the realization that if he was ever to accomplish anything major, he needed more power. The kind of power you could only get by rising up through the organization. He explained all that to Drew and myself and we took him out and toasted his ambition. Certainly neither Drew nor myself shared his ambition. We enjoyed what we did and were too cynical to think we or anyone would make much difference. Still, we encouraged Aaron. After all, he was our friend.''

At some point, Stan had reached into the bag and pinched a few corn chips, but he had never transported them to his mouth. He sat frozen in front of Cliff, eyes shining intently.

"The problem," Cliff continued, "was how could Aaron move up. There were the usual channels of bootlicking, but Aaron was too impatient for that. He needed to prove his worth with magnificent schemes and important projects. Then the higher-ups would take notice. Actually, with Drew and me helping him, he did manage to jump ahead on the corporate ladder a few rungs. After that, we began to see less and less of him. We were all still friends, but Aaron traveled around Europe more, worked late and on weekends. He was driven.

"Drew had a girlfriend, an Irish girl living in London. Drew had always been a bit of a cad, but once he met Molly it was True Love. She'd come from a little town in the Donegal section of Ireland. A place with names like Sheep Haven and Bloody Foreland. A real country girl. Drew was from Brooklyn. Jesus, what a pair. But somehow it worked. Until Aaron Leland got involved.

"Molly worked for the East German cultural attaché, teaching his children English. That's how Drew and I met her, following Herr Faber around London, hoping to discover his drop where he contacted his local agents. We even tailed Molly for a few days, thinking she might be his liaison. But she was clean. Everyone knew Herr Faber was the mastermind of the East German espionage ring in London, but we couldn't prove anything. We were pulled off for another assignment, but Drew and Molly kept seeing each other. Meantime, unknown to us, Aaron Leland, looking to make points with his superiors, had gone undercover as a double agent looking to work for the East Germans.

"To prove his authenticity, Leland had to give them someone. Desperate, afraid he was losing the whole operation, he finally gave them Molly. At first they didn't believe him. She didn't have access to any information. But Leland convinced them, using forged papers, that she had turned someone else on the staff and only she knew who the mole was. Leland was backed against the wall and saw his operation as well as his chances for promotion slipping away. But once he gave them Molly's name, they kidnapped her, tried to make her tell who the mole was. She didn't know anything. They tried harder. She died."

"Jesus," Tory said. "That's a hell of a story."

"That's not the story," Cliff said. "The story is that Drew and I knew nothing of this. When Drew found out Molly had been murdered, he went a little berserk. He asked his buddy Aaron to help find out what had happened, who had fingered

Molly. Everything with the Germans was coming to a head then, with Aaron finally on the inside. He was afraid Drew would screw it up now. I was out of the country, translating for some Greek operation, so Aaron figured it wouldn't hurt to pin the rap on me. He told Drew that Molly was an IRA terrorist, provided documents he'd had made up that proved she planned to bomb a London store. The same documents also proved that I'd turned her in to the British.

"Aaron only wanted to keep Drew out of his hair for twenty-four hours while he completed his operation, so he saw no harm in the deception. He'd straighten the whole thing out later, as soon as he had a chance to come up with a better story. Only problem was, I came home early from my assignment and went straight over to see Drew, have dinner together. I walked into Drew's flat. He looked like hell, strung out on grief and liquor. He attacked me with a knife, sliced my stomach open before I'd said hello. Drunk or not, he was the best man with a knife I'd ever seen.

"I tried to talk to him, calm him down. His anger was too great. He leaped on me, knife jabbing at my eyes." Cliff laid his finger on a small scar at the corner of his right eye. "Anyway, we fought. He shoved the knife through my hand, but I managed to crush his windpipe. He died."

Tory, horrified, shook her head. "And Leland?"

"His undercover operation was a success. He found the liaison, broke up the spy ring. He was promoted."

"But what about Molly? And Drew?"

Cliff smiled. "Dead is dead."

Stan nodded. "They'd measure the loss against the gain. The gain won. Acceptable losses."

"Yup."

"And this is the man," Tory said, "who's running the fucking Agency?"

"The same."

Stan stood up, stretched. Bones clicked in his back. He took a deep breath as if trying to shake off a sudden weariness. "That was a long time ago. He'd be the first to admit he'd made mistakes. There was nothing malicious in what he did. Circumstances got out of control. That happens all the time in this business. And don't tell me you've never been responsible for innocent people being hurt."

Cliff thought of Ginger and the kids. Lily.

"At least Aaron is trying to do something good. He wasn't ambitious for himself, he wanted to make things better."

"Yes, I believe he did. Maybe that's what makes him even more dangerous."

Stan's stomach rumbled loud enough for everyone to hear. He glared at Cliff a moment longer, then shuffled off to the bathroom.

"How can he defend that monster?" Tory asked.

"Stan wants the world to be better too. He identifies with Aaron. Don't underestimate Aaron Leland's charm. When he talks, he radiates a kind of energy. He's so sure that what he's doing is right, he makes you believe too. It's not until you walk out of his light that you start checking for your watch and wallet."

"Then he's nothing more than a con man."

"He's much more than a con man. He believes his own con."

Tory rolled her eyes. "I feel like I've wandered into some low-budget Italian sword-and-sandal film about Greek gods. The dubbing is so bad that the actors' lips are moving, but they don't match the words being said." She lifted a spatula in frustration. "What the hell is going on?"

"Dinner," Cliff said. He rooted through the cupboard for a flat pan to bake the pizza on. "Turn on the oven."

"I would if I could figure out how to get this burner lit first." She stood over the skillet, twisting the knob on and off, but no flame caught. "Maybe the pilot's out." She leaned over, examining the gas line.

"Try another burner."

"I tried them all."

Cliff reached into the cupboard and pulled out a pan and set it on the counter. He opened the cardboard box, tore open the cellophane bag and laid the pizza on the pan. The edges hung over on both sides. He shrugged. It would do.

"Oven doesn't seem to work either," Tory said, turning the dial. "I don't hear that familiar whoosh of igniting gas."

"Light the pilot."

"You light the pilot, pal. I'm not singeing my eyebrows for a lousy frozen pizza."

The kitchenette was narrow, so Cliff had to squeeze by her to look at the oven. "Pardon me, Betty Crocker."

"Betty Crocker does all her cooking in a microwave now, Chef Boyardee."

Cliff grinned, squatted down as he pulled open the oven door. There was no heat. He closed the door, then slid open the broiler drawer beneath the oven.

The plastique explosive sat on the broiler tray like a roast. Except for the calculator attached with wires. The calculator flashed 23 seconds. Then 22. Then 21.

Tory made a face. "What the hell's tha—"

Cliff's arm snagged her around the waist and dragged her backward out of the kitchenette. "Run!" he snapped. "Get out!"

Tory's eyes widened and she spun around and ran for the door.

Cliff rushed to the bathroom and flung open the door.

"Jesus Christ, Remington!" Stan said. He was standing, buckling his belt. "Do I have to lock—"

"Bomb," Cliff said, turned and ran for the door.

Stan followed in his stocking feet, his shirt flapping, his unbuckled belt clinking.

As Cliff neared the door, he could see Tory waving people away, holding back a couple of children who wanted their Frisbee. Behind him, he heard Stan muttering as he ran. "Go back," Cliff hollered at Tory as he ran. "Farther."

Tory quickly complied, yanking the stray kids with her.

The bomb exploded with a raspy growl. Cliff felt the heat on his back, prickly first then scorching. Then the concussion of air punched him off his feet and he was tumbling across the lawn. Somewhere in his somersault, he saw Stan rolling beside him.

Tory and the children were also knocked down and quickly blanketed by a thick gray smoke that blew out of the condo. Cliff squinted, his eyes stinging from the smoke, but he could barely see. There were forms on the ground, his among them, but he couldn't make out faces. He lifted his head, trying to bring the rest of his body up with it. Somehow he couldn't quite manage.

A girl screamed, the sound as shrill as a siren. "An arm. It's an arm."

Through the drifting smoke Cliff could see the little girl that Tory had been holding back screaming and shaking and pointing at the small lump on the ground.

"An arm! It's an arm!" she hollered again.

Cliff, confused, looked down at his own immobile body. That was when he noticed the blood.

26

FROM HIS HIDING PLACE in the thick garden underbrush, Kyle watched the flames and smoke erupt through the shattered doors and windows. Dark smoke hugged the ground, spreading like lava among the onlookers. The way the smoke seemed to roll across the lawn reminded Kyle of an old Doris Day movie he'd seen once where the washing machine had too much detergent in it and suds flooded the whole house, sweeping Doris across the floor and out the door. What a funny image to have now, he thought. But he did not smile.

A little girl was screaming, hopping up and down, pointing at something on the ground and yelling. Kyle couldn't quite hear what she was saying, and the smoke was too thick to see what she was pointing at. He pushed aside a clump of leaves from the hala tree he was crouching behind and leaned forward for a better look. Tourists were running out of adjacent condos, most wearing swimming suits or shorts. One man stood in his underpants with his face half-lathered with shaving cream.

Kyle identified the three agents: Victoria Fawley, Standish Ford, Clifford Remington. They were moving, so they were alive. He could do no more here.

Kyle brushed aside the spindly hala tree, cutting his hand on one of the sharp leaves. "Damn," he said, sucking the tiny incision on his palm. The hala tree leaves were thick and tough, once used by natives for weaving mats and sails. Now they grew in resort gardens with little signs identifying them for the guests.

He walked quickly back to his car. Everyone else was rushing toward the site of all the activity. He bumped against a few anxious tourists. A black tourist carrying a tennis racquet asked Kyle what had happened. Kyle shrugged and kept going.

His car was a 1969 Impala with 148,000 miles on it. Vatican had shown him how to rebuild the engine, scavenge parts from other cars, cleaning, fitting, sometimes hand-tooling a part to make it work. Nothing was wasted, nothing thrown away. Everything, Vatican taught, had more than one purpose. Just because something started life as one thing didn't mean it had to stay that way. The coconut palm produced drink and food, but it also provided leaves for thatching, nuts for dishes and wood for carpentry. A person was no different. No matter what one was before, he could be something different in the future. Kyle knew Vatican was speaking as much about his own life as he was about cars or palms.

Kyle started the engine. Each metal part, once clunky and angled when saved from the junkyard, now harmonized sweetly. Automatically, Kyle thumbed the tape cassette into the slot. The music started in the middle of "Sarah Smile" by Hall and Oates. Kyle hummed along as he shoved the gear into reverse and looked over his shoulder to back out of the parking lot.

"Hi," the man in the back seat said. The something in the man's hand whacked Kyle's head and flames even brighter and smoke even darker than those he'd seen outside filled his head.

KYLE'S EYES felt pasty. He struggled to open them, but they seemed glued shut. He tried again, but they wouldn't open.

He was sitting in a chair, hands tied behind the chair back. He was naked. That much he was sure of.

"Tape," a man's voice said.

Suddenly there was a burning pain across his right eyebrow and eyelid. He was now able to open that eye. Standing in front of him he saw the man from his car's back seat, holding a strip of white adhesive tape on the end of his fingertip. Kyle could see some eyebrow hairs and eyelashes stuck to the tape.

"Tape," the man said again. "Just so you know it's nothing permanent." He grinned at Kyle. "Go ahead, take a look. A long look. We're going to get to know each other well. I'm going to be your father confessor and you're going to tell me everything you know about Vatican Towne. Especially where he is."

"Who are you?" Kyle asked.

"Oops. First mistake. See, I ask the questions, you answer. But maybe introductions are in order here. I'm Charon, with a C. And you?"

"I don't know what you're talking about. What do you want? Who's Vatican Towne?"

"I assume he's the man who hired you to blow up those three agents. Unless you were doing that on your own, which I doubt."

"Blow up? I didn't blow anybody up. This is crazy." Kyle watched Charon's casual manner as he lit a cigarette, took two puffs, then tamped it out.

"I've quit smoking," Charon explained. "Almost quit."

Kyle looked around the room, trying to memorize details, looking for clues. He would have to tell Vatican how to get here, find this man.

"Relax," Charon said. "We're at 2768 Kipuka Street. The people who own this lovely home are away on vacation and have no idea we're here." He laughed, a high pleasant chuckle. "Can you imagine, living here in paradise and going to L.A. for a vacation. It doesn't make any sense. Of course, where *would* you go? Weird, huh?"

Kyle was encouraged by Charon's sense of humor, his broad toothy smile. This man could not be a true killer. Certainly Kyle thought he would be able to endure anything this man did, without revealing where Vatican was.

"Enough chatter," Charon said abruptly. "I don't get paid by the hour." He came toward Kyle with the adhesive tape, then paused, thinking. "There's something I want you to see before I put this tape back on. I think it will help you understand your situation a little better.'' Charon turned his back on Kyle like a stage impressionist who might suddenly whirl around with a Kirk Douglas scowl. Instead, Kyle watched him unbutton his loose cotton shirt and shrug it off his shoulders. He wore one of those blue elastic belts that Kyle had seen some older joggers with paunches wear. Only he wore it around his upper chest. Charon peeled the belt off and Kyle could see the red welts in his skin from the belt. He could also see that though the shoulders and back were narrow, they were finely etched not with thick bumpy muscles, but with long braided muscles. Kyle thought of a lizard.

Charon sighed with relief and turned around, smiling.

Kyle's one open eye blinked rapidly. He gasped. This man Charon had a woman's breasts, round and swollen. Embarrassed, Kyle looked away, looked into Charon's face. The features were oddly symmetrical. In men's clothing, talking with his educated and playful tone, he looked like a handsome, successful man. But Kyle could see that if you saw him first as a woman and made a few cosmetic changes, he would appear to be a tall, attractive woman. Kyle felt suddenly very nervous being naked.

"Hermaphroditism," Charon said. "That's what it's called." He put his shirt back on and started buttoning it. "Spooky, huh?"

Kyle didn't say anything. He didn't know what to say. He did know that he was no longer sure that this man would not kill him.

"Don't look so glum," Charon said happily. "It's not contagious."

Kyle squirmed on the wide wooden chair, pressing his legs together to hide his penis. He didn't know why he felt compelled to do so, but he did.

"True hermaphroditism is very rare. There are pseudo disorders, copycat isms, but none are quite as exotic as this.

Imagine, you're born half male, half female. Those X and Y chromosomes jingle-jangling around in the embryo. It's like Nature on LSD got all turned around and stuck the wrong parts in the wrong places. Technically, we're talking about a phallus in chordee, with a urogenital sinus opening between two labioscrotal folds and a palpable gonad on the right side. Follow me?"

Kyle nodded dumbly, as if in a trance.

"I mean, I even have a Fallopian tube, believe it or not. On the other hand, I also have a testis, which is uncommon even for my ilk." He grinned. "Makes me feel a little like an omelet, a bit of everything thrown in."

"You could do something. Fix it somehow."

"Now that's the point exactly. Yes, there are techniques. They could do a boob job, nip these suckers back to nothing." He hefted one of his breasts. "You know when a hermaphrodite baby is born, the doctors ask the parents to decide what sex they want the child to be, then they perform surgery, snip, snip, and that's what the kid is. Sometimes a child isn't diagnosed until it's older, then they simply make the kid whatever it's been raised as. You been putting it in dresses, then it must be a girl. Snip, snip. Thing is, most doctors try and convince the parents to go with a female, because it's a hell of a lot easier building a working vagina than a working dick. See what I mean?"

Kyle twisted his wrists, trying to loosen his bindings. From the texture, it felt like an extension cord.

"From what I've told you, you probably figure my parents were some backwoods yokels with straw in their teeth and hay in their hair. A couple of real pigfuckers. On the contrary, they were actually very wealthy and highly educated. My father was a corporate investment broker, with an office in New York City, though we lived on Long Island. You think *I'm* strange, boy, my dad was really odd. Worked all week making a fortune, then worked all weekend losing it by investing in

Broadway-bound shows that never quite opened, or if they did open, they closed in three days. I think there's a lesson in all that. You do something well, stick to doing just that. Don't dick around where you don't belong. Thing is, both my parents were devout Catholics, real mackerel snappers. They were on a strict body-and-blood-of-Christ diet. So along comes baby me, with all kinds of spare parts hanging out, and they nearly freaked. The doctors advised them it was best to deal with the situation right away. You know, surgery. But Mom and Pop figured that was some kind of heresy, screwing around with what God made. The doctors figured they'd come to their senses later. They didn't.''

Kyle felt fine sweat lacquering his brow. The more this man talked, the more frightened he became.

"They raised me as a boy, thanks to a dominant Y chromosome that had wiggled in there somehow. But let me tell you, gym class was no fun. They sent me to a private school, where I was excused from locker room activities. All I dreamed of the whole time was having my operation. I even saved my own money for it. When I was sixteen, I was ready. I made all the arrangements myself, checked into a hospital, forged my parents' signatures on the consent forms. Thought I was home free. Somehow they found out where I was, put a stop to the whole thing, brought me home kicking and screaming. They thought my condition was God's punishment of them for some past sins and that it would be sacrilege to try to dodge God's punishment, like Jonah did. They just sent me off to another school.''

Charon stooped in front of Kyle so they were eye to eye. "Here's the part I like. I go home one Thanksgiving vacation without telling them. Only, get this, I dress like a girl. Panty hose, pumps, a dress. I was so terrified I'd be discovered and humiliated, but inside I felt kind of thrilled too. Anyway, I knock on the door and Mom answers. She can't see past the makeup who I am. I tell her I'm supposed to meet their son here as a surprise. They get all stiff and proper thinking I'm having some sexual affair, but manners win out and they invite me in to wait for me. Well, to cut to the chase, I kill both of them, lay them out on the living room floor, hack their bodies into their individual parts and rearrange those parts on each of their bodies so you can't tell who's who." The smile vanished from Charon's face and he leaned forward and taped Kyle's eye shut again. "Dark in there, isn't it? Good, it'll help you concentrate. I don't want any distractions."

Kyle felt a loosening at his wrists, twisted them more.

"I told you all this," Charon continued, "because I want you to know who you're dealing with. I want you to be scared. You see, I know the human body. I studied it thoroughly for years. Medical texts, biology books, Oriental martial arts, acupressure, acupuncture. I know exactly where to jab needles so that I could perform open heart surgery on you and you could be wide awake and not feel a thing. Or I know where to stick one little needle and you'd be paralyzed from the waist down. You want technical language, I can discuss mullerian and wolffian ducts and the 17-ketosteroid examination. Or we could cut through all that, and I place my index finger just so..."

Kyle felt Charon's fingertip lightly touch the back of his neck, trace across the skin to where the spine stuck out, travel upward again. Kyle shivered from the touch. Then Charon's finger jabbed hard and Kyle's head exploded with sharp pain. The energy seemed to travel along his jaws and up into his brain. Everything behind his closed eyelids looked white.

Then Charon jabbed another spot and the pain stopped as abruptly as it had begun. The only aftereffect was a slight buzzing in Kyle's ears.

"You see, my friend, I'm smart. Unbelievably smart. I even know what you're thinking. You think you can endure whatever pain I give you. But that's because you can't fully imagine how badly I can make you hurt. Somewhere inside you even look forward to this test of your courage. But in the end, you'll tell me everything. The problem is you'll start with lies, hoping that will make me stop. But you see, I'll know they're lies so I'll have to continue, constantly increasing the pain. Then you'll tell me the truth, everything I ask. Only I can't be sure you're not still lying, so I have to keep increasing the pain. Then you'll start lying again, tell me anything, implicate everyone, confess to all crimes. And you know what you'll do then? You'll thank me. Yes, you will. With big tears in your eyes and snot bubbling from your nose, you'll look into my eyes and thank me. You know for what?'' He chuckled. ''For killing you. Which I most certainly will do.''

Kyle's body was chilled from sweat and fear. He had no doubt that this man would indeed do everything he promised. But not without a fight. Kyle felt the loop around his wrist loosen even more, almost enough for his hand to slip through.

Charon was directly in front of him now. He could feel his presence there, hear his shallow breathing. ''This torture business is so unstable. I read in 1984 where they'd strapped this cage to a man's face and stuck a big hairy rat in the cage. Well, it worked in the book, so I tried the same thing once. Problem was, the rat bit the guy's tongue so hard, the thing swelled up and he couldn't talk when he wanted to. He had to write everything down for us. Had the worst damned handwriting, too.''

Kyle was about to say something, anything to distract the hermaphrodite while Kyle continued to work on the cord around his wrists. But then Charon's finger was pressing against a spot on Kyle's cheek, and Kyle's sinus cavities suddenly seemed to be on fire. He thought he felt Charon's finger piercing the skin like a dagger. He couldn't breathe. Tears poured from his eyes. ''Jesus!'' he hollered.

Charon removed his finger and the pain subsided. ''Where is Vatican Towne?''

The tears had lifted the adhesive tape a little and Kyle could open his eyes just enough for a foggy view of his captor hovering in front of him. He saw Charon's finger coming toward him again and he flinched. The finger landed lightly on his solar plexis, just beneath the rib cage. Then Charon pressed and a ragged bayonet tore into Kyle's stomach, twisting and chewing until he felt the vomit swirling in his throat. Charon withdrew his finger and the pain stopped. Kyle swallowed thickly.

"Where is Vatican Towne?"

Kyle tugged on the cord. His thumb joint was almost through, sliding slowly, the plastic cord scraping away skin. Just a few more seconds. Then this freak would see what a real fight was like. Kyle was a trained kick boxer, one of the most powerful on the island. His heart pounded as he felt his hand slip free.

Charon's finger started toward him again. Kyle's eyes were open just far enough to see his target, and now that his hands were free he charged. Leaping from the chair, he bulled his shoulder into the smaller man, tackling him to the ground. Quickly, he tore away the adhesive tape, then began punching Charon's face. The first two blows landed directly, but after that, something went wrong.

Charon threw a short punch. Not at Kyle's face or stomach, not a blow to topple him. Instead it was a short but powerful punch to the hip. Yet somehow it connected with a nerve that made Kyle's whole leg twitch involuntarily then start to cramp up. Kyle hopped to his feet to fight the cramp. But Charon was on his feet before Kyle was, and threw two quick jabs, one to the cheek, which flooded Kyle's eyes with tears and blinded him, and another to the neck, which buckled Kyle's legs. Kyle had been punched and kicked much harder many times in pretty much the same locations, but these short jabs were crippling. Kyle dropped to one knee, still swinging at Charon, but missing badly.

Charon leaped behind his captive and snapped a fist into the base of Kyle's skull. Kyle's eyes rolled back and he fell face-first to the floor. He was still conscious but unable to move. He felt the hermaphrodite straddling his back, grabbing a handful of hair, and jerking Kyle's head back.

"Now," Charon said sadly, "things get ugly."

27

"FOUR MINUTES!" the driver said over his shoulder.

Cavanaugh tightened his grip on the 9 mm Astra A-80. The gun was designed to hold fifteen rounds, but only Cavanaugh and the driver of the van knew the gun was empty. The other six men sitting along both walls of the van had been told that Cavanaugh was their leader. The van's driver, Sergeant Boone, was supposed to be Cavanaugh's second in command. The difference was, Sergeant Boone's gun was loaded.

Cavanaugh assessed the readiness of his men. Two sat slouched, with their gazes drowsy. One picked at a small wart on the back of his hand. Two others discussed whether cats were smarter than dogs. The sixth sat tensely at attention, arranging his Uzi on his lap so the angle of the barrel intersected the angle of his thighs. His concentration brought sweat to his brow as he nudged the gun a few millimeters one way, then the other.

Cavanaugh studied each face as he racked his brain to find some way to explain to them what was going on. To stop them from doing what they were about to do. But he knew they wouldn't listen, wouldn't believe the truth of what he told them. They had been betrayed so often they didn't know what trust was anymore.

He leaned forward, glanced down the van's hollow belly and out the windshield. The streets of Miami were bustling with civilians. This neighborhood was run-down, trash clogged the gutters, and some of the cars used coat hangers as radio aerials. Mostly, though he noticed the odor. A damp fetid odor of human bodies and animal excrement, of dead fish and the flesh of fowl and meat frying on a thousand burners, of unfiltered

cigarettes and city bus fumes. The sweet lethal scent of insec-
ticide spray. The raw aroma of hungry sex, both willing and
unwilling. All of these swirled into one heady smell that Cavanaugh was only too familiar with.

"Three minutes," Sergeant Boone said as he wheeled the
car around the corner for a final approach to the target. He
blared the horn at a black kid on a wobbly bike. "Check your
weapons."

The men all looked at Cavanaugh. Cavanaugh could see
Sergeant Boone scowling into the rearview mirror, his jaw
working furiously on the wad of tobacco in his mouth.

"Check your weapons," Cavanaugh said quietly.

Without a word, each man examined his gun and ammu-
nition. Last check before action.

Cavanaugh went through the motions with his unloaded
weapon. When the men had finished with their checks, they
glanced at Cavanaugh for any further instructions. Sergeant
Boone might have been second in command, but he wasn't one
of them. He hadn't been over there, hadn't visited The Cave.
He was no Junkyard Dog.

Which is exactly why Aaron Leland had gone through all
this trouble to find Cavanaugh. Sergeant Boone had come to
Cavanaugh's quarters last night, unlocked the door that kept
Cavanaugh prisoner and let himself in. Boone was a big man,
everything about him was big, the features exaggerated like
someone who'd taken too many steroids. He'd sat on Cavanaugh's bunk without being invited, stretched out, bounced
a little.

"Not bad," he'd said. "Better than my bunk, I can tell ya."

Cavanaugh had been sitting at the desk, going over the plans
for tomorrow. He'd already received a long telephone call from
Aaron Leland explaining the situation in very plain terms.
Cavanaugh remembered Leland from the debriefing sessions
after their rescue in Nam. Now he was head of the CIA. He
told Cavanaugh why the group had been recalled, what was

expected of them, what would happen if they failed. There was some patriotic fanfare here and there, and Cavanaugh thought the bastard actually believed what he was saying. But the upshot was that they go in tomorrow, raid a known terrorist nest in Miami, kill everyone in that apartment, innocent civilian and terrorist alike, and leave the bodies in such a way that the warning to other terrorists is clear. He needed a group of men that couldn't be traced back to him, men who weren't afraid to get a little dirty.

"I'm here to give you the final lowdown," Boone had said from the bunk. "You guys are the last of a breed, man. Kinda like celebrities. Like those guys that die but are brought back to life and people are always asking what they saw when they were dead. That's how I look at you guys. In a way, I wish to hell I'd been there with you, seen what you seen. Man, that would've been something."

Cavanaugh's smile was grim.

Sergeant Boone didn't like the smile. "Maybe you think I couldn't've cut it? Well, fuck you. I've done my share, mister. More than my share, you want to know the truth. So fuck you."

"Is that what you came to say, Sergeant?"

Boone stood up. "I've got my orders, Cavanaugh. You're here because these guys are hard to handle. They can shoot, fight, crawl naked over barbed wire, but somewhere along the line their mechanism for following orders got fucked up. Unless you're one of them. And none of these guys is really officer material, you get my drift."

"Those that were you had killed."

Boone pretended he hadn't heard Cavanaugh. "We go in tomorrow. My job is to back you up. You give the orders you were told to, I make sure you do. Any fuck-ups and I blow your head off. Understood?"

Cavanaugh turned back to the desk as if Boone wasn't there. After several minutes, Boone walked out, locking the door behind him.

Cavanaugh had been isolated from the men except for their initial reunion and briefing sessions and at meals. At that time he'd tried talking to Darby Louden, the sharpest of the group.

"This is all wrong, Darby," Cavanaugh had said when the two of them went off to share a smoke. Sergeant Boone ate with the other men, but Cavanaugh could see him watching. "These bastards are using us."

"So?" Darby said.

"Christ, man, they murdered all the others that wouldn't fit in with their plans. Conway, Tallman, Weitz. All dead just because they'd managed to get out and adjust."

Darby dragged on his cigarette. "You saying what? Me and the rest are here 'cause we're too fucked up to give a shit about? Psycho vets on killing rampage?"

"No, man. But that's the way Leland knows the headlines will read if you get killed or caught."

"So what. It's like *Mission: Impossible*, Sarge. The secretary will disavow any knowledge of you." Darby laughed. "We know that going in."

"Then why are you doing it?"

Darby leaned against the wall and smiled. "Number one, because I guess I *am* a little crazy." His smile faded and his face sagged. "Look, I'm not one of those vets who thinks this country owes me something for what I went through. Hell, I joined in the first place back then because I was eighteen and thought going to war would be fun. We'd kick some ass, I'd come home in my uniform with a couple medals and get laid until I couldn't walk. Didn't quite turn out that way though. But I came back, and that's more than a lot can say."

Cavanaugh dropped his cigarette to the floor and stepped on it.

"Thing is, Tim, I have these relapses. Bad fucking flashbacks when I'm wide awake only I think I'm back in The Cave. Haven't had one for a year, which is why they let me out of the hospital. Like I said, I don't think the country owes me squat, and I'm tired of hearing other vets whining about how nobody treats them with respect. But I gotta tell you, Tim, you tell someone you're a Vietnam vet and they've seen so many TV shows and stuff about the wackos that they look at you like they think you're gonna go home and eat their babies. Or they want to know if you ever killed anybody. Jesus."

"Leland's no different."

"He's brought us all together, given us a chance to do something we know how to do. Yeah, a couple of the guys here, man, they are on the other side, Tim. *Twilight Zone*, man. They just want a target, any target. But me, Johnny Gonzales, Kurt Lawson, maybe even Craig Spinner, we're here because we think we can do some good. Fuck a few of these terrorist assholes. Do something for our country."

"This isn't the country doing this, man. It's Aaron Leland."

Darby shrugged. "Close enough. After tomorrow, the terrorists will get a message. Get their bony butts outta here. And we'll keep hitting them until they think twice about coming over here again.

"Terrorism against terrorists."

"Bet your ass, Sarge."

"That doesn't work. Arresting them is one thing. Even assassinating them. But what we're doing tomorrow is a massacre. Blood and guts for television. Just enough to make voters feel the government is doing something. What we're doing is getting a president reelected and securing Aaron Leland's job. These terrorists believe in jihad. They think it's their religious duty not just to kill, but to die."

Darby grinned and slapped Cavanaugh's shoulder. "Hell, Sarge, we got a jihad of our own right here. Being back with these guys, man, it's the first time I've felt comfortable in years.''

Cavanaugh was surprised to realize he felt the same way.

"WEAPONS READY," Sergeant Boone announced.

The men sat straight, turned to face the back door of the van. They were ready—more than that, they were anxious.

Cavanaugh looked them over. They weren't killers, not like mercenaries who traveled about looking for any war, any side. That was Sergeant Boone. These men were anxious because they believed, whether through false or true reasoning, that what they were about to do was for the good of the country. They felt chosen, selected for their unique skills and abilities to help a country that had ignored them. Indeed, Darby had been right. They were a jihad.

The van squealed to a stop, Darby popped open the van door and everyone leaped out. Only Kurt Lawson, who'd finally proved to Craig Spinner that dogs were smarter than cats, was left behind to circle the block in the van, having replaced Sergeant Boone behind the wheel. By the time Lawson pulled up again, they should have finished and be running back out the door. Everything had been planned and timed.

Cavanaugh felt Sergeant Boone beside him as he led the charge into the shabby apartment building. The Junkyard Dogs were all dressed in civilian clothes—polo shirts, jeans, windbreakers, sneakers—and they carried their weapons out in the open. But most of the people on the street who saw them didn't flinch. They merely assumed the armed men were part of a drug bust by cops or a rip-off by a rival gang or something else equally mundane, just part of the landscape like an overturned garbage can.

Intelligence had the main nest on the second floor, in apartment 2F. According to the reports Cavanaugh had read last night, there were three terrorists living in that two-bedroom apartment, along with their families, which included two wives, four sons, two daughters, one mother and three cousins. Two of the terrorists had been living in the United States for eight years. One, Ahmed Naji, was a Syrian-trained Libyan specialist who had slipped into the country illegally, it was believed with a group of Mexican farm workers. Naji specialized in children as targets. He and his buddies were responsible for planting a bomb on a plane carrying a Miami Little League team to play in the World Series up in Williamsport, Pennsylvania. Official investigations had blamed the airplane crash on pilot error, thanks to Aaron Leland.

"My God, Tim," Leland had said to Cavanaugh during their phone conversation. "No matter what you think of me, just read the reports on these animals. The bomb on that airplane is only one incident. Their newest wrinkle is to smuggle in dope from Syria and supply it to children in school yards. With the drug paranoia in this country right now, what will happen when they announce what they're doing and say that if we don't stop supporting Israel, release a few hundred terrorist prisoners, sell Iran a few F-16s, they'll get our kids hooked on crack. Tomorrow you guys are saving kids' lives."

Cavanaugh almost bought it too. Because a lot of it was true. Getting rid of these bastards was a community service. But there were other things to consider—such as how Leland had had other Junkyard Dogs killed.

"Move it, assholes!" Sergeant Boone shouted.

"Fuck you," Darby said, and the others laughed.

"Quiet," Cavanaugh said. "Let's get it done."

The men shut up and picked up their pace. Cavanaugh figured if they were going to do this, then it was his job to at least get his own men out safely.

The first of Naji's lookouts was at the foot of the stairs—about seventeen years old with a pump-action shotgun. He shouted something up the stairs and leveled his shotgun at the men running toward him. Sergeant Boone fired a quick burst from his MAC-10 and the kid flopped in midair, going backward over the banister.

The men looked back at Boone with contempt.

"You fuckhead," Darby spat. "Now they know we're here."

"He was going to shoot," Boone said.

"He was already dead," Cavanaugh told him.

They passed the boy's body and Cavanaugh pointed at the flat black knife sticking out of the boy's chest. Johnny Gonzales had thrown it a split second before Sergeant Boone had opened fire. Bullets had dented and twisted the knife, proving it had stuck the kid before Boone had opened fire.

"Where'd they dig you up, Boone?" Cavanaugh said. Without waiting for an answer, he signaled his men and they stormed the stairway. He and Boone backed up the stairs, covering the rear.

Even with the advance warning of the gunshots, Cavanaugh's men were too fast for the ordinary soldier. They took the stairs in six seconds and were fanning down the hall toward 2F. A few hallway doors opened, flooding the corridor with television sounds, and heads peeked out. When the curious neighbors saw the armed men running, their doors slammed shut.

Apartment 2F opened and a man with black hair and a mustache jumped into the hallway. He had a Beretta Model 12 submachine gun in his hands and opened fire. The first burst was fired in panic, and he let the gun climb in his hands so the bullets pocked high on the walls and popped a light fixture in the ceiling. Craig Spinner fired one shot with his 9 mm and the man's chest burst like a ripened plum.

Someone inside 2F stuck a shotgun out the door and fired a random round at the men. Cavanaugh felt a few pellets nick his thigh, but otherwise no one was hurt.

Cavanaugh nodded to Darby, who lobbed an M26 grenade down the hall. It rolled in a wobbly path along the dirty floor, stopped near the door and rocked there for a few seconds. Then it exploded.

The impact blew the doorjamb off 2F, but also blew open the closed door across the hall in 2G. A woman inside 2G screamed in a foreign language, not a scream of fear, but of agony. She'd been hit by some stray shrapnel.

"Let's go," Sergeant Boone said, nudging Cavanaugh.

Cavanaugh nodded to the others and they moved quickly in shifts down the hall. Darby tossed another grenade into the smoking doorway. This explosion brought more screams and children's wails. Cavanaugh's stomach twisted. He saw his men waiting for his order, but he hesitated. This was fucked, man. Wrong.

Sergeant Boone's gun prodded his back. Cavanaugh nodded to Darby, and the men charged into the room with howls and bursts of automatic fire. Boone and Cavanaugh covered the hallway for their escape.

The gunfire continued like some berserk machine grinding gears and burning oil, rattling and shaking and throwing off smoke but still insisting on running. Cavanaugh knew the rhythm of the sounds well enough to realize his men were successfully doing what they'd come to do—slaughter every man, woman and child in the apartment.

"After today," Sergeant Boone said, "there won't be anybody who'll give aid to these camel fucking shitheads when they come here."

"You think this is going to be on the news as anything but some kind of dope deal gone bad?"

"Doesn't matter. Word gets around."

Cavanaugh knew he was right. Kill entire families of terrorists and the local people who usually aid or hide terrorists would think twice about it. Most were too Americanized to swallow the jihad crap. They helped out of sympathy or fear. The point of this raid was to make them more fearful of the hit squad than of the terrorists.

One skinny kid, maybe fifteen, ran out of the apartment. He was shirtless and barefoot, carrying a Magnum too big for his hands. He was more intent on running than using the gun, until he saw Cavanaugh and Boone. He froze a second, thought about firing, decided to run instead and turned toward the open doorway of 2G. Cavanaugh recalled the fire escape on that side of the building.

Sergeant Boone raised his MAC-10 at the kid but Cavanaugh knocked his arm down. "He'll spread the word," Cavanaugh explained. Before Sergeant Boone had a chance to snap his reply, they saw Ben Russell step into the hallway out of the smoky doorway of 2F, jam his shotgun against the back of the boy's head and pull the trigger. The blast lifted the boy onto his toes. Hair ruffled at the back of his head but his skull remained surprisingly intact. But Cavanaugh was almost sure what he saw fly out the front of the head was the entire facial mask, intact, splatting against the wall like wads of wet Kleenex.

Russell turned to Cavanaugh and winked. "Want us to save a couple for you, Sarge?"

Cavanaugh must have shaken his head, because Ben shrugged and went back into the apartment.

"Don't ever fuck with me like that again," Boone threatened, pointing his gun at Cavanaugh's chest.

Cavanaugh looked into Boone's deep-set eyes. They were wide with excitement, passion, anger. Cavanaugh could see he felt robbed of killing that boy.

"Next time, Cavanaugh, I'll fucking blow your ass off. Got me, shithead?"

Cavanaugh's moves were casual. So casual that Boone misunderstood their deadliness. Cavanaugh brushed the MAC-10 aside with one wrist, grabbed Boone's hand, broke it, then broke the arm, then drove his elbow into Boone's nose, breaking that too. Boone's mouth opened to scream and Cavanaugh shoved the barrel of the MAC-10 into it and pulled the trigger. The bullets seemed to nail Boone's head to the floor.

Leaving the gun and his men behind, Cavanaugh disappeared.

28

AARON LELAND sat in his favorite leather chair in his study, head back, fingers steepled. His headphones prevented him from hearing the telephone's electric buzz. However, he did see the flashing light on the panel, waited just a dozen more notes as the organ scaled Bach's rhapsodic Toccata and Fugue in D Minor. One of the classic cantatas out of Bach's Muhlhausen period, written in the energetic Northern style.

It was not like Leland to ignore a telephone, but he was himself in such a rhapsodic mood that he hated to break the spell. The Junkyard Dogs had been successful. Yes, Sergeant Boone had been killed and Cavanaugh had escaped, but those were minor setbacks. Boone was easily replaced—in fact already had been. Renegade soldiers who know how to keep a secret weren't too hard to find. And Cavanaugh, well, he had been only really crucial for the first raid. The men had needed his familiar presence to cross back over the line, to return to what their imprisonment had made them. Now that they'd crossed it, were getting rewarded for it, they would keep at it for as long as Leland asked them.

According to the news media, the raid had been part of either a drug war or a family conflict. But there were preliminary reports that already some identified terrorists were moving out of their nests and heading for the borders or buying plane tickets. Not en masse, but enough that Leland could make a convincing oral report to the president, who was extremely pleased. His own party's polls showed his support dwindling dramatically. He'd nodded with enthusiasm at Leland's good news.

"How long before I can safely announce our program?" he had asked Leland.

"Not quite yet. Wait for a few more raids. By then there'll be a convincing pattern to report."

"Who are these guys you sent in, Aaron? Anybody among them we can give to the press, someone they can make a folk hero out of, run through the *Today* show and such?"

"That's already taken care of. Not actually one of the squad, of course. The real men must remain anonymous to be effective. But I'm grooming a soldier, a real good kid, looks like Kurt Russell. He'll do the publicity later when we go public. He'll pretend he's been on the raids and is making a statement now because he's been wounded and can no longer participate. I guarantee his face will be smiling from the covers of *People* and *Newsweek* and *Time*."

"Think he can stand up to reporters' questioning?"

"Mr. President, he's been training for media the same way those other boys train for combat. Believe me, the whole country will take him to their hearts. We're already negotiating a book contract about his life and a film deal. Through undercover parties, of course. America needs a hero, and this boy will fulfill that need."

"Yes, a hero," the president said, tugging his earlobe. "A hero is always good."

"And every time the public sees his face, they'll remember you were responsible for making them feel safer. They'll remember that come next November."

The president stiffened and Leland realized he'd made a mistake. He shouldn't have been so obvious about the votes.

"I'm not doing this just to stay in office, Aaron," the president said coldly. "I'm doing this because it's right." He stared forcefully at Leland a minute, then let his famous smile break over his face. "Of course, I wouldn't mind staying in office too. Most of my programs are just getting off the ground. I made one mistake and the country is ready to boot me, the hell with everything else I've tried to accomplish. One hijacked plane in Berlin. Shit.''

The triumphant notes of Bach erased the president's stern face from Leland's mind. The phone continued to flash. Leland punched the button stopping the compact disk, removed the headphones and picked up the receiver. ''Yes?''

''Comfy?''

Leland sighed. Charon.

Charon laughed. ''This place is great, Aaron. One day and I've already got a tan.''

''What have you found out?''

''How'd your little Junkyard Dogs do? They sit up and beg or roll over and play dead?''

''The program was a success.''

''Yeah. I called a friend of mine, a cop. He spoke to another cop who was on the scene. Said it was so bloody, even the cops were tossing their cookies.''

''We emphasized the detrimental aspects of this operation.''

Charon laughed again. ''Some of the victims had teeth marks in them, Aaron.''

Leland touched the smooth plastic compact disk case, began spinning it on the tabletop. ''What have you found out?''

''Start spreading the news. Your guys are leaving today.''

''You found him? You found Towne?''

''Got a fucking map, man. Arrows and everything.''

Leland permitted himself a smile. Everything was finally coming together. Word had come down from the computer experts that although most of Fat Boy's crucial files were still closed, no more had been shut down. That fact tied in with Charon's news. Vatican Towne must be feeling their hot breath on his neck. Now Leland could send the Junkyard Dogs in, and by tomorrow evening everything would be back to normal. Except that Aaron Leland would have much more influence in the White House.

"I'm ordering a private jet for the men now. They'll be there within hours."

"Fine. I've done my part, so don't expect me to go wading in there with them. I'm strictly an observer except for the mop-up afterward. Remington, Ford and Fawley. Unless you want me to kill them now."

Leland considered this. "No. Let's wait and see first."

"Okay with me. Towne almost did my job for me anyway. Set off a bomb under your people."

Leland was surprised. He hadn't received any report from Stan about a bombing. "Were they hurt?"

"Don't know. I was busy snagging the bomber. He's the one who drew the map. The lines are a little shaky—poor son of a bitch couldn't hold a pencil too well when I was finished with him. I mean, how many fingers do you really need to hold a pencil?"

Leland did not respond to Charon's bragging tone.

"I have to admit, I was impressed by the boy's loyalty to Vatican. Takes a hell of a man to inspire that kind of devotion."

"Give me a number where you can be reached there. My men will need to contact you upon arrival."

"Just use my Georgetown number, Aaron. I can phone in for my messages and contact them."

"You still think I'll try to kill you?"

"It's what I'd do."

"Not everyone is like you, Charon."

"Maybe not. But sooner or later everyone tries to be. That knowledge has kept me alive."

Leland hung up. Killing Charon was not a high priority right now. Capturing Vatican Towne and getting Fat Boy back was. Moscow intelligence reported some unusual movement among top government officials there. Secret meetings, arguments, military alerts. They probably suspected something was wrong in the United States, even if they didn't know what exactly.

The country's safety, indeed its existence, depended entirely on Aaron Leland now. He accepted this responsibility with a sense of joyful fulfillment he hadn't felt since his seminary days.

Most people couldn't fathom the feelings of people like him. They looked at celibacy and shuddered. They didn't understand the freedom that came with certain disciplines. To Leland, avoiding the complexities and distractions of sexual relationships was no different from Einstein buying identical suits so he didn't have to decide what to wear each day. The celibate reserved his passion—not his lust—for truly worthy subjects. Even Bach, at age twenty, anxious to study under the flamboyant composer Dietrich Buxtehude, had walked more than two hundred miles to learn from this master, a pilgrimage no less spiritual than those made to the Holy Land.

Leland wished he'd been able to make such a pilgrimage, one fraught with hardships and physical punishment. Perhaps he should go with the Junkyard Dogs to Kauai, lead the capture and interrogation of Vatican Towne. He absently touched the white island of hair at his temple, his fingers stroking lazily. No, too risky. His pilgrimage had been the slow, steady climb in his career, to a place where he had the power to do good. Knowing good from evil wasn't enough; one had to be able to *act* on behalf of good.

That was the argument that had led to his trouble back with the Jesuits. He had been the top student in the seminary, with the highest evaluations; he had been the role model for other novices. Leland hadn't minded the hard work or the strictness of the discipline. He had encouraged it, blossomed under it. In the evenings he would lead discussion groups. One hot topic was his desire to reestablish the ancient Templars, a religious military order of knighthood established during the Crusades. The formal name of the Templars was Poor Knights of Christ and the Temple of Solomon. Originally established by eight or nine French knights, their professed duty was to

protect pilgrims on their way to the Holy Land from maraud-
ing Muslims. They even had a formal set of rules written by
Saint Bernard. The group grew and grew until it was a formidable force of considerable political power. Through a series of corrupt political moves designed to steal the Templars'
wealth, however, they were unjustly declared heretics, and
their Grand master Jacques de Molay was burned at the stake.

Young Aaron Leland had proclaimed the glory of the Templars to his fellow students, professing that it was not enough
to carry just the *word* of God—one needed to wield His sword
too. Other students dismissed such musings as word games.
But Aaron Leland was serious. Even now he thought of his
agents as missionaries, not for God exactly, but for what was
right and good and just—the things this country exemplified.
And goodness could not afford to be static or complacent.
Certainly evil was not. People like Charon were everywhere.

But young Aaron Leland had not been as patient then. He'd
had no plan, merely a burning desire to make the world better. When he saw a novice stealing three stamps from another,
he sneaked into the thief's room that night, gagged him and
bound him into a painful crucified position across his bed for
the entire night, throwing water on his face whenever the boy
drifted into unconsciousness. "This is only part of the pain
Christ suffered," he told the gagged boy, "so that you
wouldn't do such things. Remember that pain and learn."

By morning, Leland released the boy and left. Leland never
mentioned the incident to anyone, nor did the boy report Leland. However, the boy confessed to a friend, and eventually
there was a formal inquiry. When the Jesuit authorities questioned Leland, he denied nothing. They were willing to forget the matter after relatively minor punishment. But Leland
would accept no punishment for what he had done because he
believed himself to be right. He left the seminary, went to
Harvard to study law. Soon after graduation, he entered
Graceland.

Leland reached over to the bookshelf and pressed the Play button of the compact disk player. Bach's rich organ music filled the study as if it were a cathedral. Once Leland had tried to discuss his passion for Bach with Cliff Remington, describing the complexities and nuances of the man's genius. Cliff had merely shrugged and said, "He's good, sure. But you know who's really a genius? The guy who invented dental floss. Simple. A piece of string. But look at how much pain and agony he's prevented. That's genius. Do you know dental problems were the number-one cause of suicide in the Middle Ages?" He'd said it all with a straight face, not a hint of a smile, so Leland hadn't been sure if Cliff was teasing or not. Not that it mattered. It was so much like Cliff to be more concerned with the physical while Leland dealt with the spiritual. Cliff wept for the hungry, Leland for the morally lost.

Aaron Leland turned down the volume and dialed the phone. Sergeant Geary, Boone's replacement answered. Leland ordered him and the Junkyard Dogs to report to the waiting jet. "How do the men feel, Sergeant?" Leland asked.

"Ready, sir," Sergeant Geary said. "Ready for action."

29

"YOU LOOK TERRIBLE," Tory said.

"History repeats itself," Cliff said.

"Huh?"

"That's what you said the first time we met. That I looked terrible."

"Yeah, but this time it's not my fault."

Cliff hopped off the emergency room gurney, carefully tucking his shirt into his pants. Dried blood stained his shirt, a long green grass stain blotched the seat of his pants. His abdomen was tightly wrapped in white gauze, the pressure relieving some of the pain. "Let's find Stan."

Tory looked at the nurses and doctors bustling around them. "You sure you can just leave? Aren't you supposed to check with somebody first, sign something official. That's fresh blood on your shirt, Cliff."

"Fresh blood, old wound. The bullet hole in my side tore open from the impact of the explosion. Otherwise, not a scratch."

"Have you seen Stan?"

"Not yet. Have you?"

"They rushed him right past me. Wheeled him down the hall, through some doors. Everything happened so fast, I don't even know how badly he's hurt."

"He's tough."

"Bombs are tougher."

At first there had been cops. Lots of them, in short-sleeved uniforms, perspiration quick to slick their skin after stepping out of their air-conditioned squad cars. They started asking questions right away. Stubby yellow pencils poised over battered clipboards. Then the ambulance drivers had carried Cliff away. He'd expected more cops to be waiting for him here, asking more questions, but so far no one had shown up.

Stan was easy to find. They just asked at the nurses' station and were directed by a tiny Oriental nurse with thick glasses. The hospital was quaint, hardly bigger than a grocery store, but everyone seemed busy, and no one paid particular attention as Cliff and Tory wandered around, peeking behind curtains.

"Over there," Tory pointed.

Stan wasn't even in bed. He was leaning against the wall talking into the pay telephone. His back was to them. He was wearing a hospital gown over his shredded trousers. The gown wasn't tied and Cliff noticed several fresh cuts amid a crowd of freckles on his back. Stan hung up the phone, but remained leaning against the wall, as if gathering strength for movement.

"Can't be too hurt," Tory said. "He's already making calls." She walked up to him and tapped him on the shoulder. Stan turned slowly, obviously in great pain. Tory saw his arm and gasped, jumping back a little.

"Why do you think they always pick on this hand?" Stan asked. He held up what remained of his left arm, which ended just below the elbow in folds of pink gummy flesh, like an exotic flower about to bloom.

"My God, Stan," Tory cried.

"Don't worry, the explosion just tore the harness straps of my prosthesis. Sent the sucker flying, scaring some little girl out of her wits. Broke the hook mechanism, though. I just phoned Honolulu for a replacement. Won't be custom fit, but it'll do until this is over."

"They flying one over?" Cliff asked.

"Take a couple of hours."

Tory put an arm around Stan and helped him walk back to his bed. Stan sat on the edge and shrugged out of his hospital gown. A few more scratches from his fall crosshatched his chest. Tory stared where the nipple should have been.

"Happened a long time ago," Stan said to her, smiling. "More or less a novelty now, a conversation piece." He reached for his shirt and Tory helped him put it on, buttoning the front for him.

"Where's all the official questioning?" Cliff asked.

"All taken care of. The cops have it down as a faulty valve in the gas line. We're free to continue enjoying our vacation."

"Leland's got a long arm."

Stan climbed slowly off the bed. "On the bright side, I think my bowels are better."

"Now we know Vatican must be around here someplace. Otherwise he wouldn't have bothered trying to kill us."

"Which brings us to the bad news." Stan reached into his blackened, torn pants and pulled out Kyle's map. "I checked this out with the local police on the ambulance drive. The map is a phony. Leads to a school yard."

"Good thing you didn't pay him yet. Do you think this Kyle really knows where Towne is?"

"He knows. He probably got greedy, wants more money. Figured we'd be more pliable after running this phony down."

Cliff stopped at the drinking fountain in the hallway and sipped some cold water. Then he dipped his head deeper into the fountain and splashed some of the icy water on his face. The cold shock tensed his muscles all the way to the bullet wound in his side. He straightened, blotted excess water with his palm. "The way it looks, you give me Kyle's address or some of his contacts, I hunt him down and get the real map, if he really knows where Towne is."

"Without money?"

"I was on the debating team in high school. I can be persuasive."

Stan stopped hobbling, but still leaned on Tory as he turned to look at Cliff. "This is a search-and-locate mission, Cliff. Not a search-and-destroy."

"Search-and-locate," Cliff repeated, nodding.

"Then we call in the experts."

"Interrogators."

"Correct. We're talking about preventing a world war here, not revenge."

"I'll call as soon as I learn anything. You wait here for your prosthesis."

Cliff could almost feel Stan's stare bumping his own eyes. Stan was doubtful, but Cliff knew he didn't have any choice. They couldn't all sit around and waste hours, yet neither could Stan comfortably go chasing after Vatican Towne with only one working hand.

"Take Tory with you," Stan finally said.

"I'll be faster without her."

"You'll also be less likely to go charging into dangerous situations. I don't care if you get killed, just as long as I get Towne's whereabouts first."

"Hey, fellas," Tory said. "Thanks for asking, but what if I don't want to go with him and I don't want to stay with you? I mean, I came along because you guys promised some protection. Pretty shabby job of it so far. I'm not so sure I wouldn't be better off disappearing up in Canada for a while."

Cliff kept walking. "Suit yourself."

THEY USED Stan's credit card to purchase new clothing. They didn't bother trying anything on—just popped into a store, grabbed some handfuls from the shelves and off the racks and tossed everything in the car.

The Kiahuna Plantation offered profuse apologies about the accident in their rooms and supplied them with an identical condo closer to the beach at no charge. The rooms were filled with fresh tropical flowers and fruit, courtesy of the management. First thing Cliff and Stan did was search the flower vases for electronic bugs, then they threw out the fruit in case it was poisoned. They scoured the rest of the rooms but found no bombs. Then everyone showered and changed into their new clothing.

Cliff pulled on his blue polo shirt, khaki shorts and Top-siders. He looked into the bathroom mirror, which was still slightly foggy from his shower. He was surprised to find his reflection smiling, cheeks slightly flushed. That had been his expression when he was about to go on assignment, at least when he was younger. The thrill of expectation. The feeling that he was challenging himself, the confidence that he would win. Eventually those good feelings had been replaced by foreboding and dull routine. But now, right this minute, he felt that old thrill again.

He opened the bathroom door and walked out into the living room. Stan and Tory were sitting on the sofa going over road maps of Kauai. Stan was marking the last place he'd seen Kyle.

Cliff picked up the car keys from the counter as well as his wallet, watch and some loose change. As he was funneling the change into his pocket, he palmed the dime and placed it on the back of his hand. He held the hand out in front of him for a couple of seconds.

"What's this?" Tory said. "Magic tricks?"

Cliff jerked his hand out from under the dime, then snatched the dime in his hand as it dropped toward the floor.

Tory applauded.

"You still do that, huh?" Stan asked.

"Doesn't everybody?"

"Some old-timers."

"You?"

"No need. I haven't been in the field in years."

"What's the game?" Tory asked. "I'll play."

"No game," Stan said. "A kind of test. A ritual really, to focus the reflexes."

"Superstitions?"

"No."

"Yes," Cliff said. "Field agents are very superstitious. One thing they've learned is that no matter how good you are, how much you prepare, survival is mostly luck."

Tory looked at Stan, then at Cliff. "Doesn't look like much of a test." She stood up, took Cliff's dime, placed it on the back of her hand. She tossed the coin up and caught it. "Not hard at all," she said, grinning.

"You tossed it up. Just pull your hand out from under it, like yanking a tablecloth."

She tried it. The dime bounced onto the carpet. She tried it again. Her fingers hit the dime, sending it flying into the sliding glass door. "Almost," she said, fetching it.

"Once you've got that mastered," Cliff said, "you can move on to this. He placed two pennies and a dime on the back of his hand, pulled the hand out, then scooped all three coins in midair.

"Big deal."

Stan chuckled.

Cliff picked up the road map from the coffee table and started for the door. "I'll call when I know something."

Tory grabbed her purse and hurried after him.

Stan got up and turned on the TV. Cliff heard Connie Francis singing "Where the Boys Are" as he stepped into the sun.

"How MANY IS THAT?" Tory asked.

"What?"

"How many people? How many people have we questioned so far?"

"I don't keep track."

"I do. Eighteen. We've stopped at every little cluster of houses and stores, you've asked about this Kyle guy, and they've stared at you like some child molester. Then they grin at me like they've been through my underwear drawer while I'm not home. Doesn't it get to you?''

Cliff steered the rented car along the Kuhio Highway. Sometime during the past hour, night had sneaked in from the ocean and dimmed the landscape. Cliff switched the headlights on.

They'd searched all the hangouts Stan had mentioned, but had seen no sign of Kyle. No one admitted knowing anything about him. Cliff had been patient, partially because he was getting used to the process again. The endless questioning, the posturing. He'd forgotten how good he was at it, how Drew had always bowed out when it came to this part of an assignment. "You're more people oriented," Drew had said. It was true. Cliff had a way with people because he generally liked them. Maybe that was why he'd always been such a language whiz.

The past few hours had been a revelation to Cliff. He'd felt his old powers coming back, the moldy instincts, the rusty reflexes. He gripped the steering wheel until his knuckles drained of blood, whitened like snow-capped peaks. His muscles enjoyed the tension. He dug his elbow against his wounded side, felt the pain spark and ignite. He did it again, concentrating. His mind absorbed the pain, sponged it up, tacked it to some bulletin board inside his head, diagramed and analyzed it, and found it to be inconsequential. The pain disappeared. He dug his side again. Felt nothing.

Finally, Cliff had an identity.

Since Moonshadow, he had been a family man. Husband, father, landscaper. He read report cards, went grocery shopping, attended PTA. He knew who he was and liked it. Then they'd taken that away, and he'd been floating ever since. In the middle of the ocean, treading water, trying not to think about the billions of threatening life forms swimming beneath his helpless body.

Now he had somehow tapped into the source within himself, found the rejuvenating springs. He had come full cycle, back to what he was in the beginning: powerful, committed, energetic. Ruthless.

Cliff eased the car off the side of the road and parked in front of Kapaa's Seafood Hut.

"This isn't on the list, is it?" Tory asked.

"On my list. I'm hungry."

"As long as they have salad. I'm dying for a good chef's salad."

"Island salads are terrible. The lettuce looks limp and wilted. You won't like it."

Tory sighed. "Perfect."

Inside they were seated at a booth, the table a thick slab of polyurethaned wood. Hurricane lamps flickered on each table. The menu was printed on the paper place mats. Cliff ordered the mahimahi, Tory the Hawaiian chicken marinated in shoyu and ginger.

Business was slow. Besides Cliff and Tory, there were two middle-aged women at the next table, and a couple with a small boy across the room.

"Excuse me," one of the women said to Cliff and Tory. "I've never had this calamari before. What is it exactly? Peg here says it's squid, for God's sake."

"Yes, ma'am," Cliff said. "Breaded and sautéed."

"Oh, God, sounds absolutely horrible. I think I'll try it." She giggled with delight at her daring.

"Our first time in the Islands," Peg said. "Lorrie's never been out of L.A."

"That's not true," Lorrie said. "I go to San Diego to visit my daughter and her family every month. I go to Palm Springs once a year."

"Okay, then, Southern California. You've never been out of Southern California."

"I went to Las Vegas last year, remember. Won thirty-four dollars on the slots. That's not in California. It's in Nevada."

Peg shook her head and looked at Cliff and Tory. "You know what I mean."

"God, imagine me eating squid. I mean, I know they must serve it in L.A., but I never eat in places that have it. Squid, my God. It's kinda like frog legs or something."

"She's excited because we won this trip. Stay at each of the islands for two days. All expenses paid." Peg tried to look droll and sophisticated about it all, but Cliff could see she was as excited as her friend Lorrie.

"What kind of contest?" Tory asked.

"Not a contest. We're Star Polishers," Lorrie said proudly.

"Beg your pardon?"

"Star Polishers. Me and Peg adopted James Garner's star at 6927 Hollywood Boulevard. Once a week we go out there and scrub his star, polish up that brass TV and the lettering. Make sure it really shines."

Peg interrupted. "After you been doing this for a year, you get to adopt the star. Not Jimbo, but the sidewalk star. And you meet all kinds of neat people. Like there's this Indian fella, Sioux, I think."

"Sioux," Lorrie agreed.

"He's adopted Jay Silverheels, Sinatra, Isaac Stern and Iron Eyes Cody. He's always out there hosing them down."

"Hosing's not enough, though," Lorrie said. "Hosing don't take the bubble gum off. You gotta get down on your hands and knees with a putty knife and some 409 or Fantastik to really do a good job. That's terrazzo marble we're talking about."

"Anyway, Mr. Garner hears about us and he just *gives* us this trip. He's personally paying for the whole thing. Had a limo drive us to the airport. You ever hear of anything so dear?"

"No," Cliff said.

"Sounds wonderful," Tory said.

"A few days ago we were at work sewing little smiling whales on the sleeves of shirts I wouldn't want my son to wear. Today I'm eating breaded squid."

"Penguins eat five or six squids a day," Cliff said.

"My goodness, that's incredible. You should go on a game show or something. You'd clean up."

"I've been meaning to," Cliff said as the women's waitress arrived, ending the conversation.

"Lucky ladies," Tory said. "They were so happy."

"One year. That's a lot of gum to scrape. Lot of spit to scrub."

"They must enjoy it. Feeling connected to a star, to the glamour."

Cliff sipped his water, somehow bumped his tender side against the edge of the table. The pain burst, then died immediately. Under control.

"I hope I have a job when this is all over. One thing law firms frown upon, it's their lawyers suddenly taking off for Hawaii in the middle of a big case."

"Stan cleared it, didn't he?"

"Oh, yes, he called, gave them some story so complex I didn't even understand it. Gave them government references. National security. Blah, blah, blah. Back at the office they're probably referring to me as Mata Hari, thinking I'm walking around in black stockings, sleeping with international spies."

"You'll be a celebrity when you get back."

"I'll be hit on by every male in the building."

Their dinner arrived and they ate mostly in silence. Cliff didn't feel like talking. He was getting used to his body, to his new strength. At one point he excused himself, went into the rest room and did fifty push-ups with hardly any effort.

When they finished eating, Cliff paid the bill and they returned to the car. Tory strapped on her seat belt with a deep sigh. "Life seems so accelerated. Like we've lived ten years in the past two days."

"We have. Ten years' worth of bad luck."

"More than that."

Cliff started the car, looking straight ahead. But out of the corner of his eye he could see her staring at him. He avoided her gaze.

"You're so strange. Sometimes I feel as if we've known each other for years, as if we went to school together or something wholesome like that. Right now I almost have trouble remembering what Ed looks like."

"He looks dead."

"Christ, I know that. Why are you being such a shit? You know what I meant."

"It's important that we remember the dead."

"Remember, sure. But not enshrine." She shook her head, smoothed back her short blond hair. "I'm sorry. Forget I said anything. I lost an ex-husband I hated. You lost a family you loved. Who am I to talk about the dos and don'ts of mourning?"

Cliff swung the car back onto the highway and headed for the next address where they might find Kyle. He avoided looking at Tory, who sat quietly looking out the window. She was a good person. He liked her. He poked his elbow against his wound. Nothing. No feeling. He was relieved.

"Actually, I never really wanted to be a lawyer," Tory said, still facing away, staring out the window. "I never really wanted to be anything. No driving ambitions. College was just a way for me to delay making any decisions. I had the grades, though, to be anything. Doctor, lawyer, engineer, architect. But I never had any talent. You know, no knack for anything, no passion. I could master the techniques of any profession, but I'd never really care about it. Guess that's why Ed was able to recruit me so easily into the Agency. Do they call it Company or Agency now?"

"I don't know. We called it Graceland."

"Yeah, I'd heard that. I like the sound of it. Anyway, Ed loved what he did so much I think I got caught up in his passion, hoped some of it would rub off on me. Didn't work out that way. So after I dumped Ed, I went to law school. Hell, I may not get shivers up and down my spine, but I'm a damned fine lawyer."

There was a long silence. She looked over at Cliff, waiting for some response.

"We're here," he said and pulled the car off the road.

CLIFF RETURNED to the car. Tory was reading *U.S. News & World Report*.

"We're all going to die of AIDS," she said, not looking up from the magazine as he slid behind the wheel. "I'm convinced. The world will end, not with a bang, but with tubes growing out of our veins. I've got to stop reading these articles."

Cliff started the car.

"Where to now?"

"Kyle's apartment."

Tory looked at him. "You finally found someone willing to talk. Impressive." She flicked the overhead light on, then off. "What happened to your knuckles? They look red."

"I fell."

"You fell on your knuckles? Where did you land, someone's jaw?"

KYLE'S APARTMENT was in Lihue, on Umi Street, the top floor of an old house converted to two apartments. Kyle's entrance was at the top of a rickety wooden stairway attached to the side of the house. The door had been added long after the house was built, apparently sawed right through the bedroom wall to make a rental unit.

Cliff parked the car and Tory immediately flipped open her magazine. "Eventually they're going to test everybody for AIDS. Schoolkids, everybody. Wait and see." She tapped the glossy page that had a color photograph of the AIDS virus. "This little fucker is going to cause the collapse of democracy as we know it."

Cliff opened the car door. "You'd better come with me."

"What for?"

"Because there's too much about what's been going on that doesn't ring true. Kyle's map. How hard it was to find his address. I get the feeling that he's not working alone, which means I don't want to leave you here in the car. Okay?"

"Okay."

They started up the stairway, which creaked and wobbled with each step. Tory grasped the weather-worn railing with both hands. Cliff marched soundlessly to the top, his gun already in his hand.

He knocked.

No answer.

He knocked again.

Nothing.

He tried the door. Unlocked. He pushed it open slowly, crouching immediately so the moonlight didn't outline him in the doorway. Tory had enough training to wait a few steps from the landing until Cliff had checked the place out. Cliff didn't move, just stared into the darkness waiting for his eyes to adjust. Nothing in the room moved. When he was finally able to identify most of the dark lumps in the room, he flipped the lights on.

He was right. The owners of the house had just cut a door in the bedroom wall and called it an apartment. The bed was empty, but neatly made. No clothes were strewn around. There were no photographs on the walls, merely a few Georgia O'Keeffe posters of skulls and flowers. The desert moti seemed somehow overwhelmed by the lush tropics outside, but perhaps that was why Kyle had hung them.

Cliff moved cautiously around the room, gun poised, using his left hand to casually poke in drawers, not really searching, just nosing about.

Tory peeked around the doorjamb, saw Cliff opening a drawer and entered. "He's not home?"

"Not in here," Cliff said, closing the drawer. Something struck him as odd. Though there were a few socks and T-shirts and such in some of the drawers, most were empty. Dust caked the furniture. There were no plants in the room. It was as if no one really lived there, but merely stayed over on occasion.

"You want me to search the closet? They taught me how to do that."

"Not necessary."

Cliff was about to look in the bathroom. The wedge of light fell over a bare foot. He nudged open the door with his gun and turned on the light. Half in the shower stall but with his legs splayed across the floor of the tiny bathroom, lay a dead young Filipino. He was naked. The various nicks and cuts, bruises and burn blisters indicated extensive torture. The caked blood around the closed eyelids proved he'd been blinded before being killed. His mouth hung open to reveal puffy white blisters and missing teeth. Beaten, then his mouth washed with lye.

Cliff's throat constricted and his stomach lurched. He slapped his hand against his wound. The pain burned away the queasy feeling. He was back in control.

Tory's shaky voice came from the bedroom. "Unless it's absolutely necessary, I'm not coming in there, okay? I see a foot and part of a leg and I've got a bad feeling he's not resting."

Cliff returned to the bedroom, closing the bathroom door behind him.

"Is it Kyle?"

Cliff nodded. "Matches Stan's description."

"What happened?"

"Tortured, then garroted. The wire nearly beheaded him."

"Jesus! Where does that leave us? If he's the only one who knows how to find Vatican Towne, we're screwed."

Heavy metal rapped wood.

They both turned to the doorway. A young Oriental woman stood there, clutching a heavy automatic with both hands in a professional stance. It wasn't her stance that convinced Cliff she knew what she was doing, it was the fact that she'd managed to climb those creaky wobbly stairs without making a sound.

She gestured with her gun at Cliff's gun. Cliff slowly laid his gun on the floor. She gestured again and he kicked it under the bed.

"Who are you?" Tory asked.

The woman said nothing, as if she hadn't heard. She kept her eyes on Cliff, and he noticed they paid particular attention to his lips. Without speaking, he mouthed the words, *Who are you?*

She shook her head as if to say it didn't matter.

Cliff signed, *Who sent you?*

She looked surprised. She released one hand from the gun and signed in alphabet letters rather than Ameslan. *V-A-T-I-C-A-N T-O-W-N-E.*

"Why?" Cliff said aloud.

She cocked the hammer on her gun.

30

HER EYES WERE FIERCE, red rimmed. Raw. She'd been crying. There was no sign of tears now, just hatred.

"Who is she?" Tory asked.

"I don't know," Cliff said. "Probably one of Towne's assassins."

Tory paused, smiled. "I thought I'd be more frightened. You know, you picture the moment of your death, hope you don't embarrass yourself. Wet your pants or worse."

"That comes after death. The bladder relaxes, the sphincter muscles open."

"So I guess it doesn't matter that I've got clean underwear on."

Cliff looked at her, impressed by her cool head. Part of it was an act, sure, but part of it was just her. He had underestimated her.

The Oriental woman waved the gun and Cliff backed up until he stood next to Tory. The woman closed the door behind her. She glanced at the bathroom, her jaw clenched firm, her eyes glistening. Then she turned away and she shut down whatever emotion she was feeling. Cliff could almost see the instant it vaporized, like a candle flame puffed out. It was the same effect he'd been striving for by prodding his bullet wound. But she did it faster, better, without pain. Just by sheer will.

"She's just a kid," Tory said.

"She's young, but no kid." Cliff figured her for about twenty-two. Her long dark hair reminded him of Lily's, but she was half Lily's size in every way. One difference, blue eyes. Ocean blue. Her Oriental features, like the Filipino's in the bathroom, had been subdued by an infusion of Caucasian blood.

Her bare feet slid slowly across the floor as if the soles were memorizing the grain pattern. Cliff had thought he knew how to walk silently; she was better.

"Now what?" Cliff asked her.

She stared at Cliff a long moment, then tossed her gun on the bed. Her hands churned with language. *Now you must find Vatican Towne and stop him!*

CLIFF DID NOT MOVE toward the gun. He stood solemnly and let her speak.

He's gone crazy, she said. *I don't understand all of it, what he's doing with the computer. He doesn't tell me everything. But he doesn't know what he's doing anymore. The consequences.*

"You know where he is?" Cliff asked.

He wanted only to help. That's what started it. Those poor boys. He'd given his word. He was honor bound. But things have gotten away from him. Out of his control. His son Bradley was killed. Now his son Kyle.

"Kyle was Vatican's son?" Tory said.

Cliff spoke with his voice and hands. Sometimes he couldn't remember the sign, so he'd spell it out with his fingers. This was too important not to be sure she knew what he was saying. "He was sent by Vatican, wasn't he? Sent here to play hard to get, but eventually lure us somewhere where Vatican would be waiting. A trap."

She nodded.

"What was your job?"

To help Kyle. Once you were in the canyon, Kyle and I would prevent your retreat.

Cliff sat on the edge of the bed. "The bomb. That wasn't meant to kill us. That was meant to convince us we were on the right track."

Yes.

"That can't be," Tory said. "I saw the timer. It was counting off seconds."

"The timer probably counted down from twenty seconds, then repeated the countdown endlessly until we went running from the house. I imagine someone was just outside waiting. When they saw we were clear, they detonated the bomb by remote control."

That was Kyle's job. Now he's dead. Tortured.

"We didn't do it."

I know. If I thought you had, I'd have killed you both already.

Cliff didn't doubt it.

However, I know you've been asking where to find Kyle all afternoon. He's been dead at least two hours, maybe longer. Killed somewhere else and brought here. Lividity has already settled in.

"You know a lot about this sort of thing."

I had the best teacher in the world. Vatican Towne.

"And now you want to betray him?"

She shook her head violently. *Not betray, save! Whoever killed Bradley and Kyle will go after Vatican next. You must save him. You're his only chance now.*

"You know who I am?" Cliff said.

Clifford Remington. Vatican thinks you killed his son.

"Did he kill my wife, my children?"

Believe me, Mr. Remington. He did not. He did not kill them.

Cliff believed she believed that. He had to admit, he had his doubts. Treachery was becoming all the rage, and now no one could be trusted. Perhaps he should just put a bullet through the woman, through Tory, through Stan. A bullet through everyone involved. Aaron. Vatican Towne. Go into the bathroom and put a bullet through Kyle. Don't miss anybody. Eventually he'd get the person responsible. He rubbed his eyes and blew out a deep breath.

"What do you want me to do?" Cliff asked.

Go with me. I'll take you to his home. We can sneak in. You can do whatever it takes with the computer. Just call off the others. Protect him from the men who did this.

Cliff didn't point out that he didn't know what to do with the computer. That expert interrogators would be flown in with all the latest drugs and sharp medical instruments and that when they were done, even Vatican Towne would talk. Everyone always talked in the end. Whether or not he believed Vatican was responsible for his family's death, Cliff did believe what Stan had told him about Fat Boy. He did believe the country was in great danger. Consequently he would call in those interrogators.

"I'll see what I can do," Cliff said.

She smiled at him gratefully, then grabbed her gun from the bed. She tucked it in her shorts and pulled her loose blouse over the butt. *Let's go.*

"What's she saying?" Tory asked.

Cliff stood up, guided Tory toward the door. "I'm going with her." He turned his back to the woman so she couldn't see his lips. "I want you to drive back and pick up Stan. We're not more than twenty minutes away. He should have his new prosthesis by now. Bring him back here."

She pulled away from his elbow. "Back here? What for?"

"For the map. I'll have her draw a detailed map, a real one this time that will allow Stan to call in backup. I'm sure he and Aaron Leland have already worked something out."

"Why not have her make the map now? I'll wait."

"Because it will take too much time. She's a little antsy."

"She's in mourning for Kyle and scared for Towne. She's not antsy about me."

"I'll show you." Cliff turned around and faced the woman. "What's your name?" he asked aloud and signed.

Dayna.

"My friend and I agree to go with you," he said, but he signed, *If you want me to help you, refuse to let her go.*

Dayna pointed at Tory and shook her head adamantly.

Cliff shrugged at Tory. "See?"

Tory looked suspicious, but accepted the car keys from Cliff. "I'll be back in an hour." She touched his arm with her fingertips, no more than a light brush. "Cliff, these guys aren't fooling around. Whoever's doing all this killing, whether it's us or Towne, they aren't done yet."

"I'll be careful."

"Don't be clever. I almost had you fooled that day we met, remember? And these people know what they're doing."

Cliff walked her to the door, inhaled. The faintest tang of baby powder tickled his nose. "Watch the roads. Don't pull over for anything. For anything."

Cliff and Dayna watched Tory slowly descend the stairs, both hands again gripping the railing as the stairs shifted noisily. When she drove off into the darkness, Cliff immediately pulled Dayna out the door. "Let's get out of here," he said.

Dayna drove the Jeep to the Lihue airport to the small helicopter pad near the tiny terminal building. She hopped out, gesturing brusquely for Cliff to stay in the Jeep. Cliff leaned back in the seat and watched her enter the square metal hut that was Whirlybird Tours. She nodded at a sleepy man in a beard and black nylon jacket with colorful patches on the sleeves. He sipped coffee from a thermos and nodded back at her, hooking a thumb over his shoulder. Obviously everything had been prearranged.

Dayna hurried out of the building, waved at Cliff to follow. They passed two MBB BO-105 CBS twin-engine helicopters before Dayna stopped at a smaller Hughes 500D. The craft's ID numbers had been taped over. Cliff stood by while she quickly checked the exterior, her face grim and efficient. She certainly seemed to know what she was doing. Cliff's flying ability was limited to small fixed-wing planes, though he'd had some helicopter training. Enough to know he didn't like them.

She climbed into the cockpit, Cliff followed and they strapped themselves in. The cockpit was snug. Cliff noted the Allison 250C20B engine and estimated the cruising speed at about 150 mph with a range of about 250 miles. The whole island of Kauai had only a 110-mile circumference, so wherever Vatican Towne was hiding, this should get them there soon.

The four rotor blades started turning overhead, and Cliff noticed that Dayna, being deaf, didn't bother putting on her headphones or communicating with the airport tower. Obviously the man inside the hut must be doing that for her. Still, she wouldn't be able to hear weather reports or aircraft warnings. Cliff squirmed a little in his seat. He signed to her that he would monitor the tower for her, but she shook her head and signed that everything was taken care of.

The helicopter lifted smoothly off the ground and rose at a slight angle into the air. Cliff felt as if a giant hand had just snatched him off the ground and was jerking him up toward some gaping toothy mouth. The helicopter leveled off and Cliff looked out the plastic bubble cockpit at the ground below. Lights shone in clumps, then barely dotted the land at all. The ground looked more like a star-studded sky than did the actual sky above them.

They flew along the southern shore for a while. Cliff had familiarized himself with the island enough that he had a vague idea where they were. When he saw the heavy floodlights and military personnel below, he knew they were passing by Barking Sands Pacific Missile Range and the Barking Sands Airfield. This was restricted airspace and likely to get them a missile as an extra passenger. Dayna coolly veered off and headed out over the ocean, away from the island.

"Are we going to another island?" he asked, signing so she could see his hands.

She didn't respond. She concentrated on the controls, flying at some odd pattern that he realized was meant to throw him off so he couldn't remember how to find the place again. Finally the helicopter dipped to the right and they darted back toward the island.

As they approached the dark mass of land, Cliff was startled by the lack of any lights at all. In the far distance a few dots of light shimmered, but the great black wall in front of them was uninhabited. Cliff realized it must be a section of the Napali Coast, with three-thousand-foot craggy cliffs so sheer that there were no roads here. The land was accessible only by sea. And helicopter.

They buzzed over the cliffs, heavy waves crashing into the rocky base, the foam and froth iridescent in the moonlight. Cliff didn't bother trying to memorize the landscape. There was no way he'd be able to find this exact location again, night or day. Besides, if he did his job properly, he would have no need to return.

Thick puffy clouds hovered ahead, crowning a couple of the taller mountain peaks. Dayna maneuvered expertly around them.

The helicopter began to descend. The tropical forest below grew clearer, more distinct. Dense branches intertwined. A skinny waterfall dropped over a thirty-foot cliff and dumped into a narrow stream. She skimmed just above the treetops, searching for her place to set down.

He tapped her shoulder. She looked over at him.

"Lost?" he said.

Misplaced.

Cliff smiled. This was a remarkable woman. Beautiful and capable. Self-reliant. She'd been highly trained, obviously by Vatican Towne himself.

She shifted the helicopter to the right and suddenly a burst of gunfire sounded. She couldn't have heard it, but she must have seen the muzzle-flash, because she yanked the bird around and started to climb. But not fast enough. Two more bursts sounded and smoke began cascading down from the rotor blades. The helicopter rattled, convulsed, began to drop toward the ground.

Cliff pulled his gun out of his waistband and set it on the floor between his feet. He braced himself for the crash. When he looked at Dayna, though, he saw that she was perfectly calm, concentrating on the controls. Despite the damage she was guiding the craft in a controlled crash. It fluttered down in a slow spin and fell into a thicket of trees. Dozens of branches slowed the fall, but the weight of the helicopter pushed it through the tree limbs to smash onto the ground.

Cliff felt himself being hurled forward and backward at the same time, his neck whipping back with a crack. His harness kept him from flying out of the seat, but it also yanked hard against his bandaged side, tearing the wound open again. The rotor blades that had been sheared by the tree branches dropped on top of the cockpit, cracking the Plexiglas bubble. Birds screamed nastily around them.

Cliff looked over at Dayna. She was dazed. A thin stream of blood trickled from the corner of her mouth. He examined her, found only a bitten lip.

"You okay?" he asked.

She knitted her brows quizzically. Her eyes were glazed and she hadn't been able to focus on his lips.

"You okay?" he repeated, signing as well.

She nodded. *Too close to Farmers' Market.*

"What?" Cliff thought she might be delirious.

Farmers' Market. I flew too close to them. Marijuana growers. We call them Farmers' Market. They shot us down.

"How far are we from Towne's?"

She looked around, checked the sky. *Not far. We can walk part of the way now. But we will have to wait for light to cross the last section. It is easy to get lost in this jungle. Also, the people who shot us down have infrared night scopes.*

"Every farmer's best friend."

Dayna and Cliff climbed out of the wreck. Dayna salvaged her purse, checked her gun, then slung the bag over her shoulder. She nodded for Cliff to follow.

They hiked deeper into brush, climbing higher and higher up the craggy mountains. Cliff did not like jungle assignments. He was not a man-versus-nature enthusiast like many of his fellow agents, whose vacation time was spent acting out the role of jungle survivalist in remote areas of the world. Cliff liked cities, cabs, restaurants, people getting on with their lives, trying to survive together. He'd grown up in a rural area, the rolling hills of northern Pennsylvania. Much of his childhood had been spent roaming the woods for hours, examining insects, flowers, poking through the creeks for crayfish and frogs, flipping rocks to catch garter snakes. He'd brought home turtles and toads, his mother patiently helping him build a pen for his new pets. He'd released them into the woods when they began to die in captivity.

After three or four hours, Dayna finally dropped her purse on the ground and sat. Cliff looked back on the area they'd just climbed. The moon illuminated enough to show a magnificent valley that sloped straight down into the sea.

A small stone bounced off his back. He turned.

Kalalau Valley. Valley of Refuge.

"I almost expect dinosaurs." Cliff sat a few feet from Dayna. She was looking at him now with curiosity.

This is where the first Hawaiian settlers came a thousand years ago. They terraced much of the land here and grew taro. They were completely invulnerable to invasion. The mountains were easy to defend and the only other way in was the turbulent sea.

"Where are they now?"

Gone.

"No one's been able to hold on to Paradise yet. Who took it away from them?"

No one. They gave it away. When white settlers established towns, the natives were drawn to them, eventually abandoning their isolation.

"Perhaps it wasn't Paradise after all if they were so willing to abandon it."

Dayna shrugged. *Perhaps not.* She settled back against a tree trunk and closed her eyes.

Cliff flattened against the ground and closed his eyes too. A few hours' sleep would be helpful right now. Over the past couple of days, his mind and body had been dragged across a potato grater so many times he wasn't sure exactly what he thought or felt about anything. All he could do now to maintain sanity was concentrate on his goal: Vatican Towne. Nothing else had any meaning.

Cliff might have drifted off—he wasn't even sure about that. He was sure that he heard sobbing, not soft melodic weeping, but choked, rib-racking crying. He listened awhile with his eyes closed, pretending to sleep.

After about ten minutes he heard her get up and walk deeper into the woods. He opened his eyes and watched, wondering if she'd changed her mind about taking him to Towne and decided to just leave him here. She marched to a spot about twenty yards away, removed her shorts and panties, squatted and peed. She looked over and caught Cliff's eyes, but he didn't turn away. She didn't seem embarrassed. She wiped herself with some leaves, dressed and returned.

You thought I would leave you here?

"Possibility."

She sat back down. *I'm counting on you to save my father.*

"Towne's your father."

She nodded.

"Where's your mother?"

Dead. Vietnam.

"She was Vietnamese."

Yes. From North Vietnam. Hon Gai.

"Not far from Haiphong."

You know the area?

"What happened to your mother?"

She was a nurse. She escaped to the south.

"And that's where she met Vatican?"

He was a patient. Ordinarily he wouldn't have even been brought to the civilian hospital, but it was an emergency. Food poisoning. The restaurant where he'd eaten had sneaked in some bad dog meat with the pork.

"Then you were born."

Then I was born. As you can see, I lived happily ever after.

"What happened to your mother?"

Killed in the evacuation of Saigon. Trampled to death on her way to the helicopters.

Cliff looked up into the dark sky. He imagined a big ceiling fan overhead.

She began sobbing again. Cliff ignored the sound, closed his eyes again and tried to sleep. If Kyle, the Filipino, was also Vatican's child, as was the Caucasian Bradley, then Vatican had gone through a lot of wives.

A few minutes later her crying stopped. Cliff looked over at her. She was curled on the ground, knees tucked up to her chest, sleeping. He stood up, walked deep into the woods until he couldn't see her anymore, pulled down his zipper and began to urinate. When he was finished, he zipped himself, turned around and saw her standing less than five feet away, watching him.

"You're very good," he said. "How can you be so silent if you can't hear the noise?"

I feel the vibrations through my feet.

He nodded and started back to camp. She followed behind him. This time they sat closer to each other, though Cliff wasn't sure who initiated that. Somehow they were lying on the ground less than three feet apart. She had her back to him. Her long black hair draped her shoulder, then spread out for another foot along the ground. He could see a few twigs and snips of dried leaves caught in her hair. Absently, he reached out and picked a twig from her hair. Startled, she immediately turned around, gun in hand.

"Twig in your hair," Cliff said.

She didn't lower the gun. Her eyes fixed on his, trying to penetrate.

The joke was on her, he thought. There's nothing there *to* penetrate. There's nothing inside.

She lowered her gun. Her eyes looked sympathetic, sad for Cliff. That surprised him. Her hand reached over, touched his hand, curled around it, the fingers long and thin and cool.

Her other hand touched his face.

Cliff felt paralyzed. If they were in a hotel room, in a bed right now, both naked, he wouldn't have done anything about it. Ginger was still too much with him. But lying here on the ground, the moistness of lava-rich soil in his nostrils, the lightness of her fingers like leaves brushing his cheeks . . . the black emptiness within him. Somehow it all combined to hypnotize him, take away his control.

They came together in a hard embrace first, just lying there in each other's arms, not kissing, not groping, just holding, feeling each other's warmth and need mingling. Kisses followed. Brief ones at first, lips barely touching. Then long, deep kissing. Dayna's hair tangled across his face, around his neck. He dug the fingers from both hands into her hair, pulled her closer to him. The clothes came off magically, without effort, each removing the closest piece, no matter who was wearing it. Flesh against flesh, his thick muscled body clutching her thin sinewy body. His bandaged ribs ached a little from the effort, but he ignored the ache. She was on her back now, his mouth on her dark brown nipples, then moving lower, between her legs, her sparse pubic hairs matted against his cheek.

She made no sound, so he watched her, her head rolling slowly back and forth in pleasure as she lifted her hips toward him, thrusting against his tongue. Finally, she opened her eyes, smiled, pulled him up on top of her and guided him into her. Birds cried out and Cliff imagined they were Dayna, that through some enchanted spell they were able to express her feelings. That was how Cliff felt, as if enchantment were possible.

Even afterward, when they were finished and sleeping in each other's arms, Cliff dreamed that Dayna could speak, but that her hands had little wings like those of a hummingbird. In his dream, they both laughed at that.

Cliff didn't know how long he'd been asleep. He knew only that it had been a deep and refreshing sleep, more like unconsciousness or a coma than a nap. When he awoke, Dayna was still in his arms, they were both naked.

They were not alone.

The old man leaning against the nearby tree had a shotgun aimed at them. He was smiling.

Cliff recognized Vatican Towne. Older, grayer, craggier. But the wizened eyes were still the same clear blue, the thin mouth still stretched halfway between grin and grimace. He looked like all his photographs, mischievous.

"Morning," he said.

Dayna opened her eyes. She quickly climbed to her feet and ran happily to him, hugging him. Somehow it wasn't the reaction Cliff had expected from her.

"Some effect you must have had on Dayna," Vatican said. "Ordinarily she would've sensed my approach and woken up."

Cliff reached for his pants and began tugging them on. Ordinarily he should have heard the old man's approach too. "Your daughter had other things on her mind."

"Daughter?" Vatican laughed. "Is that what she told you?"

Dayna was dressing, not watching their lips, so she didn't know what they were saying. But Cliff had the impression that she already knew.

"She's not your daughter?"

"Goodness no." Vatican shook his head, his smile huge and truly amused. "Dayna's my wife."

31

THE THREE OF THEM trekked for another couple of hours high into the steep mountains, then down again into another valley. Dayna led the way, Cliff followed and Vatican trailed, shotgun casually slung over his shoulder. No one spoke.

Cliff felt foolish. Definitely not the emotion he'd thought he would feel when he finally met Vatican Towne. He had expected outrage, murderous passion. Instead, he realized how easily he'd been manipulated, controlled at every turn, either by Aaron Leland or Vatican Towne. This hadn't been a quest for his family's murderer, but a blind rush through a carefully planned maze.

"The helicopter crash," Cliff said over his shoulder as he maneuvered through a clawing thicket. "Planned, of course."

"Dayna's idea. An expensive idea, I might add, but she refused to help me unless she was sure about you. She thought isolating the two of you would give her an opportunity to evaluate you. She's an amazing judge of character. You'd be surprised."

Cliff doubted that anything about Dayna would surprise him. "What's her conclusion about me?"

"That you didn't kill my son."

"And you believe her. Just like that."

"As I said, an amazing judge of character."

"Sort of a sexual lie detector, huh?"

Vatican chuckled. "You're bitter. Embarrassed. Don't be. She's not. I'm not."

"Silly me," Cliff said. He continued to climb after Dayna, watching her easily dodge the underbrush, the muscles in her thighs and calves flexing with each step. Oddly, he didn't de-

sire her anymore. That surprised him. Maybe it was knowing
that she'd deceived him, or that she was married, but he
doubted it. There was something special about last night, the
weight of the darkness on them, the depth of their mutual
grief, the thickness of the jungle. They had come together in
a dreamy passion that did not transcend daylight. Cliff didn't
feel as if he'd betrayed Ginger. He just felt somehow stronger.

Vatican's cheerfulness annoyed him. No matter why or how
they had come together, Cliff had indeed slept with the man's
wife. Cleared of killing his son, but caught in the act of cuck
olding him. Jesus, he thought, that must have been how
Ulysses felt trying to get back home after the Trojan War. Ten
years of being bounced around by irate gods he'd somehow
insulted along the way.

After a long silence, Vatican said, "You don't still think I
killed your family, do you?"

Cliff shook his head. "It would be simpler if you had."

"I think you know who's responsible, Cliff."

Calling him Cliff was an odd familiarity. This was the man
Cliff had come to kill. Yet Cliff had to admit, the familiarity
seemed natural, almost comfortable. "Aaron Leland must
want you dead very badly to have gone to so much trouble."

"He has good reason," Vatican said.

"What could you possibly hope to accomplish by sabotag
ing Fat Boy? You must know they'd never send you Aaron's
head, for Christ's sake."

"One must dream large, Cliff."

Cliff continued walking without talking for another half
hour. Either Vatican had flipped out completely, or he had
something else up his sleeve. Either way, Cliff still had a job
to do.

"Almost there," Vatican said. "Another little hill and we'll
be home."

"What exactly do you intend to do with me?" Cliff asked.

"Do?"

Cliff stopped walking and turned to face Vatican. "Kill me?"

Vatican's smile widened. He unslung the shotgun from his shoulder and tossed it to Cliff. Cliff caught it with one hand, checked to make sure it was loaded. It was. "I was under the impression you were here to save me," Vatican said and walked around Cliff. Cliff watched him catch up with Dayna, then fell in behind them. His head was dizzy with the strangeness of these people.

"You know about Kyle?" Cliff asked Vatican's back.

"That he's dead? Yes. Dayna called me from his apartment." Vatican didn't slow down or turn around. Cliff was having a hard time keeping up with both of them. "Morse code," Vatican said.

"What?"

"You were wondering how she told me over the phone. Tap, tap, tap. Morse code."

"He was tortured."

"Yes, he was tortured. So we must assume he gave Leland's assassins my location."

Cliff reached out and grabbed Vatican's arm. "That all that matters? That he gave you away?"

Vatican twisted around in a graceful way, using no force, but somehow freeing himself from Cliff's grasp. Cliff's hand was still clenched, though it held only air. He had never seen a move quite like that.

"You have no idea at all what does and doesn't matter, boy," he said, eyes cold and flinty. He turned back and kept pace with Dayna.

Cliff paused to catch his breath, but the two of them kept hiking. He had to scramble to catch up again. There was no use talking to them out here where they could run. He was like Alice chasing the rabbit into Wonderland. He would wait until they reached the house. Walls had a way of making people talk.

"Thar she blows," Vatican said from the top of the hill. "Home sweet home."

Cliff pulled himself up the slippery knoll, hand over hand on a thick vine sticking out of the ground, until he finally stood puffing beside Vatican and Dayna. His huffing and the cry of birds was the only sound. He followed the old man's pointing finger down into the valley below.

"Jesus," Cliff said. "*That's* your house?"

"What'd you expect?"

Anything, Cliff thought. Anything but that.

He built it himself, Dayna signed.

Vatican neither confirmed nor denied Dayna's boast. He was already running down the hill, leaping and hopping, dodging bushes and roots and volcanic rocks, spanking off embankments, shoving off trees, like a young boy chasing a puppy. Dayna launched herself after him with equal agility and soon caught up.

Cliff stood at the hilltop and watched them for a few moments, still catching his breath. Despite everything that was going on around them, everything that had happened to them, they looked almost playful.

Cliff inhaled deeply and followed them, his pace slower, more careful, as he picked through the unfamiliar jungle. Halfway down his feet got snared in the webbing of exposed roots and he tripped, rolling twenty yards down the hill before Vatican stopped him by standing in front of his tumbling body. Cliff banged into Vatican's shins and immediately halted. He thought his momentum alone should have knocked the older man over. But it didn't. Vatican merely reached down, snagged Cliff under one arm and hoisted him to his feet.

"You stay in shape," Cliff said, brushing twigs from his face and clothes. "What's your secret? Local herbs or something?"

"Young wife," Vatican smiled, slapping Cliff on the back.

Cliff tried to read Vatican's expression, but found no hidden meaning, no accusatory tone beneath the words. The old man had merely been joking. Still, Cliff felt defensive, somehow guilty. He gripped the shotgun tighter.

They hiked the rest of the way down the hill in a tight line. Cliff could tell that Vatican and Dayna were purposely slowing down for his sake, but he was glad. His back ached and his knees felt a bit spongy from all the climbing.

As they finally left the hill behind them and entered the flatland of the valley, the plant life seemed to rise up around them even thicker and taller than it had been before. Every step meant wrestling a stiff branch or giant leaf out of the way, disentangling from a vine or punching aside a bush. Then as suddenly as it had engulfed them, the jungle ended.

Vatican's house stood before them.

Not at all what Cliff had expected. He had pictured something exotic, a tropical home in the middle of the jungle complete with thatched roof and natural wood posts tied together with rawhide strips. A simple home that matched the spirit of paradise yet still demonstrated the ingenuity of humankind. Like the tree house in *Swiss Family Robinson*.

Instead he stood before a typical two-story white house with dark blue shutters, flower boxes outside the windows, and an honest-to-goodness white picket fence surrounding the whole place. Between the fence and the house was a real lawn, the short grass somehow dwarfed by the cornucopia of exotic plant life outside the fence. The fence was in fact some sort of demarcation between Vatican's created world and the thriving jungle all around him. Oddly the house and yard had a decidedly serene look, as if it had reached a truce with the wild chaos of life around it, each maintaining its own ground.

"There's even a birdbath," Cliff said.

"Kyle made that," Vatican said, opening the gate for Cliff. "Hmm, lawn could use some mowing."

Cliff followed then to the front door. The house and yard looked as if they'd been snatched from the center of some middle-class neighborhood in Anytown, U.S.A. A place where parents attended PTA, little girls drew hopscotch boxes on the sidewalk with colored chalk, pet cats sat sleepily in sunny window boxes crushing Mothers' flowers.

A lot like Cliff's neighborhood.

The interior was equally astounding. Each room had its own motif, New World Spanish or French Mediterranean or Early American. Cliff was led down the hallway, through the rooms, Vatican explaining about various objects, not with any tone of pride, merely with a sense of pleasure at sharing his home with someone. He seemed in no hurry to get on with their business, showed no signs of worry about where Leland's assassins might be. He continued with his leisurely tour, treating Cliff as a welcome guest.

Somewhere along the way, Dayna disappeared, reappearing when they wound their way back to the living room. She had prepared a plate with some neatly arranged raw vegetables and fresh fruit and offered glasses of iced sun tea. Cliff ate and drank in silence. Dayna again disappeared.

Cliff set his glass aside. "I appreciate the tour, Mr. Towne. You are a bona fide eccentric. But there's still the business at hand."

"Fat Boy."

"Fat Boy."

"You know my position."

"I know it, I just don't understand it. The country is in danger. The same country you devoted most of your life to protecting. Because of you, if the Soviets decided to attack us right now, they'd probably sweep over us the way Santa Ana's men swarmed the Alamo. With the same results."

"We are in worse danger from within, Cliff. Men like Aaron Leland."

"I'm not going to defend Leland. You have influence in government. You know people, talk to them. Get him thrown out."

Vatican shook his head. "I no longer have that kind of influence. It's the old 'What have you done for us lately?' dilemma. While I've been out here playing Tarzan in the jungle, my old friends have steadily been retiring. Or dying. Aaron Leland now has more clout in government circles than I have. Force is the only way."

"If you wanted him out that badly you should have just killed him. I have a hunch you've still got the knack for a little covert operation."

"Killing him isn't the point."

"It sure as hell seems like the point."

Vatican sighed. "More important than his death is that the people around him remove him. That they take back the power they gave up. That they throw him out themselves."

"You underestimate Leland."

"No, *you* underestimate him. That's why he killed your family."

Anger flooded Cliff's face. "And your sons."

Vatican nodded. "And my sons."

"Why now? Why start all this now? Be honest, man, Aaron Leland is no worse a monster than some of his predecessors. How clean were your hands when you ruled the roost?"

Vatican stood up, walked to the phone, dialed one number, said, "Come in," then hung up. He returned to his chair and sat down. He stared silently at Cliff, that grim smile stuck on his face. Cliff heard the loud footsteps clacking down the hall, heavy boots against thick tile. Definitely not Dayna.

The man marched into the room, shot an appraising look at Cliff. An edge of hostility showed in his every movement. Suspicion. Cliff figured the man was a few years younger than he, but he looked older. His coarse sandy hair was dishev-

eled, his face unshaved. There was a hard leanness to his body
that suggested soldier.

"Ah, Tim, come in," Vatican said. "Timothy Cavanaugh,
late of the U.S. Marines, this is Clifford Remington, late of the
CIA."

Neither offered to shake. Cliff nodded, content to keep distance between them until he knew what Vatican was up to.

"You asked why now, Cliff," Vatican said. "I'll let Tim explain."

Cavanaugh didn't sit. He stood behind one of the high-
backed wooden chairs, grabbed the back rail and rocked the
chair back on its hind legs. When he spoke, his voice was soft,
low, but easy to understand. His tone was flat, emotionless.
He spoke uninterrupted for twenty minutes. When he was
finished, he walked around the front of the chair and sat.

"Junkyard Dogs," Cliff said, testing the sound of the
words.

"Ever hear of them?" Vatican asked.

"No."

"Good. That was our intention. When I gave my word to
that pack of eighteen-year-old boys, it was to prevent them
from being exploited, either by the public or the government.
Can you imagine what would have happened to them if the
public had found out?"

"They'd have either made a movie about them or put them
on trial. Probably both."

"Exactly. I gave them my word, but now Leland has acti-
vated them into a personal antiterrorist hit squad. Those that
he couldn't exploit, he had assassinated. That will not be tol-
erated."

Cliff looked at Cavanaugh, then at Vatican. "Admirable
sentiment, but you've put the entire country at risk because
of your word to these guys."

"The country has to stand for something, Cliff, or it de-
serves to fall. You see the dilemma. Does Abraham do wha

God commands and kill Isaac, his son, and thereby break one of His Commandments? Or does he refuse to kill his son and disobey His direct order?''

"Which part do you play? Abraham? Isaac? Or God?"

"Perhaps more important," Vatican said, "is which part you play?"

Cliff had no answer. Vatican Towne, living in his private world, in a house that was not real, but a replica of a home. A home that represented the values he believed in. Out here, protected by a natural jungle as well as the islanders, he seemed to have evolved into some new human species. He wasn't crazy—Cliff was certain of that. But he was willing to let the country be defeated for the moral laxity of one man. To punish the world for allowing that kind of man that kind of power. Cliff didn't allow himself to ponder the moral complexities of Vatican Towne's thinking. The reasoning didn't matter. Even if he were right it wouldn't matter. Cliff was by habit or temperament a creature of simple goals, trained to win. To win now, he had to force Vatican Towne to restore Fat Boy to full capabilities.

Cliff turned to Cavanaugh. "Your raid in Miami. Successful?"

Cavanaugh nodded. "When I left they were just mopping up."

"And they were to come here next?"

"Wherever Mr. Towne was. They didn't know his exact location yet, just that they should be ready to travel at any time. From what Mr. Towne's told me, they're probably already on the island."

Cliff stood up, walked across the room. Framed on the wall was an original Edward Hopper painting. The valuable artwork was a contradiction, both to the simplicity of the house and the spirit of Vatican's speech. Certainly the painting was too expensive for any family that might actually live in a house like this to afford. The painting was of a lonely girl, alone, glumly sipping coffee, the plate glass window behind her revealing a slab of night as darkly foreboding as her obviously dim future. Its sad melancholy was a sharp contrast to Vatican's own outgoing zeal.

Cliff turned abruptly and looked at Vatican. He seemed to catch the man by surprise, because gone was the robust half-grin half-frown. Vatican's face looked pale and drained. Like Cliff's dad near the end. Presenile dementia, they'd called it. Alzheimer's disease. The disintegration of nerve cells in the frontal and temporal lobes of the cerebrum. His father holding a Camel cigarette, the brand he'd smoked for forty years, uncertain how to light it.

"You'll have to kill them, you know," Cliff said. "If Leland sent these Junkyard Dogs after you, you'll have to kill them. Even if you backed off from Fat Boy right now, restored everything, he'd still have to kill you." Cliff walked toward Vatican. "Which means you'll have to kill these same boys you've already lost two sons trying to save."

Vatican Towne smiled sadly.

"You lost two sons and I lost my family. For nothing."

"Not for nothing."

"For what, then? Your word? Morality in politics? Shit, none of that is worth my family's lives. Where's the logic?"

Vatican faced Cliff. "You know how I got my code name? Cronus. Do you know?"

"No."

"From FDR. Lot of people think Wild Bill Donovan gave it to me. We were nutty about codes back then. Hell, we had to be. Germans were eating us alive in the intelligence game. Every time one of us farted, they seemed to have a report. Anyway, in Greek mythology, Cronus was one of the Titans, sons of the king and queen of all the gods. Seems the king was jealous of his sons, so he thrust them deep into the bowels of the earth. But the queen, pissed because he'd forced her to bear so many children, forged a steel sickle and tried to incite her sons to castrate their father. None dared."

"Except Cronus."

"Except Cronus. Afterward he became king, and his reign was regarded as the Golden Age. Old Roosevelt told people I'd cut the balls off my own father if it would mean we'd win that goddamn war. He used to joke, say he had to wear his iron shorts whenever he was around me. Just to be safe." Vatican laughed. "Maybe he was right. Well, we won, didn't we?"

Cliff nodded. "Yeah, we won."

"Of course we won."

"What does that have to do with this, with right now?"

Vatican leaned back in his chair. "'Ripeness is all,' Cliff."

Cliff felt tired. Talking to Vatican Towne was like wrestling smoke. The man changed form right before his eyes, became something else, segued from Greek mythology to World War II politics to *King Lear*. Cliff wanted to drop to the floor and do fifty quick push-ups. Emerge himself in discipline. There the goals were tangible, completion of tasks. Do fifty push-ups. Run ten miles. He had to keep his mind on the task at hand: restore Fat Boy. "If Cavanaugh's buddies attack us, ripeness won't mean shit. Bazooka is all, then."

Vatican laughed again. "You have a point, Cliff."

"Can you unjam Fat Boy first? Just in case."

"I can see why Leland wants you dead. Once you grab hold of something, you don't let go. You must have been a hell of an agent."

"Yeah, a hell of an agent. Check my résumé. Can you unjam Fat Boy?"

"I can."

"Will you?"

Loud voices interrupted. Footsteps clattered down the hallway. Stan and Tory entered the living room followed by a light-skinned black man in his mid-twenties. The black man carried a sawed-off shotgun.

"Any trouble?" Vatican asked him.

"No, Dad," the black man said. "Everything just as you planned."

"My son Zack," Vatican said by way of introduction.

"Nice place," Tory said. "Didn't Donna Reed used to live here?"

VATICAN LED his son Zack and Cavanaugh out of the room, announcing that they had preparations to attend to and requesting that Cliff, Stan and Tory remain in the living room until he returned. No one responded, but he left anyway.

"How's the new hand?" Cliff asked.

Stan lifted his hook. "I'm not going to peel grapes with it, but it'll do. Who's the laughing boy with Towne?"

"A Junkyard Dog."

Tory laughed. "A what?"

Cliff explained, repeating Cavanaugh's story almost word for word. He watched Stan closely, looking for any sign of previous knowledge. But Stan's face registered the kind of shock and horror that was not acting.

"So that's the backup team Leland meant when he told me he was sending one in," Stan said. "I take it they have an interrogation expert among them."

"Considering their own experiences, they're all interrogation experts, wouldn't you say?"

Tory stood between Stan and Cliff. She didn't look frightened but outraged. "I know this sounds terribly naive, but there are laws against what Aaron Leland is doing. Laws he is answerable to."

"Technically," Stan said.

"Which means not really. Right?"

Stan nodded. "We can't think about that right now. We have to concern ourselves with Fat Boy. Getting Towne to restore the computer. Regardless of what breaches of ethics Aaron Leland may have committed, the danger to the rest of the country is real and immediate. Besides, he may be over-zealous, but he has also been effective. His antiterrorist raid will undoubtedly scare off other terrorists."

"Scare them, yes," Tory said. "Not just by killing them, but by killing their families. Children, for God's sake! Isn't that the very morality we're fighting?"

"I didn't say I agreed with his method. I'm saying he's not necessarily a bad man. Aaron wants to save this country."

"From what exactly, Stan?" Tory said. "To become what?"

Cliff interrupted. "Right now we work on keeping Towne alive until he restores Fat Boy. Nothing else matters."

"Yes," Stan said. "That's our priority."

Tory said nothing. She walked over to one of the large Spanish chairs and sat down.

"So far I've run into three sons. Bradley in L.A., who was white. Kyle, who was Filipino, and Zack, who is black, in Hawaii." Cliff gestured to Stan. "Any other kids we don't know about?"

"Nothing in our records. Vatican was married when he was young to his high school sweetheart. They had a daughter. They were driving through some rural West Virginia town on their way to visit his wife's grandmother and show off the baby. Heavy rains the week before had raised the creeks to deep tor-rents. Guess one of the wooden bridges had been weakened from the storm. Collapsed under his car, swept the car right down the river. The current sucked Vatican out the car win-dow, but his wife and daughter weren't so lucky and drowned. Crazily, he swam after them, but he got tossed around like a paper boat in the gutter. Broke a few ribs, caught pneumonia. One of his lungs collapsed.

"After that, the tabloids used to carry stories of him dating someone now and then. Our own files show that he lived with various women, all over the world. Had lots of children, but never formally married any of the women. Before he disappeared, he was still visiting each of them regularly, supporting them all with large sums of money. You know something odd, these women and children always welcomed him back. Some of the women went on to marry other men, but Vatican still visited, became friends with the new husbands, was treated as a respected member of the family." Stan shook his head. "A remarkable man. But somewhere along the line he snapped."

"Maybe," Cliff said. "It doesn't really matter."

"What about the woman at Kyle's apartment?" Tory asked. "The one who can't hear or speak."

Stan shrugged. "I don't know. Probably another daughter."

"His wife," Cliff said. "She's Vietnamese."

"She's gorgeous," Tory said. "Maybe a little young."

"More than a little," Vatican said, entering the living room again. Cavanaugh and Zack flanked him, both heavily armed with pistols, grenades and Heckler & Koch MP 5 automatic rifles. Dayna stood behind them, barefoot, in shorts, a WA-2000 Walther sniping rifle clutched in both hands. Vatican carried no weapon as he walked into the middle of the room.

"Dayna is much too young for me, I agree," he went on. "I told her that when she asked me to marry her. But she is very stubborn." He turned so Dayna could see his lips, but he spoke to Cliff, Stan and Tory. "Her mother was indeed a nurse, and was killed during the fall of Saigon. That much of what she told you was true, Cliff. But she wasn't trampled by Vietnamese storming the helicopters, she was shot by one of our soldiers, who panicked at the sight of the rushing mob. A stray bullet, really, but Dayna's mother was just as dead. I picked Dayna up and took her with me, raised her here, taught her what I knew. Then I sent her to college. Straight A student too. She could have gone anywhere she wanted. I offered to set her up in business, any kind, anywhere. She refused. She wanted to stay with me." He smiled. "You're probably wondering what kind of relationship we had. What kind of perverted dirty old man I was. Believe what you want, but I raised her with love, not sex. Nothing sexual ever happened between us. When she told me she wanted us to marry, I refused, told her I couldn't think of her that way. She said I could, in time. She was right."

Cliff looked at Dayna, but her eyes were on Vatican. He could see from her gaze that she did indeed love the man. It was the gaze Cliff had sometimes seen in Ginger's eyes when she was looking at him.

"Now Cliff," Vatican continued, "may think it cruel or cheap that Dayna seduced him in the woods."

Cliff felt everyone's eyes turn on him. He was especially aware of Tory's shocked expression.

"But I assure you, Cliff, she wouldn't have had sex with you if she hadn't liked you. In fact, she enjoyed you completely. She told me." He chuckled. "You probably think I should be jealous, or that I'm too old and doddering to get it up myself. Neither is the case. I haven't experienced jealousy in several decades. As to our sex life, Dayna and I manage very nicely."

Dayna smiled, not shyly or with embarrassment, but with genuine amusement.

Cliff didn't judge them. Whatever philosophical plane they were living on worked just fine for them. Cliff had slept with the man's wife, had enjoyed her, had comforted her and been comforted by her. He didn't desire her again, but he was grateful he had the memory of that night.

Vatican wagged a finger between Cliff and Stan. "The two of you are so concerned about Fat Boy. I'll tell you what I've done. I've programmed my computer to shut down the rest of Fat Boy unless I cancel that command in exactly—" he consulted his watch "—two hours, four minutes, eight seconds. After that time, Fat Boy will be dead. Useless to anyone. And there will be nothing you can do about it."

Stan's face went gray, but he spoke slowly and precisely, controlling his anger. "Why the delay? Why not just shut it down now?"

"Incentive, Stan. I want you all to have a reason to keep me alive. Didn't I tell you? Your Junkyard Dogs have penetrated my half-mile electronic perimeter. They're hiding right outside this place getting ready to attack."

Suddenly an explosion rocked the room, shook the wrought-iron chandelier above them. Automatic gunfire chattered outside. The window near them burst, and bullets chewed up the wallpaper on the opposite wall.

32

"THE DECISION is final, Yuri," General Kerensky said.

Yuri Danzigkov nodded.

The general walked with a limp. His left leg had been severely wounded in World War II when the tank he'd been navigating had been firebombed by the Nazis. Usually the leg was fine and he walked with a normal gait, no limp. But the hours of sitting and debating had left his joints stiff and sore, and Yuri made an effort to slow down so the general wouldn't feel any more discomfort.

"When do we strike?" Yuri asked. Technically it was not an appropriate question, not of his province. But he had spoken against attack along with General Kerensky and two other generals until he was excused from the meeting. He'd waited outside the door with the other aides and advisers for four more hours. Food and beverages had been sent in every two hours.

General Kerensky looked at Yuri, then sighed. "Once we've attacked the U.S., there's bound to be some reaction from their European allies. A few tank divisions should put an end to that. To reposition the rest of our tanks and troops at the European borders will take another two or three hours. Once that is done, we will be ready to attack."

"And our ships?"

"Yes. We must move our submarines and aircraft carriers to strategic locations. Everything will not be perfect, but good enough. If at that time the PAW satellites are still inoperative, we will launch our attack."

"I see."

The general stopped walking, laid his hand affectionately on Yuri's shoulder. "We did not agree with this decision,

Yuri, but now that it has been made, we must ensure victory. Anything less than victory would be disastrous. For both sides.''

''Yes, General.''

The two men marched silently through the chilly air.

"YOU CAME to save the world," Vatican said. "Here's your chance." He gestured at Zack and Dayna. "Get them some weapons." Stan and Tory quickly followed Zack and Dayna down the hall. Cavanaugh silently wandered out of the room on his own. Cliff remained behind with Vatican.

Another explosion shook the walls. A mirror fell off the wall and shattered on the tile floor. Vatican didn't seem to notice.

"The walls were built to withstand a little abuse," he said. "They'll hold awhile longer."

"What about the computer?" Cliff asked. "What if the power source is disrupted?"

"Boy, you really know how to chew your food, don't you?" Vatican waved for Cliff to follow him down the hallway. "We have our own generators. They'd have to get inside to cut power, and even if they did, the computer is on a separate generator built into the floor of the room."

"Nifty."

"The only thing you have to worry about is that they don't kill me and blow the whole deal."

Cliff gave him a look. "I'll try not to screw up."

"Good. Follow me." Vatican guided Cliff down a few more corridors and into a bedroom. Cliff was surprised at how sparsely furnished the room was. A simple platform bed, old-fashioned six-drawer dresser, small nightstands on either side of the bed. The wooden floor was bare, the two windows caged with wrought-iron bars like all the other windows in the house. The only decoration was a large red-and-white quilt on the wall. On the dresser was a photograph of a tiny Vietnamese woman in a white nurse's uniform. She was smiling, shading her eyes from the bright sun overhead.

Vatican opened the drawer of one of the nightstands. Cliff noticed each nightstand had a book on it. The one Vatican was hovering over held *Prick of Noon* by Peter de Vries. Dayna's nightstand displayed *The Riddle of the Dinosaurs* by John Noble Wilford. Cliff didn't try to make anything of this information, he merely observed, filed it away for a future time when he knew he would replay these events over and over, analyzing, rubbing them smooth like stones washed up from the ocean.

"Here," Vatican said, turning around. He handed Cliff a Walther P38 Military. "I used to carry this thing through Europe with me during the war. This was the official German service arm in 1938. They produced these suckers right up until 1945. Of course, toward the end the quality went down, very loose fit, rough finish."

"You took this off a dead Nazi officer, right?"

"Close. Actually, I borrowed it from General Patton and never returned it. Son of a bitch hounded me for it even after the war. I'm not certain where he got it, but if you asked him two different times you'd get two different stories." He stared solemnly at the gun in Cliff's hand. "I've killed some men with that gun. A lot during wartime, a few during peacetime. Even wore a trench coat back then, before movies made it a cliché. No snapbrim hat though. Earmuffs. My ears were always freezing and I had to be careful of colds."

Cliff checked the clip. Eight 9 mm bullets. "What about you? Where's your gun?"

"You think it's crazy, me out here in the middle of some lost valley, living in this corny house, mowing my lawn, growing tea." He didn't seem to expect an answer, so Cliff didn't give him one. "Hell, maybe I am."

Several loud explosions echoed down the corridor, followed by the sound of more glass breaking.

"Time to go," Vatican said, his impish half-grin half-frown firmly in place. Suddenly he was running off down the hall. Cliff tried to follow, but lost him during a couple of turns.

The chattering of automatic gunfire resounded throughout the house. Occasionally another explosion would shake the walls.

Cliff found Stan kneeling at a living room window, sighting down the barrel of an M-1 carbine, his new hook clamped on the wooden stock, his right finger squeezing off three-round bursts. "You're not going to believe this," Stan said, firing another burst through the wrought-iron grille. "But I have to go to the bathroom."

"Go in your pants."

"We're way past that point."

Cliff looked around the room. "Where's Tory?"

"She and Zack are in the kitchen, keeping the back of the house from being ambushed."

"How many?"

"Cavanaugh says six—five of the original squad and Leland's personal watchdog. Six of them, seven of us. Pretty good odds."

"Except they're trained soldiers, hard as diamonds," Cliff said.

Stan fired another three-round burst, popped the magazine, slapped in another and fired again. Cliff stooped beside him, thumbed new bullets from a box of .30 short rifle ammo into the empty clip. "I'm willing to admit I'm not quite their caliber," Stan said. "Zack seems pretty tough, though, and Tory's got more guts than the whole CIA. She's looking a little frazzled, but I'd be willing to bet that at least her undies are clean." He ducked as incoming bullets pinged off the window grill. "What about Cavanaugh?"

"I don't know. Hard to read him."

"Well, it's not as if we've got a lot of choices anyway. Besides, it's Towne I'm worried about. Keeping the old bastard alive."

"Last time I saw him he was running off without a weapon."

"Yeah, he and Dayna ducked outside."

"Outside without a weapon? Jesus!"

A flurry of bullets swarmed through the window, a couple clanking off the grillwork, others embedding themselves into the walls, chairs, paintings. Stan returned fire.

"At least Dayna was armed," Stan said.

"Yes, but *he's* the one who has to restore Fat Boy."

Stan fired again. "Good point. What's our status?"

"We've got good cover. I don't think Leland expected Vatican to be so well protected. Even so, with their superior firepower and experience, time is more on their side than ours. We can't afford to just sit here and wait them out. Not with Vatican on the loose outside. Besides, this gingerbread house won't hold up under much more pounding."

"Meaning?"

"Meaning Vatican and Dayna had the right idea. We have to take it to them outside." He slid the full clip across the floor to Stan. It bumped Stan's foot. "I'll go outside, see if we can't do some sniping of our own. Try to keep the old man from getting his head blown off. At least until he's fixed the computer."

"I'll hold down the fort. Ha, ha."

Cliff stood up, dashed across the room. Another crowd of bullets zipped through the window and hammered into the wall next to Cliff. Plaster flaked onto the floor.

Cliff ran through the corridors until he found the kitchen. Tory had a Winchester propped on the windowsill behind the kitchen sink. The microwave oven next to her was shattered from bullets. Zack crouched under another window, popping up to fire his Uzi, then ducking down again.

"Can you see them?" Cliff asked her.

"Two of them," she said.

Machine gun bullets flew in through Tory's window and tore open the cupboard behind her. The cupboard door exploded into splinters. A box of corn flakes was shredded and spilled flakes onto Tory's hair. She opened fire again. "I think I hit one," she said excitedly. "He fell!"

"You got him," Zack said. "You got one."

Cliff peered over Tory's shoulder, saw a rustling in the jungle, then saw one of the men rise and hobble off to a new position.

"Shit!" Tory said, firing another burst at him. But he was already hidden among the trees.

"You wounded him anyway," Zack said encouragingly. "He won't be running up here too damned fast. Easier to pick off next time."

"Or more deadly," Cliff said. He looked over at Zack. Early twenties, handsome face, a lot of Vatican's regal features. "How'd you get involved in all this, Zack?"

Zack fired a burst with his Uzi. "A few days ago I was at Berkeley studying economics. I'm two quarters away from my master's. Kyle called to tell me about Bradley's murder. They weren't going to tell me anything until that happened. They figured I was safe. No one knew I was Vatican Towne's son."

Machine gun bullets flew through the window and punched a hole in the wall next to a small cork bulletin board. There was a slip of paper pinned to the board with the heading Groceries. Cliff couldn't read what was scribbled beneath that.

"So you came here to help?" Cliff said.

"Dad didn't want me to, practically begged me to go back. But no way, man, am I going to let them get him. No fucking way. He's too—"

Another burst of gunfire. Tory and Cliff ducked. Zack screamed.

Cliff lifted his head, saw Zack drop his gun and grab his face. Blood and wet gummy bits of flesh oozed between his fingers. He cried out in agony, then stumbled backward dead.

"Oh, God!" Tory said, lowering her gun to run to him.

Cliff grabbed her by the shoulders and pushed her back into position. "Keep your eye aimed out there. That's where they're coming from."

Tory choked back a sob, poked her Winchester out the window and fired another round.

"I'll be back," Cliff said, heading for the back door.

"Cliff, don't leave me here!"

"You're fine. Just keep shooting. Don't let them get any closer." He stooped over Zack's body, grabbed the Uzi and slid it along the floor to Tory. "When I give the word, lay down some covering fire for me. Just spray the woods so I can get out that door."

Tory picked up the gun, held it tight against her ribs. She nodded at Cliff.

"Go!" Cliff shouted.

Tory popped up, squeezed the trigger and peppered the backyard with a dozen rounds. Cliff used the cover to unlock the back door and bolt through it. He dived behind a flowering bird of paradise plant, somersaulted back up to his feet, vaulted the white picket fence and ran into the jungle. A few scattered shots dug at the ground behind him as he ran, but once he was in the cover of the jungle, they stopped.

Cliff squatted next to a stand of golden shower trees, the branches adorned with clusters of white flowers. His heart banged from more than just the exertion of running. He was scared. And excited. He liked the feeling of fear burning through his body, cleansing the veins of impurities, sterilizing the tissue. Making him pure again. Perhaps Ginger had been right about him after all, perhaps he did miss the action. He stared at Vatican's old Walther clutched in his hand. Eight shots, six targets. A margin of error of two.

He sniffed the air. Rich, most smells mingled with the bitter scent of cordite in a dizzying concoction. The air was heavy with humidity. Sweat had already greased his body.

He controlled his breathing, brought the pattern down to slow deep breaths of equal length. He could feel his heart slow down, the beating less frequent but stronger. His body tingled slightly as a sudden cool breeze evaporated sweat on his skin. Every part of his body was now under perfect control, and he realized that Ginger had been wrong. The action wasn't the lure. Completion was what attracted him. Finishing was what he was good at. Discipline was merely preparation, not the end. The preparation led to the result. It was mathematical, the physics of inevitability. Preparation leads to resolution. This was what Cliff had to do because this was what Cliff did best.

He stood. The bark of the tree felt smooth. No more than thirty seconds had passed since he left Tory, but Cliff felt as if he'd changed significantly during that time. As if he'd unzipped his old corrupt skin and stepped out, his slick new skin tingling from the sting of its first touch of clean air. He felt refreshed. He wondered if this was how a snake felt after molting.

Methodically, he worked his way through the jungle toward the flashes of muzzle-fire. The two shooters were hidden in a clump of ferns. As he neared, he could see their faces streaked green, black and brown with camouflage grease. Their fatigues were dark jungle-green. One man was firing an M-60 machine gun. The other held a Soviet-made Kalashnikov AK-47. Untraceable to Leland, no doubt. Their bullets were chewing up the kitchen window where Tory stood her ground, dropping out of sight, but popping up again every few seconds to spray the jungle with bullets. When she popped up this time and fired, Cliff heard the rustle of leaves nearby as her bullets burned a path through the jungle a few feet from him. He ducked behind a tree trunk.

The man behind the machine gun sat with legs splayed straight out. Blood soaked his right leg where Tory had wounded him earlier. Cliff waited for him to fire again, using the loud mechanical clacketing as cover to sneak closer.

"We musta got the black guy," the one with the AK-47 said. He had so much black grease around his eyes he looked like a raccoon. "That just leaves the cunt."

"Maybe he's reloading," the wounded man said. "Or went for help."

"Not after the howl we heard. Like a stuck pig, man. He's fucking dead meat."

The wounded man shifted, winced from the pain. "They weren't supposed to put up this much of a fight, man. We were just supposed to waltz right in there and blow 'em away. Fuck, man."

"It's better this way. Like the old days, right? Old times there are not forgotten, right?"

"Yeah, right." They slapped palms.

Cliff fired a 9-mm bullet through the raccoon's chest. The raccoon spun around, the AK-47 dropping into a giant fern plant. "Holy fuck!" he said, looking down at his chest. There was only a tiny hole, but as he staggered around in a slow pirouette, Cliff could see the much larger hole gouged from his back where the bullet had tumbled out like a propeller. "I'm fucking shot, Kurt," he said. "Goddamn." Then he dropped to his knees, rocked back on to his feet and sat there, dead.

Kurt didn't spare a glance for his partner. He swung the M-60 around and immediately strafed the jungle where the shot had come from. But Cliff had already moved away. Leaves and branches and bark flew into a jumble as the 7.63 mm bullets chopped the flora into airborne salad.

Cliff stepped out from behind a tree and was about to shoot when Tory popped up to the window again and blasted away with her Uzi. Bullets chipped bark three inches from Cliff's shoulder and he dived to the ground. The sound alerted Kurt and he swung back again, his face clenched with pain from his leg. He saw Cliff, aimed the M-60 and opened fire.

CAVANAUGH HAD BEEN sitting high up in the tree for almost fifteen minutes. There was gunfire to the left of him, over by the kitchen, and there was more to the right of him, by the front door. From here he could see the occasional grenade arcing through the air followed by an explosion. One of the grenades had ripped the heavy wooden doors from the front of Vatican's house, but the one-armed guy inside was keeping them from charging in.

Just as Cavanaugh figured.

Now they'd have to switch tactics. They must have realized that Vatican's house was better defended than Aaron Leland had anticipated. They would have to penetrate individually, splitting off into two pairs, with two men maintaining the bombardment while the other two divided and attacked at opposing angles. According to Cavanaugh's calculations, the one-armed guy had about another four minutes before they killed him.

Cavanaugh shifted. A knot from the branch poked his butt. He shifted again. Comfortable.

He waited.

The way he figured, one of them had to pass close to this position to start their advance on the house. When they did, he would be ready.

Cavanaugh didn't actually hear him. The soldier was too good for that. But he sensed a change in the sound of the wind, maybe smelled the greasepaint. However it was, he looked down and saw Darby Louden hulking through the undergrowth with his rifle close to his chest.

Cavanaugh aimed his pistol and fired three quick shots at his friend's back. The first two shots hit their target, but the third shot caught Darby as he was falling and nicked the side of his neck. Darby flopped face forward into a bush.

Cavanaugh stared for a minute, looking for movement. There was none. He waited for some feeling to seep into his brain, relief or remorse. But nothing happened. No feeling. He dropped out of the trees and walked toward Darby's body.

Darby suddenly flipped himself over, his hand aiming a Colt pistol at Cavanaugh. Cavanaugh's pistol was aimed at Darby.

Darby's chest had two bloody holes high near the collarbone. An egg-sized chunk was missing from the side of his neck. Blood spilled heavily, funneling down his throat and disappearing into the bloodstained shirt.

"Hey, Tim," Darby said. His voice was surprisingly strong. "You made it."

"I made it."

"Other side, huh?"

Cavanaugh nodded.

"Whatever."

"Whatever," Cavanaugh said. He fired. The bullet ripped into Darby's stomach. Darby fired too. Twice. Cavanaugh didn't feel the bullets at first and thought maybe somehow Darby had missed. Then the pain seized him in the abdomen and as he looked down to inspect the damage, he noticed his legs were folding under him. One bullet had actually drilled through his canvas belt, the other entered an inch lower. He was flat on the ground now, only a couple of feet from Darby. He could hear Darby's ragged breathing. He looked over and saw Darby curled on his side, staring back at him.

"Tough ... to ... kill, aren't we?" Darby said.

Cavanaugh dragged himself over toward his friend. "Too tough."

Darby coughed. He pushed his heavy hand over the ground toward his Colt. His fingers, lazy and stupid, tried to pick up the gun.

Cavanaugh kept his left hand clamped against his leaking abdomen. He felt some slippery internal organ pressing against his fingers. With his left hand, he pulled the long knife from his leg sheath.

"Fuck you, Tim," Darby said with a pained grin, raising the gun to Cavanaugh's face.

"Fuck you, Darby," Cavanaugh said with no malice. Then he plunged the knife into Darby's heart.

Cavanaugh held on to the knife until he was certain Darby was dead. But by then he no longer had the strength to move. He felt sleepy and he thought of Audrey pinching his butt, felt her in his arms as they danced across the gym floor, her breath on his neck so warm and light. He died, hands on knife, his head dropping softly onto Darby's chest.

CLIFF ROLLED. A bullet bit into the top of his shoulder. He kept rolling. Another bullet kicked dirt into his eyes. He rolled. He didn't even know where he was rolling anymore, just that he had to keep moving.

Cliff was still rolling before he noticed the silence. The machine gun bullets were no longer chasing him. He lifted his head, felt a painful tightening across the top of his shoulder where he'd been wounded.

Vatican Towne stood over the man named Kurt, his thin arms wrapped around the man's neck. The head cradled in his arms was twisted at an absurd angle. He released the head and the body dropped limply against the ground. Vatican stepped over the body and Cliff thought he was coming over to help him up. Instead, he kept walking past Cliff. His movements were stiff, mechanical.

That was when Cliff noticed the quiet. No grenades exploding. No gunfire. A few birds chattered tentatively.

"The Junkyard Dogs?" Cliff asked.

Vatican stopped walking, bent over a fern plant. "Dead."

"All of them?"

"All of them."

"Tory?"

"Alive."

"Stan?"

Vatican stooped behind the fern.

"Stan?" Cliff repeated.

"Alive."

What was he doing in that fern? Cliff lowered his voice. "You know about Zack?"

"Dead."

"What about Cavanaugh?"

"Dead." Vatican lifted the limp form in his arms. Dayna. Her arms hung lifelessly, her head tilted way back, her eyes were closed. Vatican carried her past Cliff toward the house. "All dead," he said.

"WHERE'D HE GO?" Tory asked. She carefully applied a strip of adhesive tape to the edge of the gauze bandage over Cliff's shoulder wound. They were sitting in the kitchen. Bullets had punctured the refrigerator, but Cliff managed to salvage some milk, which he offered to share with Tory.

"I don't like milk," she said.

"Me neither. But I used to."

She sipped the milk and asked again, "Where'd he go?"

"To change his pants," Cliff said.

"Not Stan. Vatican. He carried Dayna's body out of here, then came back and carried Zack's out too. Where do you think he's taking them?"

"I don't know. Maybe to bury."

"So soon? My God, they were just killed."

Cliff didn't answer. Maybe Vatican was burying them, maybe just sitting quietly in a room with them. Cliff understood that need. If he could have, Cliff would have dug graves for Ginger, Bogie and Liza, laid them in himself and covered them. The ritual would have allowed him some sense of finality. Instead the bodies were hauled off, cut open, slapped back together and shipped to a mortuary. The funeral bought and paid for long ago by Ginger's first husband.

Stan entered the room in fresh chino pants he'd gotten from Vatican. They were too long so he'd rolled up the cuffs, and too narrow at the waist, so he'd left the top button undone and held them up with a belt. "Milk?" he said.

"Want some?" Tory asked.

Stan nodded, took a sip. "Whenever I was sick my mother used to heat this up and stir in some honey."

"In India," Cliff said, "half of the milk consumed is from the buffalo."

"Interesting," Stan said.

They spoke of milk for a few more minutes. Stan explained how milk was homogenized: forced at high pressure through small openings to distribute fat evenly throughout the milk. Tory told about the time when she was thirteen and had a bad pimple on her cheek and was afraid to go to school. She dunked her head in a bowl of milk and held her breath, hoping the milk would make the pimple go away. Cliff and Stan laughed.

"Well," she explained defensively, "everyone was always saying how good milk was for you. I thought direct application would be even better."

No one spoke of the events that had just happened. They spoke of everything but.

Vatican reappeared at the back door, though no one had seen him leave the house. This time he was carrying Cavanaugh. Again, he walked through the kitchen and down the hall. He spoke to no one, no one spoke to him.

Eventually the three of them fell silent. Cliff didn't remember putting his arm around Tory, or Tory laying her head against his chest, but somewhere along the line it had happened, because that was how they were sitting when Vatican finally returned. Stan was leaning on the counter staring at the telephone.

"You can call Washington," Vatican said. He had changed his clothes and washed the blood and dirt from his hands and face. He looked refreshed, certainly fresher than any of them. "Go ahead, Stan. You'll find that Fat Boy is back to full capacity. PAW satellites are once again beaming their information. If the Soviets had any intention to attack, they most certainly will not now."

"I'd like to take your word for it, Mr. Towne," Stan said. He reached for the phone and began dialing.

"My word has lost some of its value, I know." Vatican walked across the room, opened the bullet-riddled refrigerator, pulled out the vegetable drawer and removed a cold can of Moosehead beer. "Anyone else?"

Tory raised her hand. "Please."

He handed her a can.

She popped the top, drank deeply. "Now I remember why I gave up milk." She offered the can to Cliff. He shook his head.

Cliff studied Vatican's face. No signs of what had happened. He looked like a pleasant robust old man ready to bore the crap out of you with exaggerated stories of his adventurous youth. No grief showed. But Cliff had seen him carrying Dayna, had seen his face when he'd admitted Zack was dead. Grief and despair had hollowed his eyes then, dried up his skin, stooped his shoulders with age. Yet now he stood straight, eyes bright, shoulders square. Somehow, through sheer mental will, he had conquered his grief and despair. The ultimate discipline, the one Cliff had not yet mastered. The thought of Ginger still knotted Cliff's stomach, swelled his eyes.

Cliff listened to Stan speak to Dubus. The conversation was brief. Stan hung up the phone.

"Fat Boy is working," Stan announced.

"Then it's over," Tory sighed.

"Except Leland knows you still have the power to do it again," Cliff said to Vatican.

"I don't," Vatican said. "I've deleted my access code. Even I can't enter again. I've forfeited my power."

Stan went to the refrigerator, found the beer in the vegetable drawer. "I believe you. But Leland won't."

"That's something he'll have to live with."

"He'll send others."

"I won't be here."

"That won't matter," Stan said. "I'll do what I can for you."

Vatican smiled skeptically.

The four of them trekked for several hours to a secluded field where Vatican had another helicopter hidden. They removed the camouflage netting and Vatican flew them back to Lihue. When his three passengers disembarked, he smiled at them. Then he looked directly at Cliff, the smile turning a little sad. *"Hoomananao,"* he said. *"Hoomananao."* He waved and guided the helicopter back into the air.

"What'd he say?" Tory hollered over the sound of the rotors. Her hair whipped at her cheeks from the swirling wind.

"Was that Hawaiian?" Stan asked.

"Hawaiian," Cliff nodded. "Means 'remember.'"

PART FIVE:

HOMECOMING

34

AARON LELAND searched the entire house, but he couldn't locate where that draft was coming from. He checked the windows, crawled around the attic, poked about down in the basement. Windows were secure. Doors were snugly molded with weather stripping. The attic was amply insulated, the basement almost warmer than the rest of the house.

But when he settled back down to his baby grand piano and began to play Bach's Mass in B Minor, he felt the same cool draft blowing across the back of his neck. He flipped up the cowl collar of his sweater and settled back to play again. But then his neck got *too* warm. He wheeled the heavy piano a few feet to the left and slid the bench over in front of it. The draft was there too.

Funny how a simple thing like that could ruin even Bach. He smiled at his own annoyance. All things considered, he had very little to be upset about. Fat Boy was hard at work. The PAW satellites were fully operational, giving this country the strategic edge once again. And no one important had found out about the whole episode. There had been only a few snags. The Junkyard Dogs were all dead now—that was a setback. But they had accomplished what he'd wanted. He was proud of them, of their patriotism. The president was happy, and that happiness would be expressed tangibly in allocation of more secret funds to continue this project. Besides, Leland was now sifting through a whole new batch of possible candidates for a whole new squad. The training methods of the Cong had been crude but effective. They were worth trying again.

His fingertips flashed across the keyboard, fingers arcing and flexing. Each contraction of his muscle produced another glorious chord. Each physical movement translated into rhapsodic sound, the beastly into the beautiful. Like tapping a code to God.

Aaron Leland had been a child prodigy with the piano, astounding his parents and friends, even his many music teachers. His agility at the keyboard was truly remarkable. There was no piece of music, no matter how complicated, he could not master remarkably fast. Even as a child, with the disadvantage of small hands and short fingers, he outperformed all other students. The only criticism his teachers expressed was that his technical proficiency, though indeed awe-inspiring, somehow lacked texture. Soul. Heart. All the right notes were played at exactly the right time in exactly the right tempo with exactly the right emphasis. Yet there was a hollowness to the sound, as if what they heard was only the echo of music bouncing down a marble hallway. He didn't know what they meant; what he heard when he played was as soft and lush as if the composer were whispering in his ear, encouraging him.

The cool draft whipped across his neck again and other thoughts intruded on his playing. There were still a few loose ends in this project. Vatican Towne was alive, so was Cliff. That would have to be remedied. Soon.

He stretched his fingers across the keys, his eyes closing with the pleasure of the music. He had arranged everything with the same precision Bach had scored his compositions. Order had been restored. Domestic terrorism had received a crushing blow. He'd given them a little of their own back in their faces. The newspapers were still filled with photos of the mangled and dismembered dead women and children hauled from the smoking wreck of the Miami apartment. Some suggested a vigilante group was responsible, others maintained the same drug angle. Whatever the papers said, his private intelligence showed the country was a little safer today than it had been last week. He was proud of that accomplishment.

He almost didn't hear the doorbell, drowned out as it was by Bach's insistent chords. But the discordant notes of the bell pricked at his ears until he recognized them. Reluctantly, he pushed himself away from the piano and walked to the front door.

"Gentlemen," he said, surprised.

Stan stood in the doorway, flanked by Dubus and Collins. Their faces were grim. Leland smiled heartily to cover his surprise. They had never been to his home before. They had never been invited. Nor had they been invited this evening.

"Stan, I thought I told you to take a few days off. You and Lanie are supposed to be planning that new vacation."

Stan led the other two past Leland into the foyer. "We have to talk, Aaron."

"Must be important."

"It is."

Leland looked at Collins and Dubus, their glum eyes avoiding his. This was obviously Stan's show. Well, whatever was bothering them, he would solve the problem, soothe their worried little minds and send them on their way. Bach awaited.

"Talk, sure. Come in, gentlemen. Let me show you around the place. Modest, but comfortable. Except for a damned draft I can't quite find." Leland walked down the hall, Collins and Dubus behind him.

Stan lagged behind to lock the door and slide closed the dead bolt.

"IS IT HEAVY?" Vatican Towne asked.

Dayna shook her head, carrying the breadbox-sized package in front of her. She set it on the table next to one of their suitcases. They'd been packing for two days now, preparing their move. Vatican wouldn't tell her where they were moving to, which she found romantic. Not that it mattered. She would be perfectly happy anywhere with him.

The phone call this morning had come in from the Navy base in Honolulu. Since the phone was not listed or even registered under their real names, only Stan could have given this number to the base. The Navy man had told Vatican that a special delivery package was being rushed over to the Lihue airport and could he pick it up. Vatican had sent Dayna.

The box was heavy cardboard and weighed ten or fifteen pounds. They'd had it packed in dry ice, and the box had smoked as she'd carried it back to the Jeep. She'd strapped it into the helicopter seat next to her on the flight back here, the nylon seat harness pulled tight across the word Perishable.

Vatican had been on the phone all morning making arrangements for their move, buying land under false names, making sure their trail out of Kauai would be untraceable. Just as he had made sure that no one knew Dayna was still alive. In the jungle that day, after they had killed three of the soldiers, Vatican had injected her with a drug, knocking her unconscious and lowering her respiration. She had protested his plan at first, but he had been convincing and she had bowed to his instincts and logic. "If they think you are dead," he'd explained, "they won't send anyone to kill you."

These people are good people. They are good people.

"Aaron Leland was once a good person, Dayna."

So. He had fooled them. They had gone away thinking she had died with the others.

Open it, she said.

"Who's it from?"

It doesn't say. Open it and find out.

Vatican used his pocketknife to slit the flaps, careful not to damage whatever was inside.

Dayna sidled closer to him to watch. Because the Navy was involved, it had to be from Washington. Certainly this Aaron Leland would not be so stupid as to just send them a bomb. He must realize that Vatican was too smart for that.

He sliced open one flap, then another. Inside was yet another cardboard box heavily wrapped in packing tape and cushioned by hundreds of white Styrofoam peanuts. Vatican lifted out the box and began slicing this one open too.

When she saw the contents, Dayna gasped, backed up a few steps bumping into the wall.

Vatican lifted the thick plastic box out of the cardboard. The plastic container was a terrarium. Inside was the neatly severed head of Aaron Leland.

A press release dated tomorrow was taped to one of the sides of the terrarium. The release described the tragic death of CIA Director Aaron Leland in a boating accident. He had fallen overboard, hit by the boat's propellors. Witnesses included Leland's temporary replacement, Standish Ford, as well as CIA advisers Dubus and Collins.

Dayna stared at the handsome face, looking for the signs of evil she'd expected to find. There were none. Only a patch of white hair among the curly black ones, the white hairs looking soft as flower petals.

We are safe now, she said. *We can stay.*

"We are safe," Vatican said, kissing her lightly on the lips, "unless Standish Ford decides otherwise."

But we can trust him.

Vatican smiled, pulled open another empty suitcase and began filling it.

35

"I'M SUSPICIOUS," Tory said.

"Suspicious." Cliff smiled.

"Things are great. Life is great. I didn't even have PMS this month."

Cliff laughed. "Then why are you suspicious?"

"My life is never this great. I'm waiting for the little man who pops out and says, 'Sorry, you've been living someone else's life by mistake. Here's your old one back. Start worrying.'"

Cliff squeezed her hand. They walked along the almost deserted beach. The weather had turned unseasonably cool for the past few days and only surfers came to the beach now, and then not many to this remote beach. They had driven half the morning to get here.

About twenty yards ahead of them, Karen Fawley played with the basset hound, Mike, in the surf. Mike jumped and whirled on his short stubby legs, his long mouth hanging open, his floppy ears wet from dipping them in the ocean. He ran after Karen, nipping at the hem of her shorts.

"She looks a little like Ed, don't you think?" Tory asked.

"Not much."

"I was hoping you'd say that." Tory leaned her head against his shoulder. She purposely walked on his right side so she could do that, avoiding his wounded shoulder. "I realize now why I never got around to changing my name from Fawley after the divorce. The name was my only link with Karen. I guess I figured as long as I had the name, I had a right to see her, even if she wasn't biologically my daughter."

"She's your daughter now."

Tory smiled. "Incredible, isn't it? Ed's mom didn't object, but then she once told me she couldn't understand what I saw in her son anyway. Hell of a tough woman. And the government agencies aren't putting up a fuss."

"I think Stan may have had something to do with greasing those wheels."

"Yeah. I wonder how he's doing."

Cliff didn't pursue that topic. They'd already discussed the convenience of Aaron Leland's accidental death and decided to ignore it. Instead they concentrated on each other. Cliff took Tory and Karen everywhere. Disneyland. The San Diego Zoo. Marineland. Always crowded places. This was the first time they'd been isolated.

"Should we talk about love?" Tory asked, kicking a broken seashell back into the ocean.

"What about it?"

"Well, I'm in it. Love that is."

Mike barked, frustrated that Karen managed to continue to dance just out of his reach.

"Mike's enjoying himself," Cliff said.

"You're changing the subject."

"Not changing, avoiding." Cliff faced her. "I feel a little like an interloper. I'm always moving in on ready-made families. I'm the epitome of instant-made American society. Instant coffee, instant dinners. Instant families."

"What's your point?"

"I think you're supposed to earn those things. Love and loyalty over a period of time."

"You make it sound like weight lifting. Pump that iron until the muscles appear."

"Discipline is part of it."

"What about love?"

Cliff shrugged. "I don't know. Love's a strange brew."

"Maybe it's too soon for you. I'm expecting too much. I'm more the impulsive type."

"No, you aren't."

"Okay, so I'm not the impulsive type. After all that's happened, I feel like I've changed. Haven't you?"

"I don't know." He looked away, started leading her down the beach again. "I still miss Ginger."

Tory didn't say anything.

Cliff put his arms around her as they walked. They had finally made love a couple of days ago. The bed had squeaked, and Karen had been asleep down the hall so they'd had to be careful not to make too much noise. It hadn't been the enchanted experience he'd had with Dayna. Not as dreamy. But it had been better, more passionate, more real. He and Tory had laughed a lot, finally moving to the floor to finish what they could not do quietly in the bed. Afterward, Tory had raided the refrigerator and they had eaten banana and peanut butter sandwiches washed down with V-8 juice while watching *Zulu Dawn* on television.

Karen seemed to like Cliff. They laughed together and played games—Chinese checkers and Yahtze were her favorites. Even Mike had grudgingly gotten used to Cliff, after gnawing through a new pair of shoes and shredding the cuff of his best pants.

A pretty good life.

But like Vatican Towne, Cliff needed to bury Ginger and the kids. The funeral was long over, but he needed more than the ritual. The completion. That was not yet done.

"There's the rest room," he said, pointing to the small building ahead. "Last stop."

CHARON HELD the palm-sized binoculars to his eyes and watched Cliff and Tory walk toward the rest rooms. The little girl snapped the fat basset on a leash and joined them. Good, very good. He threw the binoculars on the car seat and climbed out of his car.

Now or never.

He'd been following them for more than a week now, looking for a pattern, waiting for an opportunity when they were alone. This was the first time. They had stayed among crowds until now and Charon had to avoid crowds. Not just for the logistics of assassination, but because Standish Ford had McQueened him. Put a bounty on Charon's head. Two hundred thousand dollars. Christ, that would bring out all the pros and amateurs alike. He didn't see much problem in avoiding or killing any would-be assassins, but there was a principle involved here. No one McQueened Charon.

Charon checked his lipstick in the car's side mirror. His hair was ratted and moussed for fullness. He wore a tight blouse to accent his breasts and a denim skirt to hide the bulge at his crotch. He slung the purse over his shoulder, unsnapping the flap for easy access to his gun.

And to the glass vial of sulfuric acid.

The gun was for Remington. The acid was for the woman and the child. A little splash in both their faces. Just enough so Remington would know how good Charon was. Then, after he'd seen their scarred blinded eyes, kill him. And maybe them too.

He walked toward the rest room, only about fifty yards behind them now.

McQueened. A cute little phrase referring to that old Steve McQueen series, *Wanted: Dead or Alive*, about a bounty hunter. So whenever intelligence slapped a bounty on someone, they called it getting McQueened. Spooks thought of themselves as great wits, Oscar Wildes with guns. Christ.

None of that mattered. Once Charon had finished business here, he had enough money to hide out for a couple of years until things blew over. When they did, he'd come back and pay a visit to Standish Ford and his family.

Charon's flat Capezio shoes filled with sand as he walked across the beach toward the rest rooms. Ahead, the woman and the girl went into the women's side. Remington took the hound by the leash and ran down the surf with him. The dog nipped at his shorts while Remington kicked water at him.

Excellent. Now he was out of the way entirely.

Charon reached into his purse, his warm fingers slipping around the cool glass vial. He could feel the acid's energy through the glass, like holding a handful of hornets. He heard the females inside, their voices echoing in the small concrete room. He looked over his shoulder. No one else was coming. He looked down at the beach. Remington was still splashing about with the dog.

Charon opened the door marked Women and entered.

The woman, Tory, was leaning over the sink, applying lipstick. One of the three stall doors was locked. Charon bent over as if to brush sand from his shoes, saw the little girl's skinny legs dangling and straightened up. He removed the vial from his purse, cupping it in his hand, his thumb edged against the cap, ready to pop it off and throw the acid.

"Tory?" Charon said softly.

"Yes?" Tory said, turning away from the mirror, the lipstick poised.

Charon thumbed the cap of the vial. The cap dropped to the cement floor, bounced, and rolled to the drain.

Tory's eyes widened with fear. "No, please . . ."

Suddenly one of the stall doors yanked open and a heavyset man burst out pointing a gun. Charon recognized him from Aaron Leland's hit list: Lieutenant Godfrey.

"Police!" Godfrey shouted, his .38 aimed at Charon's face.

Tory shrank back, obviously just as surprised by his appearance as Charon.

"Mom?" the little girl hollered. "Mom, there are men in here."

"Karen, stay where you are. Don't come out, baby." Tory's voice was calm, despite the terrified look on her face, Charon had to give her that.

Charon heard the door open behind him. He looked over his shoulder.

Remington.

Cool and casual, eyes a little sad. Gun in hand.

"You knew I was following you," Charon said.

Remington didn't answer.

Everything was clear to Charon now. Remington had purposely kept in the crowds, teasing Charon to keep following, waiting for the right time and place to lure him out. The bastard had planned this whole day, knew exactly where the best place to strike would be. Had his fat friend stake it out.

Remington gestured with his gun. "Dump that in the drain."

"What are the charges, Lieutenant?"

"Bad fashion sense," Lieutenant Godfrey said. "Now dump it. Slowly."

Charon sighed. "I have no choice, right?"

"None."

Charon grinned, shrugged, lowered his hand. Then suddenly he was moving. Spinning around to throw the acid into Remington's face.

Cliff fired while Charon was still turning. Godfrey fired an instant later. The glass vial fell, shattered against the cement floor and spilled the acid in a puddle. Charon fell backward, slamming his head against the edge of sink hard enough to leave a smear of hair and blood on the white porcelain. But he was already dead. He hit the floor and his left foot slid across the cement into the puddle of acid. The acid foamed and chewed furiously around his shoe leather.

Karen screamed hysterically, her voice so loud and piercing that Cliff couldn't understand what Godfrey was saying to Tory or what Tory was saying to him.

36

CLIFF KNOCKED on the door.

A few minutes later the door opened. "Oh," she said, standing in the doorway. Her shoulders stiffened.

"Hi," Cliff said.

"Hi."

She was wearing a business suit, still in her stockings, though no shoes. She had her reading glasses on and a pen behind her ear. Blue ink smudged her fingers.

"Busy?" he asked.

"Kinda. Briefs. You know."

He nodded. "Not much racquetball these days."

"No time. I'm a lawyer, after all. They kinda expect me to do something for my inflated salary."

"A lot of catching up to do, huh?"

"God, you're not kidding. I just got home from the office and I'm already at work." She gestured over her shoulder to indicate huge piles awaiting her attention.

"I know. I mean, I know you just got home. I've been waiting."

"Oh."

"In the car."

Tory looked over his shoulder. "I didn't see your car when I drove up."

"Parked it a few blocks away." He smiled. "Habit."

She nodded, a minute of silence followed.

"Look, Cliff, I don't want to be rude, but what do you want?"

"A visit."

"You should have called first."

"I haven't seen you in a couple of weeks."

"That was your choice. I called you, remember?"

"I wanted to call back."

She reached out and touched his forehead where she'd hit him that first day. Only a thin white line remained, unnoticeable unless you were looking for it. "All healed up."

"Is that a question?"

She withdrew her hand. "I'm not being mean, Cliff. I know you suffered. But suffering has to end sometime, we have to at least make the effort. Life takes precedence."

"Precedence. You sound like a lawyer."

"I am a lawyer, Cliff. A damn good one. But I wouldn't plead your case to a jury for anything. You want to lose."

Cliff didn't know what to say. She was right. He had been trying to lose her, to punish himself more for what he'd been unable to prevent. If he was responsible for his family's death, did he deserve happiness with another family? He'd needed time to think all that through. To bury his dead or crawl into the grave with them. He'd thought it over. Killing Charon had been the end. The completion. With Charon's death he had buried Ginger and Lily and Bogie and Liza. God, he still missed them. But he had missed Tory too. Missed her the way one misses the living. In the end, that was more powerful than mourning the dead.

"What about your business?" she asked, breaking the silence.

Cliff shrugged. "Sold it."

"What now?"

"I don't really know. I have money. Insurance money." He reached into his back pocket and pulled out three airline tickets and fanned them open. "I also have these."

She shook her head sadly. "Cliff, don't."

"Courtesy of Standish Ford. He said we could go anywhere but Mexico. He's boycotting Mexico."

"Cliff, this just isn't working out. Look, I can't talk about it now." She took a deep breath of resolution. "I have to go pick Karen up soon. She's almost done with ballet class."

Mike's droopy face appeared at the door, his big head trying to squeeze between Tory's legs.

"Mike, damn it, get back." Tory pushed at his head with her foot. He persisted, finally squirming his thick body through so he could get at Cliff. Immediately he began biting Cliff's shoelaces, untying both shoes. Tory came out of the house and grabbed him by the collar, tugging him back inside. Cliff followed them in and closed the door behind him.

"Pretty slick move," Tory said.

"I still have a few."

"That's what I'm afraid of." She looked at him solemnly. "You hurt me, Cliff. No fooling. I mean, you were great with Karen and me after that awful mess with that creep in drag. But what about the next day? And the next and the next and the next? Lieutenant Godfrey called, even came by several times. Where were you?"

"Hiding."

"From what?"

"From you. From Karen." He looked down at Mike, who was gnawing on his laces again. "But especially from Mike."

"Cut the bullshit, Cliff. Cut the charm. Don't *work* me."

"You know me too well."

"I don't goddamned know you at all. That's the scary part. I'm navigating by instinct here, pal. I told you before I'm very good at doing things, I just don't care about them. No passion, remember? Well, now I've got passion, now I care. About you. I'm just not so sure I wasn't better off before."

"I'm sure."

Tory looked at him. "Sure about what?"

Cliff kissed her. She kissed him back. His lips felt the little scar above her mouth. He kissed the scar.

When they broke apart, Cliff held up the airline tickets. "All we have to do is pick a destination. You, me, and Karen. Anywhere. Tahiti, Tokyo, London, Paris. Anywhere."

"Anywhere?"

"Anywhere."

Tory plucked the tickets from his hand. "Anywhere?"

"Except Mexico."

"Fine." Tory tore the tickets in half. She dropped the pieces on the floor and Mike immediately sniffed them, stepped on them and finally chewed them. Tory began counting on her fingers. "First, we pick Karen up from class. Then we stop off at the grocery store so we'll have something to cook for dinner tonight. Saturday is Karen's soccer game, so Tokyo will have to wait. Next week I have a guy coming over to regrout the bathroom, so Rome is out."

"How about the week after that? London?"

"The swap meet. I need some new sheets." She shrugged. "That's real life around here, Cliff. Getting Karen off to school, feeding the dog, going to work. The adventure begins every morning when the alarm clock goes off."

Cliff stooped down and petted Mike, pulling one of the ticket halves from his mouth. "How does Rome taste, pal?" He stood up, pointed at Tory's stocking feet. "Better get some shoes on or we'll be late picking Karen up."

"And the swap meet?"

"Bright and early."

"Bathroom grouting?"

"I'll get a book on grouting out of the library, do the bathroom myself."

She smiled. "I've got a two-week vacation coming in the spring. We've got plenty of time to plan."

He pulled Tory close and sniffed her baby powder scent. "I love you. I think that ought to be said."

"Yes," she agreed. "And often."

They kissed again. Tory slipped into her shoes and they walked out of the house, his arm around her shoulder, her arm around his waist, her hand buried in his back pocket. As they navigated the brick walkway on their way to her car, Cliff noticed the unkempt hedges that bordered Tory's house. At that instant he had a sudden vivid vision of himself leaning over the hedges with clippers, snipping away the stray branches and straggling leaves. Once a week fussing in the garden on hands and knees. Planting and pulling. Maintaining the order. The discipline of it appealed to him. The inevitability of weeds was thrilling. The physics of completion.

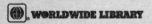

Gripping thrillers by masters of suspense . . .